Escape *to the* Irish Village

BOOKS BY ANN O'LOUGHLIN

The Irish House

My Only Daughter

Her Husband's Secret

Secrets of an Irish House

Ann O'Loughlin

Escape *to the* Irish Village

bookouture

Published by Bookouture in 2024

An imprint of Storyfire Ltd.
Carmelite House
50 Victoria Embankment
London EC4Y 0DZ

www.bookouture.com

ISBN: 978-1-83525-404-2
eBook ISBN: 978-1-83525-403-5

To John, Roshan and Zia xxx

ONE
MAY

Emma took a deep breath and looked all around her. Nobody would find her here. The big iron gates were pulled across, but there was enough space, she hoped, to squeeze through onto the avenue. She checked Google Maps. She had reached her destination after walking the mile out of Killcawley village. Pressing her handbag close to her chest, she winced with pain as she manoeuvred her body through the gap.

Straightening up, she stopped and listened. The air was still, but in the distance a dog barked, a lazy middle-of-the-day woof which did not in any way alarm her. A small gate lodge was set back to one side. The windows were shuttered, and the planters were full of weeds and flowers that had long since bloomed. It looked like nobody lived here.

Suddenly, a car passed on the road. Emma quickly stepped back out of sight behind an outcrop of brambles, before rushing up the avenue to a small bend, where she knew she could not be seen by passing traffic.

Was she mad to flee to another country? Was she mad to think she could get away; that nobody would try to find her? Shivering, even though the sun was shining, Emma told herself to keep it together. She had to make this work. Opening the camera on her phone, she checked her appearance to make sure that her face did not betray her fear. She carefully scrutinised her make-up to ensure it had successfully hidden the fading bruises on her jaw. Her hands clenched in tight fists, she steeled herself to continue up the avenue.

The stillness unnerved her; a blackbird flitted by her shoulder, before letting out a shrill warning call as it disappeared into the undergrowth. She flinched, stopping for a minute to further assess her surroundings. Banks of fuchsia and some type of wild white and magenta roses lined this part of the gravel driveway. Further on, the avenue opened out, fenced-off fields on either side. Ahead, the little road split in two and she hesitated, wondering which fork she should take.

Slowly, she continued on her way. The sun was shining, the air clear; the only sound was the bees burrowing into the foxgloves that were standing like soldiers between the roses. The horses in the field raised their heads, and two, a chestnut and a grey sauntered over. She stood and waited by the fence for them to push their heads over to say hello.

They were curious, nuzzling her hands as if they were used to getting treats and she laughed, telling them to get back.

A text buzzed on her phone.

You will have to walk up from the gate I'm afraid, but it's not far, and on a day like today, it's a lovely stroll. Take the road going left, it leads to the house. Come around to the back. These days, I hardly ever open the front door. J.

Emma texted back.

On the avenue now. Be there shortly. Thank you, E.

She worried that her sign-off was too familiar. Flattening

down her long blonde hair, she checked her blouse buttons were fastened and straightened her jacket. Slipping her phone in her handbag, she walked smartly up to the fork in the avenue. One of the horses trotted beside her, keeping her company at the other side of the fence.

As she approached the divide in the road, the house came into view. A three-storey red-brick building with long elegant windows, and a large conservatory at the side. It was set back with a sweeping view of a lake, where two swans were gliding together, creating lines on the surface. Emma stopped to take it all in. Every window was open, but there was no sound coming from inside the house. It was, she thought, as if the occupants were away for the day and had forgotten to lock up before leaving. She wandered down the small incline to the house and turned down the side as instructed.

As she was passing what looked like a sitting room, she thought she heard the faraway, faint sound of music in the air, and she stopped to listen. Peeping in the window, she saw the room was opulent, with walls papered in a heavy gold design. Cream velvet couches had cushions in pops of blue and gold. One wall was covered in paintings in different sizes with various styles of frame.

On the chimney breast was a big painting of a young woman in a ball gown. Emma wanted to press closer to the glass for a better look, but she was afraid of appearing rude, so she continued past another few windows, until she reached the back courtyard. A Border collie lying out in the sun wagged its tail but didn't bother getting up when she walked past.

At the back door, which was half open, Emma hesitated. Somebody inside had opera music blaring, and she wasn't sure whether she should knock or text the owner.

'Emma, is that you? Come in for goodness' sake, girl. Just lift the latch,' a voice inside said cheerily, and the music stopped.

Slowly, Emma opened the door.

'Come in, come in. I can't shake your hand, but just give me a few minutes,' Judith McCarthy said as she carried a tray to the oven and pushed it in.

'There's a cake sale in the village and I'm making cupcakes,' she said, reaching for a tea towel to wipe her hands, before catching Emma's hand in a firm grip.

'Don't you look lovely in your suit? I should have said this wouldn't be a formal interview. Let's sit at the table, dear. It's lovely to have you here, Emma...'

'Wilson,' she replied quickly. 'Emma Wilson.'

She nervously sat down at one end of the table, which was piled high with cookery books. She had no idea what to say. Judith, she knew, was seventy-five years of age because it said so in the ad. She was a stylish woman, her silver hair swept back, showing off her fine bone structure. She was wearing a royal blue kaftan under a white apron with chunky jewellery bunched at her neck. Her nails were long and painted purple.

'I know the place is a mess. I need somebody to organise me,' Judith said as she pulled the apron off, rolled it in a ball and threw it on the armchair beside the AGA.

Emma wasn't sure what to do next. She fingered the ad in her pocket. She had taken the card from the notice board in Killcawley post office the day before, because she didn't want anybody else to get this job, which she so desperately needed. Nervously, she waited for Judith to ask her questions.

Judith scratched her head with a long nail and laughed. 'I have never interviewed anyone. Why don't I tell you what I am looking for and see if it suits you?'

Emma nodded.

Judith sighed loudly. 'I will be frank. My son is worried about me. He doesn't like that I live here on my own. He's in New York, and he wants to put Killcawley Estate on the market. He says now is the best time when the land can be rezoned for housing, and when I am still well enough to have a say on the downsizing option,' she said.

Emma wasn't sure if she should speak and was relieved when Judith continued.

'Don't get me wrong, I love my son, but he doesn't realise the only way I will leave this place is in a coffin. He really harasses me an awful lot; he doesn't like me being in this big old house on my own, even though I tell him, who the hell would bother trying to find Killcawley Estate to come and steal stuff?

'I'm sure it's an awful lot easier to break into the housing estates all around the big towns nearby. And I am not exactly alone. There's Jack, who works the farm and runs the estate. Pete, who looks after the animals, though he is a cranky old bastard. However, I love my silly son dearly and I have agreed to have somebody – a so-called carer – in to help me.'

'I have no qualifications as a carer,' Emma interrupted anxiously.

'I jolly well hope not; I have no need of one, but I am looking for somebody who could be like a manager or a housekeeper, a companion if you will. If all that doesn't sound too confusing and odd.'

'What would I be expected to do?' Emma asked.

Judith threw back her head and guffawed. 'I am scaring you, but I don't mean to. I think I need a friend who has good organisation skills, a brain in her head, and who will put up with Judith McCarthy. Seriously, I need to have this arrangement set up and functioning well by the time my Miles comes to visit, otherwise he's going push me into someplace I can never be happy. He has the best motives, but sheltered accommodation or a luxury nursing home arrangement are not for me. I don't do old,' Judith said, striking a pose as if she were on camera.

Emma giggled despite herself.

Judith got up and switched on the kettle. 'Now, your turn;

I'm curious why somebody from London would want to move all the way here to the arsehole of nowhere?'

The question came out of the blue and Emma froze. If she told the truth, what would this woman say? If she told the truth, she might get turned down for the job she so badly needed. And, if she told the truth, she would be disclosing something she could not share with anybody else.

'I wanted a change, I guess,' she said feebly, a tremor in her voice.

Judith switched off the kettle, and swung around to face Emma. A silence descended, which Emma did not know how to handle. Judith, her voice kind, was the first to speak.

'I see in your application you were a legal secretary. Won't this job be a bit of a comedown for you?' she asked.

Emma's voice strangled in her throat. She shook her head.

'I need the job,' she said quietly, kicking herself for sounding so pathetic.

'You won't leave me in the lurch before Miles comes home, probably sometime in July or August?' Judith asked firmly.

'I won't. I give you my word.'

Judith opened a cupboard door, and took down two champagne flutes.

'Bugger tea. Sounds like we both need each other. Will you take the job as my executive assistant?'

Emma gasped. 'Really?'

'That is, if you still want it,' Judith said, twisting around to look directly at Emma.

'Yes please,' Emma said.

'OK. It's settled,' Judith said, opening the fridge and pulling out a bottle of prosecco. She expertly popped it open, like a woman who regularly had bubbly before four in the afternoon, and poured.

'Before we clink to seal the deal, tell me please you're not a murderer or running from the law,' Judith said.

Emma shook her head.

'Well, that's good enough for me for the moment,' Judith said, handing Emma a glass of bubbly.

'To the future,' she said, and they clinked lightly before sipping their drinks.

'You haven't asked about terms and conditions or pay.'

'Sorry, I forgot,' Emma said, feeling her cheeks flame with embarrassment.

'Don't worry, I intend to pay you well. How does €500 a week sound? And you will of course get free bed and board.'

'That sounds very generous.'

'It's not; I can be a bit of a dragon. I will expect you to do some light meals, housework, driving me about and maybe, if you feel OK about it, helping me out in my garden. My estate manager, Jack, looks after the walled kitchen garden and wild-flower meadows, but I like to supervise when it comes to the fruit and veg.'

'What about the horses?'

'Pete usually has a local teenager in to help out with the horses, so I am well covered.'

'It all sounds good to me. I feel I have landed on my feet,' Emma said.

'Oh, I nearly forgot. I'll need help with my social media as well.'

'Social media?' Emma asked, staring at Judith.

'Yes, you heard right. I am surprised you don't know me, but then I'm not on your radar; I don't appeal to anyone under thirty. But I'm set on the path to become quite an icon to those over fifty. I just know it. Everybody loves my vintage outfits and my wonderful collection of hats. Wait until you see my hats.'

'Do you have a blog?'

'StyleQueenJudy. Look me up on TikTok. I need help making videos, and these days you don't stand out if there isn't a professional touch to the work.'

Emma's mouth went dry, and she felt queasy. 'You won't expect me to be in any shots or videos, will you?'

Judith laughed. 'Relax, there can only be one star around here, and its granny in the corner. Are you still up to taking the job?'

Emma laughed. 'Yes, I am, as long as I am not expected to be in front of the camera.'

Judith jumped up, beaming. 'Time to talk practicalities. I presumed you might like to live here, but if you prefer, I can help you find a place in the village. Here at the big house, I can offer you bed and board, your own suite of rooms upstairs with your own bedroom, sitting room and bathroom, all with inter-connecting doors. It depends on whether you prefer to live in or not.'

'Staying here at the house sounds good,' Emma said.

'OK, but before you say yes for certain, let's take a look. Also, for the next while or so, my very good friend Marsha is in the guest bedroom across the hall, while the gate lodge, where she normally resides, is decorated. You'll like Marsha. She is gone to visit her sister in Dublin, but she will be back in a few days.'

Emma followed Judith out into the hall and up a wide staircase.

'Your quarters overlook the lake. I have a similar suite on the floor below,' she said as they tramped up to the second floor.

Emma whistled when she saw the first room. A sitting room with long windows overlooking the gardens and lake. A small bedroom and bathroom were off this main room.

'Do you like it? You can change it around or if you see anything else in the house you would like brought up here, just let me know.'

'You're very kind,' Emma said quietly.

'Nonsense, dear. But I don't know if you will be saying that after the first week. We have so much work to do.'

'It's so beautiful here.'

'Precisely the reason I don't intend to give it up. Killcawley Estate has been in my family for generations. When can you move in?'

'Today, if you like.'

'I like. You go get your things and come back when you're ready.'

Emma shifted from one foot to another.

'I don't have anything else.'

Judith, who was struggling to pull up a sash window to air out the room, turned around. 'My, you're a mystery, Emma. Do you always travel so light? And, tell me, do you always wear suits?'

'Not exactly...' Emma's voice faltered.

'Is this where I should retreat gracefully and respect your privacy?' Judith asked.

Emma didn't answer. She watched Judith walk to the door, but she called her before she stepped out into the hall.

'Mrs McCarthy, I am very grateful for this opportunity. I won't let you down.'

'I jolly well hope not; I'm depending on you, Emma. And please, no more Mrs McCarthy, it makes me sound old,' Judith said, her voice firm.

Emma frowned and made to say something, but Judith put her hand up to stop her talking.

'In time, you will tell me your story. You can't stay running forever, and I hope here at Killcawley Estate you can find peace.'

Emma turned to Judith and smiled.

'I hope so,' she said quietly.

'In the meantime, we will go with not being an axe murderer. Have a rest, settle in and come to the kitchen when you're ready,' Judith said.

TWO

Emma stood by the long window looking out at the lake. The swans had disappeared into the reeds at the far side. The sun sprinkled across the surface; a mother duck and her chicks gliding across the water; the mother duck surging forward sending back the ripple of wave for her young to follow. Emma watched, envy coursing through her that each chick was so secure in their mother's ability to keep them safe. Nobody, she thought, starts out thinking they won't be able to protect their young. Shuddering, she turned away. She had no idea what was going to happen next, but she had somewhere to live, and she was able to earn a wage. Fingering the silk curtains, she looked back into the room. The little sitting room could have come straight from an expensive country hotel. The antique furniture was well cared for, each piece picked with good taste. Every now and again, there was a pop of bright colour, a cushion or an ornament, and Emma thought these must be Judith's additions. On the bed was a cushion in the shape of a heart and another which said *Wild When Woken*.

Emma smiled despite herself. She slipped off her jacket,

and threw it across the back of an armchair, and loosened her shirt from her trousers. Scrabbling through her handbag, she took out a hairbrush. Slowly and carefully, she brushed her hair, wincing when she forgot and the bristles hit the bruising on her right side. She next sat at the mahogany dressing table, coiling her blonde hair into a low bun. Taking her pink lipstick from her bag, she slicked it across her lips. She loved the colour; the carefree frosted pink made her feel joy again. In a rash moment, she had spent too much money on the lipstick in the ferry shop. It made her feel good, but then she couldn't buy lunch. She still had her credit card, but she dared not use it. Peering closer in the mirror, she wished she had bought concealer to hide the dark patches under her eyes. She needed to sleep, sleep deeply without fear knocking her rudely awake.

She hoped at Killcawley Estate peace would, in time, come dropping slow, for her. Lifting the lid of a silver box on the dressing table, she peered inside. It was empty except for a tiny key. She fiddled with the key before she noticed a heavy-set dark wooden box to one side of the mirror. She put the key in the lock and turned it. Nervous, because she wasn't sure if she should be looking inside, she lifted the heavy lid. It was an old jewellery box; on the top tray lay a pair of small gold hoop earrings and a dangly set. Emma held the long mother-of-pearl earrings up to her ears. There was a time she would have loved to wear these, enjoying the sheen contrasting with her long hair. Quickly, she replaced the earrings but lifted out the tray. Underneath was stuffed with teenage treasures, necklaces, braids and bracelets. Emma, worried she was snooping, quickly replaced the tray, shut the box and locked it. She heard Judith call out her name from the first landing, and she stepped out to find out what she wanted.

'Forgive me, I was too lazy to come all the way up. Would you like a week's advance on your wages, Emma? I thought you might want to buy more suitable clothing. I doubt if you would be seen dead in any of my attire?'

'That would be fantastic, thank you.'

'Let's go in to Killcawley to the bank, and from there we can go on to a bigger town and the shopping centre. You'll find plenty for a...'

'I was twenty-nine years old last week.'

'And I was going to say twenty-one.' Judith laughed.

Emma followed her down the stairs.

'It's a sunny day, so I thought the Beamer with the top down. It's good for the soul to feel the wind through the hair,' Judith said, leading the way through the kitchen to the backyard and an old stable block, where a jeep, a Bentley and the BMW were parked.

'My silly son says I am too old to be driving around with the hood down. He fusses so much about me since he moved to the US. He needs to meet a nice young woman to occupy his time and then he wouldn't be putting me under the microscope all the time.'

Emma got into the car and watched as Judith slipped on a pair of Dior sunglasses before roaring down the avenue to the gate.

'I rang Jack, who looks after the farm, and he said he would have the gate open for us. We might as well keep it back; I reckon we will have a lot of trips to do. How did you get here? I hope you didn't pay for a cab.'

'I walked. It wasn't far.'

'You poor thing, you probably would have preferred a cuppa to bubbly. I'm an awful show-off; I can't help it.'

Judith suddenly applied the brakes, making Emma fall forward. The jolt frightened her. Tears rose up in her, and she couldn't stop them.

'Oh heck, I'm sorry, I didn't mean to scare you. I forgot the bloody cupcakes. Hetty in the village is going to put a topping on them for me.'

Emma swallowed hard and forced herself to smile.

'I'm sorry. It was so unexpected, and I guess I'm tired.'

Judith reached over and squeezed Emma's hand. 'I have been selfish, making you get stuck in from the start. Please feel free to say no, whenever you want.'

'OK,' Emma said, wiping the tears from her cheeks.

'I will go back for the cupcakes. Do you want to stay at home while I deliver them, and you can shop another time?'

'I'm OK, and I am beginning to feel overdressed.'

'That's my girl. Don't worry, I won't inflict Hetty on you just yet. Money and shopping for you.'

Emma waited in the car while Judith got the cupcakes. When she came back, she had a carton of orange juice and a warm cupcake on a paper plate for her.

'Just to keep you going,' she said as she started up the engine.

Emma wasn't able to drink or eat as Judith speeded down the driveway. After they pulled out on to the road, Emma gripped the door handle and tried to balance the paper plate and drink on her lap. Judith powered around the bends, pressing the horn as she went.

'I'm a bit of a speed merchant, but don't let on to Miles; I tell him I'm too afraid to go above thirty on the narrow road into the village.'

Emma swallowed hard and closed her eyes until she felt the car slow to a crawl.

'I forgot to ask if you can drive? I must put you on the insurance.'

'I have a UK licence.'

'No bother, I will get the insurance company to sort that out,' Judith said as she nipped into a parking space for the disabled in front of the bank.

'I'm seventy-five years old, for Christ's sake. Surely that is enough of a disability,' Judith snorted, and Emma wondered if this woman ever stopped fighting the world.

Emma waited in the car while Judith went into the bank. She grew nervous in case a traffic warden or police officer came along, and she began to perspire. It was a small village with a wide main street. A number of women were standing chatting outside the post office. A man cleaning the windows of the newsagents said something to them every now and again, and they laughed. A double-decker bus pulled into a stop and a number of people got off.

When Judith returned to the car, she was scowling.

'Why is it when you reach a certain age everybody thinks you are a doddery old fool. The clerk had the cheek to ask me why I wanted so much in cash, and when I wouldn't tell her, she called the manager. Of course, it was a pimply twenty something – no offence – who spoke to me in a raised voice and deliberately slow. He said he was the new manager and wanted to look out for all his customers. He asked me if I was under any duress.'

'What did you do?'

Judith laughed. 'I told him look up my balance, which is not insignificant. As he looked at the screen, I told him if he wanted to remain a bank manager past this week, he would treat me with respect and realise I can make my own banking decisions.'

'He may have just been looking out for you,' Emma said.

Judith turned to her. 'And I am a touchy old bird, I know, but I didn't close my accounts and that's thanks enough. The previous bank manager was there for thirty years, and I didn't even have to queue. Life has changed and not for the best,' she said, starting up the engine. 'Have a look in my bag – there is an envelope with five hundred cash. I will drop you at the shopping centre. Will an hour and a half be enough?'

'More than enough,' Emma replied.

She sat back in the seat, and closed her eyes again as they slipped out onto the motorway. Not long ago, she wouldn't have thought twice about spending five hundred euros on just a handbag. Now she was supposed to gather a working wardrobe for the same amount. She shook herself. Her life had changed and she was lucky to get this job. She told herself to focus on the basics. A wardrobe hardly mattered anymore. Her life was so different now, and that made her afraid.

She felt sick, and she wanted to cry. She didn't want her old life back, but she was afraid of this new one, though Judith, despite her over-the-top manner, appeared to be straight. She worried, though, that she wouldn't be able to live up to her high standards.

'I'm calling back to Hetty, and then getting my nails done. I will text you when I'm finished,' Judith said as they pulled up at the shopping centre.

'OK. But I do have to buy a new phone, so that number won't work for much longer.'

Judith gave her an odd look.

'You really are leaving the past behind. Let's make it two hours, you have a lot to do, and Hetty is such a gossip, she's bound to hold me up chatting,' she said.

Emma said goodbye to Judith and went into the first café she came across, and ordered a cappuccino. She took out a pen and paper from her handbag, hoping to write a list of what she'd need, but she found herself doodling boxes, line after line over and over again. The last time she had used this pen, she was a legal secretary, and was always writing reminder notes to stick on her desk. Now, she had no idea what to do.

She barely touched her coffee, nervous that others were watching her. She had been wearing the same clothes for the last four days. She had no need for a list; she needed everything.

A man in a denim jacket opened the café kitchen door and shouted a quick instruction to the waitress. Emma, reacting to the man's voice, got up so quickly from her chair it fell back, crashing to the ground. A woman nearby picked it up and smiled, but Emma, like a rabbit startled by the headlights, bolted from the café.

Her cheeks were burning, and she was breathing quickly. She wanted to go back to Killcawley Estate, but she had to buy clothes. She marched into Penneys and grabbed a shopping basket. Starting with underwear, she picked out four or five of everything. She stuffed three different pairs of jeans, as well as shorts, skirts, tops and hoodies, and a pack of scrunchies for her hair in the basket. She chose a waterproof jacket as well and two pairs of runners, sandals, and a multipack of socks. On impulse, she bought a mahogany brown hair dye; somehow the way she felt now didn't go with blonde.

In the phone shop, she picked the cheapest pay-as-you-go phone. She smiled, thinking she was walking around with a burner phone, but what did it matter when she had nobody she could ring?

She was walking past a boutique and spotted a cobalt blue fascinator. Beaming with delight, she imagined Judith wearing it. It resembled a deep blue dahlia and was surrounded by netting edged in the same blue. Judith, she knew, would wear it jauntily to the side. She stood for a few minutes looking at it until an old lady using a walker called out to her.

'Go on, treat yourself. It will be beautiful with your lovely tresses.'

Too embarrassed to explain she was buying it for a friend, Emma smiled and disappeared inside the shop.

The assistant made a beeline for her.

'Will I take it from the window? Do you want to try it on?' she asked, already reaching into the display, and pulling out the tiny hat.

Without asking Emma, she placed it on her head.

'It suits you. Not many can wear such a vibrant colour.'

Emma slipped it off and looked at the fifty-three-euro price tag.

'I'll take it,' she said, as Judith texted her old phone with the carpark location.

'Oh, you're a sight for sore eyes. I love to see a woman with shopping bags,' Judith said, popping open the boot.

Emma waited until they got home, and had lifted all the bags onto the kitchen table before she presented Judith with her gift.

'I just wanted to say thank you for taking a chance on me,' she said, pushing the boutique bag across the table.

'What have you done? That's such an expensive shop,' Judith exclaimed as she edged the fascinator out of the bag.

She didn't say anything for a moment, and Emma was afraid she might have got it wrong.

Judith rushed out to the hall mirror and fixed the fascinator on her head.

'Emma, it's perfect. I want to do my next video by the lake, and I was looking for a piece to go with my long, vintage, navy taffeta skirt and cream silk blouse. You're a darling,' she said, pulling Emma into a big hug.

'As tomorrow is your first official day, maybe we can pencil in the photo shoot for after breakfast. The lake shimmers in the morning light. I just know you're going to produce something divine for me.' Judith sighed and readjusted the fascinator. 'Sadly, my videos so far have not been up to scratch. It's difficult to make a professional video on your own. It has made me feel quite foolish, that I can't make the idea in my head look good in the video. Tell me, Emma, can you work an iPhone?'

Emma smiled. 'I think I can handle that.'

'Fantastic! I'll be able to dance, and you will help me look wonderful. I won't have to be overthinking all of this anymore.'

Emma laughed as Judith twirled down the hall and into the kitchen.

'I don't know what brought you here, Emma Wilson, but I'm so glad you picked Killcawley Estate,' she said, bowing low in front of Emma.

THREE

Emma woke very early. The house was quiet, but outside the birds were singing at full throttle. She pulled a chair to the window and managed to push up the bottom sash. She sat listening, luxuriating in the sound, wishing she could identify the different birds. On the lake, the two swans were floating and preening their feathers at the same time as if they were getting ready for the day. She closed her eyes, enjoying the early morning sounds.

She must have dozed off because when her alarm went off, she jumped from the chair, nearly dropping her phone out the window. She had set the alarm for 8 a.m., but she wasn't sure if this was too early or too late for Killcawley Estate. She pulled on jeans and a hoodie, and stole downstairs. Judith was nowhere to be seen, but somebody had let the dog out.

She was setting up the coffee machine when a man wearing corduroy jeans and a jacket walked in, his head stooped over a large box which he let drop on the table. Emma stood back and whispered, 'Hello.' When he looked up, the man smiled and extended his hand.

'Jack. You must be Emma,' he said.

'Yes, I wasn't sure what time to get up, so I thought eight wasn't too early or late.'

'I think you pick your own times here. I am up at dawn, but I knock off earlier. Judith never surfaces until just before nine. So it depends on what way you want to run your day.'

'I just wish I knew what I am supposed to be doing.'

'That's easy, we will start with the coffee machine; after that, the sky is the limit.'

Emma switched on the machine.

'I'm only joking. I think it's for Judith to say. We all have our individual roles, but yours is one of the hardest; Judith can be a tough woman to be around at times – her batteries never run out.'

The kitchen door swung open.

'You watch your mouth, Jack Dennehy, and don't be turning the young woman against me before we even start,' Judith said, sliding into the room in a peach silk dressing gown.

'What has you up so early?' he asked.

'I realised Emma might be stuck with the likes of you, and I came down to save her from dying of boredom.'

He laughed, and Emma looked from one to the other as they chuckled like a pair of kids.

'Don't mind us, Emma, we've known each other a long time. Seriously, I never said what time we would have breakfast. So I thought I would get up because it's such a beautiful morning. Maybe after coffee we can head off on our photo shoot.'

'Make mine a takeaway. The postman dropped off another large box for you; no doubt more clothes you insist needed rescuing,' Jack said.

'And I do it so well.' Judith laughed, taking a sharp knife, and slicing it across the top of the parcel.

Different outfits tumbled from the box.

'More work for Marsha. I have a lady in Dublin who, once a month, does the rounds of the markets for me. Some of the clothes won't suit me and I give them to the charity shop, but often there's a dream find. Last time it was a 1940s satin opera coat.'

'Just what Emma always wanted,' Jack said, before disappearing out the back door.

'Don't mind him, he gets embarrassed because they rib him down the pub when I sometimes make him appear in my videos. It is so lovely out, are you ready to do the photo shoot soon?'

'Ready when you are. Though I will warn you I have never done anything like this before.'

'Just follow my lead. Give me ten minutes to get the slap on. Feel free to have a look around the house. This is your home now,' Judith said as she hurried off to do her make-up.

Carrying her mug of coffee, Emma wandered to the front drawing room. The embossed gold wallpaper was even more lovely up close. Worried she would spill coffee on the cream velvet upholstery, she stood by the fireplace and examined the painting. The portrait was of a young girl gazing earnestly towards the artist. It must be Judith, she thought; a girl ready for whatever adventures life might bring. She was wearing a cream off-the-shoulder linen dress with flounces, each frill made of tiny linen pleats, and topped with a band of intricate crochet in the same colour, and laced with thin blue ribbon. Her hair was a soft beehive style with strands hanging down, framing her face.

'I thought that dress was a bit much for my eighteenth birthday. I had no appreciation back then of designer wear,' Judith said as she walked into the room, her long taffeta skirt swishing across the floor.

'It's so detailed.'

'My mother was a good friend of the designer, Sybil Connolly. We borrowed the dress sample for the portrait. I'm not sure it would have been my choice, but Mother was a forceful woman. I was into minis and bell-bottoms, but no way was she going to let her only child wear hip clothes. She said timeless quality was the way to go, and she was right. The dress has stood the test of time, even if I haven't.'

Emma detected a sadness in Judith's voice.

'Do you like my hairdo? I absolutely insisted on a beehive, but my mother put her foot down and said it had to be soft, otherwise it would be competing with the dress. I used up so many bobby pins. I wish I had that lovely, strong hair these days,' Judith said, gesturing to Emma to follow her.

Emma trailed behind as Judith, bunching up her long skirt, made for the lake. She had teamed the skirt with a cream silk blouse with sleeves gathered into a wide cuff, and a collar with a pussycat bow.

When they reached the little jetty that jutted out into the lake, Judith placed the cobalt blue fascinator at an angle on her head and asked Emma how it looked.

'Perfect,' Emma said as she took out her phone.

Judith tutted loudly. 'No offence, darling, but my iPhone is top-notch, so please use it. I don't fancy making a pay-as-you-go video.'

Emma took the iPhone as Judith practised her moves.

'Let me know when you're ready. Call out "action" and I will do my thing,' she said, doing her facial exercises until Emma called 'action'. Judith transformed, looking seductively at the camera and inviting her followers to come down to the lake. There, she stepped across the stones, picked up one or two and skimmed them across the water, finishing with a fascinator close up and her cheeky wink.

'Cut' Emma shouted, getting into the swing of things.

'I think you're a natural at this,' Judith said. 'What did you think of the skipping stones? Thankfully, there were a few bounces before they sank without trace.'

'It all looked wonderful,' Emma said.

'Would that all my viewers or followers were as kind as you,

Emma. No doubt there will be a few who will complain about my throwing stones near the swans. Little do they know, those two could scare off an army if they so wished,' she said, leading the way back up the hill.

When they got to the house, Judith took a dressing gown she kept on a hook on the back door, threw it over her blouse and poured some coffee.

'I have to do it; too many times I have been caught out and left with a nasty stain that love nor money wouldn't shift. Now that we have got the first job of the day out of the way, will you tell me why you picked a small place like Killcawley in County Wicklow? You must have some connection to the place,' Judith said.

Emma sat down, cradling her mug with both hands. 'I liked the name.'

'Interesting,' Judith said, looking at Emma through narrowed eyes. 'Let's try again.'

Emma hesitated as the dog settled under the table.

'My grandmother always talked about this place. She lived here once. It seemed as good a place as any to come...'

She wanted to say when she had run out of options, but instead she let her voice trail off.

'Who was she? Maybe we met,' Judith said.

'Kitty Shanahan from Main Street.'

Judith set down her mug and was quiet for a moment.

'Did you know her?' Emma was unnerved by her pause – she hadn't seen Judith with nothing to say since she arrived.

'We went to the same school, but she wasn't in the village very long.' Judith didn't offer any more information, and instead started inspecting the box of dye Emma had bought.

'Why would anyone your age want to go from blonde to mahogany brown?' she said. Emma knew she was diverting her attention, but she couldn't think why.

'I just need a change; blonde brings with it a lot of unwanted attention.'

'Darling, you're beautiful and your hair is amazing, but you don't want to end up green.'

'What do you mean?'

'I'm not sure trying such a radical move at home will work. Best wait until you can book a salon appointment.'

Emma grabbed the box.

'I need to do it now; I don't want to be blonde anymore.'

Judith got up from the table and took a pile of old towels from the airing cupboard.

'You can't do this on your own; you're going to need help.'

'I couldn't ask you to do that.'

'Why not? I know a thing or two about this, but you're going to have to accept there isn't going to be a major change on the first round, we're going to have to layer the colour so it looks good.'

'How do you know so much about this?'

Judith laughed, and began to read the back of the box of dye. 'When I was a teenager I was best friends with a girl in the village, the hairdresser's daughter. We experimented all the time, and I didn't care how my mother reacted. She blew her top so many times about my hair colour.'

Emma opened the box, and took out the dye bottle and conditioner. 'I think I can go for the full colour in one go.'

'Believe me, it's best to go for a reddish base colour at the start. I have some we can use.'

'I just need a change, anything at this stage.'

'Have you an old T-shirt you can wear?' Judith said, before correcting herself quickly. 'Of course you don't, let me find something for you to wear; you don't want to spoil any of your new clothes.'

Emma wandered about the kitchen as Judith went upstairs to get her a top.

It was an old-fashioned kitchen with oak cupboards, and a dresser, and an AGA with a big armchair where Benny, the old sheepdog, was snoozing. Emma thought the best feature of the room was the long rectangular table, which could seat ten people, or even twelve at a squeeze.

She was standing at the sink looking out at the courtyard when Judith came back holding two brightly coloured T-shirts. 'I don't possess such a thing, but Miles used these when he painted the front window frames last summer. Don't worry, they have been washed. I hope you don't object to wearing one.'

Emma picked a red T-shirt which had a Target label, and a picture of palm trees on the front.

'Your son likes bright colours?'

'It surprised me too, but he said he knew he would have to do some painting so he grabbed them at bargain price before he flew home. Miles always did like a bargain.'

Emma pulled on the T-shirt over her top.

'Don't be silly, girl. We need to save your top and let Miles' cast-off take the dye. Hop into the drawing room. There's nobody much around here, and I doubt if Jack will be looking in the windows of the big house,' Judith said.

Emma changed in the hall, too nervous to step into the drawing room which had front and side windows. Back in the kitchen, Judith draped an old towel over her shoulders and got to work, humming as she covered all the hair with the dye. Afterwards, she placed a glass beside Emma.

'You need to sip a good whiskey. It's a big change, blonde to brown,' she said.

Emma sipped the whiskey as Judith set a timer and concentrated on flicking through her recipe books.

'I need to use up all the rhubarb or it will go to waste. My husband, Stephen, used to make jam, but I don't have his touch and nothing I make sets right.'

'I like to make jam – my grandmother and I used to do it.

She loved rhubarb and ginger.'

Judith snapped the book shut.

'Well that's sorted, then; you can make rhubarb and ginger jam for us all.'

Startled, Emma shook her head.

'I have no idea of the recipe. I was always only the helper.'

'I have just the thing for you,' Judith said as she rummaged in the dresser drawer before taking out a worn leather book.

'Stephen's recipes. You will find the rhubarb and ginger recipe on the third page. His favourite was strawberry jam followed closely by blackberry and apple.'

'Are you sure? What if I don't get it right and it won't set?'

'Oh, it's like riding a bike; it will all come back to you. But let's do a small batch first,' Judith said as she checked on Emma's hair.

'Time to rinse off the dye and reveal your new colour,' she said, leading the way to the sink.

'Shouldn't I do this in the bathroom?' Emma asked.

'And risk getting dye all over the place on the way up the stairs. No way. I have a shower attachment for the tap,' Judith said.

Judith rinsed Emma's hair before applying conditioner, then rinsed again and wrapped an old towel around it.

When the towel became heavy, Emma unwrapped it and let her hair fall around her shoulders.

Judith procured a small mirror from a drawer. 'I think we have done a fine job,' she said.

Emma peered into the mirror. The woman who looked back at her was different, but the brown colour, which sat evenly across her hair, only highlighted the strained look on her face. But Emma didn't care, all that mattered was that she looked completely different.

'Do you like it?' Judith asked anxiously.

'I love it,' Emma said, and Judith clapped.

'Let's get Jack to drop in some rhubarb, and you can start your first batch of jam.'

'It will have to be tomorrow because I will have to soak the rhubarb in sugar overnight.'

'Of course, of course.' Judith waved her hand, 'Let's do it tomorrow morning after our meeting to discuss TikTok strategy,' Judith said.

The next morning, Emma was again awake at dawn. Sleep still did not come easy for her; there was too much running inside her head. She pulled on jeans and a hoodie, and tiptoed down to the kitchen. Lifting the big cauldron of rhubarb from the high dresser shelf, she set up a big stainless steel pot on the hob for the jam. There was something relaxing about standing at the cooker, watching for the sugary rhubarb mixture to bubble. There was a rhythm in the stirring which never failed to calm her brain. Her grandmother said it gave time to stop and think, and there was the bonus of jam at the end.

When Judith swept into the room, wearing a hotel dressing gown, over an hour later, Emma was testing to see if the jam would set by placing some on a cold plate.

'Oh, it looks perfect. May I taste?' Judith said, reaching for a spoon and scooping nearly all of the jam patch on the plate.

She put it in her mouth and closed her eyes.

'I never thought I would say this, but it is better than Stephen's. Just the right balance between the rhubarb, sugar and ginger.'

Emma scooped the mixture into jars she had sterilised earlier as Judith cleared a spot on the dresser shelf for them.

As the sweet smell filled the air, reminding her of her grandma, Emma realised she hadn't felt this at home in months. She felt safe here at Killcawley Estate. It was too early to hope, but maybe this really would be the start of a new life for her.

FOUR

The days melded into each other, and Judith and Emma developed a routine of sorts. Emma told Judith she would have to increase her TikTok videos to one a day so she could build up her followers and her profile.

'Well, I certainly have enough hats for a daily caper in front of the camera,' Judith said.

Emma explained that previous videos had been too long, and what they needed to do was make snapshots of her fashion, and maybe of Killcawley Estate as well.

'Sounds like you're going to make me go viral.' Judith laughed, and Emma was worried that her expectations were too high.

They had breakfast together each morning, and made a TikTok video afterwards. After lunch, Judith usually had a nap, which gave Emma time to explore the farm. Emma usually prepared the evening meal, and they spent an hour or so on chat and correspondence afterwards. Emma liked the pace of life at Killcawley, though she had little time to herself. But that also meant there wasn't much time for her to dwell on why she was here.

. . .

Even though it had only been a week, she recognised Judith's heavy step on the stairs. She poured a mug of coffee and waited for her to burst in through the kitchen door.

'What do you think?' Judith asked as she stepped into the room and twirled about.

Emma, who was sitting at the kitchen table about to butter some toast, stopped and stared.

Judith threw her hands in the air and twirled again to show off the batwing sleeves of the long pink dress, which were finished with a pearl cuff.

'Isn't it just divine? Marsha brought it back from Dublin; she does all my rescues on my second-hand beauties. It's vintage, you know.'

A woman with dyed black hair caught back in a severe bun wandered into the kitchen after Judith. She extended her hand to Emma.

'I'm Marsha. I've heard so much about you, Emma. Sorry for not meeting you sooner, I've been away, staying with a relative in the city. Judith says she thinks you'll be the one to bring life back to Killcawley Estate.'

'I wouldn't exactly say that,' Emma said, her cheeks flushing with embarrassment.

Judith twirled around the room again, almost falling over the dog.

'All eyes on me, please. This is my piece for this week. To think it was being thrown out, and all you had to do was deal with a few moth holes and fraying around the hem and sleeves,' she said.

Marsha clicked her tongue. 'I'm glad you think I had little to do, but that doesn't matter – you pay well.'

Judith stopped. 'A marvellous job, Marsha. I couldn't have such a high profile, but for you.'

'High profile my ass. Sure, who looks at that TikTok anyway?'

Judith rolled her eyes. 'You go ask any young person and they'll tell you you're nobody if you're not on TikTok. Sure, China probably has a file on me in Beijing...'

Marsha pulled out a chair at the table and sat down. 'Well, I hope they record that you have a big, fat head,' she muttered, and Emma sniggered.

Judith edged around the back of Marsha's chair and landed a kiss on her head. 'She loves me, really. And, unlike a lot of her other customers, I always pay on time. We are also the best of friends, have been forever.'

'There's that,' Marsha said.

Emma got two mugs and poured some coffee.

'Nonsense girl, we're going to have some bubbly,' Judith said.

'But it's not yet noon.'

Marsha laughed. 'Live long enough with this one, and you will be having it for breakfast, lunch and dinner. The rest of us swear it's what is keeping her looking so good.'

'I need some, so I can cavort for the camera. We TikTokers can't just stand about like a statue.'

'We know all about that; tell her about the time you persuaded Jack to dance with you. He was the laughing stock of the county afterwards.'

'That's not fair, he looked mighty fine in a gentleman's tails and top hat.'

'As if you could wear that get-up in Killcawley or anywhere else for that matter,' Marsha said with a loud sniff.

'I will wear this dress at the Estate Supper Club.'

'You do that; it will give us something to talk about,' Marsha said.

Emma looked at the others.

'What is the supper club?'

Marsha laughed. 'We meet, we eat, we drink and we gossip. And good old Ms Fancy Pants has us trying out different foods and calls us a supper club.'

Judith waved Marsha away. 'Of course you're invited Emma; tomorrow is French night.'

'Emma, don't be thinking it is anything fancy; we eat and chat and sometimes set the world to rights,' Marsha whispered as she reached for a biscuit from the packet in the middle of the table.

'I like to think of it as a high-brow supper club where we sample the cuisine from around the world and—' Judith said.

Marsha hooted with laughter. 'Get over yourself, J. Don't sound so high and mighty. We all know you have had the bucks all your life while the rest of us are left relying on the pension, and the bits we make from doing odd jobs like dressmaking.'

Judith, ignoring her friend, pulled out a deep pink headband with tassels hanging on either side and placed it on her head. 'Doesn't it go perfectly with the gown? You must join us, Emma; bring fresh new ideas to the table,' she said.

Emma smiled. She had never met anyone quite like Judith.

Marsha turned to Judith. 'I am off to do a day's work, you enjoy your photo shoot, lovelies,' she said.

When she was gone, Judith flopped down at the table and poured some milk in her coffee.

'Don't mind Marsha, she's always like that.'

'Doesn't it bother you that people might resent your wealth?'

'Not Marsha, she's a good friend. Others have no idea what it takes to run a place like Killcawley Estate. If Miles didn't inject capital into the estate every few months, I would be out on my ear.'

'The estate must give a lot back to the community, though?'

'Well, you know what they say; you're never appreciated until you're gone. Maybe they think I have outstayed my welcome. But Marsha is all right; she says it straight out, others like to mutter behind my back. Marsha is a friend; we trust each other. I know if the chips were down, she would be on my side.'

She blew on her coffee to cool it before sipping from the mug. 'Are you ready for our photo shoot?'

'What do you want me to do?' Emma said.

'Follow me for starters, and I think we will film by the purple rhododendron on the driveway. It will provide a nice contrast to the dress.'

Emma placed the mugs in the dishwasher before following Judith down the avenue to the small rhododendron grove.

'The light is perfect here. Let's get this done before Jack decides he wants a cameo and passes by in his tractor. Since our last dance routine together, he has been persecuting me, always appearing either to trim a hedge or drive his tractor when I am trying to prepare my content.'

Pinching her cheeks to pull up her colour, Judith threw a pose while Emma filmed.

Throwing her hands in the air, Judith reached for a rhododendron bloom. She showed her well-turned ankle, and the vintage silver sandals, which were way too high for walking around a garden. Suddenly, she stopped and looked directly at Emma.

'Emma, you're preoccupied,' she said, pulling a funny face.

'Maybe a little. I noticed we're picking up quite a few hundred followers every day.'

'But that's good?'

'Yes, but it is also a pressure. I just hope I can keep delivering quality content.'

Judith laughed. 'They just want to see an old lady wearing funny hats and dancing about the place; don't take it all so seriously.'

'If you believe that, why do you do it?' Emma asked.

'I want to be part of the wider world; it makes me feel

connected. At my age, there is a risk of being invisible. You're young and beautiful; it's difficult for you to fully understand.'

'I understand, I think.'

'I'm not going to start believing my own PR – give me some credit. This is fun, and believe you me, when you get old, there isn't much chance to have fun.'

Judith made a face and stuck out her tongue, making Emma laugh.

'OK, let's get this video done,' Emma said.

Later, Emma headed to the walled garden and to the bed where the rhubarb was growing. She forked some manure from the wheelbarrow under the wide leaves. Judith was an enigma, she thought. She had this beautiful estate and yet she insisted on forging a career as a social media influencer. It was as if because of her age, Judith was constantly trying to prove that she could outdo everybody, and Emma found this exhausting.

Here in the walled garden, Emma found refuge. Among the fruit trees and the vegetable garden, and the beds of flowers sown specially for their value as cut flowers in the Killcawley Estate vases, Emma found peace. Surrounded by the beds of broad beans and carrots, and the banks of perennial and annual flowers, she could think clearly.

She closed her eyes, but almost immediately opened them when she heard a branch crack nearby.

'Has madam finished her photo shoot?' Jack called out.

Startled, Emma jumped up and burst into tears.

Jack rushed to her. 'What's wrong?'

Emma shook her head.

'Did you two have a row?' he asked gently.

'Nothing like that; I am just trying to find my feet and it's difficult.'

'And Judy can be a bit overwhelming.'

Emma nodded. 'I'm all for how fit and active she is. I know I'm being a stick in the mud, but I don't see the point to the whole social media profile and all the dressing up.'

'At her age, you forgot to say,' Jack said gently.

Emma looked at him, more tears forming in her eyes. 'And now you think I am ageist.'

'I am the same age as Judy, give or take a year, and you won't see me on social media ever again. I had my fifteen seconds, and it was torture for a long time afterwards. Judy loves it. I think it's one of the things that keeps her young.'

'She has been so good to me. I shouldn't be talking like this behind her back,' Emma said, kicking out at a small group of nettles.

She thought Jack wanted to say more, but he turned away and pretended to examine the raspberry bushes.

'Is there something else? I feel I have missed something big, and you're not telling me,' she said.

He suggested they sit down at the gazebo. 'It looks away from the house, so we can't be seen,' he said, by way of an explanation. He waited until she had settled on the wooden bench inside the gazebo before he started talking.

'I suppose there's no harm telling you, but these photo shoots knock a lot out of Judith.'

'Is she ill? Oh God, no.'

'She is full of energy, and so enthusiastic about her social media, but there is a sadness about it all,' Jack said.

'I don't understand.'

'She wasn't always like this, you know. But when Stephen, her husband, got cancer, and had to have chemotherapy, she had to find a way of coping.'

'I didn't know.'

Jack continued, 'She went with Stephen to every chemo session, but instead of taking it lying down, she said she was going to fight with him all the way. She came up with this idea of dressing up for chemo.'

'Sounds macabre.'

'But it wasn't, it gave them both something else to concentrate on. Stephen was her photographer back then, and they had such a laugh at a time when everything was dark.'

Emma bent forward, her head in her hands. She couldn't even imagine what that must have been like.

'Judy is like a bird – fragile, and flapping about when injured. She and Stephen were married a very long time; you don't get over that quickly. The day she stops being outrageous is the day we'll lose her.'

'What do I do now?'

'Carry on, and tell her you will help her as much as she wants with the social media. Put up with her foibles too. Humour her; that's what the rest of us do, when she gets a little precious.'

Emma reached over and shook Jack's hand.

'You're a good friend, Jack. Thank you.'

She rushed back to the house, but Judith had already gone to her room to lie down.

Emma stole upstairs and lingered outside Judith's suite, before knocking on the door and asking if she was OK.

Judith opened the door.

'Don't be worrying, darling, we'll get to know each other well over time,' she said, reaching out and kissing Emma on the cheek. 'I know I can come across as slightly batty. Now, let me rest. Today has been stressful, and I must get ready. Miles is going to FaceTime me and I must be in top form. No point worrying the lad.'

Emma retired to her own room. Her head was thumping, and she needed to lie down. Working at Killcawley Estate was not as easy as she'd expected, and when things went wrong, there was nowhere to escape.

FIVE

A couple of hours later, Emma was dozing when a knock on her bedroom door woke her. Sleepily, she got off the bed, and opened the door.

'Let's get to know each other. I expected you to fit in without even telling you much about us. Please forgive me,' Judith said.

She bowed low to Emma.

'If I may, I would like to show you my special room.'

She led Emma down to the next landing and opened the door of a small room overlooking the courtyard.

Emma gasped when she stepped inside. The powder pink walls were lined with shelves holding different hats of all shapes and sizes. A pyramid of multicoloured hat boxes partially obscured the light coming in through one window, and special hat stands replaced curtains at another tall window.

'Welcome to my hat room,' Judith said.

'I have never seen anything like it. It's like a vintage hat shop. There are more hats here than the shop where I got the fascinator,' Emma said, before looking at Judith. 'You were very kind about the fascinator, but you have no need for another adornment for your head.'

Judith placed a black silk cloche hat with a big red silk poppy on her head, and chortled as she looked in one of the room's many mirrors.

'*Need?* I don't know about that. But I will always *want* just one more hat. I adore hats.'

'But why so many?'

Judith turned around. The hat matched her dress beautifully, the red of the flower picked out in the sparkles of her jewellery.

'Why not? I have the space, after all.'

Emma picked up a hat that looked like a mass of pink and silver feathers, but replaced it as quickly.

Judith reached for a simple blue beret.

'Here, put this on; you need to get familiar with wearing a hat before venturing forth in a sea of feathers.'

Emma pulled away. 'I don't really wear hats. Only in winter when it's cold.'

'There is no pleasure in wearing a hat out of necessity. Here, let's have some fun,' she said, taking Emma to the mirror and placing the beret on her head.'

Emma looked at herself. She was smiling as she realigned the beret.

'See, I told you. Once you put on a nice hat, doesn't it make you feel better about yourself?' Judith said.

Emma nodded, but before she could admire herself further, Judith had whipped off the beret and replaced it with an orange straw cloche with a ribbon tightly pulled around the crown and tied into a little bow at the back.

'Beautiful with your long hair and fresh young looks. I have to wear too much make-up with it, because the orange drains the colour from my face,' Judith said as Emma nervously viewed herself from all sides.

'I'm not sure it's me,' she said.

Judith stopped what she was doing and reached for a wide-brimmed straw had with a white band.

'Perfect for you for summer. I hope you know you can tell me what is going on; it always helps to talk.'

Emma smiled but tried to divert the conversation away from herself. 'Did you always love hats?'

Judith wagged her finger. 'OK, I'll let you get away with it this once. Yes, I began wearing hats in the seventies. I was always regarded as a little odd, but because I was the woman in the big house, most put up with me. '

'Wearing a hat in these parts must have appeared strange.'

'You only feel out of place if you're not comfortable. For me, a hat always adds the finishing touch to an outfit. Or it can elevate an ensemble. There were days when I put my hat on and it changed my whole outlook on the world. I felt empowered. But, most of all, it's always fun to wear a hat.'

'But you are brave. Not many of us can carry off the unusual, like you can.'

'Nonsense. It is all a state of mind,' Judith said as she placed a deep red top hat with a broad navy band on Emma's head.

'Beautiful. One of these days I hope to see you sneak in here, and steal a hat. I will be overjoyed; just don't touch anything in the hat boxes without my express permission, because they are the expensive designer hats that I treasure above most other things.'

'I don't think you need worry that I will ever steal one, but they all look lovely on you,' Emma said as she slid off the hat and put it back on its stand.

'Just promise me when you want to talk, you will come knocking on my door,' Judith said.

'Soon,' Emma said, but she was interrupted by somebody calling from the hall.

'Ladies, can I come up?' Marsha called.

Judith shouted they were in the hat room, and they heard Marsha plodding up the stairs.

She was out of puff when she got to the top of the landing.

'With all your money, do you think you could put in a lift?' she said, wiping her brow.

'It keeps us fit and trim,' Judith said as she rearranged the hat boxes, before stopping to open a silver and black one.

'I am showing Emma my collection,' she said as she carefully took out a hat covered in white tissue.

Clearing off a space on a small table, she unwrapped a purple confection adorned with delicate feathers and a silk flower and placed it on a special stand.

'Miles bought it for me for my seventieth birthday. I have only worn it once; it's a Philip Treacy.'

Carefully, she turned it over to show the label – Philip Treacy London – sewn in to the underside.

'Try it on, girl. It will be nice with the black dress,' Marsha said, pulling out a stool from the corner and sitting down.

Judith beamed as if she had been waiting for encouragement.

Standing in front of the mirror, she used her two hands to gently place the hat on her head, easing it back so that it rested neatly.

'It cost a fortune, I'm sure. I always feel I need an occasion to wear it. You don't do a grocery shop in a Philip Treacy hat,' Judith said, sounding wistful.

'Nonsense, darling. If you wait for an occasion to wear any of your good hats, we'll all be dead,' Marsha said in her matter-of-fact tone.

She turned to Emma.

'This one is mad about hats. You know, when she was in her twenties she got this crazy notion that she would like a job, and of course she landed one in Dublin as an executive assistant.

Within two months she had left because the CEO said she could not wear a hat at work.'

Judith shrugged. 'I was right, the man had no style.'

Marsha reached over and took a wide-brimmed black straw hat with large black and white flowers from its stand. Plonking it on her head, she waddled over to the mirror. With her hand on her hip, she managed to elbow Judith out of the way.

'Move over, sister,' she said as she stood making faces at the mirror.

'I'm way too short to wear a hat,' she said, and before the others had time to say anything, she added: 'That's my story and I'm sticking to it.'

Emma was battling to stop a stack of hats from toppling over, when Marsha rushed out of the room to answer her phone. A few moments later Marsha stuck her head around the door and said she had to leave.

'Are you OK, darling?' Judith asked.

'Good news. The decorator has finished at the lodge. I can move back there tomorrow.'

'Good news, indeed,' Judith said.

'No offence, but I can't wait to get home. I will see you at the supper club tomorrow,' Marsha said quickly.

Judith took a wide-brimmed straw hat and put it on before reaching over and placing the hat on Emma's head, tilting it an angle.

'Lovely. I want to see you walking around the estate wearing that hat; it is meant for somebody young like you.'

'I don't think so; I don't really know how to wear a hat,' Emma said, shrinking away.

'Nonsense, I absolutely insist. Anyone can wear a hat; the trick is to wear it with confidence.'

'Which is easy for you Judith, but not me,' Emma said stiffly.

'Darling, you're at Killcawley Estate now; it is time to open up to new possibilities. Wearing a hat might seem a tiny enough possibility, a folly even, but let's start with the small stuff.'

Emma allowed Judith to lead her to the mirror where she stood and looked at herself, a tall woman wearing a hat that was at odds with her blue jeans and T-shirt. It looked quirky and different, and she secretly liked it.

Judith came behind her and gave a thumbs up.

SIX

Emma slipped out of the house early while Judith was in the kitchen preparing her signature French dish, coq au vin, for the supper club's French evening.

She told Emma she had learned the recipe from a Parisian chef. She had also ordered bottles of a full-bodied French red wine from the wine shop in Dublin which were expected to be delivered that morning.

Emma knew she should help, but Judith was sometimes hard to take on an ordinary day. However, today she was surpassing herself by slipping in French phrases whenever she could. Slowly and quietly, Emma let herself out the front door and quickly scooted off down the hill, where there was a door directly into the walled garden.

Briskly, she walked down through the woods, and towards the wildflower meadows. She needed to be alone. The wind billowed out her skirt, and her hair fell in front of her eyes as she followed the path down the hill. She wanted to run like she had as a child and let herself go, stumbling and falling. She wanted to feel the joy of being carefree again. She had become too wary, too reticent. A rabbit zipped in front of her, and she stopped, watching it weave between the grass and the wildflowers, and out of sight.

When she got as far as the oak tree, she stood, letting her hand rest on the bark. How many had done this before her?

Shivering, she dropped to the ground, settling in with her back to the tree trunk. Closing her eyes, she listened to the sounds around her. Buzzing bees drawing up pollen from the red poppies. Somewhere up above her, there was a piercing cry. She knew it was a hawk, as all around her the little birds stopped singing. It was as if all the life in the meadow took a collective breath, and everything stood still, until the hawk spotted easier prey elsewhere and glided away. Bit by bit, the birdsong and the busyness returned; a blackbird called out and a robin came and landed to the right of Emma, watching her. She opened her eyes, and breathed in the fragrant air. She was at peace here, where history stood side by side with the wildlife, welcoming newcomers, and making them feel at home.

The sound of chatter drifting over the meadow told her Judith was coming her way. She saw her and Jack strolling down through the meadows. When Judith saw her, she waved enthusiastically.

'The coq au vin is delicious, and Jack has prepped some potatoes to roast. We are going to pick some fresh fruit as well. I don't trust Marsha will bother her arse past an apple pie,' Judith said, when they came closer.

'We have some nice cheese from the market for a cheese board,' Emma said.

'*Magnifique*. Now, does anyone know an easy French dessert as an extra?' Judith said, looking at Jack.

'I could run to profiteroles, maybe with a Baileys cream if you have the ingredients,' Jack said.

Judith whooped with excitement, and said '*magnifique*' again. Then, she took a little jar of rhubarb jam from the picnic basket slung over her arm.

'Darling, your jam is truly magnificent. Stephen always intended to have a little jam business. He planned to call it 'Killcawley Estate Preserves'. I am sure he even got labels made up and they are somewhere in the stable block. Stephen had what he called a jam shed out there.'

'I don't know if I want to take it that far. I'm just using up the rhubarb.'

'Nonsense, girl. It will be fine; the local shops can take it for starters, and who knows after that. We may conquer the world.'

Emma wanted to scream that she did not want to start a business; she was happy where she was, and she was only finding her feet, but when she saw the excitement in Judith's face, she pulled back.

'I'm not sure rhubarb and ginger jam is the key to taking over the world,' she said, and she was relieved when Jack said they had to get going.

'We're off to find wild strawberries for Judy's pavlova to go beside my profiteroles,' he said, gently directing her around the oak tree.

Emma watched as they made their way along the side of the meadow and over a stone wall in to another field.

When she got back to the house, she checked the casserole and turned down the oven, before sitting down to edit and upload a video of Judith in a purple frock walking among the roses in the walled garden. She didn't have to wait long before there were thousands of views and 3000 likes, which gave Emma a big thrill.

Emma, Judith and Jack were busy in the kitchen when Hetty and Marsha arrived for the supper club. Carrying a large box, Hetty was first in the door. She was wearing navy trousers and a white blouse, with a pink shawl over one shoulder, and she was smiling broadly.

'I am the worst in the world, but I couldn't find any French recipe I could tackle, so if nobody minds, I bought some lovely fresh baguettes and chocolate which I think has some French connection.'

Judith took the baguettes and chocolate with a stiff smile.

Marsha made a big deal of kissing everybody on both cheeks. '*Bonsoir*,' she said, laughing, and adding that she adored the continental way of greeting.

'Did you bring any dessert?' Judith asked firmly.

Marsha took a pie dish out of a plastic bag.

'My first apple pie with a French flag,' she said, placing the pie with a homemade paper flag in red, white and blue in the middle of the table.

Judith rolled her eyes.

'Marsha, couldn't you have looked up some recipes?'

'Why would I? Everybody loves my apple tart.'

'A tarte tatin would have been nice,' Judith said, before disappearing out the kitchen door.

'Where is she gone?' Hetty asked

'Judy is changing into a special dress for tonight,' Jack said, pouring out the wine and handing the glasses around.

Quite some time had passed, and Emma was placing the plates on the table when Judith swept into the room in a low-cut red dress with a skirt that swished from side to side as she walked.

'Mother of divine Jesus, what are you wearing?' Marsha said.

Judith, who gave Marsha a fierce look, sat down as Jack placed a glass of wine in her hand.

'*Bonsoir*,' she said, staring at Hetty, who was pretending to blow her nose to hide her laughter.

'You should have told us we were coming to a ball,' Marsha sniffed.

'We're starving, waiting for you – the aroma is killing us,' Hetty said.

'Let's sit and welcome Emma to her first supper club,' Judith said.

The others raised their glasses, and they all clinked.

'Let's eat. We'll all be in a better mood when we have tasted these divine dishes,' Judith said, placing the garlic roast potatoes on the table along with a simple green salad.

'Could you not have used chicken breasts? I'm afraid I will choke on the bones,' Hetty muttered, pushing the stew around her plate.

Judith looked at her severely. 'Try it; you'll find the meat falls away from the bone,' she said testily as she finished ladling out the dish.

They ate mainly in silence, Marsha announcing that the food was delicious and Jack refilling everybody's glass. They had got to the stage where they were all feeling quite full and satisfied when Hetty broke into the silence.

'Emma, tell us a little about yourself,' she said.

The women looked at her expectantly.

'There's not much to tell,' Emma said uncertainly.

Marsha leaned closer to Emma.

'What I would like to know is how somebody who was a high-flying legal secretary ended up in the arsehole of nowhere?' she said.

Judith slapped down her glass a little hard, splashing wine on the linen tablecloth. 'Hey, the supper club is where good conversation happens, it's not meant to be a bloody inquisition. I'm sure there are many other things we could discuss,' she said.

'There are, but we would love to hear about Emma, just a cosy chat,' Marsha said.

Emma went to the fridge and took out the pavlova.

Hetty said they should change the subject, because Judith didn't look too happy.

'I just think we should let Emma tell us in her own time why she came this way. Anyway, she has family connections to Killcawley.'

'What?' Jack said.

'Who? Do tell us more,' Hetty said.

Emma sat down at the table. 'My grandmother lived in the village at one time.'

'Who was she?' Marsha asked.

'Kitty Shanahan.'

'Oh, Judith, don't you remember Kitty? You two were best pals,' Hetty said.

Emma looked at Judith. 'But you said...'

Judith shifted in her chair. 'Darling, at my age, some things are buried too deep,' she said.

'Let's have dessert,' Jack said, in an attempt to change the subject.

Judith fussed about gathering up the dinner plates as Emma took dessert bowls down from the dresser.

'Wasn't there some sort of scandal?' Hetty said.

Jack placed the pavlova and profiteroles in the centre of the table. 'Ladies, a perfect pavlova and delicious profiteroles made by my own fair hands,' he said, his voice loud to drown out Hetty's mutterings.

'Good man,' Marsha said.

Emma wasn't sure what to do. She knew Judith felt uncomfortable and didn't want to discuss her grandmother at the supper club table. But she was desperate to know more. Her grandma had been the most important person in the world to her. But Judith had stuck up for her, and it didn't feel right to press her in front of the others.

'Would anyone mind if I called it a night? I have a headache,' she said.

'Oh dear, have we upset you?' Hetty asked.

'We certainly didn't mean to be firing questions at you. Stay and we'll have coffee with dessert,' Marsha said kindly.

Judith put her arm around Emma's shoulders. 'Let me bring up a whiskey to you; it will help you sleep.'

Emma nodded, then escaped upstairs. She didn't go to bed, but sat in the dark looking out over the lake where the moonbeams were dancing across the surface.

A short while later, Judith eased the door open, and stuck her head into the room.

'Darling, I have a small shot of whiskey for you,' she said.

Emma switched on a light and took the glass from Judith's hand. 'Why wouldn't you tell me you were friends with my grandmother? Did you have a falling out?'

Judith sighed loudly. 'No, I loved your grandmother, but life got in the way.'

'So, why leave me in the dark?'

Judith turned back to the door. 'It's complicated, Emma. Can you give me until tomorrow?'

'I suppose.'

She heard Judith go downstairs to her suite, and she thought she heard sobbing. Unable to listen to it, she turned up TikTok on her phone. She didn't know why Judith had pretended she didn't know her grandmother, but she didn't want to think about what she could be hiding from her.

Life had suddenly got a lot more complicated, and Emma wondered if she could really trust Judith.

SEVEN

Judith tapped on Emma's bedroom door early the next morning.

'Darling, I have a breakfast tray here for you,' she said.

Emma pulled on a dressing gown, and opened the door. Judith was holding a tray with buttered toast, a jar of rhubarb and ginger jam, a pot of freshly brewed coffee along with two mugs, and two glasses of orange juice on it.

'I would have come downstairs,' Emma said, standing back to let Judith in.

'I felt I had to make an effort. I am so sorry I didn't tell you about your grandmother earlier.'

'You're going to tell me now, I hope.'

Judith hesitated. 'You're cross, but I didn't know how to find the words; to my dying day I will regret that I stood idly by. I was young, but I could have protested.' Judith's words came out in a rush.

'I don't understand.'

Emma took the tray, and set it down on the coffee table. Judith hung back until Emma invited her to sit.

'Pour the coffee, darling. I have a lot of talking to do, if you're prepared to listen.'

Emma did as she asked, then took a slice of toast and slathered on some jam.

Judith gulped her coffee before she started her story.

'Kitty and I were such good friends. When she was around, I laughed so much.'

'So you met at school, then?'

'I saw her at school, but she stopped attending as soon as she could and went to work in the local chipper. My parents frowned on me associating with her, but I liked Kitty. Around her, life was never dull. And living in this big house when I was eighteen years of age was extremely dull.'

'I never knew why she was in Killcawley,' Emma said.

'It was all hush-hush, but everyone is dead now, so no harm talking about it.'

'What do you mean?'

'Her mother ran off with a French man. Kitty didn't react well and her poor dad found it hard to cope. She was a wild one, and I suppose he thought sending her from the UK to a village in the middle of nowhere meant she couldn't get into much trouble. His sister Megan lived in Killcawley at the time, so Kitty came to live with her.'

'She mentioned her, said she was very strict.'

'They were knocking heads all the time. I'm not sure it was the best thing sending Kitty to Ireland.' Judith sighed. 'That girl came into Killcawley like a whirlwind. Every boy in the place was after her, but she only had eyes for my friend, Justin Baker. He came to stay with our family from England every summer. I think it was expected that eventually he and I...'

'But you married—'

'My Stephen. I think I was destined for an arranged marriage one way or another. Stephen's family owned the neighbouring estate, so our union brought together two tracts of land which make up Killcawley Estate today. Kitty, though, fell madly in love with Justin, and he was infatuated with her. They spent a long summer together, and when he returned to Nottingham, they corresponded by letter.'

'I never knew it was so romantic.'

Judith slurped her coffee, and snorted. 'Your grandmother was the least romantic person I knew. Justin spilled himself out onto the page, but she hadn't a clue how to answer him. Kitty wasn't much of a writer. So she roped me in, and I wrote the letters for her.'

'But did you have feelings for him?'

Judith sighed. 'I was only eighteen, and I had feelings for another. I couldn't say no to Kitty and she was so much in love. I wanted to help her, she loved Justin so much.'

Judith stood up, and walked to the window. 'In a weird way, I liked it; I could write like I was corresponding with my beau. In the end, Justin persuaded Kitty, to join him in the UK and I lost a good friend within weeks.'

Emma thought Judith looked lonely, standing there looking out over the lake.

'Do you know what happened after that?' Emma asked quietly.

Judith remained at the window. 'I'm not sure what you have been told.'

'Nothing much. Please, tell me.'

Judith sighed, and moved back to sit beside Emma. 'Kitty stole off to the UK, leaving a note for her aunt. Justin left his home, and they moved to a small flat in Coventry. Eventually Justin's family caught up with them, and threatened to disinherit him, if he continued with the relationship. Don't underestimate what that meant; Justin's parents were serious landowners, but also total snobs. He point-blank refused to turn his back on Kitty, and his parents kept their promise.'

Emma gasped in shock. Waves of anxiety coursed through her, but she also felt angry. When Judith pushed a box of tissues in her direction, Emma batted it away too fiercely.

'I just don't understand; they were young and in love,' she cried.

Judith shook her head. 'Justin found a job working as a journalist, and the two of them managed. Kitty became pregnant, and they were very excited by that. Her dad pleaded with her to come home. He was afraid for her.'

Judith stopped. Emma wasn't sure if it was for dramatic effect, or because she was finding the subject so difficult. When she began to talk again, her voice was shaking.

'And then everything changed. Justin was walking home from his newspaper office one night when he was knocked down by a car. He was dead before the ambulance arrived.'

Emma sat up straight. 'You think it might not have been an accident?'

'I never knew what to think. Justin was dead, and Kitty was bereft. She went back to live with her dad, and your mother was born five months later.'

'And that was it? My grandad's family never bothered with her after that?'

'Kitty and her daughter were wiped from their history. Kitty was grieving and she didn't want any contact from anybody in her past. I can understand it; she had to forge a new life. We didn't have contact after that.'

'She died just before I graduated. My mother died a year later,' Emma said.

'You have had it so tough, darling,' Judith said, taking Emma's hands and squeezing them tight.

'Kitty must have spoken well about some of her time in Killcawley, if you thought of coming here,' she said.

'It was the happiest time of her life in Killcawley. She said she felt safe and very much loved.'

'Is that why you came here? Somewhere to feel safe?'

Emma shifted uncomfortably in her chair. 'Yes,' she said quietly.

'I feel I've let you down, Emma, but I buried all this so deep, I could barely think about it.'

'I understand.'

Judith shook her head.

'I feel I should have done more, but I was young, and what happened was so shocking and sad, I could hardly function afterwards. And now here you are, Emma; it's like I have been offered a second chance at friendship.

Emma got up, and stuck out her hand to Judith. 'Let's go downstairs; we have done enough talking.'

Judith pulled Emma into a hug. 'You remind me of your grandmother; you have the same kind streak.'

They walked hand in hand down the stairs, and got to the kitchen just as Marsha knocked on the window.

'Didn't you see enough of us last night?' Judith asked in a sarcastic voice.

Marsha dropped a brown paper bag on the table.

'Hetty and I were talking; we were hard on Emma and we're sorry. There are a few croissants there for breakfast. A tiny peace offering,' she said.

'Thank you,' Emma said as she placed the croissants on the plate and filled the kettle to make tea.

While Judith slipped out of the room to put on her TikTok outfit, Marsha came up behind Emma.

'While Judith is out, sweetheart, can I just say you're going to have to learn to stand up for yourself. You should have just told us to mind our own business.'

Emma concentrated on rinsing the teapot and didn't say anything.

Marsha stepped in beside her. 'You've suffered too, I can see that now. Don't worry – there won't be any more grief from me,' Marsha said, gently hugging Emma.

'Thanks,' Emma said.

'Now, let's get the tea made before the queen dowager comes back, and I am in another pickle,' Marsha laughed.

When Judith came back, she stood and observed Emma and Marsha. 'This is nice to behold. Are you two good?' she asked.

'Three of us; Hetty is here in spirit,' Marsha said.

Judith, who was wearing a long leopard-print dress and a matching light coat, said they had to get to the lake and make a video.

'We need to get a video up; there are millions waiting for me,' she said, and Emma wasn't quite sure if she was joking or not.

Judith walked ahead, laughing as the wind whipped around her dress. She danced on, gesturing to Emma to join in.

'She'll frighten away the ducks with that caper,' Marsha whispered as she diverted down the avenue.

'Is red lipstick too much, or should I tone it down?' Judith asked, as Emma joined her at the bottom of the hill. She took out her compact mirror to check her make-up.

'Tone it down, I think.'

'Because red screams "mutton dressed as lamb", I know.'

'I wasn't thinking that.'

'Of course not. If we're to get on, though, be honest with me, Emma,' Judith said as she twirled near the ducks, making them scatter, squawking across the lake.

'I am thinking frivolity and fun at Killcawley Estate,' she said, taking off the coat and throwing it at Emma. 'OK, like that at the camera?' she said.

'OK,' Emma said, picking up the coat, and handing it back to Judith.

'You're not yet very comfortable with all this social media stuff are you?'

'It's all right, as long as I don't have to appear on camera.'

Judith chortled. 'Why would I want you with your lovely young looks and long tresses in front of the camera, darling?

Nobody would look at me then. Now, say "action" when it's time to shoot.'

Emma positioned the phone and muttered 'action'. Judith danced by the shore, making the two swans veer off course and move towards the centre of the lake. When she was finished, Judith said 'cut'.

'I think that went very well,' she said, leading the way up the hill. Back at the house, Judith stepped into the drawing room to take a call, and immediately afterwards ran upstairs to change into jeans and a long-sleeved top.

'I am going out for a while. Will you upload to TikTok? I will see you later,' she said hurriedly.

Emma nodded, but she was puzzled at Judith's hasty departure.

After Emma had edited and uploaded the video, she put on her walking shoes and set off for the wildflower meadows.

It was mid-morning and the birds were quiet as she made her way through the woods and out onto the meadow. Slowly, she picked her way along the path, which had now become overgrown, patches of pink and red poppies wafting in the light breeze and cowslips spilling over in places.

The recent rain had battered the flowers, and they were beginning to look bedraggled. Soon, Jack would have to cut the meadow, but she knew that Judith had asked him to hold off another week or so.

When she got to the top of the hill, she saw Judith sitting under the oak tree. Emma hesitated for a moment, wondering whether to interrupt her meditation. She was still standing there when Jack approached the tree from the direction of the village. He rushed to Judith, who whooped loudly and threw herself into Jack's arms. He swung her around before holding her close and kissing her hair, and then gently setting her down on her feet. There was something about the two of them that made Emma think that what she was looking at was a couple who knew and loved each other deeply. Aware she was intruding, Emma backed up before she was spotted.

Quickly, she made her way through the woodland, branches snapping beneath her feet.

She shook herself to dislodge the thought and admonished herself that this was none of her business. It was nice and romantic, she thought, and she wondered why – months after her husband's death – Judith felt she had to meet Jack in secret.

Back at the house, Emma escaped to her room.

Curling up in a chair at the window, she tracked the swans on the lake as they flapped their wings and took off, circling the perimeter of the lake as if getting their bearings, before heading south. Jack said they alternated between the lake and the marsh near the beach at Kilcoole a few miles down the road.

He said the swans always came back, but sometimes stayed away a day or two. Judith fretted when they were gone, afraid she had lost them for good.

Emma wished they would come back as well. They were a reminder to her that togetherness could last forever. She needed to know there was love and devotion like that out there right now. A knock at the door interrupted her thoughts, and she thought of not answering, but she had to when Judith pleaded with her.

When Emma pulled back the door, Judith was in front of her wearing a different outfit: white palazzo pants, a crisp white linen shirt and a large straw hat trimmed in blue and white.

'There is nothing on the lake; the swans have gone for their sojourn in Kilcoole. It is an ideal time to bring the boat out and do another video.'

Panic seeped through Emma, and she tried to ignore it. 'I don't know how to row and I'm not a very good swimmer,' Emma garbled quickly.

'Don't be such a scaredy cat, it's only for a short while,' Judith said.

'What if something happens and we end up in the water?'

'We used to swim there as kids, it's not very deep.'

Emma felt like her head was bursting.

Judith pulled her to sit on the bed. 'There's something you're not telling me.'

'I had a bad experience the last time I went out in a boat.'

'What happened?'

'The person I was with thought it would be funny to jump around until the boat listed so much that we fell out.'

'Can you swim?'

'Yes, but...' Emma stopped. She couldn't talk about it anymore.

Judith took Emma's hand. 'The jetty will do just fine, let's go.'

EIGHT

JUNE

Emma wandered through to the drawing room, but Judith was nowhere to be found. It was early and the house was quiet. Still, even. She stopped when she saw Jack in the garden, digging in the agapanthus and crocosmia flower beds near the lake. Benny was lying beside him, dozing and every now and again wagging his tail.

She caught sight of Marsha driving up the avenue and shrank back, but she knew there was little chance of escaping. Marsha usually called in for coffee after her morning walk, but this morning she was extra early.

When she heard her come in the kitchen door, Emma considered exiting by the front, but afraid of being rude, she waited for her to knock.

'There you are. I thought everyone had disappeared on me,' Marsha said.

'Is there something wrong?' Emma asked, taking in Marsha's red face.

'I think there is. Is Judith about? I need to talk to her urgently.'

'I don't know where she is. When I got up, she wasn't here. I expect she will be back soon.'

Marsha slapped her sewing bag on the kitchen table. 'Well, you're going to have to find her. We need to talk urgently. She didn't pass the gate lodge; maybe she went down to the meadows and the oak tree.'

Emma switched on the kettle, hoping the sound of the water boiling would distract Marsha, but she continued to prattle on. 'Maybe she just went out to clear her head,' Emma said.

Marsha sat down at the table. 'It's all just a mess. A total mess.'

'What is?'

Marsha didn't answer, but fished out her phone and dialled Judith's number, switching on the loudspeaker.

'Where the hell is she?' she said.

'Hang on to your hair, Marsha. Can't a girl go for an early morning stroll? I thought I would come across you when I circled back by the lodge,' Judith said in a loud voice as she walked in the front door.

'Since when did you go for an early morning anything? You heard the news, didn't you?'

'I may have got a call or two.'

Emma looked from one to the other, but the women continued to stare at each other as if waiting to see who would blink first.

'What's wrong?' she asked.

'Spit it out,' Judith said to Marsha.

'Hetty works part-time in the post office, and she rang me this morning. She said it is all over social media. Remember that motorway that was proposed a while back? Everybody is saying the developers have changed the route and it's now planned to run right across Killcawley Estate lands.'

'Don't you think as the owner of the land, I would have to

be consulted? Nobody has even sent an introductory letter,' Judith said.

Marsha shook her head.

'They are saying it has been very hush-hush. A lot of land has been bought up already, and there's only your land and a few houses with big gardens to the west side of the village left. Everybody is saying they are going to be bought up under compulsory purchase orders. One of the houses is Hetty's family home and she's in bits.'

'This can't be true. It would ruin the village. And Killcawley Estate can't be cut up like that. This estate is central to this community,' Judith said, her voice shaking.

Marsha sat down. 'I'll have a cuppa. I feel we need to digest this news properly.'

Judith turned to Emma. 'We're going to need you, Emma, with the legal stuff and the social media; any support you can give.

'We wouldn't expect anything less,' Marsha said, pouring milk into her tea. 'We could do with some young blood, and new ideas. Not like us, who are too world-weary to fight.'

'Speak for yourself, Marsha. But I intend to bring this battle to the national press and to court, if necessary. First, we have to find out if this news is correct,' Judith said.

'Hetty is hardly going to get worked up about something that's not going to affect us all. She also heard the main man from the council talking to the postmaster about it. Seemingly, he says it will pull our village into the modern world,' Marsha said.

'I know him; he lives miles from here. He doesn't give a shit about life in Killcawley. I smell the stench of brown envelopes and under-the-table payments,' Judith said as she pulled out the coffee pot and poured some into a mug.

'That's a big accusation to make,' Emma said.

Judith stared at her. 'We won't get through all this by

staying on the sidelines. One important thing I learned from my father was that when it comes to Killcawley, you fight hard and loud; there's no holding back. There isn't a blade of grass in this estate that I will let a bulldozer touch, and it's completely irrelevant whether they serve me with a compulsory purchase order or not.'

'That's the fighting spirit I need to hear,' Marsha said.

The three of them sat at the kitchen table. Marsha was the first to break the silence.

'What are we going to do?' she asked nervously.

'Jack will help; he has friends in local government,' Judith said, before she went to the back door and shouted out his name.

'He would hear that screeching if he was on the other side of the estate,' Marsha quipped as they heard Jack's heavy footfall on the courtyard cobbles.

'I carry a mobile phone for a reason, Judy,' he said, his voice betraying his annoyance.

'Who the hell thinks of phoning when we're in a tizzy about the motorway news?'

'Motorway?'

'From what I hear, some of the estate lands, Hetty's cottage and those other homes on that side of the village could all be knocked down.'

Jack pulled out a chair and sat down. 'I know, it's all about making the journey into Dublin city faster. There was talk in the village this morning; but we won't know anything until the local paper publishes this afternoon.'

Judith frowned, tears dampening her eyelashes. 'What will we do if they are going to take Killcawley Estate? Even if they don't, it will ruin all that is good here. There will be no more peace and quiet, and the wildlife will disappear.' She buried her head in her hands.

Marsha rubbed her back. 'Don't sound so defeated before

we even start. Remember, we will fight it with everything we've got,' she said.

'Which is a sum total of nothing,' Judith said.

'You know a lot of people, and you're an influencer. If anyone can get publicity, you can, and a lot of this battle will be about shaming them into rerouting the road somewhere else. You know all these institutions go for the path – or in this case, the road – of least resistance,' Jack said.

Judith jumped up, and began to pace the kitchen floor. 'Hats and baubles aren't going to be enough. We have to find out who is behind all this. There are a lot of people who will gain from a fast link to the city.'

'And just as many who will want nothing to do with it. Look at all those people who have moved here because Killcawley is such a quiet spot, within spitting distance of the sea. We can't have that ruined,' Marsha said.

Emma sat listening to the others. She had only been here a short while, but the thought of anything disturbing the peace and quiet of Killcawley Estate was very upsetting.

'Why don't you ask your son, Miles? He's a lawyer, he will know what has to be done,' Emma said.

Judith shook her head. 'I have no intention of telling Miles anything; he could see this as an opportunity to sell up the estate for the highest price, and I couldn't bear that.'

Jack said he had to get back to work, and Emma also made to move from the table.

'Hey, we need to talk this through,' Marsha said.

'Until we know all the details, what can we talk about?' Judith said flatly, and waved her hand to tell Jack and Emma to go.

At a loss for what to say, Emma set about tackling her tasks for the day – one of which was to make a big batch of rhubarb and ginger jam. She began gathering together all the utensils she would need later.

'I can't help you, darling. My mind is too full of this motorway business,' Judith said.

'How can you be thinking of making jam at a time like this?' Marsha asked.

Judith put a hand up to hush her.

'Emma had a great idea to sell Killcawley jam, and we're starting up a little business trying out the homemade recipes. We should have enough jars soon to start putting out feelers to get it on the shop shelves. Life can't stop because of a stupid motorway,' Judith said.

'I always loved Stephen's jam, so I'll be your first customer,' Marsha whispered to Emma as she wiped down the worktops before leaving Judith and Marsha in the kitchen. Outside, Emma hurried away from the house, and turned into the walled garden and the little shed, where she had set up the packing operation for Killcawley Estate Preserves. Her grandmother had told her that jams and pickles were the best when homemade, and had handed down her little notebook of recipes. Emma had to leave it behind when she had fled her home, but as she made more jam, she realised that they were still etched in the back of her mind.

With this latest rhubarb and ginger jam, and the tiny preserve jars Jack had sourced at a glass factory, they would soon be able to approach local hotels and guesthouses, as well as shops. She set about stacking the glass jars in a box to carry back to the house, so she could sterilise them for the next batch of jam. She enjoyed making the jam. It gave her a kind of peace in her heart and a sense of pride that there was something she was good at doing.

The kitchen was empty when she got back. She checked the rhubarb chunks she had left soaking in sugar overnight before tipping them into a big saucepan. She turned up the heat on the hob, then wrapped half a lemon in muslin and dropped it in the mix. The memories flooded back of her grandmother standing at the cooker and stirring the jam with a wooden spoon. She loved that moment as it started to bubble and the rhubarb fell apart; the sugar turning everything a reddish brown. When she was very young, her grandmother had her standing on a chair beside the cooker helping, only letting her stir when the jam was on a low simmer. Making jam, no matter how many times she did it, calmed her brain and helped her think straight.

Jack came back in the kitchen as she stood over the large saucepan slowly stirring.

'Is Marsha gone?' he asked.

'I think so.'

'She's going to egg Judy on about this motorway, I just know it.'

'I think Judith knows how to look after herself,' Emma said, but immediately regretted it when she saw Jack walk out of the kitchen.

She wondered whether she should follow him, but the house phone in the hall rang and she answered it.

'Miles here, who is this?'

'Emma, Judith's assistant.'

'Can you put my mother on, please?'

Emma faltered; she hadn't spoken to Miles before. He sounded brusque and businesslike. 'I'm afraid she's not here at the moment. She may be out on the estate somewhere, but I can take a message.'

There was an impatient click of the tongue at the other end of the line.

'No, that won't be necessary, though I would like to chat to you a little. Ask you about yourself.'

'Excuse me?'

'My mother speaks very highly of you, Emma. No matter what Judith says or does, she is an elderly woman, and it is my job to make sure she is not taken advantage of.'

'I would never do that—'

Miles interrupted, his voice raised. 'My mother tells me you qualified, and previously worked as a legal secretary. I am wondering why somebody with your qualifications would be satisfied to be a general dogsbody in a rundown old house in an Irish village?'

Sweat prickled on Emma's back; her throat tightened. 'I'm not sure I like what you are implying, Mr McCarthy.'

'As you can appreciate, I am many miles away from home only months after my father passed, and I find you have inveigled your way in to my mother's affections.'

'It's not like that. She advertised for help and I applied.'

'Hardly a promotion. How can working at Killcawley be in any way satisfying for you?'

'I like my job here.'

'Yes, I hear you want to use the Killcawley Estate name to front your little jam enterprise.'

Emma shuddered, not out of fear, but anger. Taking a deep breath, she spoke calmly and slowly. 'Mr McCarthy, I am aware you don't know me, but I assure you what you are thinking is completely wrong. I respect your mother, and I have no intention of defrauding her in any way.'

Miles tutted loudly. 'I will be speaking at length to my mother about this, but I am warning you, I will be watching the financial situation at Killcawley Estate very closely. I will not shirk from doing my duty as a son if I see any inconsistencies. I am also advising you to not, under any circumstances, use the Killcawley Estate name for your jam business.'

The phone went dead.

Emma was still trembling when Judith found her in the hall.

'What's wrong, dear?' she asked, leading Emma to the drawing room.'

'I'm OK. Miles rang. He said he would ring you later,' Emma said.

'And he was a rude, inconsiderate ass to you. Am I right?'

'Maybe.'

'That son of mine. He is a wonderful man, but overprotective. I'll have a word with him.'

'Please don't. I understand – he's worried about you.'

Judith jumped up, and placed her hands on her hips. 'Look at me, fit and healthy; a brain that works and blessed with a magnificent sense of style. When is Miles going to realise I can look after myself?'

'He's just watching out for you.'

'Silly, interfering boy.'

'You're lucky.'

'I never thought of it like that. He irritates me so,' Judith said. She picked up a jar of jam. 'Miles darling forgets I own Killcawley Estate. We label these beauties, and we start ringing around any shop we can think of to offer samples for sale,' she said, her voice defiant.

Emma sensed this wouldn't be the last she heard on the matter. She just hoped she could keep her head down where Miles was concerned. They were already off to a bad start and this worried her.

NINE

On her way back from her walk along the far meadows, Emma stopped for a few moments at the trough in the backyard. She dipped her hands in the cool water, making sure that her wrists were submerged. Cooling down, she trickled some water on her neck, and stood watching out over the fields where the horses grazed. She liked that the only company she had were the birds and the butterflies. Sometimes Benny came with her, but more often than not, he gave up after Emma passed out of the woodland, and opened the rickety gate that led to the meadows.

This afternoon, it had taken her about half an hour to tramp through the fields. Jack, when he noticed she liked to walk in the meadows, had run the mower down the hill and made a curvy path she could follow. When she got to the old oak tree, Jack was leaning against it and dragging on a cigarette. When she tried to thank him, he brushed her off.

'If it keeps you happy, then I'm all for it, because it means you will want to stay here, and Judy has grown quite attached to you,' he said.

'She means a lot to you.'

'Is it that noticeable? She is the whole world to me. My

family has always worked on this estate. I am happy to help out. We're good friends; it feels like these days we walk side by side.'

'Nice,' Emma said.

Jack shrugged. 'Foolish stuff, that's all.'

He stubbed out the cigarette with his fingers and threw the butt into a tin can he kept behind a rock.

'Not a word to Judy about the sneaky cigarette; I'm trusting you, Emma,' he said.

She nodded. He made to walk away, but turned around to look Emma in the eye.

'Judy will give me hell if she finds out,' he said.

Emma laughed. 'I don't tittle-tattle, Jack.'

He threw his hands in the air. 'Look at me, at my age and and I'm behaving like a schoolkid. My apologies,' he said, sweeping off his hat and bowing gracefully. 'Now I had better get to the house, and help her in the kitchen for her Italian evening or she will give me even more grief,' he said, taking a shortcut across the meadow and not bothering with the paths.

Emma sat in her spot under the oak tree, which was an old bench formed from a slab of felled wood. She liked to think that many before her had done the same.

Closing her eyes, she listened to the sounds of the meadow. A bee buzzed loudly, and two birds flitted past. Somewhere a crow cawed, and there was the melodious sound of what she thought was a small bird singing its own story. Here, in this spot, she could let her mind rest; the sounds were becoming more familiar each day, and they were a comfort to her tired body and brain. Conscious that she was being observed, she opened her eyes. On the path, a hare on its hind legs was staring at her, its nose twitching as it sniffed the air. She held her breath as her eyes locked with the soft eyes of the hare, before it languidly moved away from the path and through the grass, where she lost sight of it.

The alarm on her phone pinged, alerting her that she

needed to make her way back to the house. Judith never minded when she took a break or went for a walk, but when she asked Emma to be back at a certain time, she became quite frosty if she was late.

Wandering into the kitchen, Emma was surprised to see a number of women gathered around the table, and, curiously, a small baby in Hetty's arms.

'Here she is. Emma, we badly need your help,' Judith said.

'Yes, maybe you can give us some insight into how people fight these things in the UK?' Marsha said.

Judith, who was wearing a bright yellow dress and a small fascinator bearing a black feather tinged with gold, pulled Emma towards the table, where a huge map was spread out.

'I'm afraid my soiree is to be overtaken by this motorway business.'

Marsha called them over to the table and the map.

'Look, they intend to run the new motorway to Dublin – the fast link on the east corridor – right through Killcawley lands. We will lose the two bottom estate fields, and probably will have the constant drone of a motorway in our ears morning and night,' Judith said.

Emma peered closer at the map. 'That's the edge of the woodlands and the meadows – I have just come from there. This can't be right.'

'Anyone with money can do anything in this country; there's a big developer who wants fast access to loads of housing estates he is planning to build further down the coast,' Hetty said, as she gently rocked the baby in her arms.

Emma couldn't take her eyes off the baby, who looked as if she were only a few months old. There was a time she had hoped a baby was the next logical step, but all those hopes had disappeared, and her dreams had been trampled. That was part of her past, but she still had no idea what the future promised.

'This little poppet, my granddaughter Ella, will help man

the barricades.' Hetty laughed.

'We'll lose a good part of the village, the park and the playing pitches, but they're saying we will get even better pitches to compensate us. And Hetty here will lose her home,' Marsha said.

'Over my dead body. Do you think I will let anyone steal away what is rightfully mine and this little baby's inheritance? They haven't met Hetty Fields,' she said, and the others cheered.

The baby stirred and began to cry.

'Get the bottle out of the fridge there, and warm it for me, Emma,' Hetty said as she put the baby on her shoulder. Emma didn't budge, sadness and loss crawling through her.

Judith put an arm on her shoulder and got up to fetch the bottle, before switching on the kettle so she could warm it the old-fashioned way in a jug of hot water.

Marsha made funny noises at the baby, who continued to cry until the bottle teat was placed in her mouth.

'I had forgotten about the beauty of the sound of silence, when a baby is feeding,' Judith said, and the others chuckled happily.

'I don't want to break up the love-in, but we need to come up with a plan; the word is this is going through and the bulldozers are earmarked to move in,' Marsha said.

'But wasn't there a public consultation process of some kind?' Emma asked.

Marsha shook her head. 'There is something fishy here; the last time this was brought to us, that road was going at the other side of Killcawley. Nobody came back to us with the change of plans, because they knew we would kick up a huge stink.'

'Those meadows and that part of the village have been there for centuries; how can they possibly think of digging it all up for a motorway?' Judith said, her eyes narrowing, and her cheeks flushed with anger.

'Exactly why we have to fight it,' Marsha said, and the others murmured in agreement.

Judith put up her hand. 'Can I just ask, how the hell are we going to do that?'

Nobody said a word. The grandfather clock in the hall chimed out four gongs. Judith sighed deeply and the others looked at their hands.

Marsha was the first to speak. 'There isn't one of us around this table who hasn't had a battle on her hands at one stage. Are we going to let a few sleazy politicians and greedy developers ruin our last years, the estate and village we love?' Marsha said, looking from one woman to another.

Judith began to cry. 'We can't let this happen, we just can't,' she sobbed.

'So, let's fight the bastards with everything we've got,' Hetty said, hopping up, making the bottle fall out of the baby's mouth. Marsha leapt up so fast that her chair fell back, making the dog growl and scoot out the back door.

'Let's start shouting as loud as we can, using every contact we have to get in the national press. The only way to get those politicians to do anything is to embarrass them into doing it,' Marsha shouted.

'I might know a few people,' Judith said.

'And my son-in-law works for some senator,' Hetty said.

Emma put her hand up to speak and Marsha told her to go ahead.

'I think we need legal advice. Publicity is good, but the legal advice will steer us in the right direction,' she said.

'But that costs money,' Marsha said.

'Maybe it is time to ask Miles. He's going to hear about it anyway. He can give us the broad-strokes legal advice and maybe make a recommendation for a solicitor in this country,' Judith said.

'I thought he wants you to sell up, give up the estate because it's too much for you at your age,' Hetty said.

Judith gave her a fierce look. 'Miles wants what's best for Killcawley Estate, and this state of affairs is not good,' she said stiffly.

'I'm sorry, I didn't mean to offend,' Hetty said as little Ella burped loudly, dissipating the tension that was building.

'Miles is ringing tonight, let's see what he says and meet back here in the morning,' Judith said.

The others knew by the sound of her voice that she wasn't prepared to linger on the campaign anymore.

Marsha said their ragtag committee would meet at ten the next day, but they would meet later on for the supper club.

Emma walked out to the courtyard with Hetty and Marsha.

'She's really upset, and I'm the fool who added to it,' Hetty said.

'You were only saying what I was thinking. Miles may not be a friend in this battle,' Marsha said.

'It's his family home and land; surely being in New York has not made him forget all that. And he knows how much Judith loves the place.'

Marsha harrumphed loudly. 'Money tops everything else. We'll wait and see,' she said, getting into her car.

After they had left, Emma thought about returning to the kitchen, but instead opted to go to the walled garden where Jack had stopped to pick some rhubarb.

'There is a lot there; enough for a good few more jars of jam,' he said.

'Judith says to ignore Miles, so we're going ahead with the jam. I'm adding strawberry and prosecco jam this week.'

'They used to make jam here, and sell what was left over at

the village market. The little enterprise was Stephen's pride and joy,' Jack said.

'So why is Miles so dead against it?'

'It's not personal – he and Stephen were very close. Maybe it's too soon.'

Jack picked a large bundle of rhubarb. 'I'll carry it back to the house for you,' he said.

As they neared the house, they heard the faint sounds of *La Bohème* coming from upstairs.

'Judy must be upset; she only ever listens to the opera when she is feeling down,' Jack said as he placed the rhubarb in the sink. 'Give it a good wash before you do anything with it.' He stood for a moment listening to the music, before disappearing out the back door.

Emma scrubbed and washed the chopping board and the stainless steel bowls, and was chopping the rhubarb in rows of three when Judith, dressed down in a tracksuit, came into the room.

She stood for a moment and looked at what Emma was doing.

'Your granny cut the rhubarb like that,' she said, reaching for a small glass and the bottle of whiskey.

'Are you all right?' Emma asked.

Judith slugged her drink. 'I'm not,' she said.

'Is there anything I can do?'

'Get me a new life. I'm fed up of this one. Hetty made me feel old.'

'I don't think she meant to,' Emma said, putting handfuls of rhubarb into the bowl, before reaching for more stalks to chop.

Judith came over beside her. 'I love a sneaky slurp of the rhubarb juice.'

'No sticking spoons in the bowl; I want to keep it sterile,' Emma said.

'You jam makers are all the same, no fun,' Judith said with a faint smile.

'Are you dressing up for dinner?' Emma asked, glad to change the subject.

Judith slapped Emma gently on the wrists.

'Some days, I am allowed to look and feel old. But, I suppose I should make an effort for the supper club. If I let my standards down, the others might just come in their slippers.'

'What about the food?'

'I have prosciutto and olives and bruschetta for starters, and a spaghetti carbonara for main. I am a little stuck on dessert. I got caught up with the motorway worry, and time ran away with me.'

'I have a nice strawberry dish we can pass off as Italian?'

Judith hugged Emma. 'Darling, I don't know what I would do without you. I am off to find an Italian designer dress to wear and to put on my make-up. There is limoncello, and lovely rich Italian white wine chilling.'

About two hours later, Marsha and Hetty arrived with Hetty's Baileys tiramisu and put it in the fridge.

'Where's Judith? She said to be here by six,' Marsha asked.

'No doubt she's trying to fill in the wrinkles, so she can knock the years off.' Hetty chuckled.

'Don't be so nasty; you said enough already,' Marsha snapped, and she gestured to Emma to join her in the hall.

Emma closed the kitchen door behind her, and Marsha pulled her into the drawing room.

'We need to check on Judith, but without Hetty knowing.'

'It might be a bit late for that, with all this whispering in corners.'

'You go up, and I will divert Hetty; I have a nice bit of gossip about a mutual friend, which is just down her alley.'

Emma went slowly up the stairs and knocked on Judith's door. She waited several minutes but there was no answer. She hesitated, before knocking again.

'Judith, I'm worried. I'm going to come in,' Emma said as she turned the brass door handle.

The velvet curtains were drawn and Emma stopped to let her eyes adjust to the darkness.

'Judith, are you all right?' she asked gently.

'Perfectly fine, but I need more whiskey,' Judith slurred. She was lying on the bed, looking up blearily at Emma.

'You're drunk.'

'Don't sound so shocked; a little inebriated, maybe. Go downstairs and get me another bottle of anything – vodka or gin, maybe. A change might be nice.'

'Marsha and Hetty are downstairs for the supper club. Jack will be here shortly.'

Judith sat up and let her legs dangle over the side of the bed. 'I can't let Hetty see me like this; she will dine out on the news for the next month.'

'I could say you're ill.'

'Yes! Yes, good idea. A stomach bug, nobody wants to visit a patient with the stomach flu.'

Emma turned on her heel and went downstairs.

Hetty was disappointed nobody would taste her tiramisu and Marsha asked a lot of questions, but eventually Emma managed to get the two of them out of the house, just as Jack arrived.

'Don't tell me they had a row with Judy,' he said.

'I wish,' Emma said.

'Is there something wrong?'

'Judith is upstairs knocking back alcohol.'

Jack made for the stairs. Within a few minutes he was back down with Judith's empty whiskey glass. 'She's going for a nap, but she will probably sleep through. Italian supper club is not happening,' he said. 'First time we've ever had to cancel it,' he added despondently.

TEN

Emma shrank back when Judith plodded into the kitchen the next day.

'Why didn't you take the bottle of whiskey out of my room? I have a banging headache,' she said, flopping down at the table and dropping her head into her hands.

Emma slipped a mug of coffee in beside her elbow.

'Take it away. The aroma, it makes me sick,' Judith snarled.

Jack, when he walked into the kitchen, rolled his eyes. 'Judy, you've been a bad girl', he said, wagging his finger.

'Go away, Jack Dennehy, and clean some shite from the backyard,' she snapped, reaching out for the fruit bowl and firing an orange across the room at him.

Jack backed out of the kitchen and strolled across the courtyard, whistling loudly.

'He has some cheek. He was the one who gave me the bottle of Midleton whiskey after Stephen died. He said if I was going to drink to blot out the pain, he'd make sure it was the best whiskey he could afford,' Judith said. She waved at Emma. 'Take the day off. I'm fit for nothing.'

Emma tried to suppress a giggle.

'What are you laughing at? I look a fright, don't I? I couldn't be bothered putting the slap on,' Judith said as she got up to rummage in the high cupboards.

'If you're looking for that other bottle of whiskey, I've hidden it,' Emma said.

Judith stared at her. 'On whose authority?'

'Judith, this is not you; sitting around drinking whiskey all night and looking for more for breakfast.'

Judith flopped into a chair. 'There are only so many blows a body can take. The motorway route is the last straw,' she said.

'We can fight it.'

'I'm not sure we can, and if we do, we won't succeed,' Judith said reaching for a box of painkillers.

'Why don't I leave you to it; we can talk later,' Emma said.

There was some truth to what Judith was saying, but Emma hoped that it was a tired and pickled brain that was talking, not the real Judith. When she saw Jack passing by pushing a wheelbarrow, she knocked on the window and beckoned him to come inside.

'Well, the day just got better; the man of my dreams has returned,' Judith said, lighting up a cigarette.

Jack walked over to her and pulled the cigarette from her mouth. 'Stop it, Judy. It's time to come back to the real world.'

He caught her in a bear hug and she slumped against his body.

'I will help her back to bed. She needs to rest,' he said, steering Judith towards the stairs.

When he came back downstairs a little while later, Jack asked Emma to check on Judith throughout the morning.

'Does this happen very often?' Emma asked.

'It's only the third time in her life. The first time, I remember her dad talking about it when some guy who used to come here on holiday was run over by a car and killed in England. When Stephen died, she was out for days.'

'It couldn't be what Hetty said yesterday. It was thoughtless, but surely this is an overreaction,' Emma said.

Jack spooned two sugars in a coffee Emma had placed in front of him.

'That was more of a catalyst. Judith is very good at hiding her true feelings behind all this designer wear, the hats and the TikTok carry-on, but really, she is terrified that she will have to leave Killcawley Estate. She loves this place, and the latest threat is nearly too much for her, especially now.'

'What do you mean, because of her age?'

Jack looked a bit distracted. 'I'm going on too much; Judith wouldn't want me talking about her like this.'

He slurped his coffee and stood up.

'Do you mind keeping all this between us? She wouldn't want anyone else to know of her episode, and Pete, who looks after the animals, is a fierce gossip. Marsha is OK, but I won't even start on Hetty.'

'Marsha and Hetty are due here at ten this morning for another motorway strategy meeting.'

'Put them off. We can't risk having them here, and Judith coming downstairs,' he said, throwing the last of his coffee into the sink and rinsing the mug.

When he had left, Emma went to the top shelf in the dresser, and pulled down Judith's address book. She found Marsha's number and was glad when she answered almost immediately.

Marsha was cross when she heard the meeting was off.

'We will have to go ahead without Judith. This motorway business is far too important. Can we at least have an update on the advice from Miles? We need a lawyer's perspective,' she said.

'Of course, but where will we have the meeting? Maybe I could come to the gate lodge?' Emma said sweetly.

'OK, but come straight away. Hetty is on the way, but I will divert her at the gates. Don't be late,' Marsha muttered.

Emma thought that Marsha a sounded a bit annoyed, but she put it out of her mind and went outside to find Jack.

'Marsha is insisting on the meeting, and I have to go to the lodge. Could you watch Judith?'

He nodded.

'Marsha wants an update from Miles, but Judith didn't even tell me if he had called.'

'Make it up, because those two will give Judith hell if there isn't one,' he said as he opened the car door for Emma.

She set off slowly down the avenue. Hetty was parking outside the gate lodge when she arrived. The house was freshly painted, the window boxes overflowing with puce petunias. Marsha flung the door open.

'I wasn't expecting guests, so we will have to make do in the kitchen,' Marsha said, bustling about putting cups and saucers on the table.

'There is no need to go to such bother,' Emma said.

Hetty clicked her tongue. 'You're talking to the biggest fusspot in town. Of course she's going to go to enormous trouble, and at short notice too.'

Emma watched Marsha take out a china teapot, and scald it with boiling water, before throwing in the leaf tea and the rest of the water from the kettle. Next, she put a hand knitted cosy on the teapot, and put it in the middle of the table along with a plate of homemade chocolate-chip biscuits.

'They look homemade, but I had to rush out to the bakery on Main Street. I am only just back,' she said.

Hetty pulled a little bell out of her handbag and rang it. 'Let's call this meeting to order,' she said, and Emma had to concentrate on a spot on the far wall to make sure she didn't laugh.

Marsha, her face red with irritation, turned to Emma. 'Please read out your report on the consultation with Miles.'

'I don't have anything written down.'

'Either you have a photographic memory or Judith didn't make the call after all,' Marsha said, sniffing loudly.

Emma straightened up. 'Judith is doing her best, and she gave me very definite points to bring up. The first is that we must get a solicitor to legally challenge in the High Court the plans for the motorway. That will at least delay the whole project giving us more time to raise money.'

To her delight, Emma noticed Marsha sit up and pay attention, and Hetty hastily scribbled down notes. Feeling encouraged, she continued.

'Next, we must get somebody to conduct a survey, to see if there is any unusual wildlife such as bats or a particular snail on the land that is to be taken by the motorway. That could swing the motorway away from us. And lastly, we should garner as much publicity as possible, appoint a spokesperson and pick a good name for the group so we can be quoted by news outlets.'

When she finished, Emma felt quite good about herself. She had heard this plan of action so many times as a legal secretary, but this time she got the adrenalin rush of being the one in the driving seat. It was a long time since she had felt that thrill, and she had to admit to herself that she missed the rush, missed her legal work.

Hetty slow handclapped and Marsha poured the tea. 'But where will we get a solicitor? Did Miles have any idea about that?'

Emma blanked for a moment, but she didn't let the others see her panic. 'He said he will get back to us on that; he has to make a few enquiries,' she said, taking a biscuit and biting into it.

'I can feel it in my bones; this is going to be some battle, but we will be victorious,' Hetty said, vigorously rubbing her hands together.

Marsha shook her head. 'There's going to be a huge spin against us, but if the whole village sticks together, we have a chance.'

Emma said she had to go, and they called the meeting to an end. Marsha said she would write up the minutes and send it around in an email.

'It always pays to do things right,' Marsha said primly, as she showed them to the front door.

Emma left the gate lodge, and decided to go for a drive to clear her head. Since she had arrived, she had wanted to visit the sea, three miles away. She checked in with Jack first, and he said Judith was up and eating a little, but best to give her the run of the house on her own for a while.

She followed the signs for Kilcoole beach, and parked up. She tramped along the stone and shingle strand, luxuriating in the sound of the waves as they calmly came to shore. At one stage a train passed. On impulse, she waved and immediately felt a little silly. Climbing up on the grassy bank, she walked along the sand path overlooking the marsh on one side and the Irish Sea on the other. There were very few people about, but a dog kept running up to her, and she enjoyed the company until its harassed owner managed to snap on its lead.

Checking her watch, she knew she had to be back for lunch at Killcawley Estate. She was out on the dual carriageway when Jack texted asking where she was.

He was waiting for her when she pulled in at the iron gates to the estate.

'I just wanted to warn you, Judy has just got an email from Marsha who has already picked the name of the group. She's going mad. Also, she insists she never rang Miles, and what about this plan?'

Emma grimaced. 'I was thinking on my feet. I thought I did rather well.'

'A bit too well. Judy is not good at playing second fiddle. Just tread carefully, once you go up to the house.'

'Can I give you a lift to the house?' she asked sweetly.

He laughed, and shook his finger at Emma. 'I see what you are trying to do, but I'm not getting caught in the middle of this.'

Emma drove slowly up the avenue. Judith was waiting for her at the back door.

'"No To The Motorway". What an uninspiring name,' she said.

'I agree we didn't vote on the name. I'm sure Marsha just picked it from the top of her head.'

'Her arse, more like,' Judith said, whipping inside to the kitchen. Emma was glad to see she was wearing a long silk shirt dress with peep-toe shoes. Her hair had been combed back and was held in a bun by a large tortoiseshell clip.

'Jack tells me I have behaved badly; I must apologise,' Judith said quickly. Emma was about to answer, but Judith continued to talk.

'Now you know one of my dark secrets. I try my best to have joy in my life every day, but there are some days when the dark cloud descends, and it takes a while to get rid of it. I hope you will forgive me any indiscretions during that time.'

'I do,' Emma said.

Judith clapped her hands. 'Enough of that, then. Tell me how you came up with such a marvellous plan under the guise of advice from Miles.'

'I was often taking notes at meetings where the parties were discussing plans to challenge planning applications and such like.'

'Well, I think you have given us quite a start to our

campaign. Miles is going to ring me later tonight. He tried last night a few times, but I pretended I couldn't hear him. He would be angry if he knew I hit the bottle.'

Emma took down her bowls of rhubarb. 'Is it OK if I make some jam?'

'Jam doesn't seem so important anymore,' Judith said, and Emma stepped back in surprise.

'Have I overstepped the mark? What's wrong?'

Judith banged down the glass she was carrying. 'Everything is wrong. I can't bear the thought of losing the estate, but what am I fighting for? Am I just battling to keep all this land for my son to sell it the minute I die?'

Emma put her hand on Judith's shoulder. 'You're jumping too far ahead. I think we have to take small and definite steps now.'

'I knew it was a good decision to bring you on board,' Judith said, smiling broadly. 'I think it's time to celebrate, pick a grand outfit, for when we tell the others the new name of our pressure group.'

'I didn't think we had a new name.'

'We don't, but I am damned if I'm going to let Marsha have that honour. We have to get our thinking caps on.'

Judith went upstairs to pick out her outfit, and Emma went out to the walled garden to find Jack.

He was sitting in the gazebo. She stopped and looked at him for a few moments. He was, she thought, a loyal friend who spent his whole life being underappreciated. She was finally feeling that she was finding her feet at Killcawley Estate. She had come here hoping to find an easy way of life, and now she was becoming entangled in the web that held the estate together.

Jack spotted her and waved. 'Is Judith back on track?'

'Yes, she is picking out a new outfit to wear.'

'Thank goodness. Then all is right in the world again.'

ELEVEN

Emma woke up to the sound of raised voices downstairs. She stiffened in the bed and listened intently. She could hear Judith, her voice high pitched with indignation, and what sounded like another female voice speaking quietly. Slowly, Emma got out of bed, and pulled on a cardigan over her pyjamas.

As she descended the stairs, she heard Jack's jeep pull up. Pausing on the last flight, she waited until Jack got to the kitchen. When he spoke, she was surprised by what she heard.

'Judy, this is no way to behave towards a friend. We're all on the same side, and Marsha here has our best interests at heart. It's not her fault that her brother is a chief engineer on the project.'

'She's a back-stabbing traitor,' Judith spat out.

'Would I have come out here to tell you this if that was the case? No, I would be off drinking champagne with my yellow-livered brother,' Marsha shouted.

Jack sounded exasperated when he next spoke. 'Isn't this what they want – divisions, before ye have finally agreed on a campaign? Ladies, engage the brains,' he said, his voice hard.

Emma was surprised when he opened the door to the hall and called out her name.

'How did you know I was here?' she asked.

'Those two fighting like cats would wake the dead,' he said.

When Emma hesitantly entered the kitchen, both Judith and Marsha were sitting at opposite ends of the table.

'We're defeated, before we have even got off the ground,' Judith said to nobody in particular.

Jack knocked on the table with his knuckles. 'Anyone know the phrase "divide and conquer"? You ladies are handing victory on a plate to the other side with your carry-on. If we're to save this estate and our village, we need a big group representing everybody, and most importantly, with everyone pulling in the same direction. I vote we have a public meeting this evening.'

He turned to Emma. 'Can you design a poster in the next hour that we can put up around the village? Judith can ring everyone she knows. Marsha, you and Hetty start pulling in the favours.'

Marsha nodded. She got up from the table and stopped beside Judith. 'You're not the only one who loves this place. You might own it, but the rest of us hold it dear to our hearts. We're all on the same side.'

Judith dipped her head. 'I'm sorry, it's just so much to take on; especially now, after Stephen.'

'I know,' Marsha said, patting Judith's back. 'I'll rally the troops for a 5 p.m. meeting.'

'There is something else, isn't there?' Emma said, sitting down beside Judith after Marsha had left.

Tears plopped down Judith's face, streaking through the heavy day moisturiser she had not had a chance to rub in properly. 'It's Miles, he was furious when I spoke to him last night. He says now is the time to get the best price for the estate, and that I could live my life out comfortably after that. He doesn't realise if this place goes – even any part of it – I won't have a life, and certainly not one worth living.'

'Miles needs to come home; he has been away too long. He needs to reconnect with the place and his history,' Jack said, folding his arms and sitting down.

Judith took out a lace-trimmed handkerchief and dabbed her eyes.

'He won't listen; he says the place is too much for me. He's crunching the numbers, and they don't add up. It's just so expensive to run the estate. Or so he says, anyway.'

While they were talking, Emma pulled out a sketchpad and drew up a quick meeting poster. She held it up for Jack to look at.

'I thought of putting a picture of the house on it as well. I can do it on the computer and print off from here. We can start putting them up in the next hour or so.'

Jack agreed, and said he would ring his friend Fintan, who was a solicitor, to come and address the group on the legal possibilities.

Judith reached out to Jack. 'Would you do all that for me?'

'You know me, Judy, I would do anything,' he replied, his voice soft and full of emotion.

Emma was on her way to the small office in what used to be the scullery when she turned back to ask where they should hold the meeting.

'Miles will go mad if we let anybody in the house. It will have to be at the front. Let's hope the weather holds up,' Judith said, and nobody disagreed.

Emma busied herself getting the posters fully designed and printed, before making her way back to the kitchen. Judith, wearing a long black dress with a heavy front panel of embroidery in bright red, purple and gold was standing at the hall mirror trying to fit a fascinator with a red and black feather on her head.

'Don't you think you are a tad overdressed for passing out the flyers and putting up posters?' Emma asked.

Judith, happy with the tilt of the fascinator, turned to Emma. 'One should never apologise for being overdressed. In fact, there is no such thing. There is well-dressed, and there is everybody else. We should do a TikTok – me out in my vintage clothes, putting up meeting posters and doing my bit. Capture a sense of urgency about this whole thing.'

'Are you sure?' Emma asked.

Judith straightened up to her full height. 'There's no point having all these followers if I can't call on them at a time of need. The world has to know what we are facing and how we are going to fight it, and we must use all the tools at our disposal.'

'OK, let's get to it,' Emma said.

An hour before the meeting was due to start, Judith checked her TikTok account.

'We're not viral yet, but the word is spreading. A lot are saying they want to stand with us,' she said.

Judith immediately started walking around each of the rooms downstairs, drawing the curtains shut and locking all the rooms.

'Stephen always said if people saw how we really live here, we might lose the support of the community. They indulge me and my crazy outfits, let's keep it that way,' she said, by way of explanation.

Emma was shocked, but managed to hide it. When she whispered about it to Jack, he laughed.

'Has it taken you until now to realise our Judy is a terrible snob? She's convinced if she lets anyone she doesn't know into the house, the fixtures and fittings could go missing.'

'Ridiculous,' Emma said.

Jack chuckled. 'There may be something in what she says; when the big country manor in the next county opened its gates for an open house two years ago, they say antique brass tap fittings were swiped from an en suite.'

Emma laughed. 'You don't seriously believe that.'

'Judy does,' Jack said, before locking the back door.

Over two hundred people turned up for the meeting. They came in dribs and drabs, all but one group leaving their cars on the main road and walking up the avenue. Some lingered to call the horses, and others ignored direction signs for the front of the house and tried to access the walled garden and courtyard, but Jack had put up a makeshift barrier.

Judith, Hetty and Marsha sat on stools on the top of the front steps. Judith had changed into a sober blue trouser suit and was persuaded at the last minute not to wear a navy cloche hat. She fretted that too many had descended on the grounds, but Marsha told her it was too late and they should just get on with it. Emma sat to one side of Judith and reached over to give her hand a reassuring squeeze.

'I didn't realise so many would be filming,' Judith whispered nervously to Emma, but stood up when Marsha poked her in the side.

Timidly, Judith opened the meeting by welcoming everybody to the estate, but was immediately heckled by a man standing apart from the rest of the crowd. Judith ignored him and Jack moved through the crowd to reach him, but he managed to sidestep away and run to the front.

'Why is it always those in the big house who think they can dictate to the rest of us?' he shouted.

Marsha shooed him away, but he jumped onto the steps and addressed the crowd.

'This motorway can only be good for us. Transport links is

what this village needs. It will bring more jobs and put more money in our pockets. With more people living here, all the shops will prosper. It's a no-brainer,' he shouted.

The crowd murmured in agreement, and Judith attempted to speak, but a woman told her to sit down and be quiet.

Emma shrank back from the crowd as Marsha stood up and vigorously rang her bell.

'What sort of nonsense is this from you all? You know us. Hetty here is going to lose her home. Do you really believe that any blow-ins will spend their money in our little shops? They will be off to the superstores for the big discounts and the jobs. Paddy Downey here has sold his soul. Word is, he's expecting a fierce big job on the back of mouthing off about all the good things a motorway brings. Paddy is being paid to talk a load of shit.'

The crowd laughed, and Judith tugged at Marsha's skirt to make her sit down. Judith pushed back her stool, and stood up, holding out her hands to get the crowd to quieten down.

'I think we have got off on the wrong foot. And I apologise for that. I know Mr Downey works for a building company; the same building company which wants all the land around the village rezoned to build large housing estates. If that happens, the lovely allure of our village will be gone and we will just become a commuting suburb for the city, and dead during the day,' she said.

Hetty jumped up. 'Didn't I see you driving a brand-new car in the village only days ago, Paddy Downey? It is hard not to put two and two together.'

There was a murmur of discontent through the crowd.

An elderly woman who was holding on to her daughter's arm said she didn't want the village to change.

Another man said he stood to lose his home as well.

'They won't give me one of the new houses either; they

want me to go into a local authority estate in Bray, where I won't know anyone,' he said, his voice cracking with emotion.

A woman tore up two of the steps, and waved to the crowd. 'It's time we stood up for ourselves and our community. If Mrs McCarthy here can help – and she has so much to lose – I trust her. Let's work together. Together we are unstoppable,' she shouted, to loud applause.

A car drove up the avenue, and everybody strained to have a look. A man in a suit and carrying a briefcase got out.

'This is our solicitor, Fintan O'Brien; he's going to represent us in this battle,' Judith said.

The man stood on the second step.

'I will give you all some facts on what can be done next, but the legal route is a very expensive one, and you will have to decide whether you want to proceed. Resistance can take many forms, and well-placed articles in the press might be an option. Lobbying your local politicians could also be helpful. Highlighting the matter on social media could be another way. Also, there wasn't any objection when this was in the consultation process,' he said.

'None of us realised the danger, and the plans have suspiciously changed since then,' Marsha said.

'Ignorance is never a defence, but if ye can come up with something unusual in the area – like a bat habitat, some sort of wildlife, flora or fauna – we could say they had not considered that and bring a legal challenge to the High Court.

'How the hell are we going to know about any of that?' one woman said.

A man at the back put up his hand to speak, but he was ignored as others fired out question after question.

Eventually, Judith spotted him.

'Sir, you have been waiting a long time to say something,' she said, pointing to him.

The man cleared his throat and raised his voice so he could be heard.

'I think I might have thought of it. My father always said the oak tree in that part of the estate which is earmarked for the motorway was one of the oldest in the country. It's ancient.'

The crowd hushed and listened as the man who identified himself as a local historian said they should gather stories about the tree, which might be the only way to stop the motorway.

Emma noticed that Judith was beaming in pleasure as she stood up. 'We are in your debt, sir; this is obviously the way forward for us.'

Fintan O'Brien said he had to go, but said that when they had the information, he would gladly file the judicial review papers at the High Court.

Marsha rang her bell vigorously. 'We thank you all for coming here at such short notice. Please sign up for text alerts or email updates. We hope we will have as large a turnout when we next look for your support,' she said.

'What's the name of the group, anyway?' one woman asked.

'"Hands Off Our Village",' Judith said quickly, before Marsha had time to catch her breath.

Judith reached over and rang Marsha's bell again. 'There will also be important updates and videos on TikTok. Find me at StyleQueenJudy,' she said, and the group applauded.

Jack supervised the crowd as they trooped back down the avenue, and he pulled over the gates when the last person had left.

Hetty and Marsha walked through the house with Judith to the kitchen.

'Why is the place so dark?' Marsha asked.

Judith shrugged. 'I don't know,' she said.

Emma gave her a funny look, but the others didn't notice, and Hetty pulled up the blind in the kitchen.

'We have enough dark days without making it darker,' she

said. When Jack returned, Judith invited the little group for a drink in the drawing room.

Jack pulled back the curtains, letting the evening sunlight fill the rooms. Judith poured whiskey from a decanter into crystal glasses then sank into a couch while Emma handed out the drinks.

'Why did you tell the whole world about your TikTok? I thought you didn't want Killcawley, or indeed the world, knowing your business,' Marsha said.

'In extraordinary times, one must do extraordinary things,' Judith said, and the others nodded in agreement.

'There are strange times ahead,' Marsha said.

'To the battle ahead,' Judith said solemnly, and they clinked glasses.

TWELVE

The next morning, Emma left a note on the kitchen table saying she had borrowed the jeep, and was on her way to the local library, which they were opening up especially for her. She drove slowly down the driveway, stopping when two rabbits ran across in front of her. She had to get out of the car to pull the gates back, but didn't bother to close them again. In the village, she parked near the post office. Hetty saw her and called her over.

'We've had people in asking about Judith and the big house; everybody wants to visit Killcawley Estate.'

'What sort of people?' Emma asked.

'All sorts, young and old; they know Judith from TikTok.'

'Oh.'

'I know Judith does not want strangers trooping up the avenue at Killcawley Estate, so I told them I don't know her, but there's bound to be somebody else around who will give them directions to the big house.'

'Thanks. I'll ring Jack and alert him,' Emma said, before continuing on her way to the library.

The library was an old, red-brick building at the corner of Main Street and Parnell Street. When Emma stepped in the door, the man who had spoken at the meeting the night before came over to her.

'Welcome, I am Dan Ryan, chief librarian. I was hoping somebody at the big house would do a follow-up. I have everything ready for you.'

'I didn't realise this was a library. It's such a small building,' Emma said.

'Yes, we badly need a new one. One of the carrots dangled by this developer is a new library building, which I have to say would be welcome, but not at the price of losing the heart of our village,' Dan said, leading Emma to a table.

'I have all the books which mention Killcawley Estate stacked high for you, and I have put a stickie on the relevant pages that mention the oak tree.'

'You have done the work for me.'

Dan put his hand up to stop Emma talking. 'I took the liberty of photocopying all the information you need. If you're running a campaign, I doubt you'll have time to be trawling through books,' he said, handing her an envelope with a bundle of photocopied sheets inside.

'This is so kind of you, thank you.'

'Tell Judith not to forget us when she makes it big on TikTok. Sure, she's nearly a celebrity at this stage,' he said.

Judith, wearing cream palazzo pants and a light pink shirt with a three-strand string of pearls at her neck, was walking by the lake when Emma got back to Killcawley Estate.

She followed Emma inside, and was out of breath when she got as far as the kitchen. 'I have been brainstorming. We need to raise funds to finance a huge campaign to save us from this motorway. We are up against the big guns,' Judith said.

'We could fundraise in the village, but really we need to go national on this, get the newspapers interested, get a bit of outrage brewing,' Emma replied.

'I just feel everything is going to go so well. When you were out, I rang my friend who works at the *Irish Times* newspaper, and she said they could come down, photograph me under the tree and interview me,' Judith said.

'The sooner the better because we need to keep up momentum on this,' Emma said as she emptied the envelope out on to the table, and began to look through the photocopied pages. '*This tree is believed to be the oldest in Ireland and holds a significance in the community of Killcawley and should be recognised nationwide*,' she quoted from one piece.

Judith sat down at the table and picked up another page and read a sentence aloud. '*The oak tree at the bottom of a far meadow from the Killcawley Estate house in Co Wicklow is believed to be the oldest oak tree in the country*.'

Judith's eyes brightened with excitement. 'This is it, Emma. We have something to throw in their faces.'

'I don't know how we can prove it,' Emma said.

Judith clapped her hands loudly. 'Don't you see, we don't have to prove a thing. All we have to do is create a frenzy about the oak tree on TikTok and the rest will follow.'

Emma looked at Judith. 'You're serious, aren't you?'

'Bloody hell, I am. Do you think I have lived all my life at Killcawley Estate to have greedy developers and complicit state agencies carve it up as if it were nothing? The history of my family is in every blade of grass, and I won't let anyone take that away.'

Emma took out her phone. 'Say it to the camera.'

'But we're just in the kitchen.'

'Who cares, the words are so passionate.'

Judith stared directly at the camera and repeated the

sentences, this time with even more vigour. When Emma called 'cut', Judith sighed.

'Miles is definitely going to hear about all this now, and you know, I can't say I care.'

'That's the spirit,' Emma said as she uploaded the video on TikTok, and Judith poured a small shot of whiskey each.

'To becoming a thorn in the side of those who would seek to destroy Killcawley Estate,' Judith said, and they clinked glasses, before downing their drinks in one go.

'It must be all the excitement, but I think I will lie down for a while, so I'm in fine form for the supper club this evening,' Judith said, before making her way quickly upstairs.

Emma stuffed the pages back in the envelope, and went outside. She needed to walk, to enjoy the summer sunshine, before it was time to cook for the supper club.

Jack arrived early to the house dressed in new jeans, a light blue open-neck shirt, and he had his hair tied back in a ponytail.

'You know it's only a bit of supper, not a candlelit dinner for two,' Marsha said, and Hetty sniggered.

'Leave the man alone; never make fun of a man who dresses the part,' Judith said, and Marsha and Hetty looked put out to be so chastised.

'Emma, here, has been doing some digging and has come up with the goods on the oak tree; it might just save us all,' she said.

Both Marsha and Hetty looked at Emma, who handed them each a photocopy.

'This is epic,' Marsha said.

Hetty laughed out loud. 'Since Marsha has started having her teenage nephew over at weekends, her vocabulary has expanded,' she said.

'My father always insisted that tree deserved our respect,

and that it would be around long after we were all gone,' Jack said.

'We have to get the publicity right and make sure that the tree becomes a national treasure,' Judith said.

'How do we do that? When nobody cares about anything anymore?' Marsha sighed.

Emma placed a Spanish paella in the middle of the table, accompanied by a rocket salad.

Judith rapped on the table with her spoon. 'It's not our usual supper club evening, because this is more of a strategy meeting for our campaign, but we must thank Emma for introducing us to this delicious seafood paella,' Judith said.

The others applauded, but Judith raised her hands to stop them.

'Everybody, I have arranged for the *Irish Times* to spend some time on the estate. I understand they intend to write a feature on me and the campaign. Of course, I will pose under the oak tree in one of my most exquisite outfits.'

'I should have known,' Marsha said. 'And what about the rest of us? It would be nice to be included, for once.'

'I'm sure you can be there too, but because I'm the social influencer, they want to concentrate on me. We can combine it with our new TikTok campaign, where I will report from the frontline each day,' Judith said.

Jack gathered up the dinner plates, and left them in the sink. 'We can't have it looking like it is only Killcawley Estate that is in danger,' he said.

Marsha produced an apple tart. 'I thought it would go nice with a cuppa, but now it can be dessert,' she said.

'Good idea. And may I suggest a glass of Baileys on the side,' Judith said.

They were on their second glass of Baileys when there was a loud crash at the front of the house.

'What on earth was that?' Marsha said.

'Oh my God, the sitting room chandelier,' Judith cried.

Jack got up to investigate. 'Everybody stay here,' he warned as he carefully opened the door to the hall. Judith got up and followed.

Emma called her back.

Marsha was next up. 'I have got to see this,' she said.

Emma and Hetty followed, their steps reticent on the hall tiles.

'Why would anyone do this?' they heard Judith say.

Judith was standing in the middle of the drawing room, a brick at her feet. The front bay window had been smashed, and there was glass all over the floor.

'Surely it wasn't Paddy Downey. He's not that bad, is he?' Marsha said.

'I'm calling the gardai. We can't let whoever did this get away with it,' Jack said.

Emma ran to Judith as she saw her stumble, and with the help of Jack, they managed to get her to the armchair beside the fireplace.

'At least it didn't get as far as the painting, but it chipped one of the glass drops hanging from the chandelier,' Hetty said, and Judith began to sob loudly.

Emma ran to get a dustpan and brush, but Jack told her not to clear up until detectives had a look at everything.

'There's hardly fingerprints in here,' Marsha said.

'It doesn't matter, we shouldn't touch anything,' Jack said firmly.

He offered his arm to Judith, and she leaned on him as she pulled herself up and staggered back through to the kitchen.

Ten minutes later, a squad car and an unmarked detective car pulled up at the house, and Jack let them in. A female garda came to the kitchen, and asked for everybody's name. She took Judith aside for a chat.

'This has to be Paddy Downey's work,' Marsha muttered to a detective, who was examining the broken window in the drawing room.

'Pardon?' the officer said.

Marsha's face reddened, and she pretended she had not heard.

When the detective entered the kitchen, he went straight to Judith. 'I'm sorry about what happened, Mrs McCarthy. I think you should have somebody stay in the house with you tonight.'

'I can. I'll sleep downstairs,' Jack said, and Marsha made a face.

'I don't think anyone will come back, but until you can get the window fixed properly, best to take care,' the detective said.

Emma saw the uniformed officer and detective out.

'Do you think that silly man did it?' Judith asked.

'He's the prime suspect,' Marsha said.

'He just wants to frighten us. What does he think I will do, move out and sell up?' Judith said, turning to Emma, who, feeling queasy, sat down to one side of the AGA.

'You do know this is an isolated incident; we're all right and Jack will stay for a few days,' Hetty said kindly.

Emma nodded. 'Would you mind if I called it a night? I feel a headache coming on,' she asked Judith.

'Of course, dear. But please don't worry. We'll get over this,' Judith said.

'It might help if you got a proper guard dog,' Marsha said as she got up and put on her coat.

Judith hugged Emma. 'Darling, you go and rest. And don't worry; I trust Jack completely to keep us all safe.'

'Thank you, it's just been a bit of a shock,' Emma said.

Jack said he would accompany Emma upstairs, but on the second landing, he stopped.

'If you need anything, call me or just shout out,' he said.

'Jack, are you sure it's that man who was shouting at the meeting who threw the brick?' she asked.

'I hope so, otherwise we are up against something else,' he said, before going back downstairs.

Emma couldn't stop shivering. She had to tell them why she had come to Killcawley, but she still didn't know how.

THIRTEEN

Emma managed to get inside her room before her knees buckled. Fear coursed through her, making her head thump. What if this was a coincidence; a silly, stupid coincidence? Nobody knew she was here. The rational side of her brain told her that, but the part which had been honed by fear and dread spoke otherwise. Her mouth was dry and her hands were shaking. She pulled across all the curtains and sat in the dark, afraid even on the second floor that she was being watched from the outside. She heard Jack downstairs, boarding up the drawing room window, and Judith saying goodbye to Marsha and Hetty at the front door.

When they had left, she heard Judith scurry to the linen cupboard on the first landing, before showing Jack up to the bedroom across the hall from Emma's.

Emma was glad Jack was staying in the house. She put on the little light beside her chair, and sat at the dressing table to brush her hair. It was then she noticed the dry-cleaning bag draped over the back of the bed. Judith had mentioned earlier in the day that she had sent off her trouser suit to be cleaned and it had come back like new.

'There was no need; I didn't plan to wear it again,' Emma said.

Judith had slapped Emma lightly on the wrists.

'You had it thrown over the back of a chair, Emma. You should really be more careful. That is a designer suit that should last you a lifetime.'

Emma had wanted to shout that she had no business even going into her bedroom, but she bit her tongue, knowing Judith would be bitterly hurt at such a reaction. She thought of offering her the suit – Judith had the same slim build, but she knew she would want to wear it on a TikTok video and Emma couldn't risk anybody recognising it.

She smiled to herself that she sounded so extreme and fanciful, but it was the small details which tripped up the killers and possibly the victims.

Picking up the dry cleaning, Emma ripped the plastic apart to examine the suit. Running her hand along it, she remembered how it had once made her feel. Slumping onto the bed, she recalled the day she had decided to buy it. She had got a bonus for her hard work on a case which was ready for trial. She could still feel the thrill of excitement and achievement when she was handed an envelope with a wad of cash inside and a thank-you note. She immediately went to the designer in the nearby town and asked to be measured for a bespoke suit. She chose a lightweight tweed, predominantly navy in colour with miniscule flecks of grey, light blue and every now and again, pink. The designer told her with her blonde hair and her grey-blue eyes it was the perfect colour for her, and she had to agree.

She was so excited and had brought swatches home to show Henry. They had been married a year and had known each other for two years. She thought he would share in her pride, applaud her hard work, but he was cross and snarky and complained bitterly that the money could have been used for something useful. He insisted she ring up and cancel the order, but she told him a lie that the fabric was already cut, and she would have to pay for it anyway.

She had gone to bed early, and she was still annoyed at him the next morning. She made sure to leave early before he got up. It was such a good day at work – she was told to put her name forward for promotion – that she forgot she was still cross with Henry. She stopped off to buy a bottle of wine at the local off-licence, and was humming to herself as she approached the front door.

Now, Emma twiddled a piece of ribbon tightly around her index finger, feeling nervous because she was dragging up the past. She squeezed it tight as she remembered how she had opened the front door, calling out to Henry that she had more good news.

'You're going to be so proud of me,' she'd managed to get out, before she was punched in the face, followed quickly by another fierce knuckle punch in the back as her legs were kicked from under her. She landed on the hall floor with a thud. Kicks powered by a vicious temper were aimed along her body as she gasped for breath; thinking she was shouting for help when, in reality, she was on the floor taking the punches like a rag doll.

Emma's mouth went dry as she dredged up the bad memory from deep inside her; how she'd thought she was going to die but she couldn't fight back, her body and brain paralysed in fear.

Emma curled up in a ball in the bed, her head throbbing. For so long she had blacked out the details of the attack, but they intruded upon her. She remembered so vividly the moment it had stopped. There was the distinctive ringtone of Henry's mobile phone, then the kicking stopped. She opened an eye to see his shoes as he stepped over her, and out the front door. She lay there, the pain engulfing her until she heard

Henry returning to curse over her, and bending down to check if she were alive.

Henry later said he had been sitting out in the garden, and that he must have fallen asleep in the sun. His phone had woken him up, and he had talked to his friend, before walking into the house where he had found Emma slumped in the hall.

Emma trembled now to think how even in her semi-comatose state she had recoiled from him because she thought he was going to finish her off, but he rang the emergency services.

He came in the ambulance with her, feebly holding her hand as they tried to help her and gave her morphine for the pain. He was at her bedside when the police came to talk to her. She said she remembered going in her front door and she was attacked by a man who seemed taller than her, who threw his punches from above.

She didn't tell anyone she had recognised Henry's shoes. After the attack, she was never without him by her side. He was so kind to her that she began to second-guess whether the man who wanted to kill her was in fact Henry. The shoes, though. She knew in her heart she had bought them for him the Christmas before – they were distinctive with a red stripe down one side. She clung on to the hope that it wasn't Henry, because to contemplate that he wanted to hurt her was too much for her.

As she lay on the bed now, she wondered how she could have come to that decision, and she berated herself for her cowardice for not speaking up. But back then, she didn't want to believe it; she loved him, and it was easier to believe that the man she loved and married had not done such a terrible thing to her. Before they married he had been a sweet caring man even if he were a little fussy at times.

When friends rang to see how she was, Henry blamed himself for not keeping her safe, that she had been attacked while he was in the house. He was very good at turning all the sympathy on himself. She could see clearly now that he had manipulated the situation, so that he looked as much as a victim as she was.

He showered her with gifts and kindness in hospital, and when she got home he did everything for her. He didn't want her to go back to work, but she laughed and said she was never going to be the wife at home. She thought in that moment he was cross, but he walked out of the room to make coffee.

Three months after she first ordered it, she collected the suit. The designer had a big welcome for her and when she tried it on, it was indeed beautiful. The jacket, with silver buttons, was fitted at the waist and the trousers were boot-cut, which accentuated her long legs. When she brought it home, she never told Henry, and if he thought the outfit was different to her usual black and grey trouser suits, he said nothing.

Life was good and slowly she began to put the attack behind her. That was until she came home two hours later than usual from work one Friday evening.

Henry, who had cooked dinner, was waiting for her when she came in the front door.

'Where were you?' he barked.

'Mary is leaving on maternity leave and we all went for a drink. Well, obviously, she didn't drink.'

'But you did.'

'I had a glass of prosecco.'

She didn't see his fist come through the air until it connected with her head, and pushed her up against the wall, knocking a picture sideways.

'You disrespect me by going out to a pub like that? That is not the way for a married woman to behave,' he shouted as he punched her again in the ribs.

She gasped for breath, pleading with him to stop.

'You're not worth it, but learn from this,' he said, before thundering out the front door and driving away.

She crawled to the bathroom, and stood under a warm shower, hoping to wash away the blood and pain.

She should have walked out of the house that night, she knew that now. But back then she still believed that she had done something wrong to bring out such badness in a man she loved.

She had trusted Henry when he came back in the early hours, drunk and upset and sorrowful. What was it about the word 'marriage' which had a stranglehold on her, prevented her from making rational decisions, and let her make excuses for behaviour she wouldn't accept from anybody else.

He had crept into their bed and held her tight, telling her over and over he was sorry, it would never happen again. She was too scared to tell him that his hold hurt her, and when he kissed her, she kissed him back. The next morning he had breakfast ready for her and told her she looked beautiful.

Emma shook herself to rid herself of the memories and went to sit at the dressing table.

She thought now how sly and clever Henry had been. He had never punched her full in the face; that would have left behind ugly bruising for the world to see. He only ever aimed to the side or the back of her head. She trembled to think how she could be so detached now. The assaults happened roughly once a month. She could never pinpoint the trigger. It could have been because the scrambled eggs were too dry, or, once, because she hadn't put enough salt on his baked potato. There was another time that she spent too long talking to Mr Murphy next door.

Taking the brush now, she ran it through her hair. The rhythmic movement helped to calm her nerves, though it also reminded her that for a long time after the assaults, it would hurt to brush her hair.

A gentle tapping on the bedroom door made Emma jump.

She held her breath, half suspended between the past's lingering memories and the present.

'Emma, just checking in on you after all that dreadful business,' Judith called out.

Quickly swiping tears from her face, Emma opened the door. 'I'm fine,' she said.

'Well, you don't look it, I don't mind saying. We all got a hell of a fright, and I don't know what I will do if Miles hears about it.'

'He won't, if nobody tells him.'

'I hope you're right. Make sure you get a good night's sleep. We're all rattled but we'll look at this whole thing afresh in the morning,' she said.

Emma didn't know what to say, so opted for a quiet 'Good night.'

Once closed, she waited quietly at the bedroom door listening. From what she could make out, Judith did not go back downstairs, but instead went across the landing to Jack's room, where Emma heard muffled voices and the door opening and shutting.

FOURTEEN

Judith was up bright and early, singing to herself in the kitchen, when Emma came downstairs.

'Never let the bastards get us down, darling; that's my motto. I refuse to be a victim,' she said as she placed a mug of coffee on the table.

Emma watched Judith as she appeared to glide around the kitchen. Wearing a deep blue kaftan with silver beading at the neck and her hair in a chignon, Emma thought she looked very happy.

'You were up early,' Emma said.

'Yes, Jack had to tend to the cows at his place, so I got him a bit of breakfast.' Judith, a broad smile on her face, put a finger to her mouth and laughed. 'Out of bad things come good, sometimes.'

Emma shrugged and concentrated on her coffee.

'Are you still upset by what happened? That was probably Downey letting off steam; Jack will sort it out. The gardai have been informed, and we have to put it behind us.'

'I wish it were that easy,' Emma said.

'Darling, we have been sent lemons, let's make lemonade.'

'What do you mean?'

Judith sat down at the table opposite Emma. 'I've had the most spectacular idea to turn this fine mess in our favour. The *Irish Times* journalist and photographer are due here this morning to report on the attack. Even if it is not linked to our motorway fight, we can make the link and get national headlines.'

'But you don't know any of this for sure.'

'Darling, isn't that what they call *spin*? I'm merely spinning the story to our advantage. It will get our campaign off to a rollicking good start, especially alongside the TikTok videos.'

'What does Jack think of this?'

'He's annoyed because I won't let him get the window fixed. I was thinking of wearing one of my purple or pink outfits for a good pop of colour inside the broken window.'

Emma shook her head.

'What's wrong? You do know last night was just a one-off? I doubt if anyone will be back tonight to burn the house down,' Judith whispered.

Emma slurped her coffee. 'How can you take everything so lightly?'

Judith stopped fiddling with her gold bracelet and gave Emma a big smile. 'If I didn't laugh, darling, I would never stop crying, especially these past few years. These moments pass. Keep that uppermost in your mind; it helps us get through. Now, go along and get dressed; I have a press release written, and I want you to print it out so I can give it to the reporter.'

'Remember, I don't want to be in any photographs.'

Judith laughed. 'This is my gig, darling. Don't worry, I didn't even tell Marsha and Hetty. They are due here later, and they'll be furious. Now, hurry up, we want to be presentable when the media arrives.'

As Emma turned to leave, Judith said, 'Will you be able to video me? I am sure everybody would be interested to see the damage, and how I was targeted, just because I want to save the estate and the village.'

'Of course,' she replied, and Judith blew a kiss as Emma headed for the stairs.

Upstairs, Emma pulled on a clean pair of jeans and a blouse, tied her hair back and applied some light make-up.

She stopped at the long window for a moment. Jack had somebody out on a rowing boat, pulling weeds from the lake. The ducks swam in front of the boat, like tugs guiding a ship into harbour.

Judith called up the stairs that the *Irish Times* people were on the avenue, and to come quickly. Judith had changed into an elegant purple trousers suit, and was wearing the fascinator Emma had gifted her.

'Do you think you need the headgear?' Emma asked, and she was immediately sorry when she saw Judith's face fall.

'I think it finishes off the outfit beautifully, and one thing we have to make sure of is that the picture gets used with the story. Even I know a story in a newspaper without an accompanying photograph – and especially of somebody pretty – can quickly become a story that isn't read.'

She turned and beamed at Emma. 'I once had a wonderful friendship with a newspaper editor. He stayed at the big house here for a little while. He was a friend of Stephen's, and I picked up a few tips on layout and journalism from him. I may not be a young beauty, but I have good features and a quirky side that lends itself to the camera.'

Emma didn't know how to reply, and she was glad when Jack came into the kitchen.

'They are all talking about you in the village, saying you have a hundred thousand followers on that TikTok,' he said.

Judith picked up her phone to check her TikTok account.

'This is amazing! It can only be good for us and the motorway campaign,' she said.

'You be careful, Judy – all these people are out for what they can get. You know you will only get your fingers burnt. Remember, if you let the press or social media in once, there are those who take it as a free pass forever.'

'Don't be so alarmist, Jack. Haven't you heard that there is no such thing as bad publicity?'

Jack eyed Judith up and down. 'You look as if you're going to a wedding, Judy.'

'Now stop that, Jack Dennehy. You know I look stunning. Live with it.'

Judith flounced off to open the front door.

'She's not letting me near them, so will you make sure she keeps to the motorway and doesn't invite the press in for a grand tour?' Jack said to Emma.

She nodded as she followed Judith out to the hall.

Judith was pacing back and forth across the front step. Emma stepped into the drawing room. As the front window was now boarded up, the only light was coming from the side windows, and the room looked dull. She stopped to take in the painting. The girl sitting for the artist was so full of hope, she thought; her eyes calm as if she knew the rest of her life was going to be very good, that everything was mapped out, and as it should be. She stopped to look at Judith, who was frantically pacing back and forth, the silk flower on the fascinator dancing in the light breeze, and her heart went out to the old lady – somebody had tried to frighten her out of her home. She admired Judith too, that she would persist to live in this big old house when she could have comfortably downsized. A car came up the avenue as Jack came around the front and began to take the hoarding off the window.

'I'm sure they will need to photograph the damage,' he said

gently. Judith smiled at him, making him look away, embarrassed.

The photographer whistled as he surveyed the house as he got out of the car, and began to drape his cameras and lenses over his shoulders. The reporter, his notebook sticking out of his right pocket, shook hands with Judith and Emma.

Emma saw Jack disappear into the walled garden while Judith told her story. The photographer, as Judith had predicted, had her stand inside, looking out through the shattered window.

'Can we have the two of you for the next one?' he said, and Emma began to stutter.

'My assistant does not want to be photographed. She's leaving all that fun for me,' Judith said as Emma slipped away to the kitchen.

She stole out to the courtyard garden where the bank of butterfly bushes was in full bloom, painted lady butterflies flitting between the flower buds.

'I thought of pulling out those bushes, but they hide the old outhouses,' Jack said, interrupting her thoughts.

'They're rather lovely,' Emma replied.

'Is Fleet Street gone yet?' he asked drily.

Emma laughed. 'I think bringing in the press was a very good idea.'

'It was, if she can stop at that. Judith loves being in the limelight. She's just made that way; she will do anything for publicity.'

'Which is probably what the old oak tree needs right now.'

'Fair point,' he said, turning when he heard Judith call from inside.

'They wouldn't even stay for tea. They said they had to get to another job, but the story should be online soon and in the newspaper tomorrow. Did you upload a video?' Judith asked.

'Yes, lots of views already.'

'It's a good time to do another TikTok, Emma. Let's go as far as the lake.'

'Not in those shoes, Judy, you'll break your neck,' Jack said.

Judith went inside to change her shoes. Emma wandered slowly through the walled garden, stopping at a bank of blue and white agapanthus. Tall and architectural, with a globe of delicate flowers, these were always her favourite. In her garden back in the UK, the faded stalks lasted until Christmas. One year, she picked the stalks and sprayed the globes silver, before putting them in a glass jug surrounded by twinkling lights. Henry said it looked like a child had made the arrangement and told her to throw it out.

When she ignored him, he took the jug, stood at the back door and fired it down the garden. She heard it land near the rockery, smashing into pieces she knew she would have to clear up the next morning.

Jack stood beside her. 'The event last night scared you, Emma?'

'A little.'

'My money is on Paddy Downey; he was always a bitter, grasping type.'

'You don't think it could be anybody else?'

Jack reached into his pocket and took out a small piece of red brick. 'I walked down this morning to where Downey lives, and he has this crushed decorative brick as some sort of garden path. That's good enough evidence for me.'

'Did you tell Judith?'

'She doesn't want to know the truth; she wants to be a big media star, but you should know there is nothing to worry about. It won't happen again.'

Emma stared at Jack. His face, which was normally calm but cracked with smile lines, was furrowed with anger. She was too afraid to ask him why he was so certain trouble wouldn't knock on the door of Killcawley Estate again.

Judith came out wearing a cerise pink off-the-shoulder ball gown.

'I thought if I came across as gentle and beautiful, then this motorway business would appear even worse,' she said.

Jack shook his head and said he had work to do; he wanted to put an electric fence around the oak tree and set up a camera, in case anyone thought of sneaking onto the land and causing damage.

'We're so lucky – you think of everything, Jack,' Judith said, and he smiled softly and nodded.

At the lake, Judith made a big fuss about getting the swans in the video by throwing biscuit crumbs in the water to lure them over to the jetty. As the swans glided past, she knelt down, making sure her bright pink ball gown was fanning out behind her. Turning around, she looked directly at the camera.

'This is beautiful Killcawley Estate. There are those who want to take all this away, and replace it with a motorway. Please help us fight the good fight,' she said, before indicating to Emma to cut.

'Get it out straight away, darling; I'm going to need to lie down after such a busy morning,' she said, throwing the last of the biscuits for the ducks, who had crossed the lake, quacking loudly to be fed.

'Shouldn't we include something about the oak tree?'

Judith turned around. 'We will keep the serious stuff for the print media for now, and let the social influencers get all riled up about the swans first, then the oak tree; a twin approach, if you will.'

Emma laughed, and stood watching Judith, who kicked off her shoes and carried them back up the hill to the house.

Emma lingered for about an hour beside the lake. She had never met anybody like Judith. She wasn't sure what she felt about her. Sometimes, she was so snooty it made Emma cross, but mostly she made her giggle. Emma had not felt this content in a long time. She felt safe here at Killcawley Estate. Life at the big house was quiet; dull almost, at times, but then out of nowhere it would become exciting and loud. It was this contrast that made her like it so much. She wandered up the hill, turning down the side of the house, past Jack, who was replacing the timber sheets across the drawing room window.'

'We have to get the bevelled glass from a supplier in the Midlands. It's going to take a few days,' he said.

She stopped, and helped fix the boards into place. When they heard a car on the driveway, they both swung around.

Hetty braked suddenly, and Marsha, her face red, got out of the car before it had even stopped. Hetty scrambled after her.

'Where is she?'

'Upstairs.'

'I have to read in the *Irish Times* about the motorway campaign, and not one mention of the executive committee. How could she do this to us?' Marsha said, holding up her iPad and the online version of the newspaper.

'It all happened so fast; they just arrived this morning.'

'And I suppose Judith always goes around in her fascinator to feed the hens,' Hetty said, pushing past Emma.

Jack stood in front of her. 'Hetty, Judith did what she does best; she dressed up and got a bit of publicity for the campaign. Don't take it so personally. She just answered the journalist's questions.'

'Are you her bodyguard now?' Marsha asked.

'I'm saying let's not fight over this. Let's capitalise on the publicity. Now is not the time to fight among ourselves.'

Hetty took a deep breath and pulled Marsha to the side.

They appeared to argue a little, before scooting around the back quickly, in case Jack tried to stop them.

Emma heard them call out to Judith as they went in the back door.

She had heard enough. Time to leave them to it. No doubt they would argue for an hour or so, before making up; that was their usual way of doing things.

Jack was already back working on the window. Emma slipped through a side door to the walled garden. Quickly, she made her way past the red and purple salvia, and the pale pink and white roses climbing the stone walls, past the pear tree, which had not fruited this year, and the plum tree, which was weighed down with fruit. She picked her way through the woodland path, stopping to gaze across the river and beyond to the meadows, where red poppies had appeared overnight, making it look almost like a Monet painting.

At the gate, a little bit into the wildflower meadow, she stopped and listened. Closing her eyes, she felt the breeze tickle past her, the faint swish of the flowers swaying in the long grass. She loved this peaceful spot, where nature wrapped around her, soothing her aching heart and her tired brain.

When she heard the crack of a twig behind her, Emma jumped, but it was Benny snuffling about. Calling him to heel, she set off down the windy path past the cluster of cowslips and cornflowers to the oak tree.

Staring up at the span of branches and leaves until she felt dizzy, she could understand why this tree was known in these parts as the Grand Oak. That it had been here for hundreds of years surely had to factor into any argument about rerouting the motorway. The last thing this tree needed was to be saved, only to end up situated in the middle of a motorway.

She remembered she was once on the M62 motorway in England, and saw a beautiful farmhouse between the eastbound and westbound carriageways. She didn't want that happening to the old oak tree, or to Killcawley Estate.

Emma leaned against the tree trunk, and closed her eyes,

listening to the sounds of the tree: the branches swaying, the creaking coming from the heart of the tree; the birds rustling in the leaves high above her. She wanted to remain here, to continue to feel this peace in her heart, the peace and comfort that the old oak tree brought her as it stood between her and the rest of the world.

FIFTEEN

Hetty woke the whole house the following morning as she speeded up the avenue revving her car engine, and blaring the horn. Marsha was holding the newspaper out of the passenger window, wildly flinging it from side to side.

Emma watched from her window as Hetty swerved to miss a clutch of ducklings tucked together on the avenue, and nearly ended up under the rhododendron branches.

By the time Emma got downstairs, there was uproar in the kitchen.

Judith gripped Emma by the shoulders. 'They say here an expert will have to examine the oak tree; it could very well be one of the oldest in the country. And look at the beautiful picture of me. I am on the front page.'

'Yeah, it would have been nice to read more about the campaign. Hetty here is losing her house,' Marsha said, but she had a smile on her face, and Emma thought she was secretly delighted with the publicity.

Judith took a spoon and clinked a glass, as if she were presiding over an important meeting. 'Dearest friends, I have something else to tell you all. I got a phone call from a researcher on the wonderful Joe Duffy radio show last night, and he asked me to come on to talk to Joe this afternoon.'

Nobody said a word. Hetty was the first to break the silence.

'You're getting all the fun gigs; we're the idiots who will have to do the donkey work,' she said, deflated.

'We need to talk about the oak tree,' Jack said, taking off his hat, and stepping into the kitchen. 'I have just come from the meadow. Somebody stole in this morning, and tried to carve something on it; luckily, I was down that way, and came across them. They disabled my cameras too.'

Judith gasped in fright. 'Oh my God, what have I done? That poor tree.'

'Keep your hair on, I caught them; I saw them access from the old road in to Kilcashel, and come across the fields. That's a shortcut to nowhere, so I went down and confronted them.'

'Who was it?'

'Some thugs from Bray had been promised €200 to deface the tree.'

'I hope you informed the police,' Emma said.

'The lads are being brought before the District Court later this morning, but I don't expect this to be the last of it.'

'What the hell, Jack? I hope you're mistaken,' Marsha said.

Emma noticed that Judith had drifted off to the drawing room and she followed. Loitering in the doorway, she watched her sit on the couch quietly sobbing. Emma wasn't sure what to do. Judith always seemed so strong, but these incursions onto Killcawley Estate had spooked her. Emma jumped when she felt a tap on her shoulder.

'I will look after her,' Jack said, easing past her into the room.

He put his arm around Judith, and let her lean against his chest. Emma watched for a moment as Jack gently stroked Judith's hair and murmured something Emma couldn't quite catch. Conscious she was intruding, she backed away to the kitchen.

Hetty and Marsha were making tea, and slapping butter on bread to make sandwiches.

'A cuppa and a feed is what she needs before going on national radio,' Marsha said, bustling about trying to keep busy.

'Is Jack getting her through?' Hetty asked.

'He's in there, comforting her,' Emma said.

Marsha turned around. 'Judy pretends to be as tough as nails, and while there's a lot of steel there, she takes everything to heart.'

'That's Judith for you.'

Emma watched as Marsha set a small tray with two mugs of tea, and a plate of tuna and cheddar cheese sandwiches.

'Bring that in to the two of them. Judith needs to keep her strength up. That radio interview could clinch the motorway debate for us,' she said.

'I don't know if I want to disturb them.'

'For God's sake, girl, it's only Jack in there with her. Get on with it,' Marsha said impatiently as she took out a notebook to jot down a few ideas for the interview.

Emma loitered at the drawing room door and coughed politely.

Jack got up and took the tray.

'Marsha thinks any ill can be cured with a cuppa and a sandwich, even at this hour of the morning,' Judith said, taking the sugary tea and sipping it.

'Are you OK to do the interview?' Emma asked.

'I'm going to have to be, but what Miles will think of it all, I don't know.'

'He's hardly going to be listening to Irish radio in New York.'

'Maybe not, but he reads the *Irish Times* online.'

Emma sat in an armchair at the fireplace.

Judith picked up a sandwich, and examined it before taking a tiny bite. 'Marsha always slathers on too much butter,' she said, making a face.

'Miles texted Judy. He's furious at what happened, and he wants Judy to pull back from the limelight,' Jack said as Judith attempted to hush him.

Hetty and Marsha, who had been lingering around the doorway, trooped into the drawing room, and perched along the edge of a velvet couch.

'Sure, we're only getting started. It's very easy for those far away to have an opinion,' Marsha said.

'He's not the one who will have to live here with cars and trucks at the back door,' Hetty said.

Judith straightened up on the couch. Emma could see that she didn't like anyone – other than herself – to criticise her son.

'Miles always wants the best for me. He loves his life in New York, and he wants me to sell up. He insists the latest trouble is just an example of why I should not be living here.'

'Well, that's complete nonsense,' Marsha said, folding her arms as if protecting herself from the news.

'You're not seriously thinking of selling up or moving away?' Hetty asked.

'There are times it would be nice to start a new adventure, but then I see the small places on offer; for goodness' sake, I wouldn't even fit my hat collection in those new homes in the village.'

Marsha guffawed loudly. 'Well, thank goodness that's sorted. Saved by the Killcawley Estate hat collection.'

Jack said he hadn't time to be chatting as he wanted to get back to check on the oak tree.

When he left, Hetty leaned in to Judith. 'You should tell Miles that you have a big strong man to look after you, and Emma as well.'

Judith shook her head. 'I wouldn't dare tell Miles about Jack; he wouldn't understand.'

'Is he a child or a man?' Marsha asked.

Emma, who began to feel like she was intruding on something, made to leave the room, but Judith called her back. 'Emma, don't go. You're part of the family now; you might as well know our secrets. We women share everything.'

Emma reluctantly sat back down. 'We should go over the sort of things likely to come up in the radio interview,' she said.

'Emma, do you ever stop working? Can't we just sit here and have a laugh and talk trash?' Judith said.

'It does us the power of good; since Jack joined the supper club, it has become a little polite. We need our space, where everything and everyone is fair game,' Marsha said.

Judith put her hand out to Emma. 'We are just a group of women who like to chat, and put the world to rights; no matter how bad things are, we support each other, and if you let us in, we could do the same for you.'

'Thanks, but I'm not as...' she hesitated, and Marsha burst out laughing.

'You mean you are not as opinionated, stubborn or goddamn bolshy as the rest of us,' she said.

'Speak for yourself,' Judith said in her marbles in the mouth voice, and the others laughed.

Judith's mobile phone rang loudly, and she handed it to Emma.

'It's probably another journalist looking to talk to me. Tell them to listen in to the radio or reschedule for this evening.'

Emma answered the phone.

'Mother, what is going on? Are you all right? I have told you that house is too much for you. You never answered my emails. I thought you were ill,' the caller said.

Emma looked directly at Judith, and mouthed *Miles* to her.

'Tell him I am out for coffee and getting my nails done,' she whispered as she led the ladies through to the kitchen.

Emma took a deep breath before she spoke.

'I am sorry, Judith is not here at the moment. This is Emma, can I help you?'

Miles sighed deeply. 'Do you know where she is, or when she will be back?'

'She went into the village to get her nails done; she shouldn't be too long. Can I take a message?'

'So somebody targets Killcawley Estate and throws a rock in the window, and my mother goes to have a manicure.'

'That is hardly fair. Judith is doing her best to save Killcawley Estate from the motorway and is regarded as quite a heroine in these parts.'

'Emma, tell me what you would have done if the rock had hit my mother or anyone else? It is not safe to be part of this. This motorway lark is putting too much of a spotlight on Judith and the estate. You should be helping to talk her out of it, instead of indulging her silly whims.'

Anger streaked through Emma. She stood up and began to pace the drawing room.

'Miles. I know it must be hard for you to trust me, given we've never met, but your mother is the most wonderful person I know. She carries on, no matter what. Yes, the incident with the rock was very frightening, but what is Judith supposed to do, pack up and go into a nursing home, because others think that is where she should be? You should be celebrating that your mother is a sprightly seventy-five-year-old who does her best to get some good out of every day.'

Emma wanted to end the call, but instead she hurried to the kitchen and gestured to Judith.

'Tell him anything; he will only put me in a bad mood,' Judith whispered.

'Emma, if you really care for my mother, you will get her to give up this silly crusade,' Miles said.

'Don't you care about Killcawley Estate? If you did, you would not call to belittle Judith's efforts and the efforts of everybody here to save this wonderful place.'

'Emma, you don't know me, my mother or even Killcawley Estate well enough to speak like this. Let me remind you who pays your wages,' Miles snarled down the line.

Emma opened the front door, and stood out on the steps. 'Miles, I love your mother; she has been very good to me. There is nothing I wouldn't do for her. She loves Killcawley Estate, it means everything to her, and she is prepared to fight for it. I will be there at her side whether you like it or not,' Emma said calmly and firmly before ending the call.

A rush of adrenalin surged through Emma. She was buzzing. She may have talked herself out of a job, but at this particular moment, she didn't care. She headed down to the lake. As she walked along the jetty, the ducks tracked across the water, quacking as they went. She had nothing in her pockets, and tried to ignore them by concentrating on the view, but the ducks were unhappy. A mallard got onto the jetty and pecked at Emma's shoes. Two others joined in, and she had to stamp her feet to force them back in the water. Four ducklings struggled to get on the jetty, but tumbled back into the water, making Emma laugh out loud.

When she heard Judith call her, she hurried back to the house.

'I can imagine what Miles had to say. Silly boy, you just ignore him. Now, please help me pick something to wear for the interview,' Judith said.

'But it's on the radio?'

'Clothes maketh the woman. I need to feel empowered, so you must help me. If I stay in a kaftan, I will be airy-fairy, but a business suit will give me strength.'

Emma laughed. 'I never thought of it like that.'

'Like when you were wearing that suit, you oozed business. Maybe you should wear it more often.'

Emma said they had better get on with picking an outfit as there was only an hour to go for the interview.

'Marsha and Hetty have gone home; they read somewhere that you can't listen to the radio in the same house, if somebody is being interviewed from there. They will be back on Thursday for the Estate Supper Club. It's Indian night.'

'That should be interesting; how will they cope with Indian night?'

'Bizarrely, Marsha spent a year in India. She's remarkable when it comes to Indian cooking; the rest of us won't be able to keep up with her,' Judith said, leading the way to her room.

Emma would never cease to be amazed by all of the surprises these women had in store for her. What next? she thought. Hetty in her youth had a fling with a celebrity?

SIXTEEN

JULY

Judith was so tired after the radio interview, which had lasted over fifteen minutes, that she spent all of the next day, Wednesday and Thursday morning in bed.

Emma knocked on her bedroom door at midday and offered tea, but Judith didn't answer. A while later, she rang Emma on her mobile.

'Darling, I don't think I will be able to make the supper club this evening. Can you tell the others and cancel.'

'Are you sure? You love Indian food.'

'Darling, I couldn't face company. I need a total recharge.'

Emma wasn't entirely sure what was going on, but she rang and left messages for Jack, Hetty and Marsha.

Within a half an hour, Marsha's car pulled up at the house, and she got out looking worried.

'Where is she?'

'In bed, since the radio interview.'

'What? We'll have to put a stop to this,' Marsha said, pushing past Emma.

Emma ran ahead and stopped her at the bottom of the

stairs. 'I think we have to respect Judith's wishes. Please, Marsha, you can't go up there.'

'Darling, you have been here a wet week, and I like you very much, but I'm going upstairs to talk to my friend. She needs me right now.'

Emma stepped back. She had never heard that tone from Marsha before. Halfway up the stairs, Marsha turned around.

'Don't think badly of me. We're like twins, J and I – we stick together, no matter what.'

'As long as Judith doesn't get cross at me over this,' Emma replied, retreating to the kitchen.

She heard Marsha knock on Judith's bedroom door, and the door opening to admit her. Suddenly, for the first time since she'd moved here, Emma felt all alone. There was always somebody bustling around, and needing something from her, but now, as the door shut between them, there was nothing but quiet.

Pulling on her straw hat, she set off to the horses, deliberately leaving her phone behind. She tramped across the fields, her head down, holding her hat against the slight breeze pushing across the fields. The grass was high, just a while out from the saving of the hay, and she followed a makeshift path where the grass had been flattened so that the young lad who exercised the horses could canter across the fields.

She stopped at the midway point because from here, she knew she couldn't be seen from the side windows of the house. In this very spot, she felt she was far away, with nothing but the sky above her, and meadows all around her. Here, she felt free of everybody and everything. Here, she felt there was no judgment; nobody who had eyes on her; nobody about to criticise and nobody to praise. It was a neutral zone, and her recharging port to get through every week. Here, she felt like a child again able to run free. Throwing her hat to one side, she twirled until she felt dizzy, allowing herself to stumble and fall, and lie down and look at the sky.

When she opened her eyes, the sky was all around her, the clouds drifting too fast, the horizon zig-zagging. She had done the very same thing with her mother. They held hands and raced around in circles until they fell over laughing. She felt safe falling with her mother, knowing that when she landed, they would meld together and watch the sky.

Remember, there is a big world out there to be discovered, her mother always said. She would hug Emma until their backs hurt, and their necks ached from watching the clouds.

Her mother had told her that the clouds were special dispatches and they had to spend time looking up and reading the messages.

Clouds help you use your imagination; they calm you down. When things aren't right, take time to stop and stare. Most of the time, the answer will come from the everchanging canvas we call the sky.

Emma took a deep breath, and watched the blue, silver, grey clouds crowding over the mountains.

She wished she could talk to her mother now; that she had been around to help her get away from Henry. She so needed to be able to lean on someone who knew her inside and out. Here at Killcawley Estate she was happy, but the day would come when Judith would not need an assistant anymore. She dreaded that day coming soon, especially after her conversation with Miles.

She heard the horses neighing in the paddock. Jumping up, she retrieved her hat and went off to give them the treats she always carried in her jeans pocket.

When the two horses saw her, they ambled over, the chestnut nudging at her pocket, the grey shy and standing back. She fed them the treats, but when they realised there were all gone, they wandered away, munching the grass.

Turning back for the house, she scurried when the first drops of rain began to fall. Pulling off her hat and pushing it under her jacket to protect it from the rain, she ran faster, and was out of breath by the time she reached the rhododendron grove.

Back at the house, Emma found Judith in the hat room.

'Where were you, that you got caught in the rain?'

'I just went for a walk to clear my head.'

'I drive you demented, I guess. I know my son is always quite grumpy around me. I irritate people and I take everything to heart,' Judith said.

'I listened back to the radio interview; you were great.'

'I was asked some questions I didn't expect.'

'Are you talking about your husband?'

'Yes, they had done their homework, knew he died recently.'

'To be honest, it made you sound so real, you spoke so well about your grief.'

Judith shook her head. 'Perhaps I shouldn't have spoken about Stephen or his illness. I hope hearing it doesn't upset Miles.'

'What I heard was a woman who is grieving, and who is now having to fight to prevent a motorway ploughing through her family land.'

Judith placed a red cloche hat on her head, and looked at herself in the mirror.

'Dear Emma, you're so loyal, and you never cease to make me feel good. I should pay you even more.'

'I doubt Miles would be very happy about that.'

'Miles is never happy with me, but that's life as you get older; your children become rather disenchanted.'

'Maybe it's because he's living so far away.'

'That's his decision; he could easily take over Killcawley

Estate and live here, or have a job in the city or even London. Sometimes, I think if he'd had the chance to work in Hong Kong, he would have taken it so he could be far away from me,' Judith said quietly.

'You need to walk the fields and look at the sky,' Emma said.

'What are you talking about?'

Emma pulled Judith's coat from the hook and threw it to her. 'Come with me,' she said, leading the way out the back door.

Judith laughed. 'You know, I think you're as crazy as I am.'

They walked hand in hand across the courtyard, and down to the rhododendron grove, where they slipped behind the trees, pushing the heavy branches out of the way to access a gap in the wall to the meadows.

Emma skipped ahead to pick the spot, pulling Judith gently along.

'Lucky I didn't choose my new high heels this morning,' Judith said as she ran alongside Emma.

Emma threw her arms wide and looked at the sky. This was the perfect spot. Gently taking Judith by her hands, she led her round and round in circles.

'Why are we doing this dance?' Judith called out.

'To help set you free; you appear so stressed,' Emma said.

They circled together, throwing back their heads and laughing.

'This is so fun, like "Ring a Ring o' Roses",' Judith said.

Emma was laughing out loud when she opened her eyes to look at the clouds.

'Everything is swirling, Emma, I haven't felt so alive since I was a kid,' Judith shouted, and flopped to the ground. 'The clouds look different from here, don't they? I adore that one which is almost in the shape of an elephant's head. See, there's the trunk.'

'And the blots of white over the mountain,' Emma said.

'I don't care that the ground is wet. I only care about the sky. Gosh, I have been so small in my thinking.'

'Nobody could ever accuse you of thinking small, Judith.'

Judith propped herself up on her elbow. 'Miles accuses me of everything. He never will forgive me that he wasn't there when his father died.'

'There was nothing you could have done about that.'

Judith shook her head. 'Except there was. I deliberately didn't call Miles, until Stephen had passed away.'

'You had your reasons, I'm sure.'

Judith stroked Emma's face. 'So kind, always so kind. Yes, I had my reasons.'

'He will come around.'

Judith jumped up and twirled again, this time slowly, her head back watching the sky. 'I can't change anything now. I did what I thought was right at the time.' She stopped, took off her hat and flung it in the air. 'Miles won't forgive me, but it's what Stephen wanted. He wanted his son to remember the father he loved, not the shadow of a man ground down by pain.'

'Tell Miles that; it might help.'

Judith scooped up her hat. 'Sometimes if you try to explain, it can make everything worse.' She dusted herself off. 'Are we going to visit the horses on the way back to the house?'

'You know I visit the horses?'

Judith laughed. 'It's Killcawley Estate, everybody tells me everything. Be careful with the grey, Rocco, she can be naughty and she can nip, when the mood is on her.'

'Maybe another time,' Emma said.

They tramped back across the fields to the gap in the wall, where they slipped past the rhododendron out onto the avenue.

'Emma, I want you to email everybody we know and tell them about the motorway. We have to keep up the momentum. We will hold a public vigil at the oak tree on Sunday afternoon, and ask everybody to come along,' Judith said.

'Are you sure you want people tramping on Killcawley Estate lands?'

'Jack is going to put up a makeshift fence, and tell people to access from the public road behind the oak tree. He has lined up an expert to address the crowd on the historical significance of the tree, and we will get the media out as well.'

'What about parking?'

'They can park at the side of the public road – the more disruption the better,' Judith said as they entered the courtyard. 'We must go sky-walking again another day, Emma; I feel so good now.'

'I like that phrase, sky-walking,' Emma said quietly.

Judith skipped ahead.

'Let's go to the oak tree and do a TikTok. We can invite everyone to the vigil, and ask them to create a noise to save the tree.'

'We can make a video. But even if one quarter of your followers came, that might cause problems. Judith, you now have two hundred and fifty thousand followers.'

'Crikey, I had no idea! But surely we can use it to our advantage?' Judith said.

'I suppose.'

Judith looked thoughtful for a moment. 'I will wear a sumptuous ball gown,' she finally said.

SEVENTEEN

Emma spent days sending out emails informing people of Sunday's vigil by the oak tree, and she and Marsha put up posters all around Killcawley.

Marsha wanted to drive to other towns, but Emma turned back towards Killcawley Estate.

'Who the hell will come to the meeting if they don't know about it?' Marsha asked.

'Just you wait and see; TikTok will do the work for us, and Judith has organised for it to be announced on local radio,' Emma said.

Marsha harrumphed loudly, and didn't say anything for the journey back to the estate. When Emma pulled up outside the gate lodge, Marsha said in a stiff voice that she wanted to stay put until the big house. 'I presume Lady Muck is at home,' she said.

'Judith is working on her speech and she has to pick an outfit for our next TikTok video.'

'That's hardly a priority,' Marsha grumbled.

Judith was humming to herself, and standing over a pot of simmering pasta on the hob when they got into the kitchen.

'Marsha, Emma, what would I do without you two?'

'Get another bloody pair to do your dirty work,' Marsha mumbled.

Judith poured prosecco into glasses and handed them out.

'Darlings, we are the A-Team. Let's toast to success for the vigil,' she said, holding up her champagne flute.

'And that's supposed to make us feel better? I could murder a cup of tea instead,' Marsha grumbled.

'Darling, down the prosecco; it might sweeten your delivery,' Judith said, pouring a little more into her own glass. Emma, who was sipping her drink, tried to stop the giggles, but ended up spluttering and coughing.

'J, you're losing the run of yourself. Put on the kettle like a good woman,' Marsha said, sitting at the table and pushing her glass of prosecco to the side.

Emma got down some bowls, and dished out the pasta. Judith switched to a bottle of red wine, making Marsha tut loudly.

'I didn't think it was supper club?'

'That's after the vigil. Indian night again, seeing as we had to cancel the last one, we expect your best,' Judith said.

'Bloody slave driver,' Marsha retorted, taking down the red wine glasses.

'I am so worried about the vigil. The *Irish Times* are sending a reporter and photographer, and what if nobody turns up. I hope the TikTok plan works,' Judith said.

Emma turned to Marsha. 'We're hoping to make two TikToks, after we've eaten. One here of the two of you at the kitchen table discussing the motorway, and another of yourself and Judith down by the oak tree, asking people to come along to the vigil.'

'I haven't got my hair done, and I wouldn't have anything to wear for something like that,' Marsha said, her eyes wide with surprise.

Judith laughed out loud. 'I knew you would say that, but rest assured, I have found the most divine pink outfit that will be perfect for you.'

'I don't wear pink. And what about my hair?'

'Which is why the straw pillbox hat I've picked out for you is so good. It's divine and covers a multitude,' Judith said.

'But I won't know what to say?'

'When were you ever stuck for words, M?' Judith laughed.

'I can't get out of this, can I?' Marsha muttered, but Emma suspected she was secretly delighted.

After their quick lunch, they trooped upstairs to Judith's suite, where there was a floaty, light pink dress and a fuchsia linen jacket laid out on the bed.

'I think that colour looks way too young for me,' Marsha said nervously.

'Nonsense. With some nice gold accessories and the little hat, you'll look beautiful,' Judith said, ushering her friend into the bathroom to change.

When Marsha stepped out of the bathroom, Judith had already slipped into a long straight skirt embroidered with deep puce and luminous pink flowers. She had teamed it with a tight-fitting black linen jacket, a pink straw fedora and a long, thick necklace in pink and orange.

'They'll need to wear sunglasses around us,' Marsha said.

'Darling, the pink is so wonderful with your dark hair, and you still have a nice figure,' Judith said, making Marsha blush.

'I still think it's a bit too much, though there's a lovely swing to the skirt,' Marsha said, striking a pose in front of the long mirror.

Judith picked up the pillbox straw hat, and placed it an angle on Marsha's head.

Marsha pulled away.

'I would rather my hair have had a salon blow-dry, but even looking like a scarecrow, I'm not wearing that hat,' she said firmly.

Judith knew better than to argue, and threw the hat on the bed. 'What about we find one that suits better,' Judith said, taking Marsha by the hand and leading her to the hat room.

'I'm not really a hat person; you know that,' Marsha said as she reluctantly let Judith pull her along.

'I have a spliced cotton linen bucket hat in cream and very light pink. I don't know why I didn't think of it before,' she said.

Judith marched into the hat room, went straight to a stack of boxes, and pulled off the lid from the top one.

'I knew it was here,' she said gleefully.

Marsha gingerly placed the hat on her head. 'It feels nice; how does it look?' she said.

'Like it was made for you, and the outfit,' Judith said, the excitement in her voice growing.

Marsha twisted herself in front of the mirror to look at the outfit and hat from all angles. 'I have to hand it to you, J, but this get-up looks mighty fine on me,' she said

'I think we need to get started on this video, ladies,' Emma said, and she led the two women downstairs.

'Wouldn't it be nicer in the drawing room?' Marsha asked.

Judith shook her head. 'We need to get across the message that we are somewhat helpless but brave, not that we are style queens who live in opulence,' Judith replied.

'If you say so,' Marsha said, as she made her way to the kitchen.

Emma set up her phone on a tripod, and placed Judith and Marsha opposite each other at the kitchen table, china cups and saucers in front of them, and a tray with a china teapot, milk jug and sugar bowl in the centre of the table.

'Are you going to give me my lines?' Marsha said.

'Why don't you two just sit and have a normal chinwag. I'll

call out "action" when I start filming, and "cut" when we have finished.'

Marsha fanned her dress around her as she waited for Emma to give the signal. When it came, Judith sprang into action.

'Marsha, we are at our wits' end. What the hell can we do?'

Marsha shifted uncomfortably on her chair.

'That's easy; we ask all those people out there to support our campaign by plastering us all over social media. Nobody in their right mind would put a big road through a beautiful village and estate. It's downright—'

'Criminal,' Judith interjected.

'Certainly. Vandalism of the highest order,' Marsha said, getting into her stride.

'Do you remember when we were young, playing hide and seek at the oak tree?' Judith asked.

'Yeah, bloody frustrating because you always nipped into the bushes, and I was left circling the tree,' Marsha said.

'Silly goose,' Judith said, pointing at Marsha.

'Getaway with your painted nails. We all have our memories of that tree; special memories, whether good or bad.'

'Too true,' Judith said, flicking out her foot as a signal to Emma to finish.

'Well, I'm glad that's over,' Marsha said as Emma stopped recording.

'Now for the second take at the oak tree,' Judith said.

They headed off through the walled garden and the woods to the meadows. Emma stopped them at the top of the hill.

'Ladies, I will go down, and if you hold hands, maybe you can skip down the hill together,' Emma said.

'And break our bloody ankles? Are you mad?' Marsha said.

'Come on, we could do a fast walk or something,' Judith said, coaxing Marsha to take her hand.

Emma filmed them as they tittered all the way down the hill.

Almost forgetting the camera, Judith stopped to pluck a daisy, and began to tug at the white petals as she chanted: 'He loves me, he loves me not...' She raised her hand in triumph at the last petal: 'He loves me.'

Marsha grasped a dandelion seed head and began to blow as Judith called out one o'clock, two o'clock and three o'clock. By the time they got to the oak tree, they were laughing heartily.

Judith pulled her friend in beside the tree. 'Let's play hide and seek,' she said.

Marsha shook her head. 'Time to be serious now; to look all around us and imagine a motorway and traffic speeding through here.'

'Unthinkable,' Judith said, rubbing her hand along the bark of the oak tree.

Linking hands, they looked at the camera.

'Please join our vigil at the oak tree off the Killcawley Road, starting at noon this Sunday. Details below,' they said together.

'Cut,' Emma said, and both Judith and Marsha applauded.

'I could get used to this. Did you see me dance down that hill?' Marsha said, as they tramped back to the house.

Judith hurried on ahead.

'It's her only failing; she never likes anyone to steal her thunder. She is an only child; it probably has something to do with it,' Marsha said, walking beside Emma.

At the top of the hill, Judith was waiting for Emma and Marsha. 'I think the last TikTok should go out tomorrow and the first can be put up tonight. We have to get a lot of people here; otherwise our campaign will fizzle out before it's even started.,' she said.

'Why are you upset? We all did so well, even me,' Marsha said.

'I'm just worried. What if nobody comes and the newspaper is here and possibly a TV crew? What will we do?' Judith said.

'Don't be silly, darling. Even if only a tenth of your TikTok followers turn up, it will stop the traffic this side of Dublin,' Marsha said, taking her friend's elbow and leading her through the wood.

'Why do I suddenly feel like a little girl who has been stopped mid-tantrum?' Judith said.

Marsha walked on ahead. 'I am right and you know it. J, you always fuss too much, and it always works out in the end.'

Judith leaned into Marsha. 'You're a good friend, even if you tell the truth,' she said.

'I will take that as a compliment.' Marsha laughed, and they made their way back to the house.

Emma disappeared to her room where she worked on the videos, before uploading the first one on TikTok.

She was sorting out her laundry an hour later when Judith shouted upstairs. Emma rushed out onto the landing to see what the commotion was about, to find Judith and Marsha besides themselves in excitement.

'Emma, Emma, we have *millions* of views and people are saying all sorts and wishing us well.'

Marsha, who had downloaded TikTok just for the occasion, was holding up her phone. 'There's going to be a huge traffic snarl up if they all come, but who cares. We've done it!' she said.

Emma joined them downstairs. Seven million views and counting. Maybe there was a chance for them after all.

EIGHTEEN

On Sunday, Emma was awoken by a commotion coming from the hat room.

She jumped out of bed, and pulled on a hoodie, before making her way to the first landing. The door to the hat room was closed. Nervously, she turned the handle.

'Oh, Emma, I'm so glad you're awake. I need help; I need to find my lucky hat,' said Judith, who was still in her pyjamas.

Emma looked around the room. There were hats and empty boxes strewn all over the floor, and Judith was frantically rifling through her stack of hat boxes containing the expensive, designer creations.

'What has happened?' Emma asked.

'I got a bit carried away, and maybe a little frustrated. I need my lucky hat,' Judith muttered.

Emma began to pick hats off the floor as she made her way towards Judith. 'What are you wearing to the vigil?'

'My purple trouser suit and pink silk blouse, with pearl earrings and choker.'

'What about the Philip Treacy fascinator?'

'Do you think it might be too much?'

Emma laughed. 'You're already wearing silk and pearls, I think a Philip Treacy creation will fit right in and it will look good in the photographs.'

Judith clenched and unclenched her hands. 'I am a silly woman, but I'm so nervous.'

'But you have spoken to crowds before, done radio interviews.'

Judith tried to straighten a stack of hats on a shelf, but they fell off. 'It's not that; I'm afraid nobody will come – only a few locals ready to have a good laugh at my expense.'

'Silly goose, our biggest problem will be the crowds who do turn up.'

'Do you think so?"

'Of course. Now, go and have breakfast. I will tidy up this mess,' Emma said.

Judith, carrying her Philip Treacy hat still in its hat box, went downstairs.

Emma quickly scooped up the hats from the floor, stopping briefly to try on the red cloche hat Judith had worn the day before. Making faces in the mirror, she thought it suited her.

It took another twenty minutes to clear the floor, and put all the hats back in their places. She went to her room, and pulled on a clean pair of jeans. Nobody was going to be interested in photographing her, and she was glad of that.

Downstairs, Marsha and Judith were sitting at the kitchen table. Marsha was wearing a bright blue suit.

'I am hoping the photographs will be in colour and J here won't hog all the attention. I have a liking for more colour all of a sudden,' she said, chuckling,

Jack stuck his head in and said: 'People have already started to arrive at the oak tree. There is even a bit of a build-up of traffic on the Killcawley Road. Hetty said she will meet ye there.'

'I hope the photographers and newspaper reporters are able

to get through,' Judith fretted.

'They can follow us on TikTok; we will be live-streaming,' Emma said, and Marsha clapped in excitement.

A short while later, they walked together to the oak tree, picking their way carefully through the woodland and across the stream to the meadows. At the top of the hill, they stood and watched as crowds of people circled the oak tree.

Judith gasped in amazement.

'And they're still coming; some are parking about a mile away and walking back to the oak tree. The gardai have been called in to direct traffic,' Jack said.

Judith took a deep breath and, taking Jack's hand, she led the party down through the meadow, where the poppies and cornflowers were swaying in the light breeze, and the borage blooms added a delicate blueish purple blur to the field.

When the crowd saw Judith coming, they clapped. It was as if a switch had clicked in Judith and she responded to the crowd, throwing her arms in the air, and blowing kisses all round. She mingled, and answered questions put by reporters, and posed for photographs as if she were a big celebrity.

Eventually, Judith stepped up onto a makeshift stage that Jack had built the night before.

'Welcome to each of you who have come from near and far. This oak tree has seen more of history than all of us, and we are here today to make sure that it survives the hideous plans for a motorway through our beautiful Killcawley. We know there are some people in the village who are also facing losing their homes. This cannot happen,' Judith said, punching the air with her fist. The crowd roared with approval and Hetty held up a placard which said *Save Our Homes*.

'We will not let anyone cut down this tree. They must find an alternative route, because this one through Killcawley lands is not available. The decision to bring the motorway across this land is not a good one, and must be made null and void. We will bring our fight all the way to the courts, and this week, we lodge papers challenging the permission given for this motorway. Today, I ask you to sign the petition here and online saying no to the motorway. Please help up save our homes, our land, our meadows and this amazing old oak tree.'

She called on a local historian to speak, who said there was evidence that this may be the oldest oak tree in the country.

Judith clapped her hands in excitement and the crowds whooped. A wind rustled through the leaves, and a palpable surge of enthusiasm rippled among the crowd that they might, after all, force a change of the motorway route.

A young man standing at the front put his hand up to speak.

'But if they reroute the motorway, won't that put other land and houses at risk? Or is anywhere else fine as long as it's not Killcawley Estate?' he shouted.

Judith stepped forward and pointed to the young man. 'Where you're standing is where the white line will be on the Dublin side of the motorway. Look around you; all of this will be gone. Yes, we need progress, but at what cost to homes and irreplaceable greenery and wildlife? Our village was built around this estate. The oak tree provided shelter for many in bad times. There is history here, and we have a duty to discover it and protect it,' she said.

The crowd roared in unison.

When the speeches were finished, people came up and grabbed Judith's hand, and thanked her. Marsha stood to the side, watching.

A photographer asked if he could photograph Emma and Marsha. Emma shrank back.

'What's wrong? It's the local newspaper – we have to,' Marsha said, grabbing Emma by the elbow, and pinning her to the spot.

The photographer snapped his shot, before asking for their names.

Emma's throat was dry; she could hardly speak.

'She's starstruck. Let me give you all the details you want,' Marsha said, pointing to the photographer's notebook.

Emma pulled away, and set off up the hill. She told herself over and over to calm down. Her heart thumped loudly as she stepped across the little stream and headed to the house. It was only a local newspaper, and maybe they wouldn't use the photograph. Didn't photographers always take more pictures than they needed?

When she got to the kitchen, she filled a glass with water, and drank it down in one go. Leaning against the sink, she closed her eyes and counted to ten.

When Marsha darted in, Emma pretended to be washing her hands.

'What's up, you rushed off?'

'I just wasn't feeling very well, and it is over anyway, isn't it?'

'I wasn't sure of your surname, and the photographer says he can't use the picture unless he has it.'

'I didn't want to be in a photo.'

'You could have said. What have you against it? It will help our campaign; the more attention we get, the better.'

'That is Judith's forte, not mine,' Emma said, her voice strained because she was afraid she was going to burst out crying.

'Anyway, it's all a matter. The photographer deleted it, and I had to pose on my own in the meadow. It has all worked out swimmingly.'

'Well, that's good. If you could excuse me, I have to catch up on a few administrative things,' Emma said.

Marsha stepped back to let her pass.

'Judith and Jack are on their way up; we can have the supper club early. I must heat up the dhal and rice,' Marsha said.

'I'm pretty beat after today; it was an early start with Judith.'

'I have done an amazing brinjal curry. My recipe is from Udaipur, near the Thar Desert; you'll love it.'

'Brinjal?'

'Aubergine, deep-fried in a spicy tomato sauce with basil to soften the flavour.'

'Sounds good. Just let me have a quick nap,' Emma said.

She took the stairs two at a time. Her head hurt, and all she wanted to do was hide. She heard Judith and Jack walk through the courtyard as she climbed into bed. Pushing her head into the pillow, she let the tears take over. There was remorse for what was gone and fear that Henry may one day find her. Her heart hurt, and she felt stupid, because in some way she missed him. She missed being with someone, she missed being part of a couple. She didn't want to be alone; she wanted to be somebody again.

When she woke up, it was dark and the house was quiet. She made her way down to the kitchen. A note with her name on it was propped against a bunch of flowers on the kitchen table.

'The flowers are to say thank you, and we love you. Marsha has left a plate of food in the fridge for you. Just heat it in the microwave.'

The bouquet was made up of cerise pink roses and eucalyptus branches. She reached up high in the cupboard for the crystal vase, and arranged the flowers in it.

Feeling a little peckish, she put the plate of food in the microwave.

Sitting at the kitchen table, she let the aroma of spices, fennel and fresh basil caress her. Slowly savouring the food, she thought life at Killcawley Estate was good. That had to be enough for now.

NINETEEN

Emma was awoken the next morning by the hall phone ringing, and Judith going downstairs to answer it. She buried her head under the pillow, but still the words drifted around her.

As the conversation continued, she could hear Judith becoming more agitated, her voice wavering. Emma pulled on a dressing gown, and crept out onto the second-floor landing. Leaning forward, she listened intently.

'Darling, you should hear what people are saying, and everybody is behind us for the court battle. I think we can win it. Everybody says the motorway can't go ahead. We have all become local celebrities.'

There was a long pause when Miles was talking. Every now and again, Judith tried to interject, but she was not successful. When she eventually did get to talk, her voice was subdued.

'Miles, I love you, but please don't ever put my devotion to Killcawley Estate in doubt. I resent all the things you have said about my very good friends, who are here standing firm with me at a time of the most serious crisis for Killcawley Estate. We may just save it from this hideous motorway. There was a time you would not have spoken to me like that, but New York has changed you, and not for the better.'

The phone in the hall clicked as the receiver was replaced. Emma heard Judith run up the stairs, and her bedroom door bang shut, the vibrations shuddering through the house.

Emma dressed quickly and stole downstairs. She had not intended to phone Miles, but the sound of Judith weeping incensed her. As she passed the phone in the hall, she noticed the little contacts book which was open under M. She stopped; Miles was the only name in this section. On impulse, she picked up the phone, and punched out the New York number.

Miles answered on the first ring.

'Mother, I was about to call you. Let's not fight. But you have to stop all this nonsense, and that TikTok business. Hordes of people are traipsing through Killcawley Estate; anything could happen to you or the house. It is not safe. This is not what my father would want, and deep down, it's not what you want either. This is a grief reaction. All of it is. Let this assistant go, and let's get back to normal. She is leading you on a needless dance, and social media is leading you astray. For Christ's sake, my secretary here at the firm is one of your followers.'

Emma swallowed hard. 'Mr McCarthy, this is Emma speaking.'

'Where is my mother?'

'She's really upset and has gone to lie down.'

'Why on earth are you ringing me? Don't you think you have caused enough mayhem at Killcawley Estate, inviting crowds through our land, and luring my mother into dangerous situations, and now a potentially costly legal battle?'

Anger surged through Emma.

Miles launched into his next tirade.

'Is that what you want, to have my mother embroiled in a legal battle that will drain the estate of all its money? Let's see how long you stick around then, Emma.' Emma thought of ending the call, but instead she raised her voice.

'What are you trying to imply, Mr McCarthy? I love your mother dearly, and there's nothing I wouldn't do for her. I resent your accusations. You have no idea what has been happening here at Killcawley Estate. I imagine everything looks a certain way from your ivory tower. Yes, your mother is old; yes, she is still grieving, but that woman wants to live life the best way she can, and I sure as hell will help her do that. You can fire me, but I will always be Judith McCarthy's friend. You can't stop that.'

She cut off the call before Miles had a chance to reply.

Emma was still shaking when Judith came downstairs.

'I heard you on the phone. Were you talking to Miles?'

'I'm sorry, Judith, I just couldn't bear you being so upset.'

'So you rang him to tell him off?'

'I rang him. Everything sort of developed from there. I hated that he made you cry.'

'Children can always make a mother cry, but he's a good man, Emma. It's hard for both of us, him being so far away.'

'Have I overstepped the mark?' Emma asked.

Judith sat down on the armchair. 'Beautifully, but for all the right reasons.'

'He just makes me so cross.' Emma leaned against the sink, her back to Judith.

She knew she was going to have to leave. Her heart hurt as if it were swollen to twice its size. She could not imagine being anywhere but this old house and estate. She loved making the jam, and some local shops had agreed to stock it. She also enjoyed making the TikTok videos and, even though it was stressful, fighting to save the estate from the motorway. This life had saved her, and now she was to be pushed out by a man who thought the worst of her, even though he didn't know her.

Turning around to Judith, Emma straightened to her full height to give her courage as she began to speak.

'The last thing I want to do is come between you and your son. I can leave this evening, get a train to Dublin, stay somewhere near the airport, and get a flight back to the UK tomorrow.'

Judith stared at Emma. 'Why on earth would you do that?'

'Don't you want me to leave?'

Judith shook her head. 'You think because Miles wants you gone, I will fire you?'

'Won't you?'

'I have never done anything in my life because a man wants me to do it, and I am not going to start now,' Judith said.

'I don't feel right about causing a rift between you.'

'You haven't. His insistence that he knows best has done that,' Judith said, before getting up and putting her arms around Emma.

Emma pulled away. 'I have to leave, I'm sorry.'

Judith gripped Emma's shoulders tight. 'Do you really want to go?' she asked.

'I have to, Judith; the last thing I want is to cause you all this trouble.'

'Is it the money? You have to know if my son stops your wages, I can step into the breach,' Judith said.

'It's not that. Don't you see? While I stay here, Miles will be in constant confrontation with you. I don't want you to have that stress in your life.'

'At my age, is what you really mean,' Judith said, before whipping out of the kitchen to the drawing room.

Emma stayed by the sink. Absent-mindedly, she took some mugs and rinsed them under the cold tap, and placed them on the draining board. She needed to give Judith her space, but more than anything she wanted to sort this out with her. Grabbing a paper towel, she dried her hands and moved to the drawing room. She dithered nervously at the door before stepping into the room, talking too fast and loud.

'Judith, I will always be grateful for the opportunity you gave me at a difficult time in my life, when I needed it most. However, it would be wrong of me now to stay for my own selfish reasons: that I love you and this estate so much. I have decided to go; it's for the best.'

Judith, who was standing looking at the portrait, spun around. 'Can I be frank, Emma?'

'What's wrong?'

Judith shuddered. 'Can I trust you to keep a secret?'

'Of course, anything.'

Emma saw the odd look in Judith's eyes, and she suddenly felt fearful.

Judith led her to the couch, and when they were both sitting down, she began to speak in a low voice.

'I want you to stay because I am happiest when you're here, and these days, I grasp at any little bit of joy life offers.'

'What do you mean?'

'I mean that my time may be more limited than I thought.'

'What?'

Time stood still between them. Emma heard the grandfather clock tick.

'I am ill, Emma.'

'Ill? What do you mean?'

'Exactly what you are trying not to think; I just hope I can see this motorway business finished before I am.'

Emma got up and stood at the bay window. From here, she could see as far as the rhododendron bend at one side, with the lake shimmering at the other side. Killcawley Estate was Judith, and she was Killcawley Estate. She felt so lonely and so selfish at this moment. Judith came to stand beside her, and Emma reached out and took her hand.

'What do you need from me, Judith?' she said, tears flowing down her face.

Judith, her lip trembling, continued to look out the window. 'I want you to stay.'

'But what about Miles?'

'He can't know, it would destroy him.'

'What is it exactly?'

'The breast cancer from a few years ago has come back with a vengeance, and spread into my lungs. I am terminal, I have months, maybe just weeks.'

'You should tell Miles.'

'I can't bear to tell him; he'll be devastated.'

'He will want to know,' Emma said gently.

'I will tell him, and Jack, when I'm ready, and only then. Please, Emma, you have to promise me you won't betray my confidence.'

'But—'

Judith looked fiercely at Emma. 'You have to keep this secret, until I am ready to share it.'

Emma nodded.

'I need to hear you say it.'

'I will keep your secret, but I think you're wrong to keep this from those who love you most. They would want to know and to help you in every way possible.'

'Yes, fuss over me, but I want to continue life as best I can to fight this motorway; let that be my legacy – that I have saved Killcawley Estate.'

'We'll make it happen,' Emma said.

'And I would like to think I have also given a sense of style to the world,' she said.

'You've certainly done that,' Emma said, and Judith twirled, the silk dress she was wearing floating around her.

When they saw Marsha scurrying up the driveway, Emma looked at Judith in alarm.

'Not a word. We're here together the day after the vigil, and all is well,' she said.

'Except, Miles is so angry.'

'Which means he will not support our campaign any further. We have been relying on him to fund everything, and now we need to ramp up our own fundraising efforts,' Judith said.

They heard Marsha step into the kitchen.

'Hello, anyone at home?' she called out.

Judith yanked Emma aside. 'Not a word, remember.'

'Not a word to anybody,' Emma said.

Marsha, wearing a dark suit, was pacing up and down the kitchen floor.

'Apologies for the early intrusion, but I wanted to get you both before you planned your day,' she said.

'How come you're in black? I rather liked when you wore bright colours,' Judith said.

'I am here to discuss business, and this suit seemed like a good idea,' Marsha said.

Emma began to make scrambled eggs as Marsha sat at the table, opened her notebook and put on a pair of reading glasses.

'I have good news,' she said, looking out over the top of her glasses at both Emma and Judith.

'Well, it had better be good, getting in the way of my coffee. Let's have it,' Judith said in a mock cross voice.

'I know we had been talking about how to fund a legal campaign and we weren't getting anywhere. Well...' – Marsha stopped, to make sure she had their full attention – 'before the vigil, I took the liberty of setting up a GoFundMe page for the campaign.'

'You what?' Judith exclaimed.

'My nephew was home for the weekend from university and I called in a favour. There was no time to tell you all, and I didn't think it would raise much, but last night Ian rang me to say we have raised €80,000 so far. It is probably more as I even speak.'

'Get out of here,' Judith crowed.

'So I think that will get us to the High Court with a high-flying barrister and a solicitor to represent us. We can step up to the next level,' Marsha said.

Looking shocked, Judith sat down. 'We can prove that we're not just all talk,' she said.

'I have a plan, and I hope Emma here can help me,' Marsha said.

'If I can,' Emma said nervously.

'We need to set up a select committee meeting at short notice – just the people who are prepared to be named on the legal papers.'

'I don't want to be named,' Emma said quickly.

'I thought of that, and I wanted you to be here so you can be a secretary to the committee,' Marsha said.

'I presume you will want my name and that of Killcawley Estate,' Judith enquired, her lips curling.

'Don't be silly, of course I do,' Marsha said. She leaned over the table to be closer to Judith. 'The vigil and publicity have been fantastic, but now it's time to go down the legal road,' she said. 'I want to host the meeting at the lodge,' she said quietly, and quickly continued before Judith had a chance to reply. 'J, you can't take this on your shoulders alone. Let the rest of us take some of the weight.'

'I hope Jack is also invited,' Judith said.

Marsha cocked her head to one side. 'What are you going on about? Of course he is, and Hetty too; we will leave it at that. The fewer people on the bandwagon, the better.'

Judith turned to Emma. 'What do you think of court action?' she asked

'We need to do it; it's the next logical step,' Emma said.

'Exactly, and to that end I have arranged for the solicitor, Fintan O'Brien, to attend the lodge this afternoon,' Marsha said.

'Why the lodge?' Judith asked.

Marsha shrugged as she tidied away her reading glasses. 'I want to do my bit, so I picked the lodge. See you all at 4.30 p.m.,' she said.

When Marsha had left, Judith grumbled that she had become insufferable since she had moved into the lodge.

'Thank God I didn't let her move in permanently to this house; she would be trying to run the estate by now and probably succeeding,' she said.

'You're not regretting letting her take the lodge, are you?' Emma asked.

'No, I owed her. We're friends for life, but some days, just some days, she drives me mad,' Judith said.

TWENTY

Judith took extra care picking out her outfit for the meeting and insisted that Emma help her.

'Good old Marsha is going to expect me to be over the top and batty. It's time for dignified elegance, and let's hit her with the crown jewels,' she said.

'What do you mean?' Emma asked.

Judith led the way upstairs. 'I have a beautiful grey cashmere dress. Miles bought it for me in a wonderful boutique in Manhattan. It is so flattering, and with my white hair, it is quite sensational. My Mary Jane shoes with the small heel and, I think, the long gold antique Chanel chain with the chucky cross,' she said.

'Why go to all the bother? We're only going to a meeting?'

'Because everyone must realise I am Judith McCarthy of Killcawley Estate, and nobody steals the limelight from me.'

'But it's just Marsha.'

'And next time it will be another Marsha, until soon I will be seen solely as another little old lady trying to fill in time.'

Pushing the bedroom door open, she swept across to the

wardrobe, and rummaged among the hangers until she had found what she was looking for.

'I have had no reason to wear this dress, and the meeting is the perfect occasion; it screams luxury and elegance.'

Judith slipped on the dress before going to her dressing table and pulling out a necklace drawer.

'Stephen bought me this Chanel chain just a year before he died. I wore it once or twice, but never seemed to get it right, until Miles bought me this dress last Christmas.

'Miles has good taste.'

'Or his secretary has, but it's perfect.'

'Stephen had an eye for beautiful jewellery,' Emma said.

Judith stared at the necklace. 'I'm glad you think so. But while my husband did not have a secretary, he had a hotline to a jeweller in Dublin who sourced every piece for him. I would have loved if he had gone himself and picked something out, but Stephen was not a sentimental man; it was a financial transaction, nothing more.'

Emma took the Chanel chain Judith handed to her. 'It's heavy.'

'And ostentatious. I didn't say I liked it, but for today, it's perfect.'

'Does Marsha deserve this?' Emma asked.

Judith punched Emma playfully in the tummy. 'It's a thing between us. We like getting one over on each other. She certainly did that with the funding page and the meeting with the solicitor. Maybe I have been concentrating too much on getting the word out there, and not putting enough into strategy.'

'Which is why if we work together, we'll be a winning team,' Emma said.

Judith picked out a gold and pearl bracelet, and snapped it on her right wrist. 'I think I look very much the lady of the manor, don't you?'

'If that's the look you want, yes.'

'Of course it is, darling; let me have my little bit of fun. At my stage of life, there are so few competitions, so few laughs, I have to find it wherever I can.'

Emma pulled the Bentley to the front of the house just a few minutes before the meeting so she could drive Judith down to the gate lodge.

Judith clapped her hands. 'Wonderful choice of wheels, darling. Definitely sets the right tone,' she said.

'I'm surprised you're not wearing fur,' Emma mumbled, but Judith only laughed.

'Way too hot, darling. Fur is purely a winter fallback,' she said as she got into the back of the car.

At they pulled up to the lodge, Marsha opened her front door, eyeing Judith up and down as she got out of the Bentley.

'Dressing down today, darling?' she said with a glint in her eyes.

Judith harrumphed, and said she had no idea what Marsha was talking about, she had just rushed out the door at the last minute.

Emma giggled, and Judith elbowed her playfully. 'Hush, girl.'

Marsha led them into the dining room, where Fintan O'Brien, Jack and Hetty were sitting at the long table.

'Fashionably late as usual,' Hetty grumbled, but Judith ignored her.

Emma sat by the solicitor, and took notes while he went into detail on how they could bring a legal challenge to the motorway in the High Court.

'How soon before the case is heard by a judge?' Marsha asked.

'If we are allowed to bring the case, it could be weeks, maybe longer.'

'Surely we'll be allowed if we raise the issue of the oak tree? Have you seen my TikToks?' Judith asked.

'TikTok has no place in a court of law, but if we can get an expert on our side, then yes, we might have a chance of success,' the solicitor said.

'Are you saying we could win this?' Jack asked.

Fintan O'Brien straightened up. 'I am saying we have good points to argue, but it would be up to the judge. We will apply to the court on Monday.'

'We must go to the Four Courts. I can film from there. We will show the world what is happening,' Judith said, and those around the table agreed.

The solicitor stood up. 'Mrs McCarthy, you will do no such thing. You can't attempt to interfere with the legal system on your social media accounts,' he said, his voice cross.

Marsha, afraid that Judith was taking over, called for a recess. 'Let's think on it while I serve coffee,' she said.

Emma followed her to the kitchen.

'What's with all the grandstanding by Judith?' Marsha asked as she prepared a tray to carry through to the dining room.

'You know she likes to dress up.'

'Hardly for a quick meeting at the lodge. Is there something else I don't know about? She's acting funny,' Marsha said.

Emma picked up the tray to carry it through to the meeting table, and didn't say a word.

'Ever-faithful Emma. When she found you, she found a gem. But doesn't the silly woman realise we are all on the one side?' Marsha said.

'You of all people should know Judith; she likes to be the queen bee,' Emma said as she made her way back to the dining room.

'Well, I'm tired of being the worker bee all the time,' Marsha said, following behind.

Emma set the tray down on the table, while Marsha announced a secret ballot on whether to use the GoFundMe money towards their legal battle.

'What nonsense! We all know it's the logical next step,' Judith said, and everybody agreed.

Looking miffed, Marsha said they could go with a show of hands.

'We must publicise this and have journalists and photographers at the Four Courts. We can surely TikTok from outside the building,' Judith said. Fintan O'Brien shook his head and sighed saying he had to leave for another client meeting. Hetty rapped her knuckles on the table. 'I hope, Judith, you are not forgetting that some of us are losing our homes, and not just a wildflower meadow and a gnarly old oak tree. This is not merely a Judith McCarthy problem, it's a problem for the whole village and you would do well to remember that.'

Judith turned her chair so that she was facing Hetty. 'That oak tree has been part of this village for so long, and those meadows are the life blood of Killcawley Estate, an estate which has long provided employment in this village. The village of Killcawley and all its citizens are of paramount importance.'

'As long as you remember that,' Hetty sniffed, before getting up to leave.

TWENTY-ONE

The day before the court hearing, Judith proposed they use the Bentley to travel to the Four Courts in Dublin.

'Where will we find parking for that monstrosity of a car?' Marsha asked.

'We will be a target for sure – the car will be broken into, and then what will we do?' Hetty said.

Jack suggested going by train, but Judith gave him a withering look.

'I can count on one hand the amount of times I have been on public transport, and I do not intend to move onto the second hand. I'm sure we can park within the confines of the Four Courts.'

Marsha shook her head. 'There won't be a hope, J, and we'll look foolish,' she said.

'I'm sure there won't be a problem when they hear who we are.'

'You mean, who *you* are: landowner, social influencer and TikToker.' Marsha sniggered.

'The Bentley it is,' Judith declared loudly.

'But what about secure parking?' Emma asked.

'Darling. When you drive a car like a Bentley, everybody wants to help; just trust me,' Judith snapped.

'I suppose you expect us to dress to the nines, because we're accompanying you,' Marsha said.

'One should always dress appropriately for court. I shall be wearing my black suit with a touch of colour in the blouse.'

'What about a hat?'

'A well-dressed woman always finishes off an outfit with a hat and gloves,' Judith said, making Marsha and Hetty giggle.

The morning of the court case, Judith was up early and dressed before 8 a.m. She was standing in front of the mirror in the hall when Emma came downstairs.

'Perfect timing. You can help me pick a hat. Or should I go for a discreet look? Though my heart is drawn to the red and black feather fascinator.'

'The pop of red would work well, but do you think it is too much for a courtroom?'

'Not at all, we want to be noticed. What are you wearing?'

Emma looked down at her jeans and hoodie.

'This.'

Judith threw her eyes to the ceiling.

'Emma, for God's sake, have you nothing more formal?'

'Formality is from my past, this is what I am now.'

'Well, I suppose it will have to do. Make sure you sit at the back of the group.'

Emma didn't react. 'I will get the Bentley around to the front,' she said.

'Darling, a quick TikTok video first; I am going to ask people to join us at the Four Courts.'

'Do you think that is a good idea?'

'We have to keep up the pressure.'

Judith stepped out onto the front steps and made a big deal

of closing the front door, before turning and looking directly at the camera.

'Join us outside the Four Courts today, where we will be shouting, "Save Killcawley from greedy developers",' she said, before repeating the chant.

'I didn't realise we were protesting as well,' Emma said.

'Neither did I.' Judith laughed.

'What will we do if a lot of people turn up?' Emma asked.

'No idea, we'll just have to improvise,' she said, getting into the front seat of the Bentley.

Hetty squished in the back with Jack and Marsha when they picked her up in the village. Once Emma pulled out on to the main road everybody quietened down. Hetty fell asleep on Jack's shoulder and Marsha concentrated on her morning prayers, quietly muttering to herself.

At the Four Courts, Judith insisted Emma drive around to the side entrance, the judges' yard. 'We can park there.'

'I don't think it's allowed,' Emma said.

'Nonsense, darling. Where else can we park the Bentley?'

At the barrier, Judith signalled with a gloved hand to the security man to come around to her window.

'The daughter-in-law of Judge Anthony McCarthy, since deceased.'

'What? Who?' the security guard asked.

'The daughter-in-law of Judge McCarthy. I have an appointment in court,' Judith said, her voice high pitched with exasperation. She looked severely at the young man. 'Kindly open the gate, and let us through,' Judith said, and the guard, a little confused, did as he was told.

Judith prodded Emma in the side to get her to drive on.

'Was Miles' grandad a judge?' Emma said.

'Good Lord, no. A gentleman farmer, but that young man doesn't know.'

Jack gently woke up Hetty and they all got out of the car, and made their way inside the building.

As they entered the round hall, Emma heard the chanting outside.

'*Save Killcawley from greedy developers*!'

Gripping Judith's arm, she checked TikTok.

'There's a crowd outside the main entrance, Judith; they must have answered your call. You should go out.'

Judith took a deep breath and stepped out the front entrance of the Four Courts.

When the crowd saw her, they went quiet, and a few raised their phones to record her.

Emma stepped back behind a column, but watched as Judith moved forward to address the crowd.

A uniformed garda asked to speak to her, and a few in the crowd hissed and booed.

Judith held her hands up and asked for silence. 'My dear friends, it gladdens my heart that you have turned up to support this important cause. I have been asked by the gardai that we confine ourselves to the footpath and not interrupt traffic flow. We are so grateful you are all here, and we will go now into court to stand firm against this motorway. I will update you on the struggle after the case comes before the judge.'

As they turned back into the building, the chanting started up again, only this time louder.

Fintan O'Brien gestured frantically at them as they walked towards him.

'You should have been here ten minutes ago. There is no time to introduce you to our barrister, Declan Simons, and the judge put your case back for second calling,' he snapped, ushering them into court.

They sat squished up together on a hard bench at the back of the court as the judge looked out over his glasses and ordered that all windows be shut, because of the din coming from outside.

Emma felt Judith squirm beside her as Killcawley Estate was mentioned several times but in a cursory way.

The judge was just about to speak when Judith jumped up.

'Excuse me, I am Judith McCarthy, the owner of Killcawley Estate, County Wicklow. I am here with my friends and neighbours, and we want to be heard,' she said primly.

'All in good time,' the judge said, before staring at the barrister and telling him to keep his client under control.

'We merely require that you listen to our side. We have come all this way,' Judith said as Marsha tugged at her skirt to try to get her to sit back down.

The judge glared at Judith and the barrister.

'Mr Simons, could you please ask your client to quieten down or I will have to have her removed from the court,' the judge said, his voice booming through the courtroom.

Fintan O'Brien was in front of Judith in two strides, snarling at her to sit down and be quiet.

Emma put a protective arm around her and coaxed Judith to sit.

'This is preposterous! I merely wanted to point out the salient facts. That judge does not live anywhere near a motorway, I'm sure of that,' Judith protested as she reluctantly sat down.

Jack took her hand and held it to comfort her as the judge said he was going to adjourn the case, until the opposing side could be represented in court.

Emma held Judith's other hand.

'What a complete waste of time,' Judith said loudly as the solicitor quickly ushered them from the courtroom.

'Mrs McCarthy, you should not have interrupted the proceedings of the court like that. It wasn't appropriate,' he said.

'We won't stand idly by,' Emma said.

'Well at least be quiet and call off the troops outside,' he said.

'But we want the judge to know how all this is impacting on our lives; this could kill our village and break up the estate and...' Judith said, before the solicitor interrupted.

'Mrs McCarthy, I have every sympathy for your viewpoint. In fact, I grew up playing in the fields of Killcawley Estate, but these things have to be done a certain way to be effective and if you make another show in court, you will make it ten times harder for us to get the right outcome,' Fintan O'Brien said.

Emma nudged in beside Judith. 'Listen to him; he is in court every day. He knows what he is talking about and he's on our side,' she said softly.

'No more dramatic outbursts or we will have lost before we even start. Please make sure you keep your followers from coming to court,' Fintan said firmly.

Judith fixed her fascinator. 'There is nothing wrong with our social media campaign; it has got us this far, after all,' she said haughtily, and the others followed her out of the Four Courts round hall to where the crowd was still chanting on the street.

Beside the big stone columns at the front of the building, Judith instructed Emma to film a TikTok video.

'Friends, we are here at the Four Courts at the start of our legal battle against the abomination of a motorway, and next we write to our government to save our village from devastation. We ask you all to continue to join us in highlighting the plight of Killcawley.

'Help us save the village homes, meadows, nature and the old oak tree,' Judith went on, and the others clapped as Emma finished filming, and quickly uploaded the video.

Marsha and Hetty said they wanted to go shopping, and they would get home by train.

As Emma walked back to the car, she saw Judith stagger,

and Jack help her, letting her lean on his arm. When Jack had tucked Judith into the front seat, Emma slipped her a pain killer.

Back at Killcawley Estate, Judith said she needed to rest. She asked Jack to help her upstairs as Emma said she had to catch up on the jam orders.

'Since the campaign started there has been a rush of orders for the jam, and I need to get off a few boxes today,' she said.

About an hour later, Jack stopped by the jam shed. He stood in the doorway, and he didn't need to say a word for Emma to understand his expression.

'She told you,' Emma said gently.

'She didn't want to at first, but it was only when I became insistent about getting her a doctor that she...' Jack stopped, his voice shaky.

'She is well at the moment. Today was a long day for her, and stressful.'

Jack sat down on the bench beside Emma. 'That's it. It is all too stressful for her; she should let the rest take on the fight about the motorway.'

'Judith wants to be part of it, and without her would we have got so far? Her TikTok videos have pushed the campaign to another level.'

Jack slapped his hand down on the table in exasperation.

'But at what cost? She insists she won't go down the chemo road again. She was so ill with it last time. Her time is limited. Shouldn't she be taking it easy, doing the things she loves?'

'I'm not sure that Judith knows the meaning of taking it easy, and this motorway battle has in so many ways reinvigorated her.'

Jack shook his head. 'Judy is such a stubborn woman. I want her to tell Miles.'

'What did she say?'

'She nearly bit the head off me. Said I was not, under any

circumstances, to tell him and that you had also promised to keep silent. This, she says, is between the three of us.'

'We have to respect her wishes; maybe in a week or so she will change her mind.'

Jack got up. 'I very much doubt that. And what will happen when Miles finds out we knew all along and never told him?'

They heard the phone in the big house ringing out.

'That's Miles now; he always rings the house phone because Judy refuses to answer his calls on the mobile. She tells him she prefers the hall where she can sit in her armchair.'

'Should I answer it?'

'Do, she has just gone to sleep, and she needs to rest,' Jack said.

Emma ran into the house, and picked up the phone.

'Hello, can I speak to Judith please?'

'Um, I'm afraid she's resting; we're just back from Dublin. Is that Miles?'

'I know well you're back from Dublin; I've seen it all over TikTok. I know all about the court case too, and everybody in this office has been watching my mother and her antics at the Four Courts. I am astounded that you let this happen, Emma. I gave specific instructions to both you and my mother that all this nonsense had to stop, but instead you have added fuel to the fire. Do you seriously think I am going to let this go? Do you really think my mother should be inciting all these people to protest outside the High Court?'

'Miles, we weren't breaking the law, and Judith isn't responsible for how many people turned up,' Emma said.

'You and my mother are making Killcawley and Killcawley Estate a laughing stock, not just of the county and the country, but of the whole damn world,' he shouted.

Emma tried to stay calm, but her voice was firm when she spoke.

'Miles, I think you're looking at this the wrong way. A lot of people came to support the campaign. It was amazing to see, and there were no incidents. It was a good thing,' she said.

'You don't understand, do you? My mother should not be embroiled in all this. This is not good enough.'

'I think we have to fight this motorway in the best way we can, and I think your mother is being amazing.'

'You don't give up, do you, Emma... whatever you say your name is?'

'What are you talking about? What do you mean?' Emma said, her voice shaking.

'You surely knew I would look into to your background?'

'I don't understand.'

'You will soon enough. And your time at Killcawley Estate will be over, no matter what my mother says.'

Emma didn't reply and Miles continued.

'You've brought an old lady along this long and dangerous road, and I, as her son, will not stand for it. Please tell my mother I will ring later.'

Emma replaced the receiver and massaged her throbbing head. The last thing she wanted was to be caught up in this family dispute. She listened, but there was no sound from upstairs. She went back out to the jam shed to continue getting her order ready for dispatch by courier in the morning.

She understood Miles was far away and worried about his mother, but there was no reason for him to be so confrontational. It was almost as if he were treating her like an opponent and he was ready to push and push, until she walked. There was no way she was going to walk out on Judith, especially not now. She just wasn't sure how she was going to handle Miles in the meantime.

TWENTY-TWO

It was a week later, and Emma was out in the field with the horses when a Mercedes drove up the drive.

She moved to the far side of the chestnut, nervous of who it might be. The gates were pulled over these days to deter curious day trippers who knew the estate from TikTok, but this visitor must have yanked them back to access the driveway.

The Mercedes stopped, and a man with dark hair and wearing designer shades got out. He stood looking around him as he rolled up the sleeves of his loose linen shirt.

When he noticed Emma, he waved to summon her to the fence.

She walked over, the horse ambling along beside her.

'Is that your horse? It seems to like you?' the man asked.

'I doubt that is any of your business. May I ask why you pulled open the gates?'

'Why did the chicken cross the road? To get to the other side, of course. What? You're not going to laugh. All right, I opened the gate so I could drive up to the house.'

'Mrs McCarthy is not taking visitors, and the avenue is closed to the public,' Emma said stiffly.

'That's going to make it difficult. I don't fancy trying to drive this top-of-the-range car over the fields.' He laughed.

She noted there was an American twang to his accent.

'Can you please turn around and go back down the avenue.'

'That's a mighty fine welcome to give somebody who has flown all the way from New York to be here. Is my mother really indisposed?'

'Your mother?'

'Hi, I'm Miles,' he said pulling off his sunglasses and reaching across the fence. The horse nuzzled at his fingers.

Emma stepped back, hitting against the chestnut who then moved off to munch some grass.

'Miles McCarthy?'

'That's me. And you are?'

Emma shook her head.

'Are you Emma?'

She didn't answer as she saw his face sour.

Miles turned back to the car.

'May I offer you a ride to the house?' he said, his tone noticeably cooler.

'Are you sure?'

Miles spun around, his face impatient.

'We may have our differences, but I don't draw the line at letting you in my car. Anyway, I would like to ask you about my mother, if you don't mind.'

'OK,' Emma said warily as she climbed the fence, and got in the car.

'You should have told Judith you were coming; she would have liked time to prepare.'

She saw Miles smile, but just as quick, his face changed. 'I was concerned that it would make her anxious; she has had enough to contend with – all this stress about the motorway. We will talk later about that. Let's get to the house,' he said gruffly.

Miles drove slowly, and stopped a little after the rhododendron bend.

'Every time I come home, I linger here to observe the house. It's as if nothing has changed and yet everything has,' he said almost to himself, as if he had forgotten Emma was there.

Emma couldn't quite figure him out – it was as though there were two of him. Sensitive Miles who stopped to take in the big house, and the estate he obviously loved, and the untrusting man who berated her over the phone.

'Tell me truthfully, how is the old bird?' Miles asked as he started up the engine again.

Emma felt nervous. What would she say? That his mother badly needed him to step up to the plate right now, that hers was no longer a battle to keep the estate intact? She had her own private battle, after all.

'Your mother is a wonderful woman and still going strong,' she said quietly.

Emma saw Miles look at her oddly as he turned the car into the courtyard.

They could see Judith through the window, bent over the kitchen sink and stirring a big pot.

Miles rushed to the back door to steal up behind her and catch her by the waist. Judith screamed, and turned at the same time as Miles caught her up. He danced around the kitchen with his mother in his arms. Judith laughed, tears flowing down her cheeks.

Emma dithered in the doorway, afraid of interrupting this private moment between mother and son.

'Miles, what are you doing here?' Judith asked as he placed her back beside the sink.

'I thought I had to see everything for myself, find out what has been going on around here,' he said.

Judith pulled away from him. 'Miles, we're on top of this; we won't be beaten.'

'And you certainly have been getting the publicity, but let's talk about the nitty-gritty later, Mother. I'm here for the next few weeks.'

Emma said she was going back out to the horses, but Judith called her to join them.

'Emma is my right-hand woman; I would not be able to continue here without her.'

'You have me here now, Mum,' Miles said pointedly.

'Don't take this the wrong way, but Emma is my trusted friend and advisor, and she's here for the foreseeable.'

Emma backed away, not wanting to be part of the conversation. 'I really have to get on with my work,' she muttered as she disappeared into the courtyard, but she knew neither mother nor son heard her.

She didn't go back to the horses but disappeared to the walled garden. Holding a bowl she had taken from the kitchen table, she made for the strawberry drills, and began to feverishly pick the succulent fruit. She didn't want to leave here. She loved Killcawley Estate, and the little business she was building up was doing so well. Her latest concoction of strawberry and prosecco jam was going to be a bestseller; she just knew it. On TikTok, they were going mad for her jam, ever since Judith had made a big deal about having it on a scone one afternoon.

Emma didn't want to risk running into Miles again, so once she'd finished picking the strawberries, she wandered off towards the lake. She was becoming too involved in life here, and that worried her, because if she lost her job, she would lose everything; she would be back at zero.

She sat down on the jetty watching the water. The swans floated by, loitering for a moment to see what was on offer, before continuing on their journey. The water lapped against the wooden poles of the pier and she closed her eyes, feeling a comfort in its slow, dependable rhythm. The low breeze ruffled across the lake and every now and again a wave would splash against the poles. When she heard the crunch of gravel on the driveway, she momentarily froze, until she heard a familiar call.

Judith, dressed in an ankle-grazing emerald green dress, was making her way towards Emma. She had set off the dress with red strappy sandals, chunky jewellery and a trilby hat, which had been customised with pops of red, yellow and green to give it a feminine look.

'Miles says I should wear this on St Patrick's Day next year. Isn't it beautiful?' she said.

Emma touched the vintage linen dress. 'It's beautiful on you,' she said, feeling herself choke up as she wondered whether either of them would still be at the estate then.

'I brought my phone – do you think you could film me feeding the ducks? I have some bread for them.'

She took out three pieces of a sliced pan from her side pocket and began to toss chunks into the water.

The swans, sensing the offering had changed, turned around and glided faster back to the jetty.

'Wait for the swans,' Judith said as Emma prepared to film.

Judith clapped her hands when she was ready, and Emma raised the phone and began to video. Emma filmed, while Judith danced dangerously close to the edge of the jetty as she threw bread to the swans and the ducks, who were squabbling over every piece.

Emma finished filming, and Judith slipped off her sandals. 'What did you think of Miles?' she asked as they walked back to the house.

'I think he's a son who is protective of his mother.'

'Yes, he's a sweetheart, but a pompous ass to boot. I apologise if he has been rude to you; I have told him you're staying and there's not an awful lot he can do about it.'

Emma should have felt reassured, but Judith's insistence made her even more nervous.

'Do you want me to move out, give you two some time on your own?' Emma asked.

'God no, you're my protection against Miles and his crazy ideas. Anyway, the campaign is at too much of a crucial stage to be worried over what Miles thinks,' Judith said, quickening her step as she reached the house.

'And what about the other thing?'

Judith stopped. 'You promised, Emma.'

'I did, but he's going to be here a while, he is going to notice things.'

Judith took off her hat and ran her fingers through her hair.

'Let's cross that bridge when we have to,' she said.

They found Miles in the kitchen. Emma dawdled in the doorway. He was scrambling eggs in a saucepan on the hob, but pushed it off the heat when he saw Emma.

'I will be out of your way shortly,' he said.

Judith looked in the pot and said there was enough for three. 'Darlings, you both are my favourite people in the world. I want you to shake hands and agree to disagree, and maybe you two can get to know each other.'

Miles fumbled with the tea towel and Emma, looking for a distraction, leaned down to stroke the dog.

'Darlings, my word still goes around here,' Judith said firmly, gesturing to the two of them to stand beside her. She elbowed Miles.

He extended his hand. Gingerly, Emma placed her hand in his, immediately noticing his grip was strong.

'I am rustling up some scrambled eggs on toast, if you care to join us. We're jazzing it up with a glass of wine for an early lunch,' Miles said.

'No, thank you. I have a batch of jam to make, if you don't mind me using the kitchen,' she said.

'I see you are persisting with the jam making,' he said cooly.

'Darling, be nice to Emma,' Judith said in a mock serious voice which diffused the tension.

'Anyway, it's so nice to have the smell of jam bubbling on the hob again,' she added. Emma slipped past Miles to get the bowl of rhubarb chunks, which had been soaking in sugar all night.

She noticed that his hair fell into his eyes when he went back to stand over the hob, and he hummed a tune as he worked. She figured he was in his mid to late thirties, and she shook her head because she was thinking too much about this man. This man who didn't even want her here.

Conscious of her eyes on him, he laughed.

'I am more used to living on my own; I don't have a singing voice, so please forgive me.'

Embarrassed, she looked away, but she wanted to tell him how much she liked it. Despite his attitude towards her, there was something about him that intrigued her.

Judith disappeared upstairs.

'I imagine she is dressing for scrambled eggs on toast. My mum is really special,' he said in such a kindly way that Emma smiled.

He served up the eggs, and was pouring the wine when Judith came in wearing brilliant white trousers and a stripy blouse.

'Decidedly low-key for you, Mother, if I may say so,' Miles said, and Emma found herself grinning again.

Miles had left a glass of wine beside the hob for her, and she joined them as they raised a glass to Killcawley Estate.

Judith began to brief Miles on the motorway, lavishing praise on Emma for her plan to raise their profile on TikTok, and the decision to go legal.

'Being back home has made me realise this motorway plan

might not be the best idea for Killcawley and the estate. Your idea for a legal challenge is very good; it must be your legal training,' he said to Emma.

Embarrassed, she wiped her hands on the tea towel before speaking.

'Yes, I was a legal secretary in the UK.'

He didn't say anything for a few minutes.

'Yes, my mother told me. So how come you ended up here at Killcawley?'

Emma in a panic glanced at Judith, who knocked over her wine glass.

'Oh dear, I'm so clumsy. Emma, can you clean this up, dear? I will walk Miles down, to the meadows and show him where the motorway would go. He will then understand more our passion for the campaign.'

Gratefully, Emma pulled at the kitchen towel and began to mop up the wine.

'Mum, I'm not sure you should have asked Emma to clean up after you,' Miles said, a little annoyed.

'Nonsense, darling, she doesn't mind,' she said, winking at Emma.

When they left, Emma sat down, and sipped her wine. Judith was a very good friend, but they all knew that Miles would return to his cross examination about her past soon enough.

TWENTY-THREE

On Friday morning, Emma was up extra early as she could not sleep. She quietly made her way downstairs for fear of waking up anybody else in the house. She was sitting with a cup of coffee when Miles came into the kitchen, a hoodie on over his pyjamas.

'I hope I didn't wake you,' she said.

'It always takes me a few days before I get into the rhythm of the big house, and Mother has been running me into the ground. I rather imagine she doesn't want us having a serious talk just yet.'

'You want me to leave?' Emma said.

'Emma, you appear to be a perfectly nice person, and I am sure we can arrange a very good reference, but my mother does not have any future need for your services.'

'Have you spoken to Judith about this?'

'I don't need to; I am, after all, paying your wages.'

'Judith isn't going to be very happy.'

'That is not your concern; for the next few weeks I can offer all the help she needs.'

'And what happens after that?'

'I'm sure Jack and Marsha can step into the breach when needed.'

Emma stood up, pushing the table so hard her coffee spilled.

'You know nothing.'

'Or how much I value Emma,' Judith said, appearing in the doorway, her voice shaking with anger.

'Mother, why are you up so early?' Miles asked.

'I could ask the same of you two. Anyway, I want Emma to go to Dublin today. She has an appointment with a department store manager and she needs to get away early to beat the traffic.'

'There is hardly any point persisting with the jam sales if she is leaving anyway,' Miles said pointedly.

Judith stood in front of her son. 'While I remain at Kill-cawley Estate, Emma Wilson will stay here too; if that is what she wants.'

'There it is. She's not Emma Wilson. I bet you didn't know that,' Miles shouted.

For the first time since Emma had known her, Judith looked dumbfounded. She instinctively looked over to Emma, a questioning behind her eyes. Emma bolted from the room and ran upstairs.

Miles and Judith were shouting at each other downstairs, then the back door banged loudly as it was slammed shut.

A few minutes later, there was a tap on her bedroom door.

'Emma, please let me in,' Judith said.

When Emma opened the door, Judith was out of breath and leaning against the wall. Emma helped her to a chair and got her a glass of water. Judith at first gulped the water, but as her breathing regulated, she sipped from the glass.

'Do I need to call the doctor?' Emma asked.

Judith looked at Emma directly. 'You need to tell me the truth. Is Miles right about your name?'

Emma sat on the bed. 'He is. Murray is my married name. When my marriage ended, I went back to my maiden name.'

'I didn't think young people changed their names anymore, on marrying.'

'My husband wanted it, but after I walked away, I couldn't bear to have his name anymore.'

Judith got up off the chair and joined Emma on the bed. 'I'm sorry for demanding an explanation and making you reveal such personal details; Miles is set on having you gone, but I have told him that nothing will separate us.'

'We can always be friends, but maybe I should leave rather than you risk your relationship with Miles.'

'Take the day off, bring the car to Dublin; have a day out. It will give me time to work on Miles.'

'There isn't an appointment with a buyer, then?'

'Good Lord, no; I was thinking on my feet.' Judith laughed.

'Pity, that would be great for the business,' Emma said.

'Throw some of the jam in the back seat; maybe you can just walk in somewhere. It would be nice to show Miles that we mean business. But first, help me back to bed. A body this old can't be up so early,' Judith said as she leaned on Emma, who guided her down the stairs to her suite.

Emma threw a few cases of jam in the boot before she set off for Dublin. She wasn't sure what she was going to do, but she liked the idea of being able to drive to the city on her own.

Judith told her of the department store that was the Harrods of Dublin, and that was her plan today, if she felt brave enough. She parked off Grafton Street, and walked by the store twice, but hadn't the courage to go inside. It was the first time she'd felt brave enough to be out somewhere busy on her own; it was the first time she'd walked up a busy street in a city without worrying that Henry might be trailing her. Not wanting to traipse through endless shops, she headed for St Stephen's Green, where she sat on a park bench watching the birds on the lake.

She should never have agreed to marry Henry so early on but he had been so attentive; always buying her little gifts. She considered him thoughtful, but her friend Sarah labelled him controlling. Slowly but surely, she dropped Sarah as a friend. Henry didn't approve of her clubbing and her stories of the men she was dating. Emma laughed and said Sarah would settle down once she found a man like Henry. Loneliness seeped through Emma when she realised she had no idea where Sarah lived now.

Observing a young couple cuddle as they watched the swans and the ducks, she recalled the time she and Henry had been in Roundhay Park on a day out to Leeds. Henry, in a temper, had fired stones at the black swans. Emma was shocked, but he passed it off as only a bit of fun. When Emma remonstrated with him that he was being thuggish and cruel, Henry had caught her tight by the arm and marched her out of the park.

Emma tingled with anger now, not at Henry, but at herself that she had given him a second chance after that incident. She should have known just a few months into their relationship to break it off, there and then, but he had stopped at a stall at the far end of the park and bought a bunch of flowers and presented them to her with profuse apologies.

She wondered if there would ever be a day when she wasn't overwhelmed by the bad memories. Henry invaded every space around her and every thought, especially at night when she was alone in the dark. She'd thought if she ran away from him, all the memories would be automatically banished as well, but she was wrong. She was tired of running in her head, tired of worrying that he would turn up, and weary of having him invade her brain.

Jumping up, she shook herself fiercely. The only way she would truly escape Henry was to do well, forge her own path where he had no part to play, not even in her thoughts. Flattening down her summer dress and fixing her hair, she walked into the department store and asked to make an appointment to see a food buyer.

She was surprised when she was given an appointment for 2 p.m. and rushed back to the car so she could drive to the store car park. By the time she found it, Emma was sweating profusely. Taking deep breaths to calm down, she stopped off at the perfume counter to liberally spray herself with Chanel No 5. She wasn't going to let this opportunity pass her by.

When the buyer exclaimed that everything looked so cute and tasted divine, Emma thought she might collapse with excitement. The buyer's eyes also lit up when Emma explained the TikTok hype for the brand and showed her their last month's sales numbers. The meeting was over quickly, but she left some jam for the buyer to test.

As she drove back from Dublin, a tingle of excitement shot through her as she thought about the buyer's positive response to the Killcawley Estate jam. She knew Judith would be pleased.

She parked up in the courtyard, and made her way inside. Miles was sitting at the kitchen table reading headlines on his iPad.

'You're back early; we didn't expect you until later,' he said.

'I don't really like the city; I just did what I had to do, and came home.'

Miles shut his iPad and gave her a look she couldn't decipher.

'I was reading about the plans for the motorway; it appears that the link into the capital is badly needed; I just wish it didn't have to destroy our land at the same time.'

Emma didn't respond to that, not wanting to be drawn into anything controversial. 'Is Judith about,' she asked.

'Gone into Bray with Marsha. They are getting supplies for the supper club on Sunday.'

'What country this time?'

'I believe in my honour they are doing something akin to a Thanksgiving meal. I gave them a few recipes from the *New York Times*, and they are getting the ingredients. Their biggest challenge might be getting a decent turkey to roast at this time of year.'

He laughed lightly, and poured a cup of coffee and indicated to Emma to sit.

'Why do I think this is not just a friendly chat?' Emma said.

'I confess I am taking advantage of Mother being away. She thinks very highly of you, Emma, and I want to think that your motives are good, but it's difficult.'

'Your mother advertised a position, and I applied. I admire Judith, and I love working here.'

'But the question remains, why would somebody who is young and... and with your qualifications want to waste your time here at Killcawley Estate?'

Emma gulped her coffee. 'Have you ever wanted to retreat from the world, Miles? I like the peace and quiet here.'

'Usually, those who want to retreat are hiding away for a particular reason.'

'I don't think you should be cross-examining me like this.'

He got up from the table. 'Emma, if there is something that is going to put my mother or Killcawley Estate in danger, you need to tell us. Let me put it this way, you appear a little too good to be true. And my mother would never tell you this, but we've been burned before. Judith is a magnet for all sorts; her heart is too big by far. I can't let that happen again. I would prefer if you told me yourself; it would save the time and effort of engaging somebody to look into your background.'

Emma stood up so fast, her chair fell back on the floor. 'Judith is my employer, and she is perfectly happy with my work and with me living here. I think you have already looked into my past anyway, if you know about my name change.'

'Yes, Mother explained that to me.'

'What else do I have to do, then?'

Miles drummed the table with his fingers. 'The problem is Judith is so trusting. Let's face it, she would be happy with anyone who indulges her silly fetish for hats and social media,' Miles said sternly.

He walked across the kitchen and stood with his back to the AGA.

'I am the future owner of Killcawley Estate, and I will do whatever I see fit to protect both my mother and this estate.'

Tears rolled down Emma's cheeks.

'I have already told you, more than once, of the high regard in which I hold your mother. I have no intention of doing anything to hurt her. It is not my problem that you don't believe me, 'She couldn't take any more and ran out of the kitchen, bursting through the courtyard and dashing through the walled garden. When Jack called out to her, she ignored him and continued to the woodland. Here, she had to slow down for fear of falling over the tree roots that protruded on the path.

Swiping away the tears, she pushed on to the wildflower meadows. When a rabbit ran across her path, she didn't slow down. She ran too fast down the hill and tripped, landing among the poppies and daisies, whose heads had faded and turned brown.

She lay there looking at the sky, but she didn't feel like sky walking; she was too upset and angry. Picking herself up, she saw Miles emerge from the woods and into the meadow. She hurried to the oak tree sitting at the far side, where he would not immediately see her. With any luck he would not bother coming down the hill, and she could be alone.

She was incensed to think he believed she was out to cheat the one woman who had taken her in and given her a roof over her head when she'd needed it.

Slumping on the ground, she leaned back against the tree and closed her eyes. The leaves rustled and the branches creaked and somewhere high in the sky a red kite called out.

She stopped crying and her breathing regulated. She would have to leave Killcawley Estate, and this hurt her heart so much. She felt foolish, and she didn't know how she would break the news to Judith.

When a branch on the ground cracked loudly, she started; opening her eyes too quickly, she was blinded by the sunlight.

'Can I interrupt please?' Miles asked.

He was standing with his hands in his pockets and she thought he looked a little ashamed. 'I have a message for you. Your cell phone rang and I answered it.'

She patted her pockets for her phone. It wasn't there.

'Why would you do that?'

'I don't know, I apologise.'

'What's the message?'

He smiled broadly, and she thought he looked so different in that moment.

'That department store rang. They asked if you could deliver thirty jars of strawberry and prosecco jam, and thirty of rhubarb and ginger as soon as possible?'

'You're joking?'

'No, for real.'

Emma jumped up. 'I don't know if I have that much jam.' Her head was swimming, and she had no idea what she was going to do. 'It's my first big order. Maybe I have enough. Should I drive up straight away?' she shouted as she spun around in circles, not knowing what to do.

'I am going up to Dublin tomorrow. I can drop them in for you if you like?'

Emma stared at Miles. 'Would you do that?'

'Judith will kill me if I don't.'

'Have you renamed the jam?' he asked.

'Judith is my boss and she wants the Killcawley Estate name on the jam. Now that it's going to be stocked by a Dublin city store, she will certainly want to keep the estate name on the jars.'

Miles threw his arms in the air. 'Looks like you have won round one, Emma,' he said before walking off.

She wandered back to the house, and was relieved when she saw Judith and Marsha taking boxes from the Bentley.

'We were so lucky! This woman decided to get rid of her complete collection of vintage clothes, and asked me to come and sort through them. When we got there, she had a room full of the most fantastic pieces, and all for free. I took the lot,' Judith said.

'She's not the only one who was thrilled; the woman in Bray couldn't believe there was someone to take away all the junk for free,' Marsha said as she dumped a refuse sack overflowing with silk blouses out onto the cobbles.

Judith donned a floppy hat and turned around to face Emma.

She immediately stopped. 'What's wrong?'

Emma tried to smile, but Judith took her by the arm and sat her on the little bench beside the small herb bed.

'Has that son of mine said something to you?'

Emma didn't answer, but the tears trickled down her face.

Judith jumped up. 'I told him to park it. That boy never knows when to leave well enough alone. I will give him a piece of my mind,' she thundered as she made to go in the house.

Emma pulled her back. 'Please, he is only trying to look after you.'

'But he simply cannot talk to you like this.'

Marsha made to say something, but Judith hushed her.

'This is between me and Miles, but for now I will concentrate on getting all these vintage finds indoors.'

Emma stood up. 'I have other news.'

'Oh, don't tell me you're leaving, please don't let that be the news,' Judith said, holding her hands to her lips as if in prayer.

'That fancy Dublin store has placed an order for the strawberry and prosecco, and the rhubarb and ginger jam,' she said, her voice trembling with excitement.

'Heaven forbid, now we will never hear the end of it,' Marsha said as Judith punched the air in her excitement

'We will have to travel up to see it on the shelves. They had better give it a good display. This is so exciting; we have to celebrate,' Judith said, and the others laughed.

TWENTY-FOUR

Emma, who had picked a huge bowl of strawberries stopped in the yard to pet Benny. She smiled as she heard Miles in the kitchen insist on helping with the preparations for the 'Thanksgiving' supper.

'The kitchen is no place for a man. We have a lot of new recipes to conquer and we want to be able to gossip in peace,' Marsha said.

'I would love to hear all the gossip; it would be a chance to get up to speed with things around here,' Miles said a little too sharply.

'We just want to surprise you,' Judith said, leading her son away from the table, which had become a large preparation area.

Miles pulled away from his mother. 'Mother, please don't treat me like a kid, and stop tiptoeing around me,' he said testily.

Judith looked taken aback. 'I'm sorry, but until you start accepting Emma is part of Killcawley Estate, that is the way it is going to be.'

Emma stayed with the dog, afraid she would draw attention to herself if she made to walk away.

'Aren't you just a little bit worried that a stranger is leading the way on the motorway challenge, handling your profile on social media and pushing ahead with a business from this address?' he said.

'But she's not a stranger to us; she's our Emma,' Marsha said.

'What she said,' Judith said glibly.

Emma smiled happily as she saw Miles through the window pick four sweet potatoes and placed them on a chopping board. 'Why don't I get to work and you ladies can catch me up on all that Emma does around here,' he said.

'I would rather you took my word on this. If Emma wasn't here, we would have JCBs digging up the Killcawley Estate lands,' Judith muttered.

'You won't move on this, Mother?'

'Just get to know Emma; give it a bit of time. I know you will end up feeling as we do,' Judith said.

Miles shrugged and nodded. 'A good lawyer always knows when it's time for negotiation and mediation. But it doesn't mean I am backing down; I am just agreeing to a small ceasefire.'

'Call it whatever you like, darling, but once you get to know Emma, you'll love her.' Judith laughed.

'OK, but let me make my signature dish. You can't have a Thanksgiving dinner without my sweet potato and marshmallow casserole,' Miles said.

'Fine, if you insist on hanging with us old fogies, but you're going to be bored,' Judith said.

'Come on, Mum, let's have fun,' Miles said, and she smiled, despite herself.

He hummed a tune as he peeled the sweet potatoes and cubed them, before putting them in a saucepan and setting them to boil.

'Mashed sweet potato – interesting,' Judith said, making a face.

'Wait until I bake it with marshmallows, you'll change your tune,' Miles said.

Heads were down and they were all busy in the kitchen when Emma finally walked into the kitchen, cradling the bowl of strawberries.

'I suppose I can't have any space to make some more jam,' she said.

'You're going to have to get a proper premises if the orders keep coming in,' Miles said.

'The jam has proved a lot more popular than we at first envisaged. We thought we would be supplying country markets mainly. We may be the victims of our own success,' Emma replied.

Judith, who was basting the turkey, asked Miles if he had any ideas.

'To convert the stables would cost too much, and we still have the nags using a lot of the space in winter. Maybe you should look into getting space in the nearest town or industrial unit, but that would only be if you are insisting on continuing with this enterprise,' Miles said.

Judith closed the oven door. 'All of this is going to cost a lot of money, unless you are prepared to invest, Miles.'

He looked up from his casserole dish. 'Why does this feel like an ambush?' he said.

'Can't be, you insisted on staying.' Marsha sniggered.

'Let's continue to talk jam. We are getting orders in so quickly. Emma is making jam at all hours, and we're running out of storage space,' Judith said as she walked over to the dresser and opened the two doors in the bottom cupboard.

The shelves were filled to overflowing with jars of jam.

'That is only last week's batch, it goes out to shops tomorrow. We also have boxes of the stuff in the jam shed,' she said.

'Sounds like you need to organise the business, and quickly,' Miles said.

Judith went over to her son. 'Which is where you come in, Miles; you've a good business head and we need your help.'

'Mother, I'm here to support you, but not to run a business.'

'And this isn't helping me?' she said.

Miles wrapped his dish in foil and placed it in the fridge.

'OK, I will have a look at the orders and can you give me your projections for the coming year,' he said to Emma.

She flushed with embarrassment.

'It's all right, he has agreed to a ceasefire,' Judith said.

'I don't have a business plan as such. It was a hobby and it just has mushroomed, and now I am getting enquiries from all over, especially after Judith showed the range on TikTok. Now with a department store on the books, I feel I will be making jam morning, noon and night and I still won't be able to keep up with orders.'

Miles looked at his mother. 'You are as bad as each other. OK, I am not promising anything, but I will look at the orders, I want to know exactly what everything costs. There is a jam and relish factory in the county. Maybe they would be willing to sell you some space a few times a week until you can get on your feet. Or they could make the jam for you, and you would just have to label it.'

'But our jam is homemade, we do it here in the kitchen,' Emma said.

Miles looked all around. 'It's not as if people will know. The fruit is from the farm and as long as the factory adheres to our requirements, it will be fine.'

Emma turned away. She wasn't happy to hand over the enterprise to somebody else. It was the first thing that had really felt like her own since the whole Henry business.

Judith, detecting her dissatisfaction, said they were not moving out of Killcawley Estate. 'Miles, dear, it is time to source the equipment, and renovate one of the old stables as a stand-alone unit serving the needs of our thriving business,' she said.

'Mother, that will cost too much, and I'm not throwing away bucks on doing up the stable. That's final,' Miles said as he made for the back door.

When he was gone, Emma slumped on a chair at the table.

'I think he's going to come back with confirmation that we shouldn't continue with the business,' she said, her voice flat.

'Nonsense, darling. He may be in line to inherit Killcawley Estate, but until then the final say is mine. I always have the last word,' Judith said, before heading upstairs to change into her latest outfit for a TikTok video.

Marsha checked to make sure there was nobody loitering in the hall before she spoke.

'Don't worry, Emma. Miles is all talk, but J is right. She is the real decision maker in this house, and he knows it. It's why he comes across as so grumpy at times. He chooses to live in New York with his big job, but I think the lad needs to move back here. He's never going to be happy pulled between the two.'

'Why doesn't he move back? I would have thought to own and run a place like Killcawley Estate would be very satisfying.'

Marsha shrugged. 'Who knows? That lad needs to meet a nice young woman who would talk sense into him.' She got her coat. 'Will you keep an eye on the turkey? I am off home. I have to find an outfit to wear tonight. No doubt Judith will be looking splendid in her designer wear.'

Emma enjoyed the quiet of the kitchen for ten minutes, until Judith came downstairs. She bustled into the room wearing a long, straight, navy blue dress with white stripes. She looked hassled.

'Emma, you must help. I can't go out without a hat to complete the outfit, but it's difficult with this long narrow dress to get one that suits. Will you look at a few alternatives for me?'

Emma followed her upstairs to the hat room.

'I am torn between my zebra-print hat – but the navy is a

different shade – or the navy block hat with a white bobble. What do you think?'

'I think they are too much. How about this one?' Emma said, reaching for a white top hat with navy netting, and a red rim. 'It will give a nice pop of colour,' she said.

'It might just do it,' Judith said, placing it at a jaunty angle. 'It will be nice to wear these colours for Thanksgiving dinner afterwards too.'

'But it's not Thanksgiving; it's just pretend Thanksgiving,' Emma said.

Judith laughed. 'You think we're so odd, don't you? Enjoy the moment, Emma. When you're my age, you will do anything for a bit of fun. Anyway, Marsha said everybody, including you, is dressing up. This, I have got to see.'

'Don't worry, nobody will upstage you,' Emma said.

'I'm not at all worried,' Judith said as she led the way out of the house and to the far meadow.

'Why so far away?' Emma asked.

'I thought if I twirled and held my hat aloft...'

'Like *The Sound of Music*?'

'Maybe, but you have to admit, I am infinitely more stylish than whatshername.'

Judith skipped through the field playing peek-a-boo from behind the hay bales as Emma filmed.

Scrambling up onto a particularly large bale, she looked directly at the camera.

'Live and laugh every day; it's my secret to a long life,' Judith said, her voice almost musical.

Emma was just about to wrap up when Judith rushed past her and climbed on top of another large bale.

'What are thinking of, Judith, you could hurt yourself?'

'Nonsense, I have been doing this sort of thing since I was a nipper,' Judith said as she jumped to the ground. She turned to the camera and said: 'Please don't let a horrid motorway ruin what is best about Killcawley and Killcawley Estate.'

'I hope you got it all on film,' she said, winking at Emma.

'Just.'

'I could do a second take?'

'What will Miles say when he sees this?'

Judith laughed. 'Who cares what Miles thinks; he's too much of a fuddy-duddy.'

They both laughed as they walked back to the house. Miles, in the drawing room, saw them pass the window and met them in the kitchen.

'Red, white and blue, Mother. You look stunning,' he said.

'Darling, you always have the best compliments, which is why I am so surprised you have not met some nice woman yet. You're not getting any younger; you need to be planning the future.'

'Mother, do we have to have this conversation now?'

'Why? Please don't mind Emma; I tell her everything, anyway.'

Feeling as if she were to be dragged into a conversation she would rather not be having, Emma excused herself to get ready for dinner.

As she went upstairs, she heard Judith chastise her son gently: 'She is one of the best things to happen to me in a long time, Miles. She may have walked in off the street, but I feel very lucky to have Emma here,' she heard her say.

Emma couldn't catch Miles' reply, and anxious not to be caught eavesdropping, hurried to her room. She opened her wardrobe. It contained mainly jeans and hoodies, but the last time she was in Bray she had bought a dress that she'd not yet had an opportunity to wear. It was a simple tea dress, light blue with a delicate flower pattern and a thin velvet ribbon at the waist.

It reminded her of a dress she had left behind, which was

why she'd bought it. She took off her hoodie, and slipped on the dress over her jeans. Stepping out of the jeans, she realised she didn't have any high shoes, but she pulled on her pair of cream Converse shoes. No doubt Judith wouldn't approve, but she didn't care. The woman in the dress shop had persuaded her to go for a silver wrap, which she threw over her shoulders.

She heard Judith go to her room, and she waited to make sure she was well inside before going downstairs.

Miles was chopping chives when she walked in.

'Wow, you look stunning,' he said before catching himself, and immediately turning back to his chopping.

Feeling herself blush, Emma grabbed an apron, and asked how she could help.

'Everything is under control. I took the turkey out and it is resting,' Miles said.

'I thought Judith said you couldn't cook.'

Miles laughed. 'What would Mother know? I left home when I was twenty-one and these days she hardly knows me. It's not my fault either. I keep asking her to visit me in New York, but she always comes up with an excuse. I thought when my dad passed, she would be itching to spend time with me in Manhattan, but she doesn't like to be away from Killcawley Estate.'

'Sometimes, nothing can replace home,' Emma said.

'It depends on where you call home, I guess.'

'Surely, it's Killcawley Estate – this place is so wonderful.'

He took the plates and started to lay the table. 'Easy for you to say; you don't have to pay the bills.'

'But the farm is not running at its optimum, and there is surely land and stables that can be leased?'

'All of which takes time and money, and not to mention the insurance implications.'

'Your father managed to keep on the place.'

Miles shook his head. 'My father was an engineer. He spent

a lot of his time in Holland. He even bought an apartment in Amsterdam. His salaried job kept the estate going.'

'Judith never mentioned he worked elsewhere.'

'Best not to bring it up with her; it was a constant bone of contention between the two of them. We were left for weeks on end, while he fulfilled his obligations elsewhere.'

'But you could return and get a job in Dublin, which is a commutable distance.'

'Don't think I haven't considered it, but it's a vicious circle. If I get a high-powered, well-paying job in finance here, it will take all my time, and I will only end up using this place at vacation time or weekends.'

Emma got down the wine glasses.

'And not being here at all and working in New York is preferable? I feel that there will always be arguments for and against taking over the estate, but you just have to follow your heart.'

Miles poured two glasses of merlot and handed one to Emma. 'I wish I had that luxury, but following your heart is rarely a sound financial decision,' he said.

They heard Judith open the front door for Jack, before the two of them disappeared to her suite.

'Why does she skulk around? I have always known how fond she is of Jack,' he said.

Emma didn't know how to answer.

At that moment, Marsha and Hetty arrived.

Marsha was wearing a navy trouser suit with a USA pin on the lapel.

Hetty, coming in behind her, was sniggering. 'Doesn't she look the elegant lady? Judy will have a hard job competing with this one,' she said.

Jack opened the kitchen door for Judith, who swept down the stairs and into the kitchen. She was wearing her navy taffeta skirt and white satin blouse, along with a discreet fascinator with three feathers in blue, white and red.

'Where do you think you're going, the White House?' Miles said as he twirled his mother across the floor.

'I thought you were wearing your TikTok outfit,' Marsha said.

'The element of surprise works every time,' Judith replied, and winked at Emma.

TWENTY-FIVE

AUGUST

Two days later, Emma felt embarrassed standing beside Judith, who was wearing an elaborate wide-brimmed straw hat and a pink gingham dress, which had a skirt puffed out with bunches of netting underneath. They had decided to have a Killcawley Estate Preserves stall at the special village fundraiser for the legal battle against the motorway. Marsha had rallied the crowds, because she said they couldn't rely solely on social media for funding. She got local businesses to offer prizes, and local children were selling raffle tickets.

Emma had spent the morning in the village hall setting up the stand, and stacking the different jams on the display table. She wasn't too happy when Judith swanned in a half an hour before opening.

'Looking really well, darling. Tell me what to do,' she said without a hint of remorse that she was two hours later than she had promised.

Emma handed her a red apron with Killcawley Estate Preserves printed in gold.

'Can you help me at the till? They are expecting the first two hours and the last two to be busiest.'

'Darling, the apron is not going to fit over this dress,' Judith said.

'But we agreed.'

'I'm sorry, but this dress came in from a supplier this morning, and I couldn't resist it. It fits in beautifully with the summer theme. Nobody is expecting to see me wearing an apron.'

Annoyed, Emma snatched it back, and stuffed it under the counter out of the way.

'Miles said he will be here to help later. I told him these old legs won't last the day,' Judith said, before disappearing to talk to the man selling watercolours at the next stall.

Emma breathed in deeply in an attempt to hide her frustration. She loved Judith dearly, but there were times – and this was one of them – she really pushed Emma's buttons.

When she saw Marsha approach, she reached for the apron, hoping to persuade her to help out.

'Emma, you are the popular young woman these days. A man has been asking about town for you,' Marsha said, smiling brightly.

'What?'

'He seemed to know you. A very handsome chap he is too.'

'I don't really know anyone around here.'

'Oh no, he's a stranger. A visitor from the UK, I would say. You're a dark horse, he said he wasn't sure whether you were still using your married name,' Marsha said digging Emma in the ribs.

Emma's knees knocked together and her hands began to tremble. She turned away, busying herself with bubble-wrapping three jam gift sets for a customer flying to Boston the next day.

She tried to speak, but her throat felt like cardboard. When she could get out a few words, she croaked, 'Did you say anything about Killcawley Estate?' she asked.

Marsha, who was serving another customer, made to answer, but suddenly stopped, and stared at Emma.

'Did I do wrong? I only gave him directions. He seemed very anxious to meet up. He thought you were Emma Murray, but I put him right on that.'

Emma's eyes darted in panic across the hall.

Marsha stood beside her. 'I tried to get it out of him why he wanted to talk to you so urgently, but he was keeping his cards close to his chest.'

Judith, who had been earwigging on the conversation as she examined the paintings in the next stand, leaned over and tipped Marsha's elbow.

'Did he ask for Emma by name?' she said.

'Oh yes, he knew her, just not her full name. He had an English accent. I was helping out Bernard in the post office. He came in this afternoon; said he was an old friend.'

Emma froze. All she could hear was Marsha droning on. Her ears were ringing; daggers of pain ripped through her body. She wanted to shout, but she was unable to utter a word. She felt Judith's hand take hers and squeeze hard. Judith was saying something, but she could not hear. She saw her lips move, and Marsha push through with a glass of water and, like a priest with holy water, sprinkle something on her face. Pain speared across her chest.

Emma was breathing quickly, her body hurt all over. The only voice she could hear was *his*, telling her she had disrespected him and she would have to pay. She closed her eyes as fear coursed through her, making her scream inside her head.

There was only one reason he had come all this way. He was going to hurt her.

She got up, shouting she had to leave town, but the sea of people around her seemed to press closer and closer, until she felt she could not breathe anymore. Her knees buckled and she heard the thud of her body as she hit the floor.

. . .

It took Emma a few moments for her eyes to adjust to the light in her bedroom. Judith was dozing in a chair at her bedside.

Miles, who was standing at the window watching the swans trail across the lake, swung around when he heard Emma move in the bed.

'How are you feeling? The doctor says you may be groggy for a while. He gave you something to make you sleep.'

'How long have I...'

'Been asleep since yesterday. Mother hasn't left your side. Marsha only moved a while ago.'

Emma struggled to sit up in the bed. 'I need to leave; I have to leave.'

'You will do no such thing,' he said.

She fell back on the pillow, tears of shame rolling down her cheeks. 'I have to leave; he's looking for me. I don't want to bring this trouble to your door.'

'Who are you talking about, Emma? Whoever he is, he will have all of us to contend with first,' Miles said.

Emma grimaced. 'No offence, but a lawyer from Manhattan and an elderly lady wearing stylish clothes will be no match for Henry. He is a nasty piece of work. I can't do this to your mother.'

Judith stirred and scowled. 'Very noble, Emma, but we won't let you go,' she said, her voice determined.

Miles said he had to leave for an appointment, but would be back by evening. 'Jack is on duty in case you ladies need any help,' he said.

After he had left, Emma made to get out of bed, but Judith stopped her.

'This is the best place for you now. You have had such a scare. Let us look after you.'

Emma shook her head. 'I only know one way of dealing

with this and that is to escape. I can't stay here; you have no idea what he's like.'

'Maybe it's time to let us in on this story that has been hurting your heart and consuming your brain since you arrived here,' Judith said.

Emma sat back on her pillows. Clenching and unclenching her fists, she opened her mouth to speak, but no words came. She turned her head away from Judith.

'I'm not leaving here until you tell me about this man. We are all involved now, whether you like it or not,' Judith said.

'I don't know where to start.' Emma turned away clutching her stomach. Cramps gripped her and she could not speak.

'He must have beaten you black and blue for you to leave him, because, Emma, I have never met somebody so loyal in my life,' Judith said.

'He was nasty and horrible...' Emma choked back tears.

'Abuse takes all forms, I know that. I am so sorry you have had to suffer at the hands of this nasty, violent man. Let us help you now and protect you.'

Emma sat up straight. 'You can't do that. He is angry; he hates me for leaving. He won't let me get away with that. He's found me all these months later; he doesn't give up.'

'And neither do we. Jack is staying over, and Miles will be back later. Hetty is going to stay with Marsha for a while, and they will keep a lookout from the gate lodge. You will not be going anywhere on your own, until we get this sorted.'

'What do you mean?'

'We may have to go to court and get a protection order, but let's see if he is stupid enough to come to the house looking for you.'

'I don't want to cause any trouble for anyone here,' Emma said, her lip trembling.

'Nonsense, darling. It is high time that man got his comeuppance,' Judith said, getting up and pacing the floor. 'Which is why Miles is meeting with a solicitor as we speak.'

'You don't know what he is capable of,' Emma whispered.

'I know enough that lovely, kind Emma has been reduced to a jabbering wreck because of this man. If the thought of him anywhere near you can do this to you, I shudder to think what he could do in person.'

'Do we know how he found me?' Emma asked, her voice high pitched with tension.

Judith pulled her chair closer to the bed. 'Marsha said he was asking about the jam-making business.'

'How did he know about that?'

Judith fidgeted with the duvet, tracing the different fronds of a palm tree.

'There was an article about the jam online.'

Emma sat up. 'What article? I didn't know about this.'

Judith kept her head down.

'Was there a picture? I said no pictures.'

Judith got up off the chair and sat on the bed. 'Darling, that nice one I took in the courtyard of the pyramid of jam jars. I didn't realise you were in the background.'

'Where was it published?'

'The *Daily Record*, Irish edition.'

Emma hit her head against the headboard.

'I don't understand why it matters,' Judith said.

'Sometimes stories from the Irish edition end up in the English paper. That's probably where he came across it.'

Judith got up from the bed, pacing the floor back and forth.

'Did he hit you?' Judith asked.

Emma gasped. It was such a direct question, but slowly she nodded.

Judith rushed across the room. 'Oh, you poor darling,' she said, taking Emma into her arms.

'You shouldn't have released a photo without running it by me,' she sobbed.

'Darling, I wasn't thinking. You know me when it comes to publicity, I get all silly,' Judith said, stroking Emma's hair.

'What am I going to do now?'

'Miles is trying to sort out a safety order.'

'It won't matter to Henry.'

'It will have to mean something – we can have him arrested if he breaks it,' Judith said, squeezing Emma tight.

Emma pulled away, threw back the duvet, and got out of bed. Sitting down at the dressing table, she peered closely at her reflection. She looked so different now. Back then, she had long blonde hair. Henry liked her to keep it curled and wavy. Her nails used to always be painted red, and her eyes... Emma moved closer to the mirror. Her eyes were bright now. Before, they were dull, always watchful, always looking for the thing that could trigger Henry. She saw Judith come behind her and reach for the brush.

'May I brush your hair, sweetheart? I find it very relaxing to brush my hair when I am stressed, and if I could find somebody to do it for me regularly, I would even pay them,' she said.

'Please, that would be nice.'

'You have such beautiful, straight hair,' Judith said.

'Henry liked it curled.'

'What did he know?' Judith replied as she stroked Emma's hair gently with the brush.

'You talk when you're ready,' she whispered.

'Henry was never happy with my appearance. That should have been a big red flag, I guess.'

'When we love somebody, we often ignore the red flags, until they are shoved in our face.'

Emma held out her hands in front of her and looked at her nails. A few days earlier Judith had insisted on a visit to the nail salon. Emma had chosen a lovely French tip, which she knew was not going to last long, but somehow that didn't matter; she had picked what she wanted, and it felt good.

'It was a silly change of nail colour from red to pink which ignited Henry's rage that last time I saw him. I was wearing the tweed suit, and the nail technician suggested a light pink to match the pink fleck in the tweed. Henry didn't notice at first. We were sitting eating a chicken salad dinner when he took my hand.

'I thought he was being loving. He asked me why I'd changed the colour of my nails. He said I hadn't asked for his opinion on the matter. When I explained about my nails matching the pink in my suit...'

Emma stopped and swallowed hard.

Judith pressed Emma gently on the shoulders.

'You don't have to continue, darling; I get the picture.'

Emma shuddered, throwing off Judith's hands.

'He said I was stupid, and I should have asked his permission. Next, he upended my dinner and started shouting. I tried to run from the room, but he caught me by my ponytail.'

Judith stopped brushing.

'I got as far as the bedroom, and managed to lock the door. He was yelling at me, that I had disobeyed him, that I was useless. He kept kicking the door.'

'How did you get away from him?' Judith said, her hands to her face, her eyes full of concern.

'I prayed that Mr Murphy next door would ring the police. He must have, but by then I was barely conscious. I woke up in hospital, and was told that when the police had got into the house, Henry was gone.

He never came to the hospital, and he didn't turn up at work, but I knew when I was discharged from hospital that if I went back to the house, he would appear. I thought he might kill me the next time he came across me. A nurse at the hospital helped me, gave me an old handbag and purse, and enough money so I could get the ferry to Ireland. She even gave me make-up to cover the bruises on my face. I still had my phone but I was afraid to use it. I ended up in Killcawley, because it was the only place I knew in this country. I was just lucky I saw your advert.'

Judith pulled over a chair, and sat down, her face grey.

'Emma, what have I done?'

'It's my fault. I should have told you at the start, but I was ashamed.'

'Ashamed? But you're the victim.'

'Shame does not differentiate; it's a feeling that pervades and is very hard to shake.'

'I hope you know none of us here believe you have anything to be ashamed about. We love you, and we have your back.'

Emma turned, and looked at Judith. 'The best decision I ever made was to get as far as Killcawley, and to answer your advert, Judith. It has changed my life.'

'I am glad of that, but now we must deal with Henry. But there's one crucial difference this time round.'

'And what is that?' Emma asked wearily.

'You're not on your own,' Judith said. She reached over, and took Emma into an extra tight hug. 'Now, let's get you downstairs for something to eat.'

Emma let Judith lead her downstairs to the kitchen, where Marsha had returned with enough hot food to feed a small army.

'Just vegetable curry and rice, good comfort food,' Marsha said, piling some on a plate.

'Thank you,' Emma said as she sat at the table and began to eat.

Marsha and Judith sat opposite her.

'We sold all the jam, and got a lot more orders. And we have raised a lot of money for the final push on the motorway campaign,' Marsha said, before Judith hushed her.

'Emma has more important things on her mind right now,' she said.

Emma looked at Judith and Marsha. She felt lucky to be here, and with these two, who were more than family to her at this stage.

TWENTY-SIX

Emma stood outside the drawing room listening to Miles arguing with his mother.

'Forget the motorway; forget everything. Our most immediate problem is this man who has been asking about Emma. We know he is violent; what if he turns up one day, and it is only you and Emma in the house, Mother?'

Judith didn't say anything for a few minutes. Emma heard Miles pacing up and down the polished parquet floor. Every now and again, he sighed loudly.

When Judith spoke, it was in her prim voice. 'Miles, I wish I could answer all the questions you have, but at the moment Fintan O'Brien has emailed to say there is a settlement proposal going to be put on the table. He expects to have it shortly, and I need to gather the troops.'

'Mother, that whole motorway thing is going to sort itself out, but this situation with Emma...'

She heard Judith impatiently rustle her newspaper.

'Miles, we stand behind Emma, and in front of her if necessary, but don't even think of asking me to abandon her, because that's not going to happen,' she said.

Emma heard Judith walk smartly across the room, so she scooted to the front door, and out onto the steps.

It had been three days since she had collapsed at the village fair, and there had been no sign of Henry. She didn't dare hope he had moved on; Henry, she knew, was not a man who liked to give up. He was very good at hiding in plain sight. Emma shivered to think what he was planning next, but she put him firmly out of her mind as she wandered down to the jetty.

The swans glided towards her, but she ignored them. Instead, she sat down at the end of the pier. Slipping off her sandals, she dangled her feet in the water. A few ducklings made a beeline towards her, but drifted off into the rushes when she had no scraps to throw for them.

There was a mid-afternoon slumber about the lake. Even the swans appeared to dawdle, stopping to preen their feathers, letting the breeze over the lake push them a little off course. It was her favourite time of day here, when the work was done and everybody was waiting for the evening meal and the days' end.

A footfall on the jetty behind her made her jump and scramble to her feet.

'I'm sorry, I didn't mean to startle you,' Miles said, looking embarrassed.

'It's OK, I was leaving anyway,' she said, scooping up her sandals.

'I came down to talk to you,' he said.

She stood waiting for him to speak, but he remained on the jetty, his hands in his pockets.

She heard the ducklings scramble up the bank beside him.

'They think you have food for them.'

'Mother says you feed them most days.'

'I like to do it.'

'Do you think we could talk about your situation?' he asked.

'Is this about Henry?'

'Mother said he was violent.'

'Yes,' she said, turning away to concentrate on the lake.

When Miles moved closer, she shuddered. 'I'm sorry, I'm a bit out of my depth here. Mother wants you to stay, and to do that, we have to make sure you're protected. I met with a local solicitor, and I think the best course of action is to take out a protection order first and then apply for a safety order.'

'What exactly will that mean?'

'This Henry can be arrested if he comes near you. Local gardai will come straight away if you call them.'

'I thought you were going to ask me to leave,' she said, looking directly at Miles. She noticed his eyes clouded and he averted his gaze.

'If it were purely my decision, I would ask you to go, but Judith is resolute that you must stay.'

He kicked a few pebbles from the bank into the lake, making the ducks scatter.

'This motorway campaign, and the success of the jams along with all the TikTok exposure has put Killcawley Estate in the spotlight – I'm not sure that is the best thing,' he said.

'I never intended for any of this to happen.'

'I believe you. But my relationship with Mother has been tense since my father died. I want what is best for her, and handling this rambling estate is not good for her anymore.'

'I don't think Judith could live without Killcawley Estate.'

'She may have to; we have to do what is best,' he said, his tone clipped.

Emma said she had to get back to the house, that she had to make jam. Miles stepped aside to let her pass.

'My mother tells me to leave you alone about the jam,' he said.

'It is doing well; I have also got word that a luxury hotel chain is taking on the small pots.

'I have examined the numbers. You're going to have to expand to keep up with demand.'

'But that will cost so much.'

'Trying telling my mother that,' he sighed.

'I know you don't believe me, but we are happy with things as they area. Judith and I are content making jam, having the supper club, fighting the motorway and doing her social media. We fit well together, and I would have thought, considering you live so far away, that would be a comfort to you. I know this Henry thing complicates everything, but I will do whatever you ask to keep him away from here. What more can I say?'

'Judith doesn't want you to leave. She says if I kick you out, she will throw me out after you.'

Emma couldn't help but giggle, and she saw a smile creep across Miles' face.

'My mother is a very forceful woman, and I believe she would.'

'So, you're stuck with me.'

'It appears so,' Miles said, walking towards her. 'I don't want anything to happen to you, Emma, and I feel for your situation. However, my priority has to be my mother. What happens if this whole business with this man escalates? This is why we have to get the protection order sorted. We have to be ready, and not caught off guard.'

'Spoken like a true lawyer.'

'I can't help it, it's who I am.'

She could tell that Miles sensed she didn't want to talk about Henry anymore. They strolled back to the house together.

Judith called them both to join her in the kitchen.

'My favourite team. Darlings, together we can overcome anything.'

Miles said he had to catch up on some emails and disappeared upstairs.

'He's not all bad, is he?' Judith asked Emma.

'No, he's a decent man, but I can see he is worried about you.'

'Miles is always worried about me; he fails to understand I have managed to stick it out for seventy-five years, and that's not because I'm a shrinking violet.'

She took a bottle of prosecco out of the fridge and poured a glass.

'Miles doesn't like me drinking during the day; he says it's bad for my health. But, between us, who cares?'

She downed her prosecco quickly, before refilling her glass.

'Now, what are we going to do about that Henry?' she said.

Emma grabbed a glass and poured herself some bubbly.

'Miles has everything set up legally, but...'

'That's not going to be much good if he comes in the dark of the night.'

Emma shivered.

Judith slapped down her glass on the table, prosecco splashing over the rim.

'Me and my big mouth. Marsha thinks we should have the buddy system for you. Every time you go out, it has to be with one of us. We can plan the shifts at breakfast time each day.'

'And we would all be miserable; I could go to Scotland, or Wales even, for a short while.'

'You will do no such thing; Killcawley Estate would be nothing without you.'

'But...'

'We'll all keep a keen eye. Marsha has even bought CCTV cameras for the gate. Maybe he won't come back.'

Emma shook her head. 'I have to get cooking for supper club. Will Miles join us?'

'Anybody staying in this house cannot miss supper club and I have persuaded Jack to come along even though he and Miles butt heads from time to time.'

Emma got the ingredients together for a seafood paella and began making her dish.

Judith said she was off to make a TikTok video in the drawing room.

'Give me a half an hour or so and I will help you,' Emma said.

'No, this is a little head and shoulders update. With the settlement offer on the way, I have to tell our supporters to expect big news'.

'But until we see the offer, how do you know we are going to take it?'

'I don't, but it won't do any harm to show we can keep the pressure on. I am afraid the last few days, with all that has been going on, I haven't posted a thing,' she said, before disappearing to make her video.

TWENTY-SEVEN

Judith had gathered everybody together to view the settlement offer.

Marsha snorted. 'Is that it?'

Judith flung the pages of the email on the table.

'Not worth the paper it is printed on,' she said despondently.

'It's a bloody insult,' Jack said.

Miles took the email and read it carefully.

'This is definitely an insult. They are offering to save Hetty's house, but it will be on the edge of the motorway, and they are offering to build a big island roundabout with the oak tree as the centrepiece. If this wasn't so pathetic, it would be funny,' Miles said.

'It's definitely not funny,' Emma said.

'Fintan bloody O'Brien says it's a compromise at least,' Judith said.

'Fire that solicitor,' Miles said quietly.

'And what will we do then? Represent ourselves?'

Miles looked around the table.

'I can help, if you are willing to let me do the job, I might even enjoy it,' he said.

'Would you really do it for us?' Marsha asked.

Miles stood up.

'From what I understand, we can press ahead as lay litigants, and with my training, Emma as back-up, and you lot behaving yourselves, we can take them on.'

'But to be clear, we do not accept this settlement,' Jack said.

'Of course not. Mother, tell Fintan O'Brien he is no longer required. Emma, find out if we have to formally tell the court about the change in representation or is Fintan going to come off record? Can you also draft a suitable response and tell the other side we reject their offer?' he said.

'What about us two?' Marsha asked, pointing to herself and Hetty.

'You ladies will help Judith with her TikTok campaign. Let's publicise this shameful settlement offer, and embarrass the other side and enrage the whole of Killcawley and beyond,' he said, his voice forceful.

Emma noticed his face had changed to match his voice.

Judith threw her arms around Miles. 'I knew you would come good eventually, my son.'

'Is there a compliment in there?' Miles asked, and Emma smiled.

Marsha put up her hand as if she were in class.

'Does this mean we will have a legal battle on our hands?'

Miles leaned on the table as if it were a court bench.

'What this means is we will prepare, and prepare well, for a court case, while we wage the social media battle. Let's show these greedy developers what we have got. This motorway route has to be stopped, and the whole of Killcawley saved,' he said and Emma felt a rush of excitement and a renewed vigour, which she knew the others felt as well.

Judith stood beside her son. 'This, friends, is exactly the

distraction we need from the other nasty business. Let's throw our backs into it. Marsha and Hetty, come along, I must find a stupendous outfit and hat to wear as I tell the world about the sleazy settlement that they are trying to sneak in through the back door.'

When the three women had gone upstairs, Jack turned to Miles.

'I hope you know what you are doing, son, because Judy is convinced of victory now that you are on board.'

Miles put his hand on Jack's shoulder.

'It's like a game of chess. We just have to hold our ground and contemplate the complex moves, and make sure we make the right one.'

'If you say so,' Jack said, before heading off to check on the oak tree.

When Miles turned to Emma, she saw he was looking a little nervous.

'You know the drill. Talk to our expert and see if he can rope anybody else in as well to back us on the oak tree. We can't depend on this case settling, so we start building up the blocks towards success. With any luck, we will get an adjournment tomorrow, which will give me more time to prepare.'

As Emma watched him work frantically, a small smile crept across her lips. He looked up at her quizzically.

'You're trying to play it cool and not get our hopes up, but I know the truth. You can do it; you can win, because Killcawley Estate means too much to you,' she said.

He grinned. 'I sure hope you're right. When there is a personal involvement, it cuts deeper at every setback.'

'What do you need from me?'

'The emails rejecting the settlement and informing the court of the change of representation need to be sent today. We also need to get those emails out before Mother uploads her thing on TikTok.'

'No need to worry on that front, they are picking an outfit by consensus, and that's going to take time.'

'I think I need to get up to speed on the motorway project, go through the plans, all documentation and the permissions so far.'

'I have all that in a file.'

'I reckon you were very good at your job, because nothing seems to faze you.'

She felt herself blush and excused herself so she could locate the documents. She was busy in the drawing room searching through her file to make sure she had everything, when she heard a noise behind her. She jumped, dropping the file to the floor.

Miles immediately got down on his knees and picked up the pages. 'I'm sorry. I didn't mean to startle you,' he said, his face full of concern.

'I am a little jumpy.'

'And for good reason; we may be going full tilt on the motorway challenge, but we haven't forgotten about this man. I have asked the solicitor in Bray to go ahead with the protection order preparation, I hope you don't mind.'

'Thank you.'

'I don't think you will thank me when I tell you that you'll have to meet with the solicitor, and go to court with him tomorrow.'

Emma stood up. 'I knew it would come to this; it's just so...'

'Final, I know, but also necessary,' Miles said, leading the way back to the kitchen.

Marsha called out as she came down the stairs. 'Look, please don't shoot the messenger, but I have just heard from Bernard in the post office that a man has been back in asking about Emma.'

'What?'

Judith came downstairs wearing a bright red ball gown with a sweetheart neckline.

'Who? What did Marsha say?'

'Henry,' Emma said.

'Oh, good Lord; I had better ring Jack.'

Miles put his hand out to stop his mother. 'There's no need to panic. Nothing has happened yet.'

'Jack will have to hear it too, and assess the threat,' Judith said, reaching across her son for the phone.

Emma went to the kitchen, and sat down. Miles followed her.

'In the panic, I think we've forgotten about you, Emma. How are you holding up?' he asked.

'I don't know. The last thing I want is that man coming here and...'

'It is very important you get that protection order tomorrow, until the court decides to grant a full safety order.'

Emma put her hands to her ears.

'He is no respecter of the law.' She stopped; her voice choking up with tears.

Miles put his arm around her shoulders, and she let herself lean against him.

'We will not let anybody hurt you,' he murmured as Judith came back into the room.

'Jack will be here in ten minutes,' she said, looking at Miles and Emma oddly.

Miles said he was going to walk through the house to check windows and doors were locked.

Judith sat opposite Emma. 'You will get through this, we all will; you have to believe that.'

Emma nodded.

Marsha came in and looked at the others sheepishly.

'I am afraid there's more.'

'What could be worse than to find out that nasty piece of work is back in town,' Judith snapped.

'Hey, I'm only passing on what Bernard is texting me. He

said the fellah came in and was very friendly; he is staying in a bed and breakfast further out this road and enjoying the local area.'

'Did he ask about Emma?'

'Not by name, but he said a friend of his had moved here recently and he was over visiting her.'

Emma froze. She knew Henry had spoken in his fake friendly voice, and charmed the locals. They probably all thought he was the perfect English gentleman. She knew what he was really like: the feel of his punches on her upper body, the pain of his kicks as she lay on the floor.

'We will go to the gardai, get them to do something,' Judith said.

'Mother, what to do we say? A man who is on holiday here is a danger to us all? They won't do anything until he does something. We will get the protection order tomorrow and we will be ready,' Miles said firmly.

'You mean let our Emma be a sitting duck,' Marsha said.

'We're not going to do that,' Judith said.

'If he comes on the property, and causes any trouble, we can call the gardai straight away; once they see the protection order they will sort him out,' Miles said.

'So, we sit and wait?' Jack muttered.

'Yes, after we get the protection order, there is nothing else we can do.'

'He must be staying in the guest house a mile south. Couldn't we go, and have a word in his shell-like?' Judith said.

'I know we all feel a bit helpless in this situation, but that would be the worst thing to do. If we are patient, he'll come to us. It is quite possible he knew the word would get back to Emma, and he was sending her a message—'

The thought of Henry sending her a message made Emma double over. Miles stopped.

'I am sorry, Emma, but we have to play this clever and make

sure we don't give him any reason to claim assault or threatening behaviour against us.'

He poured out some coffee.

'This is agonising for Emma, and bloody unsettling for us all,' Marsha said.

'Does this man have a job?' Miles asked.

Emma nodded. 'He had a good job with an insurance company when I was in the UK.'

'Why don't I ring the firm, and ask for him personally, and we may be able to find out if he is on holiday, and for how long. It will give us a timeframe for this business at least.'

Emma gave the name of the company, and Miles googled it and dialled the number.

They heard him ask for Henry as he left the room to speak in private.

'That son of yours is a smart fellow,' Marsha said.

'Let's hope it works in our favour,' Jack said.

Emma jumped again when Miles returned to the kitchen.

'He is on a ten-day holiday, so there are quite a few more days before he has to travel back to the UK.'

'If he is going to make his move, it's likely he'll do so soon, before leaving Killcawley for good,' Jack said.

'Meg Hannon owes me a big favour, and it is time to call it in,' Marsha said, pulling out her phone, and dialling the number before anybody could say anything.

Imitating Miles, she walked through the hall to the drawing room as she spoke.

Judith shook her head. 'I hope she has the sense not to let Meg Hannon in on any of this,' she mumbled.

They sat in silence and waited for Marsha to return.

When she came back into the kitchen, she was bursting with excitement.

'Meg says he booked in for eight nights, and will stay overnight in Dublin before flying home.

'It shows he is telling the truth,' Miles said.

Emma stood up. When she spoke, her voice was low. 'Thank you all for wanting to take such good care of me. I don't think you will ever know how much I appreciate it. I truly believe the best thing for me now is to leave Killcawley Estate and move on. I am sure Judith will give me a reference, and I can find employment somewhere more anonymous, like Dublin.'

'You will not. Sit down like a good girl,' Judith ordered.

Emma didn't move.

'I know you think I am running away, but the last thing I want to do is bring a man like that to Killcawley Estate.'

Miles placed his hands on Emma's shoulder, and gently leaned on her to get her to sit back down.

'If you run now, you will run for the rest of your life. Please take the help we are offering. We all care about you and want the best for you.'

Judith said, 'Hear, hear,' and the others followed.

Emma turned to Miles. 'Coming from you, that means a lot.'

He smiled. 'Now, let's get back to the work we have to do,' he said. Then, turning to the others, he said, 'May I suggest that we all stay at the big house – including you, Marsha –until we can get this matter settled once and for all?'

Marsha exhaled slowly. 'Thank God. Hetty can't stay in the gate lodge with me, as her nephew is visiting from tomorrow and I don't want to be there on my own, with the likes of that Henry on the loose.'

'It will be a house party with a difference,' Judith said, and the others looked at her oddly.

'My apologies, I am merely trying to raise a laugh, but maybe it's too early for that sort of thing,' she said.

Jack said he would alert Peter to be on the lookout for strangers, and he would walk the land twice a day.

'Let's check in with you while you are doing that,' Miles said.

The phone rang and everybody froze.

Judith went out to answer it and the others strained to listen in, while she took instructions.

When she came back into the kitchen, she looked at everyone before speaking.

'It never rains, but it pours. That was Fintan. He rang as a courtesy to tell us our challenge against the motorway is listed for hearing in court in two days.'

'That's doesn't give us long to prepare; what will we do?' Marsha said.

'We will go along, of course. We will be in the Four Courts; sure there's nowhere safer than that.'

'But we can't leave the house unattended,' Jack said.

'Why? Who would come... Ohh,' Judith said.

Emma made to speak, but everybody told her to hush.

'I know, I will stay back, and the rest of you go to the hearing. How long will it take?' Jack asked.

'We may be able to get an adjournment considering the change in representation, but we will have to work toward a hearing regardless,' said Miles.

'But we don't know what to do?' Marsha said.

Miles straightened his shoulders. 'Lucky you have the A-team who does. Now somebody get that historian from the village on the phone, and tell him get his ass here; we will need him to substantiate our claim.'

Emma said she would do that and request the file from Fintan to be collected later today.

Marsha winked at Judith.

'I think they may be right; they are an A-team,' she said and Emma blushed.

Miles asked Jack to find an old table, and set it up in the

drawing room, and to find some way to extend the phone line from the hall so he could set up an office.

'I know this may not be entirely correct to say out loud; but thank heavens we have this motorway distraction. I am going to TikTok you in your office, Miles,' Judith said.

'You will do no such thing, Mother; the last thing I need is TikTok on my shoulder,' Miles snapped.

Marsha said she needed company going back to the gate lodge to collect her clothes for the next few days, and Jack volunteered, saying he had to put a good lock on the main gates, anyway.

Judith handed Emma her phone.

'We won't go outside, but I was thinking of standing near the portrait in the drawing room, and telling the world about the false and bizarre settlement offer. I am going to rip up the email in front of the camera.'

TWENTY-EIGHT

It was a busy time. Emma, with Jack as her bodyguard, went to the local district court, and secured her protection order against Henry. Miles was up early each day working in his drawing room office. He kept the door closed, and only Emma was allowed to walk in without knocking.

Judith and Marsha were put out at first but, as Judith said, they were prepared to stay in their lane, even if they found living in such close proximity to each other so difficult.

Marsha, the early riser, turned up the radio loud in the kitchen every morning, so the sound wafted through the house. When Judith complained, Marsha became grumpy, and said she couldn't bear the quiet as she imagined Henry was hiding around every corner.

'If I feel like this, God knows what it's like for poor Emma,' she said to Miles, and he told her to hush; Emma didn't need reminding of the danger.

Jack took to walking the land at dawn. He also ran a trip wire across the top step to the front door because a stranger would go to the front, and not the back.

'People are going to find it strange that the back door is locked,' Judith said.

'They will, but they will have to get past the locked gates on the avenue first. You should tell the postman we will collect the big house post at the post office, for the next while,' Jack said.

Emma didn't get much sleep these days, and she liked to sit at her bedroom window at dawn, and watch the lake. She took part in life at Killcawley Estate as much as she could but with the threat of Henry in the air, she was only going to venture outside when necessary. Even with the protection order, she preferred above anything to be in this suite, where she knew every corner; where she knew how everything was arranged on the dressing table; where she knew if anything was out of place.

Miles said Henry was already winning if she stayed cooped up in her room, but Emma was comforted by the fact that this was the first place she had completely felt at home and at ease. Henry might be inside her head, but he was never in this room.

She watched the swans glide across the lake, envying their tranquillity. Judith said swans were a fraud, frantically pedalling underneath the water, but Emma suspected her dislike was because they never seemed to do what she wanted for her videos. It was time to go back to the High Court at the Four Courts. Judith knocked on the door and asked Emma if she was ready to drive them.

Judith had chosen to wear a black trouser suit teamed with a simple black cloche hat with a discreet red flower at the side. Her only other pop of colour was the red gloves and shoes she was wearing.

'Why don't we take the BMW this time round? I am sure there are a lot of them parked around the Four Courts, and we won't stand out so much,' Judith said, and Emma had to stop herself smiling.

Jack had opted to stay back at the big house in case of any

visitors, and Emma felt a tingle of fear run through her that Henry might confront Jack.

At the Four Courts, they had to wait until the afternoon for their case to be called. Miles, who was wearing a suit, addressed the court, and asked for a short adjournment as he needed more time to prepare the case. The other side objected, but the judge relented and set the hearing for two weeks' time.

Judith and Marsha were disappointed.

'There were no followers this time, but I did say it probably would be adjourned,' Judith said despondently.

'Mother, I have told you not to mention anything about the court proceedings,' Miles snapped.

'Darling, I doubt if the fuddy-duddy judges look at TikTok,' she said, and Miles sighed and said they had better get back to Killcawley Estate.

When they got home, Jack was snoozing on the drawing room couch.

'Sorry, I didn't sleep too well last night, and it has been as dead as a doornail here,' he said.

Judith poured out some whiskey.

'It's all a waiting game now. We're waiting for Henry and for a decision on the motorway.'

Emma said she was thinking of going for a stroll to the lake to clear her head, but stepped back when everybody turned around and said no.

'Darling, you can't leave yourself so exposed,' Judith said.

Emma walked out of the drawing room, and up the stairs to her room.

She was tired of waiting for Henry; the stress was making her chest tighten, and she never seemed to be able to shake off the headaches. The lake looked beautiful in the evening sunlight, the sinking sun sprinkling across the water as the swans did a tour of the perimeter.

When there was a tap on her bedroom door, she ignored it, expecting it to be Marsha offering her a cup of tea.

'Emma, it's Miles. Would you mind letting me in?'

She walked across the room and opened the door a little.

'I thought you could do with some company, or at least my mother did.'

Emma grinned. 'Let me guess, Judith thinks because we are roughly the same age, give or take a few years, we may have something in common.'

'Something like that. Now would you mind letting me in even for a few minutes, so Mother can be happy her plan is working.'

'Her plan?'

'My mother likes to think that if I am your protector, we may become friends, and if we become friends, I may want to stay on at Killcawley Estate.'

Emma stepped back.

'I had no idea.'

'Don't worry, I'm onto her, and nothing like that is going to happen. But if you want to while away a little time with me, I have a pack of playing cards.'

'I don't know how to play any card games.'

'Didn't you play when you were young?'

'Only go fish and snap.'

'Snap can get rowdy. Go fish it is.'

'Are you serious?'

Miles cleared some ornaments and books from the coffee table and spread the pack.

'You go first,' he said.

'I took you more as a poker type of guy.'

Miles laughed. 'I live quite a boring life in Manhattan. I work, I jog and when I can, I go hiking. Poker doesn't feature. Go fish doesn't either, but I bet I can beat you.'

'Don't be so sure,' she said, pulling up a chair.

They picked pairs, and they laughed for the next ten or fifteen minutes.

'I've never seen this side of you before. You seem more... relaxed somehow,' Emma said.

'I suppose we all have a façade.'

'I don't know, I figure I'm much the same.'

'Except for the secrets.'

Emma sighed. 'Look, I'm sorry for not telling you guys the full story, but hopefully you know why I couldn't—'

'Emma, Emma,' Miles interrupted, holding his hands up. 'You don't have to say any more, okay? I was a jerk before. That's also why I wanted to come up here... to...' he hesitated. 'To apologise for the way I treated you.'

Emma looked back at him, her mouth open in surprise.

'I love my mother more than anything in this world, and while I want to protect her, I should have realised you were just doing the same thing.'

'Thank you,' Emma said quietly.

'Is there something wrong?' he asked.

'I have a splitting headache, and I need to rest.'

He appeared to hesitate, but said he would let himself out.

After Miles had gone, Emma lay down on the bed.

Her head was thumping. When Marsha called up the stairs that dinner was ready, she ignored her.

Ten minutes later, Marsha stuck her head around the door.

'I have put a small bowl of spaghetti bolognese, and a little garlic bread on a tray for you, dear.'

Emma knew there was no point arguing with Marsha, and she said thank you, and pretended to sit up to receive it.

Once Marsha was safely down the stairs, Emma fired the bowl across the room, where it hit the wall beside the dressing table. Exhilaration coursed through her and she wanted to scream, but almost immediately her great worry returned, nagging at her soul. And now, also, she didn't know how she would explain the big red stain on the wallpaper to Judith.

At this particular moment, she didn't care much. She lay on the bed hugging her pillow tight.

She must have fallen asleep as she awoke to lowered voices: Jack was saying goodnight to Judith on the landing. It was nearly midnight. Emma went back to her spot at the window.

She kept the light off. Moonlight was streaking across the lake. The sleeping swans had their heads tucked under their wings.

It was still, the house quiet. She opened the window for some fresh air, but quickly closed it. A sense of foreboding came over her.

She was walking back to the bed when she heard the first crack. Turning around, she saw the second stone hit the window. Slinking back along the wall she peeked outside.

Henry was standing in the front drive throwing another stone.

Emma froze. Her mouth dried up. Fear gripped her hard, and she slid to the floor. She managed to pull her phone from the coffee table because she wasn't able to shout for help. She punched at Jack's number, but it went to voicemail.

Two more stones hit the window. She wedged herself in between the bedside table and the bed, her head down as if she were waiting for the blows to rain on her. Henry must have moved to the front door, because she heard him cursing when he fell over the trip wire. A loud alarm went off downstairs.

Emma heard Jack shout, and run down the stairs, followed by Miles. Judith knocked on her bedroom door, and asked if she was all right.

When Emma didn't answer, she and Marsha opened the door and rushed in.

'Jack and Miles have gone down to the front door,' Marsha said, attempting to get a proper look out the window.

'Darling, what are you doing?' Judith said as she pulled Emma onto the bed.

'Please ring the police. Jack and Miles won't be able to stop Henry,' she whispered,

'Our men know exactly what to do,' Judith said and Marsha made the sign of the cross.

They heard shouting, and the sound of some sort of scuffle, before the front door banged shut. The quiet that descended on the house was too hard to bear, and Emma sat shivering, Marsha and Judith both holding her tight.

Fifteen minutes later, Miles came up the stairs to say Henry had gone.

'He won't come back. I told him if he comes anywhere near you, Emma, or Killcawley Estate, he will not only have to deal with the law, but we will also lodge a complaint with his employer.'

'And I told him he will meet me, and a few of my friends if he comes near us again,' Jack said.

'It's not like Henry to give up so easily,' Emma said.

Judith caught both her hands.

'We will also stay together until we know he is gone from here, but sometimes the bully moves on when they are threatened themselves. Let's hope that is the case. Miles rang the gardai and they will pay him a visit.'

Miles said he was going downstairs to make some coffee and Jack went with him.

It had begun to rain heavily, a sudden wind throwing the rain against the drawing room windows.

'Let's hope he gets drenched on the way home,' Marsha said as Judith suggested hot whiskies instead of coffee, and they trooped downstairs.

Emma looked at Miles. 'What are you not telling me?'

'He's gone, that's all you need to know'.

Jack placed a hot whiskey in front of her.

Emma stood up. 'I need to know what happened; please do not treat me like an idiot.'

'OK, if you must,' he sighed. 'He had a baseball bat and he threatened me, and tried to get into the house. We pushed him back and he fell down the steps. We shut the door, and when we checked again, he was gone. Jack went down the avenue, and he saw him ahead, so he ran him off the property.'

'Was he hurt?'

'Not that I could see,' Jack said.

'Is it over?' Marsha asked.

'I certainly hope so,' Miles said, drinking his whiskey.

'Let's get back to bed,' Marsha said.

Emma hoped it was over, but if she knew anything about Henry, it was probably only just beginning. Back in her room she curled up in a ball on her bed, and kept her eyes clenched shut, every part of her on high alert.

TWENTY-NINE

Emma, unable to sleep, tossed and turned, and eventually hours later worked up the courage to go downstairs, and make a hot chocolate. The dog was whining, and she moved to the kitchen door to let him out. She stopped as she put her hand on the door handle.

Fear prickled up her back.

'Who's there?' she croaked as she pushed into the wall, cowering down.

'I am so sorry. I must have fallen asleep. It's me, Marsha.'

There was a scuffle of chairs and Marsha turned on the light.

'Oh dear, I never meant to frighten you; please forgive me. I am an ass,' Marsha said.

'What are you doing sitting in the dark?' Emma asked,

Marsha looked directly at Emma. 'Trying to work out how I can get myself out of an awkward situation.'

Emma let the dog out before steering Marsha back to her chair.

'Can I help at all?'

Marsha looked dejected. 'I think I have come across information which would blow this whole motorway thing apart, but if I reveal it, it could sink my brother and put him in jail.'

'What do you mean?'

'My brother is the engineer on the motorway project.'

'And?'

Marsha bowed her head. 'I honestly don't know what to do, Emma. I don't know if I can tell you.'

'Tell her what,' Miles said as he walked into the kitchen in his pyjamas. 'I heard a racket. Why are you even up?' he asked.

Marsha mumbled something about getting back to bed.

'If there's something wrong, let's hear it.' Miles said.

'It's about the motorway,' Emma said.

Marsha gave Emma a dirty look. 'I have obviously said too much already. I was never here. I am going home,' she said as she made a beeline for the back door.

Miles put his hand across the door to stop her. 'Marsha, you can't walk down the avenue on your own, or go home to an empty house. Stay here, please.'

Emma took Marsha by the elbow and sat her on the armchair beside the AGA. 'He's right, let's not take any chances.'

'But I can't stay here, knowing what I know.'

Miles pulled up a chair beside Marsha. 'I think I have a way around this. Have you got a five euro note?'

'What?'

'A five euro note.'

Marsha fished in her handbag and opened her purse. 'I only have a ten euro note.'

'That will do,' Miles said, taking it from her hand.

'What's going on?' Emma asked.

'Marsha, here, has got herself a lawyer, so anything she tells me is privileged and I can't divulge it until she gives me permission.'

'And what about Emma?'

'Emma is not covered.'

Sensing she should leave them to it, Emma said she was going back to bed.

She didn't eavesdrop at the door, because she knew both Marsha and Miles would get very cross if she did.

The next morning, Miles knocked on everyone's door at 8 a.m. and asked them to meet him in the drawing room in half an hour. Judith stuck her head out the door and asked was there something wrong?

'The opposite, but I want to tell everybody together,' he said.

'Jack is out on the estate, I will ring him.'

When they all trooped into the drawing room, Miles was sitting at his desk, which fitted nicely into the bay window.

He asked everybody to take a seat on the chairs he had arranged around the desk.

'Marsha has important information for us all. She was conflicted on whether to tell us, but I have agreed to help her brother get a proper deal for himself, and if everything goes right we might just save Killcawley Estate and village from this motorway and stop Hugh going to jail.'

'What is going on?' Judith asked.

Miles cleared his throat, before asking Marsha to tell her story.

Marsha, who looked very pale, stood up as if she were at a meeting. Clenching and unclenching her hands, she kept her eyes on the portrait as she spoke.

'Miles here has assured me that I can tell you this in absolute confidence. I know that he is taking care of everything. I trust him.'

'Get on with it, M. We are on pins here wanting to know,' Judith said impatiently.

Marsha, who would normally have had a retort for Judith, just looked even more nervous.

'As you all know, my brother Hugh is an engineer on the motorway project. He is a good man, but I fear he is embroiled in something nasty that is going to pull him down. I had dinner over at his place in Bray last night, and we didn't have any fresh basil for the dish he was cooking, so he nipped out to the local shop.

'There was a knock at the door, and a man asked for Hugh. Well, I did the usual, and asked if I could take a message, and told him that I was his sister.

'The man identified himself as representing the motorway developer, and he handed me a brown envelope and said to tell Hugh the next instalment would be after the court case.

'I can tell you, it took everything in me not to catch the man by the throat, and ask him what the hell he was talking about. After the guy left I took a picture on my phone of him standing by his car outside the house.'

Judith gasped loudly. Marsha held up her phone.

'I am not ashamed to say I unsealed the envelope and looked inside. She handed around her phone for everyone to see the picture of the bank notes spilling out of the envelope.'

'Why would Hugh do this?'

'When he came back from the shop, I confronted him. He put up a pretence at first, saying the person must have called to the wrong house. What did he think – that I came down with the last shower? I told him to cop himself on, that he was in deep trouble.'

'He definitely is,' Judith said quietly.

Miles knocked on his desk. 'Can I just say, I have talked to Hugh this morning on the phone and he is coming to the house for a meeting later.'

Judith looked shocked. 'But why?'

'All this augurs very well for our campaign. We have the

pictures, and if Hugh is prepared to become a whistle-blower, he can give evidence about any corruption on the planning side. We can arrange for him to make a protected disclosure.'

Marsha, warming to her subject, interjected.

'He can tell a story of brown envelopes full of money being handed out for favours all over the place. This is the first time he was approached, but he knew it was going on. He was asked to recommend the present route of the motorway, and not the one previously put forward. He says he knows of other cases too where thousands of euros have been passed under the table,' she said.

'But how is all this going to help us?' Judith said.

Miles stood up. 'This is where the A-team comes in. Hugh is prepared to make a protected disclosure, which means his identity is to remain secret. As his attorney and representative, I cannot reveal his identity either. However, Mother, if you go on TikTok and allude to bad practices, people will start asking questions.'

'But wouldn't that leave me open to being sued,' Judith asked, her face fearful.

Miles shook his head. 'We can start off with the promise of explosive news to impart. Any settlement offered will have to put the motorway back on the original route which is at the very far side of the village and estate.

'But are you sure you can pull it off?' Jack asked.

'Certain. Only a fool wouldn't settle with a threat like that in the air.'

'Are you doubly sure, darling? I feel the way things are done in America are quite different,' Judith said.

Emma, who had been sitting to the side of the group, spoke up.

'The strategy is bold, but remember what Miles is doing is getting us what we want, saving Hugh, and making sure that corruption is rooted out. It's a win–win all round,' she said.

Miles put up his hand and high-fived Emma. 'I told you she is a very good legal secretary, and probably would be an excellent lawyer, if she ever wanted to go down that road,' he said.

Marsha turned to Judith. 'I am ashamed over what has happened, J, and if you want me to move out, I will.'

Judith took her friend's hand and squeezed it. 'It is even worse for you because Hugh's your brother. I just hope we can all do our bit and get a satisfactory solution.'

'I was a fool, defending Hugh to you. I am so sorry.'

'You didn't know. And now it will work out in the end for us,' Judith said as she got up and gave Marsha a big hug. 'Now, we will go out and make some strong coffee and let the legal eagles get on with their work,' she said.

Jack stopped at Miles' desk.

'We are so lucky you came back to us; you have done us proud,' he said.

'Thanks, Jack. Your approval means a lot to me,' Miles said.

When Jack left the drawing room, Miles turned to Emma.

'I have known Jack Dennehy all my life; I have always been able to see in his eyes how he feels about my mother, and she about him. I wish now they would do something about it.'

'Maybe you should tell Jack,' Emma suggested.

The phone rang, and Miles took the call. Emma slipped away upstairs.

When he came out to the hall and called her name, Emma immediately responded.

'Hugh is on the way over. He is all set to make his protected disclosure tomorrow. I will need to go over everything with him, and I would like you to sit in on the meeting and take notes.'

'When are you going to approach the other side?'

'No point showing our hand too early. Let's hear what Hugh has to say first. This could be bigger than him, and if that is the case it will give us more ammunition.'

Marsha bustled up the hall with a tray of tea and sandwiches.

'Nothing as fancy as anything from a New York deli, but with all that brainpower being used, you two have got to eat,' she said.

'Tell them the news,' Judith shouted from the kitchen.

Marsha placed the tray on the desk. 'Meg from the guest-house texted me. Our friend checked out this morning. Told her he was cutting his stay short. I wonder why.'

'Great news. This is shaping up to be a good day,' Miles said as he tucked into a cheese and ham sandwich.

Judith called Emma to help her.

'Go, her TikTok video has to be convincing, so you had better do it for her,' Miles said.

Judith pulled Marsha and Emma upstairs. 'I'm not sure if I should go over the top with my outfit,' she said.

'I think elegant, but maybe we could do it at the oak tree; it will have more impact,' Emma said.

'But I thought we were under curfew?'

'We will be watchful,' Emma said.

'Anyway, there are three of us, and it is a sad man who would pick on this group,' Judith said firmly.

Marsha looked a little uncertain, but she said nothing.

Judith pulled out the black suit she had worn to court. 'With a pop of colour in the blouse, like my high-neck pink silk shirt and the black feather fascinator with the red poppy,' she said.

'Very nice,' Marsha said, seemingly still a bit put out.

Emma asked Marsha to go downstairs with her, and they could wait together in the kitchen for Judith. 'You're worried about your brother,' she said.

'Terrified for him, and I feel so let down as well, but I will have to get over it.'

'You know you're in good hands, and so is Hugh, with Miles.'

'I hope you're right; he does seem like the old Miles I knew when he was growing up, rather than the Manhattan Maestro,' she said.

'We are going to need a bit of Manhattan Maestro as well,' Emma chuckled.

The three of them on the way to the oak tree walked hand in hand, only letting go as they stepped carefully through the woodland. Judith insisted that Emma be in the middle as they walked single file to the top meadows.

'Let's run together, let's have some fun,' Judith said, taking hold of both Marsha's and Emma's hands.

They skipped down through the grass, laughing as they went, falling against each other as they reached the oak tree.

Judith pulled a brown manilla envelope from her pocket.

'The most important prop of all. I'm going to wave it in front of the camera. I think everybody will get the message,' she said.

'A bit too close to the bone,' Marsha said, shivering.

'We have to be close to the bone; this is our one opportunity to scupper the motorway plan that could change all our lives forever,' Judith said.

'I can't be in the video, no way,' Marsha said, scooting out of the way.

Judith practised her lines while Emma got Judith's phone ready.

After she called 'action', Emma did a long shot of the meadows before zooming in on the oak tree and Judith.

Judith took a deep breath.

'I come to you from Killcawley Estate, and this beautiful oak tree which is such an important part of this country's history. I am delighted to tell you today that soon we will be revealing the most wonderful news. We are going to save Killcawley Estate; we're going to do it. I promise you,' she said as she waved the brown envelope about. 'Please share this video, and tell everyone to expect big news about Killcawley village, and Killcawley Estate in the coming days. Love and kisses from the oak tree.'

Afterwards, they walked back up through the meadows and towards the house, chatting as they went. Walking through the woods, Emma began to feel fearful that somebody was watching her. She stopped to scan all around but couldn't pinpoint anything or anybody.

'What's wrong?' Judith asked.

'I don't know, I just got a funny feeling.'

'This wooded area always gives me the creeps,' Marsha said, and they moved on a little faster. When they got back to the house, Hugh was talking to Miles, the drawing room door locked. Emma knocked and she slipped in to take notes.

THIRTY

Two days had passed, and so much had happened they could hardly keep up at Killcawley Estate. As expected, Judith's TikTok generated a lot of interest, with journalists contacting her for updates. Emma handled the calls, and said they would release a statement when ready. Miles became crabby because there had been no contact from the developer or local officials. Hugh had made his protected disclosures, and Marsha was happy that he would be able to keep his job.

Miles was out for his run when the house phone rang. The man at the other end only wanted to talk to Miles McCarthy, but refused to leave his name, only a number. When Miles got back to the house, Judith stood over him as he dialled the number.

Emma, who was waiting at the drawing room door, grew frustrated with Miles' short responses that revealed nothing about the caller.

When he got off the phone, Miles grabbed Judith around the waist, and waltzed her across the drawing room.

'They are sending over a draft settlement. We have them where we want them; they are running scared,' he shouted.

'Fantastic, I can tell everyone,' Judith said.

Emma walked into the room, wagging her finger. 'We have to see it all down in black and white first; let's see if they come up with the goods,' she said.

'I am so glad she is on my side,' Miles said, and added: 'But Emma is right, we don't want to come across as idiots who believe the first thing they are told. When we get it over the line, that is the time to shout about it.'

'I would never have achieved this. You have a will of steel, Miles,' Judith said.

'And a heart of gold, Mother; I know you're thinking it,' he said, laughing.

'You certainly are the joker,' she replied.

Marsha and Jack came in just as the settlement popped into Miles' inbox. He quickly scanned through the document.

'Let me read out the most important line. *We agree to revert to the original plan for the motorway route, and we agree that Killcawley Estate and village will not be considered in any shape or form to facilitate road expansion in the future.*

'Further, by way of compensation, it is agreed that a new library at a significant cost of one million euros will be provided to the town and built within two years.'

'Oh my goodness!' Emma cried, beaming. 'It's better than we could have hoped!'

'You haven't just saved an oak tree, Miles; you have saved all of us,' Jack said.

Marsha sat down, saying she suddenly felt quite weak.

'I have to be the first with this news,' Judith said.

Miles put his hands up, asking for everybody to hush. 'Yes, it is very good news but I would like to copper-fasten the funding for the library, and to expand on the commitment about future development. I would prefer a more specific pledge to ensure it not only for my lifetime but for future generations,' he said.

'My son, he thinks of everything,' Judith said proudly.

'Emma is very good on this nitty-gritty detail, and she will draft a response along with suggested changes to the other side by this evening. It will take a bit of time yet to fully finalise everything, but we are nearly there,' he said and began to slow clap.

The others joined in and Miles bowed in front of his mother, and asked her to dance. Emma watched, the excitement rising in her as Judith and Miles waltzed around the drawing room until Miles stopped, and asked Jack to take over. He then walked over, and put his hand out to Emma. 'I would very much like the pleasure of this dance,' he said, and Emma felt herself go pink with embarrassment.

'I don't want to leave Marsha out,' she stuttered.

'Nonsense, darling, I want to see you two having fun. You've worked hard enough,' Marsha said.

Miles hesitated a little, but ever the gentleman, he twirled Emma around in rhythm with their own imaginary music. Judith whispered to Marsha, who took a picture before she went off to the kitchen to get a bottle of champagne and glasses.

When she came back, Miles took the bottle and put it on the mantelpiece, saying they had better not tempt fate.

'Time enough to fully celebrate when everybody has signed on the dotted line and the court is told the case has settled. We won't, in this house, count our chickens until they are hatched,' he said.

'Smart move, ever the chess player,' Marsha said, her voice light and happy.

Emma excused herself to begin drafting the response, and Miles said he would continue to work towards the court date just in case.

Judith, Jack and Marsha tiptoed out of the drawing room and left the other two working.

. . .

Emma worked side by side with Miles for the next two hours. They only talked about the case, but she enjoyed his company, and she knew he liked being with her too. When they were finished, Miles turned off the desk light.

'I think I should spend time with Mother; I feel this campaign has knocked a lot out of her. She looked very tired today, and when I was dancing with her, I felt she was struggling to keep up,' he said.

'It has been a very stressful time,' Emma said, but she tried to avoid his gaze lest he read anything in her eyes.

Miles left to find his mother in the walled garden, and Emma slipped out the front door to go for a walk. Nobody noticed her leave so she was able to walk free without a plethora of warnings. Maybe Henry had really left Killcawley after all. She had to believe it or her life would be frozen in time.

She strolled, enjoying the solitude, and not worrying about the time as she took the long circuit around the paddocks to nuzzle the horses, before making her way across the far fields to the oak tree, approaching it from a different side.

When she saw Miles sitting under the tree, she hesitated. She didn't know why, but she stopped to rearrange her hair. Taking a deep breath, she took long slow strides, so she didn't appear as if she were rushing to meet him. The sun was high in the sky, its rays piercing through the gaps in the branches and flashing off the leaves of the oak tree.

The tree stood tall. its branches pointing to all corners of the meadows, while a squirrel darted up the trunk and disappeared into the foliage.

She wanted to call out to Miles, but a reticence crowded in on her heart when she saw his slouched shoulders, his head bowed. A part of her felt she should leave him with his own thoughts, but her concern drew her towards him.

Miles looked up at her. His face was grey, tears rolling down his cheeks.

She stumbled, wishing she had turned away earlier.

He jumped up. 'I didn't hear you coming,' he said as he pulled his hands down his face to wipe away the tears.

'Has something happened? Is Judith all right?'

'She is no doubt planning one of her outfits,' he said, kicking the grass.

'Miles, what has happened; has the offer been pulled?'

He looked at her, and Emma sensed a coldness in his eyes.

'Emma, I have to go away. I don't know when I will be back here again.'

'Are you returning to New York?'

'That is the plan, yeah,' he said, before swallowing hard.

'But what about the motorway settlement, and the finalisation of the agreement?'

'You can do that, Emma; you know you can.'

'But I don't want to do it without you.'

'Judith is happy to have won. It's time for me to go. Look after Mother for me.'

'Miles, Judith needs you here. You can't go.'

'That woman doesn't need anyone. I know that now.'

'You're wrong,' she said, but immediately stopped herself saying anything further. She put her hand on his arm to restrain him, but he pulled away.

'Look after her for me, Emma,' he said again, lingering too long looking in her eyes, before taking off at a quick pace up through the meadows and towards the house.

Emma sat down. What could have happened to make Miles so upset, and to make him want to leave the estate? She wanted to cry, but she wouldn't let herself. She tried to concentrate on her breathing because she felt more angry than upset; angry that he was prepared to bolt. She was angry at herself too, that she had not been able to tell Miles the truth about Judith.

Slowly, she got up, and began to make her way back up the hill. Two baby rabbits that were playing on the path ran behind a mound of mowed grass. Normally, she would have stopped to watch them run for home, but she was too preoccupied to bother. She knew she must talk to Judith.

Everything was still as she walked through the walled garden, except for the bees sucking up the pollen from stray poppies. Jack was nowhere to be seen, and there was no sign of Benny, who was usually spread out under the apple trees.

She slowed down as she reached the house, hoping Judith would emerge in one of her fancy outfits, and start talking nonsense about photo shoots and followers.

The back door was slightly ajar, making her feel uneasy. Tentatively, she pushed it back and stepped into the kitchen. She called out Judith's name, but there was no answer. She put on the kettle, and walked down the hall. Glancing into the drawing room, Emma was surprised to see Judith dressed in a silk black dress, sitting on a couch, and staring at the painting. Emma stood for a moment and observed her, the well-cut, plain, long-sleeve dress falling just below her knee. The only hint of decoration was a discreet silver embroidery around the high collar.

She wore the same silver colour in her sandals, Emma noticed.

Cautiously, Emma approached Judith, who appeared to be mesmerised by the painting as if she were looking at it for the first time.

As she neared the sofa, Judith patted the seat beside her, but did not turn around.

'Sit down. Did you happen to meet Miles?' she whispered.

'Yes, by the oak tree.'

'When he was a child, he always ran to the oak tree when he was upset. Was he upset?'

'Yes.'

Judith, keeping her eyes on the painting, pulled a handkerchief from her pocket, and blotted away her tears.

'Judith, are you all right?'

She didn't answer immediately but concentrated on smoothing the silk of her dress across her knees.

'I thought I heard Miles driving down the avenue,' she said.

'Yes.'

More tears rolled down Judith's face, but this time she didn't bother to wipe them away. The tears glistened on her skin, highlighting the wrinkles around her mouth.

'What has happened?' Emma asked. When there was no answer, Emma sat back, and examined the painting. They sat in silence, each assessing in detail the tight linen pleats of the borrowed dress, and counting the little squares of blue made by the interwoven ribbon.

'I looked so beautiful back then, and I thought there was a good life ahead of me,' Judith said.

'Young and carefree,' Emma said.

Judith looked at Emma. 'Not quite, but it does look that way,' she said, her voice so low, Emma could barely make out what she was saying.

'Will I make some tea?' Emma suggested.

Judith smiled. 'I think a large whiskey would be more appropriate,' she said.

Emma went over to the walnut bureau where a number of bottles were laid out, along with a crystal decanter of whiskey and crystal tumblers. She poured a double measure in each glass, and handed one to Judith, who took a long sip.

'I owe you some explanation. I am, at the moment, in the worst position anybody could be in,' Judith said, then stopped for a moment. 'It sounds like I'm challenging you to a competition as to who has the worst story to tell, and who comes out the highest in the victimhood stakes, but I'm not.'

'I didn't think that.'

Judith took Emma's hand. 'You're far too kind, Emma, and I know Miles thinks a great deal of you, even if he has not fully realised it yet. Unfortunately, he thinks the worst of me at the moment.'

Emma didn't know what to say, so she remained on the couch, her whiskey in one hand, Judith gripping the other.

Judith didn't appear to notice, but started to talk as if nobody was listening.

'Your grandmother was mad about Justin, and I had eyes only for Jack. We were lucky, the guys felt the same. You know when I wrote those letters from Kitty, I pretended I was writing to Jack. I poured my heart out onto the page, and it was really for him. Justin and Kitty were made for each other, we all knew that, but only Jack and I knew we were meant to be together.'

Judith took a shaky sip from her tumbler.

There was a real problem. Jack's father worked as a labourer on the estate. His family had always worked for us. Jack was the first to go to university. His education mattered little to my father, though. He might have accepted it if Justin and I were an item, but Jack was never going to be offered a place at the Killcawley Estate table.

'When Justin and Kitty ran off together, my father moved to come between Jack and me. Anyone could see we were close, and the awful events surrounding Justin's death brought us closer. We spent every day together, spent a lot of time down the meadow under the oak tree.'

Emma saw Judith's face soften as she remembered the good times.

'I ran down to the meadow in that dress of linen pleats. If Jack wasn't in love with me, he was after he saw me running barefoot through the meadow in that confection of a dress. Of course, my mother went mad, and our housekeeper afterwards had to soak the dress, and scrub it to get out the grass stains. I didn't care; it was worth it.'

Judith pointed to the painting. 'It looks a bit much there, but the dress was beautiful to wear. The linen was so soft, and I shouldn't say this, but it was very easy to slip off.'

She guffawed, and Emma thought maybe the old Judith was back, until she saw her eyes cloud over.

'That day Jack made love to me under the canopy of the oak tree. I went home in a daze, secure in his love. We had planned to meet back there the next day.'

Emma shook her head. 'Don't tell me they sent you away?'

Judith smiled. 'Where were they going to send me? Justin's parents were dealing with the loss of their son. No, my father was always a businessman first. He hatched a grand plan to save Killcawley Estate, and make sure the near-empty coffers were filled again.'

Emma got up to examine the painting. 'You look so happy.'

'I was. My life didn't change until the night after I modelled that dress for the painting. When I came back from the oak tree, my mother and father brought me into this very room. My mother was cross I had worn the dress outside, and I thought I was going to get a telling off. Instead, my father did all the talking.

'They had decided that since I was eighteen years old, it was time that I did my bit for the family and the estate. We weren't able to pay the bills. The roof of the big house had to be replaced, and there wasn't the money for it. He said the estate had remained intact for generations, and it was not going to be divided up, and sold off on his watch.'

Emma sat back down beside Judith, who nervously fiddled with a loose thread on the embroidered part of her neckline.

'The adjoining estate belonged to the McCarthy family, and Stephen McCarthy was the same age as me. He went to a private school. I only knew him to see. We tried to include him in our group that summer, but he was a bit of a loner.'

Emma got the whiskey bottle, and poured some more into Judith's glass.

'I definitely need this. Well, you can guess, the marriage of Judith and Stephen was arranged, and that meant the estates joined, which, of course, is why we own such a huge tract of land today.'

Emma stared at Judith. 'Did nobody ask for your opinion?'

'I was only a young woman; I wasn't allowed to have opinions. The wedding was arranged very quickly, so fast people gossiped on whether I was pregnant. Within two weeks, I was Mrs McCarthy.'

'Did you go to live in his house?'

'It was a horrible, cold damp place, and his mother was half mad. She hated me, and I hated her. However, within two months his parents were wiped out in a car accident, and Stephen took the opportunity to sell the manor house and a few acres and we moved back to Killcawley Estate.'

'Wasn't it strange coming back to live with your parents as a married woman?'

Judith laughed. 'The second good thing Stephen did was do up the gate lodge for my parents. He also gave me free rein here in the house to decorate it my way. He was a dull man, but he was kind to me. The only thing he insisted on was that I stay away from Jack.'

Emma looked at Judith's face. Her eyes were hollow and sad, the wrinkles sunk deep. She was staring again at the painting as if it represented the turning point of her life; the time when she started running from herself; the time she turned her back on a true love.

'What happened with Jack?' Emma asked gently.

'I managed to sneak out to him one night, and I told him what was going to happen. He wanted us to run away like Kitty and Justin, but I had a duty to look after Killcawley Estate. I couldn't shirk that responsibility.

'He wasn't happy; he went off to university, and I didn't see him for many years until he came back to the village, and became a teacher at the school. Our friendship reignited and I fell pregnant, which was a real delight for me. I was an older mother but I didn't care, it was like this baby was my miracle. We continued to meet secretly but we had to pull back after Miles was born.'

Judith took in Emma's expression. 'I know it seems mercenary, but Miles needed a stable family and that is what he got. Stephen was decent about the whole thing, and I remain grateful to him for that. He kept on Jack's father too, and never let what happened influence him in that regard. Jack, whenever I bumped into him, was an absolute gentleman, but I found myself looking forward to meeting him. Ours became the relationship that never was and never could be.'

'Jack, did he marry?'

'No, he never married. He became principal of the school, and he travelled a lot in his spare time. He and Stephen shared an interest in football, and developed a sort of friendship. I began to see him more. When the time came when Jack could take redundancy, Stephen offered him a job overseeing work on the estate. When Stephen was ill, he was at his side all the time.'

Emma got up, and walked to the window. Outside, Jack was pushing his wheelbarrow toward the walled garden. He saw Emma and waved.

'That can't be why Miles left,' Emma said.

Judith gasped. 'No, Miles always knew there was something special between Jack and me. Miles felt he had to leave after we had discussed a much more serious matter relating to Stephen. Miles came for Stephen's funeral, but he was so furious I had not called him home before Stephen passed away. We never really talked about it until today.

'I thought it was going so well. We managed to rebuild our relationship over the phone in the last while, and to have him here at Killcawley Estate has been wonderful.'

'Don't worry, he'll come back.'

Judith pulled away. 'He won't, and it is entirely my fault. I know he can never forgive me for what I have done.'

Emma wasn't sure what to say or do next, but before she had a chance to ask any questions, Judith said she wanted to be alone and whisked out of the room and up the stairs.

Emma felt deflated. Just now, when she had decided that she loved Killcawley Estate beyond anything, trouble had once more shaken her about, and a man she had grown to like very much had left in a hurry, and possibly would not return. A sadness crept through Emma, and she worried that she was in some way cursed with bad luck.

THIRTY-ONE

Judith took to her bed for days, and not even Jack could persuade her at first to get up, and greet the world. Emma brought trays of tea and food, and placed them on the floor outside her bedroom door, but Judith never touched them. The sound of a *La Bohème* love duet filled the house, but the only time Judith communicated with Emma was to ring her and demand that the decanter of whiskey, and a clean tumbler be delivered to her room. Jack spent every night with Judith. Emma always had a pot of coffee made when he came downstairs in the morning.

'Can't you just persuade her to come down to the kitchen at least?' Emma said.

'She will when she's ready. For the moment, she wants to hide away from the world, and we have to respect that,' he said.

Emma dialled Miles in New York several times, but when there was no answer, she didn't leave a message. The signed settlement came through; she pleaded with Fintan and eventually he agreed to represent the group in court for the announcement.

The settlement had gone before a judge yesterday, and now

Killcawley Estate and the oak tree, along with all the other properties in Killcawley were safe. It was a fantastic victory, but without Miles, it felt hollow. She needed to tell Judith and the others that it was over.

Jack said that Judith should know first but they should wait until she was ready to receive any news.

'Do you know exactly why Miles left in such a hurry?' Emma asked.

Jack shovelled two tablespoons of sugar into his coffee. 'It's Judy's story to tell, not mine.'

'Tell what story?' Judith said from the hall.

Emma spun around. 'I hope you have returned permanently to the ground floor.'

'What a nice way to put it, and yes, life goes on.'

Jack whispered in Judith's ear.

She shook her head. 'I'm not ready yet, Emma, to discuss why Miles left. It hurts, and being here in the house is all I can cope with right now.'

Emma poured a cup of coffee and handed it to Judith, who pushed it away.

'I don't mean to pry,' Emma said.

'I know, but the truth is at the moment I can hardly get my head around it, never mind find words to explain it.'

'I think I might have something that will cheer you up,' Emma said.

'Have you heard from Miles?' Judith asked, and Emma immediately felt bad.

'The settlement has come through; signed and delivered. I got Fintan O'Brien to represent us in court for the announcement. We have done it.'

Judith smiled. 'Time for me to get the slap on and crow about this on TikTok,' she said, calling Jack to go tell Marsha the news.

'Jack, you must accompany me in the video,' Judith said.

Emma stared at Jack, who shrugged and said, 'If it gets my Judy back on track, then so be it.'

'I insist you wear a suit. Meet us at the oak tree in an hour,' Judith said.

'And what will I do until then?'

'Buff your nails and smarten yourself up, man,' she said, going out the door, and gesturing for Emma to follow.

Judith stopped before they went upstairs.

'I want to pick something frivolous and fun. I know Miles watches my TikToks, and I don't want to give him the satisfaction of thinking I miss him. Everything must be fun with a capital F for the next while or so.'

'Why don't you ring him, and the two of you can chat it out?'

'He's the one who walked out; he's the one who has to make the first move,' Judith said primly.

Emma lingered on the landing to look out the window at the lake. She so wanted to shout at Judith that she was being a stupid old woman. She missed Miles. He was cranky and grumpy, fun and chatty, sometimes all at the same time; but she had got used to having him around, and now she missed him.

Judith impatiently called out her name, and Emma bristled as she continued upstairs.

'Did you get lost? I really need help if I'm going to get down to the oak tree in an hour. If I don't get there on time, Jack will use it as an excuse to leave.'

'I don't think it's Jack you should be worrying about right now.'

'You think I'm being a stupid old fool, don't you?' Judith said.

'Stubbornness is something you may regret later. He's your son, Judith.'

'Which is why he should believe that I love him, and every

decision I have made in my life has been out of love for my family and Killcawley Estate.'

'Have you told him that?'

Judith turned away and didn't answer.

'I have a beautiful shell-pink dress which I have never worn. It's not designer or anything, but it is so pretty,' she said, speaking too fast as she tried to change the subject. Emma threw her eyes to the ceiling when she saw the off-the-shoulder pink tulle dress.

'Too much, even for me?' Judith asked.

Emma reached over and gently took the hanger from Judith and put it back in the wardrobe.

'Let's pick something more flattering,' she said.

Judith sat down at the dressing table. 'I'm feeling old, Emma; I'm not thinking straight.'

'You miss Miles.'

'Every minute, but there is nothing I can do or undo. I just have to try and go on.'

'Maybe the social media is not a good idea.'

'If I don't go back to what I like doing, old age will grip me, and once that happens, it's downhill.'

Emma picked out a royal blue taffeta skirt with a black silk jacket.

'More my age,' Judith said a little despondently.

'Maybe a hat would be a good idea?' Emma said.

Judith brightened and got into the outfit quickly, before moving to the hat room.

'I have a perfect feature hat highlighted with cream ostrich feathers. I've never had a chance to wear it, so today is the day.'

She opened a few boxes before she found the hat and placed it on her head.

'It looks faintly ridiculous, I know, but I adore the ostrich feathers,' she said.

Downstairs, they pulled on comfortable shoes and called the dog as they headed off for the oak tree.

Emma thought they looked a sight as they trooped away from the big house. There wasn't time to linger in the walled garden, where the roses on the far wall were in a second flush of bloom, or in the meadows which had their own strange beauty as the wildflowers faded, and scattered their seeds about.

Jack, who was leaning against the tree, whistled when he saw Judith arrive, her taffeta skirt hitched high with one hand, and holding onto her hat with the other.

'I am a very lucky man,' he said, and Judith beamed with delight.

They were halfway through the shoot when Marsha, calling out at the top of her voice, ran down the hill.

'I thought the house had been abandoned. What are ye doing down here?'

'Come, join us,' Judith said.

'What's with the hat? Can you see out under those feathers?' Marsha sniggered.

Judith gave Marsha a severe stare, which made her blab on even more to hide the loaded silence that followed.

'I came to celebrate our win,' she said.

After she had made the video, Judith linked arms with Marsha. 'You and I must sip prosecco and talk about another matter. I'm sure Emma and Jack will excuse us.'

They all drifted up the hill. Jack followed, before disappearing into the sheds near the walled garden. When they got to the house, Emma said she was going to go for a walk. She knew she was not going to be included in this chat between the two friends.

She decided to make her way to the far side of the lake. Passing by the jetty, she set off into the wood, the stillness no longer a threat but a comfort to her, now Henry was gone.

Pushing the branches out of her way, she concentrated on

the path. It was darker in this part of the woods, the track barely discernible. It was clear nobody bothered to come this way very often.

She edged along at the side of the lake until she reached a stone wall and a stile, which led out to a clearing.

She felt herself sink into the mossy ground, where the going was boggy in places, the rushes clumped tightly together on the edge of the lake. A heron, disturbed by her presence, rose up from the rushes and sounded a warning call, before it flew off low over the lake. Overhead, a red kite spanned its wings wide, and drifted across the sky, lazily looking out below for easy prey.

Emma plodded on, though she felt the damp and wet seeping into her canvas shoes, making cold seep up through her. Midway across, she came to the old boat house. Two boats were tied up; one of them had sunk and was filled with water, the other looked as if it only needed a small repair.

Looking across the lake, Emma gasped to see the big house of Killcawley Estate bathed in the afternoon light, which was sheeting gold across the top windows and glinting on the downstairs bay windows.

The two swans, who had been drifting nearby, suddenly appeared to run across the water, frantically flapping their wings as if they suddenly remembered they needed to be elsewhere. Emma watched as twice they tried to launch into the air before successfully taking off, the sound of the wind whistling through their wings loud across the water now ruffled with their exertion. She expected the swans to disappear, but they circled back, skittering across the water as they landed closer to the boat house, tucking in their wings to resume drifting on the lake.

She was observing the swans bob gently with the rhythm of the current when she saw Jack approach.

'You have found the best spot in the whole estate,' he said.

'It is so peaceful here.'

'It's my thinking spot,' he said.

'I'm sorry to have intruded.'

'It's big enough for both of us, and I guess we both have a lot to think about.'

He pointed to the trunk of an old tree. 'Let's sit. The way the light hits the windows on the house can be quite mesmeric.'

Emma sat down.

After a few moments sitting quietly, Jack said he had to continue his walk of the estate perimeter.

Emma closed her eyes, and listened to the water lapping against the boathouse. How lucky Miles was to have grown up here. She would never have traded Killcawley Estate for Manhattan. She missed Miles; she wanted to hear his voice. Taking her phone out of her pocket, she dialled him in New York. This time she left a message.

'Miles, Emma here. I don't know why you left Killcawley Estate in such a hurry, and I know you will say it's none of my business, but Judith misses you so much. You know she will never admit it. I miss you too; we all do. Please make contact. Thanks, goodbye.'

THIRTY-TWO

'I'll answer it,' Judith called out, when the phone in the hall rang the following evening.

Emma saw Judith, the phone still in her hand, slump against the wall, her head bent down, her body trembling uncontrollably.

'What's wrong? What has happened?' Emma shouted.

Judith pushed the receiver towards her. 'Take it, I can't talk to her.'

The person at the other end sighed loudly and said, 'Hello, ma'am. Are you there, ma'am?'

Nervously, Emma answered.

'I apologise. This is Miles McCarthy's personal assistant. I have just informed Mrs McCarthy that Miles has been reported missing. He did not turn up for work yesterday or today. He is not at home. The police have been informed.'

'What?' Emma said, trying to decipher the words as she helped Judith scrabble to sit down.

The assistant repeated the news.

'What should we do?' Emma asked.

'There is nothing you can do at the moment. We will update when we have any news.' The assistant hung up.

Judith was moaning. Emma grabbed and held her in a tight hug, rocking her back and forth like a baby. Judith gripped her cardigan.

'I have to make things right. When he left, we were so angry with each other. May God forgive me.'

She fell on her knees and began to mumble prayers.

Emma gently pulled Judith to her feet, and slowly led her to the drawing room, where she let her sink into the velvet couch.

Quickly, she tipped whiskey into a crystal tumbler, and handed it to Judith, who was trembling so much, she could hardly hold the glass.

'I can't take it; I will only drop it,' Judith whispered,

Emma sat beside her, and held the whiskey glass to her lips. Judith took small sips before turning away to cough.

'Will you please ring Jack?' she said.

Emma didn't argue, but got out her mobile phone and rang Jack's number.

There was no answer.

Tears plopped down Judith's face, and she shook her head. 'Jack has to be here; he has to know,' she said.

'He's probably left his phone somewhere on the farm; you know what he's like. Will I get Marsha?' Emma said.

'No, it has to be Jack,' Judith said fiercely.

They sat in the drawing room; the only noise was the grandfather clock to one side of the china cabinet. Normally, they never heard the ticking of the clock, but now it was an intrusive noise on the worst of their thoughts.

When they heard a car on the avenue, they both jumped. Emma checked out the window.

'It's Jack,' she said quietly.

Next, they heard the kitchen door open, and Jack call out Judith's name.

'Judy, I have another big package full of nonsense for you,' he said brightly.

Emma tore down the hall to meet him in the kitchen, where he was muttering that they should get a new coffee machine.

'Jack,' Emma said softly, and the tone of her voice made him spin around and look in her eyes.

'Has something happened? Where's Judy?' he said.

'Drawing room, you should go to her. Miles is missing.'

Jack dropped the coffee cup in his hand, letting the liquid flow across the worktop. He ran to Judith. Emma stood in the hallway watching as the two of them sobbed in each other's arms.

Hesitantly, she joined them. Jack asked Emma to tell him every detail, and she did her best, trying to hold back the tears. Slipping away to the kitchen, she prayed that Miles was all right. There was no doubt he was contrary at times, but he was also fiercely loyal and loving, and she knew he cared deeply for Killcawley Estate. A dull ache had taken over her heart, and it took all her power not to collapse in tears as well.

Emma poured strong coffee for both Jack and Judith, and placed the mugs on a small tray.

As she walked to the drawing room, she heard them whispering. She could only make out what Jack was saying, because he was not somebody who knew how to speak in a low voice.

'It's time people know Miles is my son. You should have told him directly. Do you think I can do a normal day's work on the estate with Miles in danger?'

Emma stopped. She wasn't sure if she should retreat to the kitchen or continue to the drawing room as if she had heard nothing. Moving from one foot to the other, she remained in the hall, until she heard Jack get up off the sofa.

'Judy, I can't bear the pain. We should have told him the last time he was home. Stephen is gone, and he knew one day Miles would be told.'

'I'm sorry, Jack, I was stupid. But Miles was so angry already with me for employing an assistant and getting involved in the motorway campaign, and then the other stuff too.'

Emma took a quick step back, but she stumbled against the hall chair, which had been pulled out from its usual spot. Losing her balance, the tray tipped, and the mugs crashed to the ground.

Jack rushed into the hall.

'Don't worry. It's only two old mugs,' he said as he helped Emma back to her feet.

'I'm sorry, I was just bringing coffee but I didn't want to intrude.'

Judith passed to the kitchen, and got a mop as Jack collected the broken crockery.

'Let's all sit at the kitchen table,' Judith said.

Emma got down three smaller cups, and managed to drain the last of the coffee pot into them.

'You heard what we were saying,' Jack said quietly.

'I didn't mean to, I'm sorry.'

'I regret so deeply that Miles doesn't know the truth,' Judith said, her voice trailing off. Emma watched as she spooned too much sugar into her coffee.

'You don't usually take sugar,' she said.

Judith shrugged. 'Better sugar than alcohol, I suppose. What are we going to do, Emma?'

'Wait for news, I guess,'

Judith moaned. 'It's bloody torture.'

Jack banged on the table with his fist in exasperation, and Judith placed her head in her hands, and cried.

Jack took her in his arms, and she collapsed against his chest. 'We have to stay strong, believe that our son will be brought home to us. We can't stop believing,' he said, tears rolling down his cheeks, and wetting his shirt collar.

Emma, distracted, said she would make more coffee.

Jack put his hand out, and pulled her into the hug.

'Miles means so much to you. I know you're feeling this too,' he said.

Judith pulled away. 'What do you mean?'

Jack smiled. 'Judith, for a woman who is so au fait with the world, sometimes you don't even notice what is happening right under your nose.'

'What happened?' she asked, looking perplexed.

'Nothing has happened; it hardly matters now,' Emma said.

Jack hugged her close.

'There can often be more in the realm of what might have been. You are taking this hard, Emma.'

She nodded. 'Would either of you mind if I take a bit of time out, walk to the lake?'

Judith stroked Emma's face. 'We all have to get through this, the way we see fit. You do what you need to do.'

Emma set off out the front door to the jetty.

Was Jack right? Was there something between them? There must have been, because the hurt in her heart was so big, she thought she would collapse. There was a rustling in the reeds near the boathouse, and she hesitated, glancing right and left, but she only saw the ducklings, pecking at the reeds. Feeling uneasy, she left the lake, and quickly walked back to the big house.

Marsha was at the kitchen table with Judith, when Emma got back to the house. Jack had gone to walk the land because that was the only way he could keep sane.

'Emma, we've been talking, and we thought it was time you knew why Miles left so suddenly,' Marsha said.

Emma made to sit down at the table, but Judith suggested they should move to the drawing room.

'Can't we sit here? The drawing room is so formal,' Emma asked.

'No, let's move. When one divulges a big a secret, it must be in the best possible setting.'

Judith walked ahead to the drawing room, and sat down on a velvet chair at the fireplace.

Marsha followed, and placed the tray of tea on a marble table between the couch and the fireside chair.

Judith, who was wearing an orange and blue kaftan with tassels on the sleeves, made a big deal of pouring the tea and offering the milk and sugar cubes.

Emma accepted a cup of tea, but refused milk and sugar.

'We have spooked you,' Judith said.

'Yes, just a little.'

'Judith likes her mystery and drama, but you surely know that,' Marsha said, trying to fill the silence.

Judith delicately sipped her tea, before putting down her cup and saucer. 'I realise I am being overly mysterious, but at my age it's allowed. With this dastardly thing that has happened to Miles, I feel I need to set the background for you. It is not fair otherwise; I know how much my son means to you. Marsha is the only person who knows what I am going to tell you, besides Jack. All I ask is that it remains between the four of us.'

'Why do I need to know?'

'Because you live here, and I trust you.'

Marsha put her hand up to stop Judith talking. 'What Ms Fancy Pants is trying to say is that we have a secret which binds us together, and if you feel you can, you could also give us a bit of legal advice.'

'I was a legal secretary. I'm not a lawyer.'

'But we can't ask anyone else,' Marsha said.

'What did you do? Rob a bank?' Emma asked.

'Nothing as bad as that,' Judith said.

Marsha snorted. 'Some might think what we did was worse,'

she said.

Emma put down her cup and saucer and looked at the two women. 'Tell me,' she said.

'It's about Stephen,' Marsha said.

Judith perched on the edge of her armchair.

'You have to understand, in my own way, I loved Stephen and he loved me. We learned to accommodate one another over the years, and he was my best friend. I still miss him.

'First, he was struck down by prostate cancer. He had chemotherapy, but when the secondary cancer took hold, he didn't want to undergo all that chemo and the awful sickness that came with it. Instead, we tried to enjoy life and making the TikTok videos, which I had started during his first round of chemo. The social media and the dressing up gave a little respite from all the bad stuff.'

Marsha made to say something, but Judith continued with her monologue. 'We loved to travel. Marsha used to stay here in the house, and we went all over Europe, New Zealand, Australia and the United States. When Stephen brought up the idea of going to mainland Europe, and looking up an assisted dying clinic, it was no surprise.

'We picked a really nice place in Belgium. Marsha even came along to have a look, and do a tour. Of course, she didn't come the weekend Stephen had picked to die; she and Jack stayed back, looking after Killcawley Estate.'

'He was in such pain, that last time I saw him,' Marsha said.

'Why are you telling me all this now?' Emma said.

Judith dabbed at the tears flowing down her cheeks.

'I told Miles. He kept pushing me and pushing me because he was so angry at me. He was livid that I had not told him his father was at death's door. He said I had deprived him of a last talk, a last goodbye. He failed to understand that I was abiding by Stephen's wishes.

'I told him everything – how his father was in so much pain, that he had shrivelled to skin and bone.'

Judith stopped to catch her breath. Nobody spoke. Emma shifted in her chair until Judith began talking again.

'Miles accused me of killing his father, and he insisted the authorities had to be informed. He packed his bags, and left. What will I do, Emma? Will I be arrested and charged, do you think? And is it very bad of me to be even thinking of all this when Miles is missing?'

Marsha hushed Judith, and she took over the story.

'What we did is not allowed in Ireland. Do you think will we face charges?'

Emma tried to compose herself. 'We don't know if Miles told anyone; he might have said all that in the heat of the moment.'

Judith shook her head. 'My son never says anything he doesn't mean. He will never forgive me,' she said.

'That's not true; you know Miles could not stay angry with you for long,' Emma said.

Judith shook her head. 'Since he left, I have been having nightmares where Miles calls to ask me why I didn't include him; why I left it until now to tell him his father wanted to die on his own terms? I can't bear it anymore.'

'You did what you thought was right,' Emma said.

'Stephen picked a Sunday morning to die. He died listening to the church bells ringing. It reminded him of the old estate church.'

Judith got up and stood at the window.

'Stephen was in this very spot the morning we left for Belgium. He loved Killcawley Estate. If he could have carried on, he would have.'

Emma joined her at the window.

'I don't think Miles did or will do anything to bring trouble on you and Killcawley Estate,' she said.

'I hope you're right,' Judith whispered.

THIRTY-THREE

They waited for news of Miles for another twenty-four hours. Jack and Emma took turns staying with Judith, who insisted on camping out in the hall beside the phone. When they persuaded her to move, she would only walk to the drawing room or the kitchen.

'There will be plenty of time for sleep when this is all over. I can't do anything, but at least when they phone with news, I am present and available,' she said.

Jack insisted on placing a stool for her feet, and a blanket over her knees.

Hetty called around to the back door with a shepherd's pie.

'I heard it in the post office. Rose Deegan, the garda's wife, knew about it. Don't let on to J that I know, but if there's anything I can do to help...' she said, pushing the large dish into Emma's hands.

Jack never slept. Sitting in the kitchen where Emma had put a plate of food in front of him, he dipped his head, unable to eat.

'I wish to God I had a chance to have a few words with him,

to explain why we never told him. He so adored his father. Stephen was his father, the man who moulded him.'

Emma thought she saw a tear slip down Jack's cheek as he reached for his handkerchief, and blew his nose.

'I'm here, if you want to talk,' she said.

'I know Judy has told you everything, but if I don't talk to someone, I will explode.'

She reached for the bottle of whiskey, and pushed it towards Jack.

He opened it, and took a slug from the bottle. 'My, things must be bad; Judy would murder me if she saw me.'

'Jack, you know all my secrets. Whatever you say here stays with me,' Emma said.

'I know that; you're a good one, Emma,' he said, taking another slug of the whiskey.

'I have been a fool. I should have fought for her all those years ago. I am a coward who stayed on the sidelines.'

'Reflection makes everything appear easier.'

'Judy deserved more from me. I have loved her from the first moment I saw her, on her first day ever of school. I don't think she really noticed me, until we were travelling on the bus to secondary school.'

He was quiet a while, lost in reminiscence. He took another slurp from the whiskey bottle then stood up. 'I should go to America, see if I can help look for Miles.'

'It's not the way it works, Jack. Judith needs you here, and—'

'I will only be in the way over there, I know.'

Pacing the floor, he stopped to look at the wedding photograph of Judith and Stephen.

'I wanted to walk up the aisle, shout out that I love her. The day of their wedding, my father locked me in the house. He was right, my family would have been ruined, and where would we go?'

'You left Killcawley then?'

'I had no choice; my father and uncle worked on the estate and my mother came in twice a week to do her cleaning job. We couldn't afford to fall out with the big house. There was nothing else in the village, and my parents couldn't believe their luck.'

'But you didn't give up seeing each other.'

Jack laughed.

'Judy had ballet lessons once a week in Bray. We had one hour, and we created our own dance.'

He sat down at the table again. 'Neither of us were made for that sort of deception; we couldn't keep it up, and slowly but surely we drifted away from each other. Judy knew she had to try and make a go of the marriage as well.'

'Did you know Miles was yours?'

Jack hesitated. 'When Miles was born, everything was more difficult. The boy needed a father. I was qualified and working as a teacher in the village, and it is my shame that I didn't try to take the love of my life and my son, and get a job somewhere else.'

Judith, who had been asleep on the hall chair, woke up.

'Have some shepherd's pie, Judith. You have to eat,' Emma said.

'Don't tell me I need to keep up my strength. I have never heard anything so ridiculous,' Judith snapped.

As she came in to the kitchen, she looked at Jack and Emma. 'I'm sorry but I desperately want to be put out of this misery, the misery of not knowing.'

'Me too,' Emma said.

Judith came and sat at the table. 'Maybe a small portion,' she said.

Jack put away the whiskey bottle and said he needed to check on a few things outside. Emma pushed a small plate of pie towards Judith.

'Are you shocked about Jack and me?' Judith asked.

'No, I think it's lovely you have found each other again.'

'This is tearing us apart,' Judith mumbled.

'You will get through it.'

Judith put her head in her hands. 'I am tired of fighting, Emma, constantly trying to battle my way through.'

'We have to keep positive.'

'You're right, but I keep thinking he's trapped somewhere, calling for help.'

Emma, in an effort to divert Judith, asked how it had been between her and Stephen.

'You have to believe me, I loved Stephen too, but in a different way. We had a good marriage. We were best friends. He never wanted to marry – not a woman at least, but his father insisted on it.'

'He was gay?'

'Oh yes, and he was always upfront to me about it. We knew why we had married, to knit the two estates together and to save Killcawley Estate. There was no out for me.'

Emma shook her head and wiped a tear away.

Judith gripped the sides of the chair. 'What will I do if Miles is gone?'

'Don't think like that right now.'

'I have to set everything right with him. He has to realise what I did, I did for Stephen; I did it out of love... He has to know that this is what Stephen wanted. He also must know that Jack is his father.'

'We have to get through this first, Judith. Small steps,' Emma said.

'I'm afraid, afraid of tripping along the way. I have been a foolish woman. I should have told Miles this a long time ago.'

When the phone in the hall rang, everybody froze. After three or four rings, Emma got up and answered it.

'Is this Mrs McCarthy?' the caller asked.

'She is here and has asked me, her executive assistant, to take the call,' Emma said, her voice croaking with tension.

'Let me first check if that is OK,' the caller said.

'Can you just tell us has Miles been found?' Emma asked, but the caller had already disappeared and she could hear hushed tones a distance away.

'What is it? Is it bad news?' Judith shouted impatiently.

Emma called hello a few times down the line, each time her voice becoming more high pitched.

'Thank you for holding. I have checked with my boss, and I am authorised to speak to you about Miles McCarthy.'

'Have you found him?' Emma shouted, her heart beating faster and her throat dry.

Judith ran to the phone, and leaned in beside Emma to hear.

'I am happy to say Miles has been found. No major injuries that we know of, but he is currently receiving medical attention. Apparently he was mugged as he walked in the Tribeca district and was found slumped on a street sometime after. His wallet, cards, and cell phone had been taken. They had to wait for him to wake up before being able to identify him.'

Judith ran to Jack and Marsha, who were passing through the courtyard.

'He's alive! Our boy is alive,' she shouted.

Emma ordered them to quieten down as she listened on the line. When she got off the phone, she was crying.

'Oh, God no, what's wrong now?' Judith asked.

'Nothing, nothing is wrong. They said they are arranging for him to phone home in the next short while.'

'But why are you crying, dear?' Marsha asked.

'I don't know,' Emma said.

Judith asked Jack to open the magnum of champagne on the top shelf of the cabinet in the drawing room.

'I have had it ten years, and I was waiting for a special occasion. This sure as hell is it,' she laughed.

Jack didn't object, and went off to get the bottle, while Marsha took down the fancy champagne flutes from the top shelf of the glass cupboard. Jack popped the cork from the bottle, and nobody complained when the champagne overflowed onto the floor. After filling each glass, he proposed a toast.

'To the best friends in the world, who help us through hard times. And to Miles, and his continued health,' he said.

They clinked glasses loudly before downing the champagne in one.

When the phone rang again, Judith ran to answer it.

Emma closed the door to give her some privacy and she, Marsha and Jack sat at the kitchen table, waiting.

Marsha leaned over and clinked Jack's glass.

'Don't let them slip away this time, Jack,' she said.

'You knew?'

'You've known Judith long enough to know we're almost sisters; we tell each other everything, and I mean everything.'

'I am not sure how Miles will take it after all these years, and so soon after his... Stephen died.'

'Speak from the heart and what happens, happens,' Marsha said as she poured another glass of bubbly each.

When Judith came back into the room, her face was pink with excitement.

'Who would ever believe that Miles could survive something like that?'

'He's tough, like his dad,' Marsha said.

Jack, his lower lip trembling, said he had better get back to the outside jobs.

Emma looked at Marsha and Judith.

'Maybe I have to catch up with the jam organisation,' she said, and slipped away to leave the two women to talk. As she passed the kitchen window, she saw the two of them hugging each other and crying.

There was something so deep between those women, even though they spent most of their days trying to outdo each other.

She shook her head; if she was here forever, she was never going to understand their relationship.

Two hours later, as she was moving boxes of jam to the kitchen dresser, Judith swept down the hall wearing a turquoise lace dress, high heels and a top hat.

'Tell me, do these dangly earrings work with the hat?' she said.

'Where did you get the outfit? It's very out there.'

'The Bray haul, and I'm feeling out there. Today is a day to celebrate,' Judith said, holding up the earrings to her ears.

'Yeah, they work,' Emma said.

'Don't mind her, she's so happy, you couldn't insult her today,' Marsha said.

'Let's get down to the lake, I want to do a video,' Judith said.

Emma followed her out the door and pulled her phone from her pocket.

'Are you going to say anything about Miles?' she said.

'God no, I don't want them knowing my personal details, just the outfits. I think this one tells everyone I am a happy woman today.'

'It certainly does that,' Emma said.

'Let's spread the news about the motorway victory, now that Miles is safe,' Judith said.

Marsha said she was off home, that she couldn't face seeing Judith cavorting around the lake like one of those ladies in a Bollywood movie.

'A little harsh, Marsha,' Judith said.

'You can take it, dear, you're on top of the world,' Marsha said as she headed down the avenue, a spring in her step.

THIRTY-FOUR

SEPTEMBER

A week had passed and things were back to normal at Killcawley Estate. Miles talked to his mother every evening, and Judith wondered if she was well enough to visit him in Manhattan.

Emma got into the habit of getting up early, and starting her day with a long walk. She usually woke at eight but this morning she was up and about earlier. It was nice out, so she decided to steal out of the house to see the horses. Moving away from the usual route down to the oak tree, she headed off through the stile at the back of the rhododendrons, to the paddocks where the horses were quietly grazing. When they saw her, they trotted over in expectation of their bucket of feed. A blackbird sounded a warning call as she tramped down by the brambles, which were still heavy with blackberries. She saw a fox at the other side of the paddock, nosing around the grass. She stopped to look at him, and, sensing he was being watched, the fox quickened his pace. He locked eyes with her, before disappearing into the ditch.

It was time for some sky-walking. Emma needed to let her mind go; let the clouds take the lead. She climbed the fence into the far paddock, and the horses followed her to the fence, lingering down the far end to munch the grass. She picked her steps carefully across the field, muddy from last night's rain.

It was an overcast morning; the sky full of slate grey and white clouds, tucked together as if to shield her from what was to come. She didn't need a sunny day for sky-walking. Her mother told her the sky revealed its secrets if you were willing to look hard enough.

In the heavy days of summer, this was one of her favourite spots among the cornflowers, daisies and poppies, but now the meadow looked tired, except for a daisy here and there struggling to keep upright, despite the westerly breeze. The last of the poppies had lost their leaves, the seed heads sodden and brown.

From here she could see the house, and in the far, far distance, the glint of the Irish Sea. This was her home now. She closed her eyes and twirled around, slowly at first and then faster, until her head felt like it would burst, and she let herself fall to the ground. Gradually, she opened her eyes to see the clouds dancing in front of her, but never colliding. She followed their lead, letting her brain spin out of control. Slowly, everything righted itself, and she began to think of Miles and how glad she was that he was going to be all right.

Emma held her hands up in the air reaching for the clouds. When she was young, she wanted to pull one down so she could curl up on it and go to sleep. Now, she wanted to do the same – to sleep, to rest and recharge after a fraught few weeks.

She cleared her mind, letting her eyes wander with the clouds, and her brain take in only what it wanted.

When the horses began trotting towards her, she presumed that Pete was bringing them their feed for the day.

She got up to walk home. Somebody shouted her name loudly. She thought it was Marsha, who often went walking in the early morning, so she ignored it.

When the person called louder, she turned around.

Emma felt her throat tighten, and fear crossed her heart.

Henry was waving and walking towards her as if he were greeting an old friend. She felt for her phone but realised she had left it on her bed.

For a moment, she was rooted to the spot. Millie, the chestnut, nudged in beside her and the grey moved in front.

'So you thought I had gone forever?' Henry said as he pulled up short of the horses. Millie breathed deeply, and shuffled; the grey craned her neck at the stranger.

'The holiday is over now, Emma; it is time to come home with your husband.'

'Go away, Henry, or I will call the police.'

He laughed loud; the horses grew agitated and stamped the ground.

Emma moved towards a fence, hoping to scale it and run for the big house, but Henry pushed towards her.

'Fat lot of good it will do when you call the gardai; how long does it take to get here anyway? Now, I suggest you bring me back to that fine house, cook me a nice breakfast, and you can pack and we will be on our way.'

'I am not going anywhere with you,' Emma shouted. The horses, picking up on the tension, began to pace around faster.

'It can be done the easy way or the hard way. Your choice,' Henry said in a strange, calm voice; the voice that he always used before striking out at her.

Emma inched closer to where the horses' lead ropes were hanging on the fence. She picked one up, and lashed out with it hard, connecting with Henry's face.

The horses galloped off, neighing in fear.

Momentarily stunned, Henry staggered, but he quickly regained his composure and lunged at Emma as she tried to climb the fence. Fiercely, he pulled her to the ground as she shrieked for help.

Henry kicked out, hitting her in the stomach. When Emma heard the two horses gallop back towards them, she shouted again, and tried to break free. Millie skidded to a halt, pushing against Henry, and knocking him over; the grey reared up, and neighed. Emma, realising that the horses had created an opportunity for her, scrambled to the fence, and stepped on the first rung. Henry pulled at her feet, but Millie positioned herself in between Emma and her assailant, all the time kicking with her back feet, and nudging Emma. She climbed to the top of the fence. The horse pushed Emma so that she fell against its body, and Emma climbed on her back.

Millie turned, and trotted out of the field. Emma, who had never been on a horse in her life, grabbed the mare around her neck, and hung on for dear life as the horse broke into a canter.

She managed to change her grip to the horse's mane as she saw Henry chase after them. Millie galloped across the paddocks; Emma could barely see where they were going, but she held on tight, because she knew the only way back to the house was to jump the paddock fence out onto the avenue.

She felt the adrenalin pump through the horse as it made straight for the fence, raising its front legs, and propelling its body through the air. Emma clenched her eyes shut.

There was a blaring of a car horn, and the sound of brakes on the gravel as a car came to an abrupt stop. Millie, who had not slowed down, continued to canter at pace down the hill, and towards the lake.

Emma managed to shout '*Whoa!*' a few times, and the horse responded, slowing to a trot and coming to a halt.

Emma slid off the horse, and stood panting, her head buried in the horse's neck. Millie turned her head, and nuzzled Emma, before wandering over to a patch of grass at the edge of the lake.

Emma slumped to the ground, and sat shaking as the car came down the hill.

The driver stopped short of the horse, and got out.

'What the hell were you playing at? You could have been killed?' the driver shouted.

Emma looked up to see a man walk towards her. A familiar, lovely, if a bit grouchy man. *Miles*.

'Emma? Emma? What happened?'

He got to her in two paces, and pulled her into his arms. Emma couldn't even get her words out. Between the attack and her surprise that Miles was here, actually here, her mind was spinning. Eventually, she managed to speak.

'It's Henry – he tried to attack me in the top paddock. Millie saved me.'

'Have you phoned the gardai?'

Emma shook her head as Jack ran from the house.

'What is going on. Emma, are you OK?'

Miles stood up. 'Call the gardai, Henry is back. Bring Emma into the house.'

Judith opened the front door. 'Miles, my son. Is it you? What are you doing here?'

'Later, Mother. Get Emma in and lock the doors. Stay upstairs.'

Judith, seeing the fear in her son's face said she would.

Emma turned to Miles. 'Please don't go after him. He's angry and dangerous, and you're only just out of hospital.'

'She's right,' Jack said.

'Don't worry,' Miles said, brushing past them.

Judith stepped out onto the front steps. 'You will do no such thing. Neither of you will. I hear sirens – let the gardai do their job.'

Millie grew nervous, snorting and stamping. Miles said he would bring her to the stables. He went over to Millie and gently placed his hand on her back. Talking to her quietly, he led her down to the stable block.

Jack went out to meet the garda car as Judith helped Emma into the house.

Miles and Jack arrived in the kitchen at the same time.

'I was told to come back, and look after you all here,' Jack said.

Judith put her arms around Miles, and hugged him gently. 'I don't know why you're here, son, but I am so thankful that you are.'

'Me too,' Jack said.

They all jumped at a loud rapping at the kitchen window.

Marsha, her face red from running up the avenue, could barely speak. 'The gardai have just arrested a man, and put him in the back of their car,' she said.

Emma flopped down, exhausted.

A few minutes later, a garda came to the front door. Miles spoke to him, and returned to the kitchen to report back.

'Henry is being brought before the District Court tomorrow morning for breaching the protection order, and also for assault and destruction to property.'

Emma shook her head. 'Does this mean I will have to give evidence in court against him? He will come back and kill me.'

Miles put his arm around Emma. 'I have told them we will press charges, but if he signs a bond to leave the country and never come back, which is akin to deportation, we will let the charges against the property go.'

'Will he take the deal?' Judith asked.

'The garda said they can have a word with the prosecuting solicitor.'

'Henry won't agree,' Emma said.

Miles laughed. 'From what I hear, he is crying like a baby and will agree to anything.'

'Well, I think after that scare, we all need a coffee and a sandwich,' Marsha said, and Emma managed a smile.

Miles continued to hold her, and she leaned against him as the others fussed about her. She felt at home here in Killcawley Estate, and had never felt safer.

'There is just one thing,' Miles said. 'When did you learn to ride a horse bareback?'

'I have never been on a horse in my life.'

Jack stared at her, agog.

'And you managed to stay on down through the fields, and over the fence? You must be a natural.'

'Pete is always going on that we should sell Millie. Tell him Millie is the Killcawley Estate horse for life. She has earned it,' Judith said.

Emma saw Judith knock Jack's elbow first, and then motion to Miles to follow them to the drawing room. With all her heart, Emma hoped that Miles took the news about Jack being his father well. Jack could finally show his love for his son, and she hoped nothing spoiled that for him.

THIRTY-FIVE

The next day gardai called to the house to inform Emma that Henry Murray had left the country, and signed a bond that prevented him from returning.

Judith invited the officers in for coffee.

'We have plenty of sandwiches if you men are hungry,' she said, winking at Emma. They had not time to stay, but Judith wrapped the sandwiches in foil so they could bring them back to the station. When they had waved off the two gardai, she asked Emma to accompany her to her room.

'I'm a little tired, and I was hoping you could help me dress. This is a very special supper club tonight with all of my favourite people together, and I am thinking a fancy ball gown.'

'A bit over the top, don't you think?' Emma said.

'I jolly well hope so,' Judith said, pointing to a wardrobe at the far end of the room.

'It's time to pick one of my expensive gowns; I don't know why I held on to them all these years hoping for a special occasion. More fool me,' she said wistfully.

Emma unlocked the wardrobe, which was stuffed with long

dresses in silk, taffeta, velvet and one cream crocheted gown over gold satin.

She took out the crocheted gown, holding it high so its skirt fell in folds onto the floor.

Judith gasped. 'I didn't know I still had that dress. I loved it so.'

Fingering the delicate silk weave of the crochet and the gold satin underneath, tears rolled down her cheeks.

'What's wrong? Should I put it back?' Emma said.

Judith shook her head and wiped away her tears. 'I can't wear it, Emma. That's the dress Stephen asked me to wear the night he died.'

'I'm so sorry, I had no idea.'

'It's not your fault, I should have pushed it to the back or thrown it out even, but after he took his last breath, I peeled it off, and just managed to get it in the case. I don't even remember putting it in the wardrobe when I got home. She looked at Emma. 'I have never opened that wardrobe until now.'

Emma swept the dress away, and shoved it to the back of the wardrobe, before firmly closing the door.

'You don't need to wear an elaborate gown. It's all the usual suspects for dinner, and with the welcome addition of Miles.'

Judith took Emma's hand.

'It is a special occasion. I will sit down not just with my friends, but with the man I love, and our son. I also need a ball gown to give me courage. Can you find the velvet and satin dark navy Dior dress?'

Emma rummaged through the various hangers until she felt the velvet right at the back of the rack. Pushing past the other dresses, she managed to tug at the Dior outfit and dislodge it.

'Careful, it's from the last collection by Dior himself,' Judith instructed.

Emma unwrapped the plastic which was cloaking the outfit, and shook out the dress.

'Hold it up, so I can have a proper look,' Judith said.

The off-the-shoulder dress was nipped in at the waist; the velvet skirt was lined with satin, and held up in such a way at the sides that the purple satin flashed as the dress moved.

'There should be a velvet shrug tied with a safety pin to the label,' Judith said, and Emma found it.

'This gown would be divine on you, Emma,' she said.

Judith got up, and slipped the dress from the hanger. Placing it carefully in front of her, she stood at the long mirror by the window. Emma watched as she swished the dress from side to side slowly and carefully, and she knew there was something wrong. Usually, when Judith chose a gown, she waltzed about, and preened herself in front of the mirror. Today felt different, and Emma felt uneasy. Judith had been so tired the last few weeks.

'Definitely over the top, but beautiful,' she said, and was disappointed when Judith didn't smile in appreciation.

'My days of looking good in anything are long gone, I fear,' Judith whispered.

'Nonsense, it accentuates your long neck. Maybe wear your hair in a bun,' Emma said.

'Emma, you're a darling, but there are days when even the finest jewellery and make-up can't hide the march of time, and the imprint it has left on Judith McCarthy.'

Emma giggled nervously, and helped Judith slip off her dressing gown.

'Time to get this show on the road,' Judith said.

'Everybody loves you, and nobody expects all this,' Emma said, spanning her hand along the velvet.

Judith, who had stepped into strappy silver sandals, took the dress and put it on over her head, letting the fabric slither down her small frame.

'Zip me up, darling, and let me tell you how I came to possess this ravishing piece,' she said.

Emma zipped the dress up, and helped Judith on with the shrug.

'I must tell you my Dior story.'

'How am I not surprised that you have a Dior story?'

'It's not mine exactly, but if you're going to own this dress one day, you have to know it.'

Before Emma had time to protest, Judith launched into her story.

'I think this is the only time my mother ever confided in me. She told me that before she met my father, she had a fling with a French man. Her family were aghast when he whisked her away to Paris. They lived in an apartment near Canal Saint-Martin. He knew everybody in Paris, and was a personal friend of Christian Dior. My mother didn't much like the designer, she said she felt under scrutiny every time they met, and he had such a fixation about hemlines. He held these divine soirees and dinner parties at his home in Boulevard Jules-Sandeau.

'At one of his get-togethers, Dior invited my mother to his salon the next day. She wasn't sure if she should go, whether he would remember the invite, but he welcomed her and asked her to try on the velvet dress.'

Judith shook her head.

'How I wish it had been me. He asked her to do him the honour of modelling his latest creation. She said he walked all around her, checking the seams, straightening the shrug and mumbling to himself. When he was finished, he told her to keep the gown, it was perfect on her. When she got the news Dior died, years later, my mother wore the dress to a special evening in his memory.'

Emma dabbed at her eyes.

'That is some story. She must have felt amazing wearing it.'

Judith laughed out loud. 'Silly woman always felt the dress was too precious to wear. And look at me – I have practically fallen into the same trap. I have been a silly goose, pulled down at my age by the expectations of the designer and my mother.'

Emma took a brush, and stood behind Judith and gently brushed her hair.

'It must be a big occasion, then, for you to want to wear this dress,' she said gently.

'I am going to announce my cancer diagnosis. It's time, and I can't face telling Miles on my own, so I thought I would tell you all at the supper club. Jack has agreed, and you must also agree, to pretend to be surprised.'

'Are you sure this is the best way of doing this?'

'No, I'm not, and it probably isn't, but it's the only way I can contemplate at this stage. Now, go downstairs and when Jack comes, send him up to me. And darling, make sure everybody has a drink.'

Miles was already in the kitchen, standing in the doorway smoking a cigarette.

'Don't tell Mother,' he said, before laughing out loud. 'Judith McCarthy may be a nice old lady who lives in the big house, but she can roar like a lion when her son steps out of line.'

Emma felt sad to think of what was to come. Looking away from Miles, she busied herself with checking the stew on the hob, and the bread-and-butter pudding in the oven.

'I take it you have heard the news?' he said.

Emma froze. 'What news?'

'About Jack?'

'Yes, Judith told me,' she said nervously.

'Don't be so worried, Emma. It is what it is. Jack is a good man, and we have always been close. Maybe now, I know why.' Miles quicky stubbed out his cigarette when Marsha's car turned into the courtyard.

'No point giving Mum's trusted lieutenant any ammunition,' he said, before running across the courtyard to help Marsha with her bags.

Marsha bustled in holding a big casserole dish wrapped in foil.

'Bacon and cabbage in parsley sauce, keep it warm in the oven,' she instructed Emma.

Jack, dressed in a dark suit with a shirt and tie, came to the front door.

'Wow, you look handsome, Jack,' Emma said.

'I am merely following orders,' he said, before heading up the stairs.

Emma diverted to the drawing room. Standing at the window, she looked out over the avenue towards the lake. She had a sense that everything was going to change once Judith came down the stairs, and she didn't know if she was ready, or if she would ever be ready, for life at Killcawley Estate to change.

'Am I the only one who cares about the supper club meeting? I could do with some help out here,' Marsha called from the kitchen.

Emma sighed, and scurried to where Marsha, carrying a stack of plates, was trying to reach a bunch of flowers on the worktop.

'Thank goodness. Judith said she had to have flowers on the table; you can sort them out,' she said.

Emma picked up the bouquet of pink roses, and took them to the sink.'

'She's insisting on her Waterford crystal vase. Where is Lady Muck, anyway?' Marsha asked.

'Putting on a ball gown.'

'You're joking.'

'No, I'm not,' Emma said as she reached high in the cupboard for Judith's favourite vase.

Miles, who was reading a newspaper, shut it quickly. 'Why is she dressing up? What the hell is happening?' he asked.

Marsha gave him a severe stare. 'I'm sure Judith has her reasons, and so what if she wants to wear a ball gown. She will look stunning, no doubt.'

Emma laid the table, and set down two candles beside the vase of flowers.

She had just finished when the kitchen door opened, and Judith, linking Jack's arm, stepped into the room.

Miles let out a low whistle. Marsha stood back to let Judith sweep by her, but reached out to stroke the rich velvet.

'I have never seen this dress before, it's a beauty,' she said.

Emma pulled out two chairs for Jack and Judith, and they sat down.

'We should have champagne,' Miles said, reaching for the last bottle of expensive champagne on the top of the dresser.

He popped the cork as Emma pushed glasses towards the bottle to catch the flow of bubbly.

Holding up his glass, Miles stood in front of Judith. 'To the most beautiful woman in the room, my mother,' he said.

He clinked her glass and then Jack's.

Judith glowed. 'May I please have the floor? You are my nearest and dearest and at this moment, I am at my happiest with the people I love around me.'

Miles stepped forward. 'Mum, is there something wrong?'

'Considering I am two months short of my seventy-sixth birthday, I would say that everything is as it should be.'

Marsha pushed in beside Judith. 'Girl, what's wrong?'

Jack put his arms around Judith.

Emma stepped back; she knew by Judith's eyes that when she did reveal all, it would be devastating. She wanted to scream.

Judith told everyone to sit, and after checking with Marsha that the dinner could hold, she took a spoon, and, tapping her glass gently as if she were calling a meeting to attention, she began to speak.

'You know how much I like a little drama, hence the dress. There are a number of things I would like to tell you all. Firstly, I want each one of you to know how much I love Jack, and from tonight, he will be living here full time at Killcawley Estate. He practically does anyway, and we're too old to be skulking about.' When Miles shifted on his chair, she put her hand up to stop him saying anything.

'I'm sure everybody will want to say something, but I must ask you to indulge me now. Jack and I have loved each other a long time. We don't want to waste another minute apart. I need to be with Jack because the next few months are likely to get difficult.'

Judith stopped to compose herself, and Jack moved closer so she could lean into him.

She shook her head, and cleared her throat. 'Remember that breast cancer I thought I beat a while back? Well, it has returned, and this time it is aggressive and raging in my lungs.'

For a moment, nobody spoke. Miles stared at his mother. Emma concentrated on a point over Judith's head.

'Why is this happening now?' Marsha cried out.

Emma sank her head into her hands. Miles sat ramrod straight, his hands trembling on the table.

'Are you sure? Have you been for tests?' he asked.

'Last weekend, my last round of tests.'

Miles looked from his mother to Jack, and back.

'I should have been there with you, Mother.'

Judith drummed her fingers on the table. 'Hush, Miles. I needed time to think, to take all this in, and decide on my life and death plan. I want you all to listen carefully. This is not such bad news. I have decided to be here at Killcawley Estate. Chemotherapy will only give me a short time more, and leave me unable to enjoy it, so I am relying on you to help me get as much as possible out of the next while. It is palliative care for me, and I need you all to support my decision.'

'But J, why not go for the treatment that will help?' Marsha whispered.

'Because I saw how Stephen suffered trying to prolong his life. He was around longer, but he had given up expecting any enjoyment in life, long before he died. I refuse to let that happen to me.'

Agitated, Miles got up, and paced between the AGA and the window.

Judith put her hand out to him as he passed her, but he brushed her off. Benny the dog settled at Judith's feet.

Clearing her throat, Judith spoke again, her voice low. 'I would also ask you to accept that Jack is a big part of my life, and it is my great joy to spend the last days I have with him and with you all.'

Miles brought his fist down on the worktop so hard, the satsumas in the fruit bowl hopped.

'I will bring you to the States, get you the best treatment. We can get you a few years more, or at least a few months, and...'

'Stop,' Judith barked as she struggled to her feet. 'Miles, I know you mean well, but I have made my decision. I am asking all of you to respect that it was made after a great deal of thought.'

She stroked her son's head as if he were a young child who had spoken out of turn.

'I saw my Stephen suffer such pain as he tried to cling on to life, and I saw his mind at peace once he had decided it was time to stop fighting. I have learned from that.'

'Is there any chance of changing your mind?' Miles asked, his voice broken.

'No,' Judith said firmly.

She stood up. 'This will be the last time I talk about the cancer. I have no intention of wasting time on false hope.

Terminal cancer is just that; it would be foolish of me to imagine otherwise.'

She turned to Marsha, who was blubbering again into her handkerchief.

'Darling, I need my Marsha to be just the way you've always been. It's why I picked Irish night, because I knew you would prepare the most delicious meal, and now can you please serve it?'

'I am not sure anyone feels like eating after this news,' Marsha said, blowing her nose.

Jack leaned forward. 'You heard the lady; it's time for the supper club,' he said gently.

Marsha, holding back her tears, nodded and got up to take the food from the oven.

Miles bolted out the back door; Emma followed him.

Standing in the courtyard, which was full of the scent of the herb garden, he turned to her.

'Why won't she let me help her?' he asked.

'Judith has made the most difficult decision of her life to go for quality over quantity. She was always a woman who put quality first.'

Miles allowed himself to smile as he brushed away his tears. 'You know her well.'

'And I know how much it means to her to make this decision, and whether – for selfish reasons – we agree with her or not, we have to respect it,' Emma said as she moved closer to Miles and placed her hand on his shoulder.

'Come in and eat; be with your mother.'

'But she won't let me help her. I have the money. Why would she do this to us?'

'Money can't solve this. Please don't lose this time in anger. Respect her decision, and enjoy being with her. Your mother loves you so much, and you have a lot of catching up to do.'

She reached over to comfort him, but he drew her into an

embrace, and kissed her softly on the lips. When he pulled back, he seemed as surprised by it as she was.

'Thank you, Emma,' he said before going back inside.

She waited for a few moments, savouring still the kiss, unsure what had just happened. When she went back into the kitchen, Miles was sitting beside his mother, and holding her hand. Emma's heart lurched, because she had never seen Judith look so happy.

THIRTY-SIX

Two weeks passed and Judith was well, so well that at times everybody forgot about the diagnosis, but they were cruelly brought back to reality when they heard her coughing until she threw up, the noise reaching every corner of the big house. Judith insisted on uploading a TikTok video every second day, picking her favourite outfits for what she called one last outing.

It was a bright, dry morning, and Emma was ready, and set up by the lake waiting for Judith to appear in a confection of net and feathers.

She had set out the brief the night before: a sumptuous gown to wear strolling by the lake, and could somebody quieten down or drive the ducks away – they rather took from the calm serenity of the swans.

Emma was ready to offload a big bag of crumbs in the rushes away from the jetty when filming was about to start, though she wasn't sure how she would get the swans to stay in the shot.

She was due to prepare a jam delivery, and she was anxious to get the TikTok video out of the way.

Sitting on the grass, she let her mind wander past the lake

and the estate, to a time when she had a job, where she was challenged every day and had ambitions for promotion.

Here, she was hiding out still, and glad to have any paid work, and a roof over her head, but she needed to carve out a proper niche for herself. She had to stop hiding, but even the thought of stepping out strangled at her throat, and made her afraid all over again.

Emma didn't know what would happen to her after; she couldn't even articulate what was to come. Tears pricked at her eyelids, and when she heard Judith calling from the front door, she pretended not to hear so she had time to compose herself.

'Yoo-hoo, can you come back up, and help me with my outfit?'

When Emma came closer, Judith gestured to her to hurry up.

'Darling, I have a conundrum. Do I go wonderfully vintage or with a Marsha copy? She dropped it up yesterday as a gift, and it is divine; tulle net, sparkles, the lot. She is a genius with the sewing machine.'

'Why did she make a dress?'

'To say thank you and to give me joy; she knows me so well.'

Judith led the way to the kitchen where the dress, a confection in blue and silver beads, was laid across the table.

'Isn't it magnificent? It's her copy of a Dior dress, just look at the detail.'

'What's the conundrum? It's beautiful.'

Judith grimaced. 'I had my jewellery and headpiece set out for another dress, and now I don't think I will have time to get ready for our photo shoot and we want the morning light on the lake...'

Emma put her hands on Judith's shoulders.

'We can do it all; it won't take long. And if we can't, we can try another day. Are you sure there isn't something else wrong?'

'I am just being silly, wanting to look pretty.'

Emma took the dress, and examined the exquisite detailing around the bodice, the two underskirts of tulle which would give it a nice kick out when Judith walked. 'I think for the sake of peaceful relations with the gate lodge, it might be wise to TikTok with this dress,' she said.

Judith took her dress. 'It is why I employed you in the first place; you're so calm and sensible.' She looked directly at Emma. 'I wonder if you are like our swans? All calm for everybody to see, gliding through life, but pedalling furiously in secret.'

'I hope you don't expect me to answer that. Let's get you down to the lake while the light is still good.'

'First, help me get into the dress and pick some nice jewellery to complement it.'

Emma followed Judith upstairs.

'It is time to show you one of my favourite pieces in my jewellery collection, and it should set off Marsha's dress beautifully,' she said as she sat down at her dressing table. Opening a silver jewellery box, she took out a key, and unlocked a drawer in her mahogany dressing table.

'Miles says I should keep my pieces in a safe or a bank vault, but I tell him what good are they to me locked away. I humour him by locking this drawer, but really, I love to wear them. Down through the years, whenever he came to visit, I wore a beautiful necklace, doing the most basic things around the house.'

'You shouldn't have teased him so.'

'My son, I always say, is wonderful, but he needs to lighten up,' Judith said, snapping open a box to show an elaborate heart-shaped old gold pendant on a yellow gold chain.

'Antique diamond and amethyst pendant. It was my mother's, and I hoped someday to pass it on to my son's wife for her wedding day, though I am hardly going to get that honour.'

Emma put her hand out to touch the necklace.

'Eighteen-carat yellow gold. Note the clarity of the stone; it is a beautiful piece. My mother said her mother gave it to her on her wedding morning. My grandfather had it designed for his bride to be.'

Emma pulled her hand away.

'I think Miles might be right; you shouldn't just have it in a drawer.'

'Nonsense, girl. This necklace needs to be appreciated, to be touching skin. Here, try it on.'

She held up the necklace, letting it sway on the chain, catching the sunshine streaming in through the window.

'I can't wear it,' Emma said, pulling away.

'Why not? Putting on something beautiful and expensive is such a special feeling.'

'But this is an important family piece, it wouldn't feel right.'

Judith placed the necklace at her neck. 'You can at least fasten the clasp for me,' she said. Dropping her dressing gown, she then took Marsha's dress and pulled it over her head.

'It makes me feel young again.' Judith twirled in front of the mirror. 'I don't think I need anything on my head. Are we ready for the shoot?' she asked, slipping on a flat pair of shoes.

'They will be hidden under the hem – no point wearing high heels if I don't have to,' she said, leading the way downstairs.

On the front steps, Judith stopped and looked out over the lake.

'The lake is where you will find me, when I am gone,' she said, before setting off down the hill.

Judith did a pirouette half way down. 'Hopefully the swans cooperate. The sun is out, so hurry; it will catch the sparkle on the dress.'

'Yes ma'am.'

'I am sounding like a sergeant major, I apologise.' She shimmied down to the lake, and smiled broadly.

'Let me dance along the water's edge,' Judith said, and Emma laughed, holding up the phone to film her in her long ball gown and wedding necklace, beside the lake at Killcawley Estate.

'And cut,' Judith said after she had twirled and cavorted at the water's edge.

She told Emma she wanted to say something special to her followers.

When Emma called out 'action', Judith turned to the camera, a big smile on her face.

'My darlings, with your help, we have stopped the motorway, and saved Killcawley Estate, the wonderful old oak tree and our beautiful village. I thank you all from the bottom of my heart,' she said, bowing low to the camera.

Miles had been out riding, and was leading his horse back to the stables when he spotted them coming up the hill.

'Why are you so elaborately dressed?' he asked his mother.

'Isn't it divine? Marsha made it for me.'

Miles laughed. 'Honestly, you're as bad as each other.'

'Miles, darling, you need to enjoy life; live a little. We all have our ways of making ourselves happy, and this is mine.'

'I have to untack the horse. But Mother, I need to talk to you,' he said.

'I will be resting in my room, but still wearing this magnificent dress. There is something I want to talk about too,' Judith said, before petting Millie, then heading inside.

'She is looking tired,' Miles said to Emma.

'She gave her all for a TikTok by the lake.'

'Please make sure she rests,' Miles said as he led the horse around to the stables.

Emma checked that Judith was OK, before heading off for the meadows and the oak tree.

A sadness had been growing inside her. She knew nobody at Killcawley Estate owed her anything. These fields she loved were not hers; she was merely passing through. The jam business was Killcawley Estate's business, and the TikTok videos and account which had gained millions of followers was not hers either. All she had from Killcawley Estate were cherished memories of a time when she had nothing, and an old lady took her in and helped her piece her life back together again.

Leaning up against the oak tree, she thought of Judith. She knew she was being selfish worrying about herself right now, but she didn't know what she could do, where she could go; she didn't know how she could be happy away from Killcawley Estate.

When she heard someone frantically shouting for her from the top of the wildflower meadow, Emma knew something was badly wrong. Jack was gesturing madly at her. Her phone rang; it was Miles.

'Emma, come quickly. Mother has collapsed.'

The phone went dead. Fear paralysed her for a moment, but then she sprinted up the hill. When she ran through the walled garden, she saw the courier van outside the jam shed, and she dithered.

Who cares about jam now, she thought. She was about to rush in the back door, when Miles called her around to the front.

Judith, still in her ball gown, was lying on the ground, a pillow under her head.

'The ambulance is on the way,' Miles said gruffly as Emma collapsed to her knees, and took Judith's hands.

The courier said he had to leave but would call back for the order tomorrow.

Miles asked Emma to go and get the package. 'Mum had done most of it, and was out here talking to the man before they went around to collect it, when she suddenly collapsed,' he said.

'I meant to do it, but I forgot.'

Emma, tears streaming down her face, ran to the shed to get the two boxes of jam.

Judith had not only packed them, but she had also addressed them. When she got back to the front of the house, the ambulance had arrived, and Judith was on a trolley and about to be transported to hospital.

Jack asked to go in the ambulance.

Miles kissed his mother softly.

'I will follow behind in the car,' he said. He jumped in the front seat, and drove off after the ambulance, leaving Emma on her own.

Wrapping her arms around herself, she stood alone, the big house behind her, and the long, lonely avenue ahead of her.

Marsha hurried up the driveway. 'What has happened? Is it Judith?' she cried.

Emma nodded.

'What exactly happened?"

Emma shook her head.

Marsha put her arm around her waist, and led Emma inside.

'We will sit and compose ourselves, and then we will lock up and I will drive us to the hospital. We need to be there,' she said.

A half an hour later they walked down the avenue together and got into Marsha's car.

At the hospital, Emma made to walk to the reception desk, but Marsha pulled her back.

'We'll ring Jack. They will never let us up to see J; we're not relatives.'

Jack answered on the second ring, and offered to come downstairs to them.

When he came down in the lift, Emma thought he looked old and haggard.

'She is being kept in overnight. She is on oxygen and they will let her home tomorrow, providing all her care is in place,' he said.

'What exactly is it?' Marsha asked,

'Does it matter? It's the beginning of the end,' Jack said, tears flowing down his face.

'What do you need?' Emma asked.

'I am going to stay with her overnight. Can you go home and get her room ready? Also, she will need somewhere comfortable in the drawing room and kitchen. Her days of doing TikTok are over. Miles will follow home later.'

Marsha wrapped Jack in a tight hug. 'Don't you worry about a thing, the A-team are on it,' she said.

They waited until Jack had got in the lift before they left.

'That poor man. Life is so unfair,' Marsha said as they made their way back to the car.

They were only just in the gates of Killcawley Estate when Miles pulled in after them.

Emma crossed the courtyard to talk to him, but Miles brushed her off, saying he needed to be on his own.

Emma followed him at a slow pace. He headed to the field where the horses were grazing. She saw him walk up to Millie and bury his head in her neck. Not sure whether she should approach him, Emma turned away, but immediately fell over a drinking trough. Miles turned around as the horses galloped off.

'What are you doing here?' he asked.

'I came to see if you were all right.'

'And nearly caused a stampede.'

'I'm sorry,' she said, scrambling to her feet.

He opened the paddock gate for her. 'Emma, I upset you earlier, and I apologise. I just got such a fright.'

'I know, I feel it was my fault. I should have done the jam order. I feel awful she had to bother herself with it. How is she?'

'She was complaining fiercely when I was leaving that

nobody had brought her a nightgown, so I think we can take it she's picked up a bit.'

Emma threw her hands in the air. 'I should have brought one, I completely forgot.'

Miles laughed. 'It is such a relief to think our Emma is not as perfect as my mother makes her out to be.'

They walked back to the house side by side, not needing to talk further, but his hand found hers and she liked that.

THIRTY-SEVEN

By the time Judith was brought home by ambulance the next day, a single bed had been set up in the drawing room, and another in the kitchen, to one side of the AGA.

'Darling, I can't go in the drawing room. That painting of the eighteen-year-old girl would look down on me, and mock seventy-five-year-old Judith, who couldn't stay forever young. I need a bubble bath, to get the hospital out of my pores. I need to feel silk near my skin; I may be an old lady, but I will not wear a hospital gown longer than I have to,' Judith said as Jack picked her up and carried her upstairs.

Marsha called after them not to forget supper club was now a late lunch club, and served at 3 p.m.

'The poor thing will be too tired if we wait until the late evening. I have cooked all J's favourite Indian dishes,' Marsha said to nobody in particular. Miles said he had to check on the horses, and he went off, while Emma escaped to her own room.

A sadness had descended on the big house, and it was hard to handle. Nobody acknowledged it, but everyone was afraid of what was to come; afraid when they wasted time on normal things, but at the same time, craving a normality that would never be achieved again. Emma leaned against the window, and looked out at the lake, where it seemed even the ducks weren't their usual selves. She heard Judith give out to Jack, complaining that he was treating her like a baby by running a lukewarm bath. Emma left the room, unable to listen to the banter, knowing that in a short period of time, Judith's voice would not be heard at Killcawley Estate. That thought was unbearable.

She darted down the stairs to go outside for a walk. She needed to clear her head, to recharge. She needed to sky-walk, even if the sky was blanketed with cloud with no spaces between. It mirrored her brain, like a thick fog had descended everywhere.

Grabbing a jacket from the hook in the hall, she slipped out the front door in case Marsha roped her into the cooking. Moving quickly towards the rhododendrons, she headed for the paddocks and distant wild meadows.

The last time she had been here with Judith, they had laughed and giggled as they walked across the first paddock, and through the wildflower meadows. Emma smiled to think of Judith sky-walking with her, and she wondered why they had not got to do it together any other time. So much had happened since then. Putting her head down against the breeze blowing in from the Irish Sea, she concentrated on her steps. Moving through the stile to the meadows, she stopped in her tracks when she saw the tractor and mower in the middle of the field, where Jack had left it when he got the call about Judith's collapse. Walking over to the mower, she noticed Jack's jacket was thrown over the side because he had forgotten it in his panic. The time could be marked in hours since everything had changed, but it felt like weeks. The pain of what was happening to Judith was heavy on her heart.

Glancing up the at the sky, she saw the cloud cover had moved from grey to silvery white. Holding her hands out, she moved in circles, slowly picking up speed until she felt as if her head might burst. She dropped to the ground. She wanted to curl up and keep her eyes closed, to blot out the last while, to go back to the lazy, boring days at Killcawley Estate, when all she did was video Judith in vintage outfits.

Opening her eyes, she willed the clouds to break free of each other, so that they could receive her thoughts and prayers. She stayed like this for a while, staring up at the sky, squinting through the brightness, and hoping to feel the relief and joy that sky-walking usually brought.

'What happened? Are you OK?'

Emma turned to see Miles running towards her. She scrambled to her feet as Miles, out of breath with Benny running beside him and barking in excitement, reached her.

'Did you trip? It didn't look like you tripped?'

'Were you watching me?'

'I was checking on the horses.'

'I'm OK, I was just looking at the clouds.'

'Lying on the ground looking at the clouds? Hardly a day for it, but I guess it takes all sorts,' he said lightly.

Embarrassed, Emma said she had to get back to help Marsha.

Miles reached out, and took her hand. 'Can I walk you back to the house?' he asked.

She agreed and they tramped, mainly single file, across the fields, stopping to watch the horses, who were feeding on haylage in the near paddock. When they got back to the big house, they heard Marsha and Judith laughing upstairs.

'She has brought saris for all the women to wear; she says you're to join them, and she will dress you,' said Jack, who was sitting at the table drinking a glass of wine.

As she walked up the stairs, Emma was surprised to hear more laughter coming from Judith's rooms. After the quiet sadness in the house, it was a welcome sound. Tentatively, she knocked on the door.

Marsha, who was wearing a saffron yellow sari with a rich red and gold border, swung back the door, and pulled her into the room.

'Please tell this silly woman she will look amazing in a sari. I have the most exquisite purple silk sari with a rich green sparkling border for her. And look, I've even got a green blouse for underneath,' Marsha said.

Judith said she didn't want to dress for dinner.

'Judith McCarthy, I never thought I would hear those words come from your mouth. We three women are going to dress up in these gorgeous saris for our Indian supper club. We will all look sensational.'

Judith pointed to the oxygen tank.

'Nothing is going to look sensational on me when I have to drag this about.'

'I am sure we can tie a silk bow on it. And anyway, what does it matter? You're with family.'

Marsha turned to Emma. 'I have a lovely pink sari for you; do you know how to wear one?'

'I'm afraid I don't.'

'Well, let's get you done first, and when J here sees how lovely a sari is on, she will be persuaded,' Marsha said.

After Emma had stepped into the underskirt and put on the blouse, Marsha unfurled the pink sari, which had a deep border of silver. Deftly, she tucked in the fabric all around the waist of the underskirt. Emma giggled at the feel of Marsha's cold fingers as she pulled, tucked and pinned until the skirt and pleats were in place, and the fabric was also draped over one of Emma's shoulders, the *pallu* hanging down her back, the pink and silver glinting in the light.

'I don't know if I can walk in it,' Emma said.

'Nonsense, girl; you'll get used to it and then you won't want to take it off.'

'It makes me feel very elegant and tall,' Emma said.

'I told you; soon it will feel like a second skin,' Marsha said, and Emma had to agree there was a style and comfort about the sari which she had not known about until now.

'How do you know how to wear a sari?' she asked Marsha

'When you live in India and you want to fit in, one must learn a lot of new things, but this was the most enjoyable,' she said.

Judith walked all around Emma, examining the garment. 'Quite beautiful. I am ready, Marsha, for you to do your magic,' she said.

Marsha unfurled the purple sari, and Judith gasped.

'I have a feeling if I were to do another TikTok video, it would be in a sari. It is simply divine, and I love the softness of the silk. And look how it drapes,' Judith said, making sure to stand in front of the long mirror, so she could watch Marsha closely as she tucked and arranged the fabric.

When she was finished, Marsha stood back, a satisfied look on her face.

'Now we are ready for my special biryani and my brinjal curry with a nice beef curry as well,' she said, clapping as the others shuffled out of the room. Emma stepped back, and let Marsha first down the stairs, her hands out in case anyone tripped. Emma brought the oxygen carrier for Judith.

In the kitchen, Jack waltzed Judith across the floor slowly, but they had to stop half way when she began to cough. They put her sitting up in the bed beside the AGA with silk cushions behind her and a hospital tray on wheels, so she could at least try the biryani and curry. The food was delicious, but everybody noticed that Judith barely picked at it. Hetty tried to coax her to have a little more, but Judith said she was full.

Marsha gabbled on about India, and the others indulged

her, because nobody felt much like being in any way entertaining.

Judith asked for a spoon and glass, and clinked them loudly.

'I want to thank Marsha for this wonderful spread, and I want to say to all of you, snap out of it. I want to fight over politics, gossip about people I know, and laugh at celebrities. Hetty, you surely have some gossip for us all. Darlings, in time this supper club will have an empty chair where I once held court. But I am here now, and I want – for this day – things to be back to almost normal.'

Marsha clicked her tongue, and muttered it was difficult because they were so worried.

'I have a way for getting around worry,' Judith said, but Marsha looked at her doubtfully.

Judith pulled herself up on her pillows.

'Jack, get yourself a whiskey. Miles, I'm sure I have a duty-free bottle of crémant hidden in the cupboard under the sink. It should be chill enough from being there against the outside wall. While Miles pours us all some bubbly, please, Emma, put on some nice jazz music to get the mood going.'

Miles popped the crémant, and poured it into flutes.

'To my mother, who even now can be the life and soul of the party and the supper club,' Miles said, and they all cheered.

Jack got the hospital wheelchair, and helped Judith into it then rolled it across the room, making her laugh with delight. Miles asked Marsha to dance, but she told him not to be stupid, and to pick on a girl more his age.

Emma was both embarrassed and exhilarated when Miles waltzed her around the room. Marsha and Hetty moved like ballet dancers between them, making everyone laugh. They were all on the second glass of crémant when Judith said she would have to be a party pooper, and call it a day.

'Darlings, thank you for making such a supreme effort to

accommodate me and my oxygen tank,' she said as Jack carried her up the stairs.

Marsha offered to help clear up, but Miles insisted he was on dish duty, and Hetty said she would help him.

Emma and Marsha wandered to the drawing room to have a coffee.

'I feel it in my bones, it won't be long now,' Marsha said.

'How do you know?' Emma asked.

'I don't, but for Judith's sake it should be soon, before she becomes totally incapacitated. She would hate that.'

Marsha texted her nephew to drive up the avenue, and collect her and Hetty, and Emma saw them off at the front door.

She was halfway up the stairs to bed when Miles asked would she like to join him for a drink. He poured a Baileys for Emma, and a small brandy for himself.

'Can we talk jam?' he said.

'Yes, but why?'

'Your little business has done extraordinarily well, and I would like it to continue.'

'It's Judith's jam business, and it's your jam business.'

'But it would be nothing without you.'

He sat on the couch beside Emma. 'You're going to have to expand, and we won't have capacity for that in this kitchen-table enterprise. I have had talks with a factory in the next town, and I think they'll be able to keep up to the production levels required.'

'What do you mean?'

'Emma, you don't honestly expect to keep up with demand? Even if you stayed up all night, you still wouldn't be able to make enough jam. It really is time to consider moving the enterprise to a bigger premises.

'But isn't the whole point that it's homemade?'

Miles shook his head.

'I am astounded how alike you and Judith are. You're using

a homemade recipe, but even for health and safety standards, you need to be in the proper environment.'

'Have you talked to Judith about this?'

'I was rather hoping to get your agreement first, and you can help me persuade my mother. She can be a stubborn fool at times.'

Emma petted Benny who had wandered in to sit at her feet.

'I'm not sure what my role would be in this new enterprise?'

'I think Killcawley Estate Preserves needs a public face, and you can be that; especially now that everything else is out of the way. We would of course pay you a salary.'

'And what would be your role?'

'I will look after the advertising and the finance, as well as looking after the farm; I have taken a sabbatical from my New York office, but I am hoping if everything goes well here, I won't have to go back to my Manhattan job.'

Emma stopped stroking the dog.

'Have you told Judith?'

'I have only just decided, but let's get back to you. We will agree a salary, and put everything in a contract,' he said.

'Thank you, but can I have some time to think about it?'

'Please do, but you know it will make my mother the happiest woman in the world to know you are staying on at Kill-cawley Estate.'

'I know,' Emma said.

'I would also like to say, I can't imagine trying to run the place without, not only Mother, but you too.'

'Thank you for saying that,' she said, her voice full of emotion, as she inched closer to him.

'I mean it, Emma. You're part of Killcawley Estate now.'

'If feels like that for me too,' she said.

His eyes flicked up to meet hers. She hadn't realised they were a hazel colour.

'I like having you around, Emma,' he said.

'I like being here.'

He reached over, and kissed her softly on the lips.

She kissed him back, and that moment, she felt at home. When he eventually pulled away, she was disappointed.

'I have to meet the solicitor to make sure Judith's will is in order,' he said.

She watched him walk away, but she wanted more than anything to call him back.

THIRTY-EIGHT

Emma spent most of her days after that by Judith's bed upstairs. Jack barely rested and spent nights with Judith, only allowing himself to sleep for a few hours when Emma and Miles took over. They were meant to do it in shifts, but more often than not, they both stayed, sometimes sitting in silence, and other times talking quietly to each other.

Sometimes, they sat beside each other or on either side of Judith's bed as she slept, providing a drink with a straw when she needed, and oxygen when required.

Miles didn't talk much at first. There was between them a quiet, working silence; the sort of silence of those watching over the sick. Emma found it strangely comforting.

One night, when Judith was sleeping peacefully, they pulled their chairs together at the window, looking at the moonlight streaking across the lake.

'She wants to make a last TikTok down by the lake tomorrow,' Emma said.

'Is she going to pretend that all is well?'

'No, she is going to wear the oxygen mask and say goodbye.'

'No doubt she will wear something extraordinary, and manage to look exquisite at the same time.'

'She has picked a ball gown for the occasion,' Emma said.

Miles shook his head. 'Of course she has; my mother always makes her statements in fashion. She once came to a parent–teacher meeting dressed in crimson, and a large black hat with red ostrich feathers. Seemingly, she was protesting at the introduction of a school uniform, which she said would stifle all creativity. I was dreadfully embarrassed, but everybody else said she was great. I know now, she was amazing.'

'Is that why you went to the States?'

'What do you mean?'

'It can be hard to live with somebody so flamboyant.'

'There was a bit of that; but I wanted to make my own life. As a young man, I didn't want to be tied to Killcawley Estate.'

'Judith has really missed you.'

He wiped his hands down his face. 'I know that.'

They sat quietly for a while, until Miles began to speak again.

'I know now my mother lived with the expectation of saving Killcawley Estate. I felt that too as I grew older. I needed to run away from it; I needed to know there was something else I could do, that I was good at. Does any of that make sense?'

'Yes, it does, but you're back now, when it matters.'

Tears flowed down Emma's face.

'Hey, what's wrong?' Miles asked.

'It's so unfair that Judith became ill again.'

'It's almost as if she needed permission to stand down.'

Emma spotted Jack walking by the lake. 'I bet he couldn't sleep; he's taking this so hard,' she said.

Miles looked down at Jack, who was skimming stones across the lake, ripples of water breaking through the reflected moonbeams.

'Jack is a good man; Judith would never have managed all these years if it were not for him.'

'I know.'

'Hey, can we lighten things up?' Miles asked.

'I'm not sure we can; these days here are hard.'

Miles reached over, and took Emma's hand. 'I have an idea. Like you have your timeout looking at the sky, I want to show you what I used to do when I lived here in the big house, when everybody was asleep,' he said. 'When the house was quiet, I always slipped out of bed, and the estate was mine, and mine only. Let me show you.'

He pulled her up from the chair.

'Mother is sleeping soundly, we have a few minutes.'

They padded out of the room together, Miles still holding her hand.

'First, we go to the top landing,' he said.

She giggled like a young girl playing hooky. At the top landing, Miles looked at Emma.

'The best high in the world is sliding down these banisters from floor to floor. My mother always said it was too dangerous, and that made it even more exciting.'

He straddled the banister, and slid down to the next landing, laughing.

'Come on, don't be a chicken, follow me,' he said.

Emma hesitated.

'Come on, it's fun,' he said.

She trusted Miles, so she got on the banister, screeching as she slid down.

He caught her and they both laughed.

'Could you have been any louder?' he said, grinning.

'Do you think we woke Judith?'

'If we did, I think this is one occasion where she would approve,' he said. 'Now, for the second set of banisters.'

'Are you sure?'

He slid down to the next floor. Emma followed, both of them trying to hide their giggles as they moved on the third banister down to the hall.

In the hall, Miles caught Emma, setting her down gently. She turned around giggling. She was looking into his eyes when Jack came through from the kitchen.

'What are you two doing?' he asked.

'Having a little bit of fun,' Miles said, and Emma detected his reluctance to let her go.

'I'm glad you're both here. I was wondering if I could have a private word?' he said, gesturing for them to follow him into the drawing room.

Indicating to Miles and Emma to sit on the couch, Jack sat on the velvet armchair opposite.

'I wanted to ask your permission, Miles, and your opinion, Emma, on whether at this late stage, I should ask for Judy's hand in marriage.'

Emma grinned. 'Definitely yes, it's so romantic.'

Jack smiled broadly at Emma. 'I know, and I think it would be a beautiful focus for us both, but I know Miles you are a legal expert, and you may have your reservations.'

Miles scratched his head, and looked at Jack. 'It makes everything complicated.'

'I am willing to sign anything to say I have no claim over Killcawley Estate, anything to ease your mind to make sure the wedding can go ahead. I am fairly confident Judy will say yes.'

Miles moved to the window. 'This is a lot to take in,' he said.

Emma got up and put her hand on his shoulder. 'It's what Judith would want, more than anything.'

Miles caught Emma's hand, and squeezed it tight. He kept hold of her as he turned to Jack.

'This is not complicated at all. You're my father, and you love each other. You have my blessing, Jack. I have known you all my life. I know you are a man of your word. You will always have a home here.'

Jack walked over, and hugged Miles hard.

'Thank you, my son,' he whispered as he reached into his pocket, and took out a green velvet box.

Snapping it open, he held up the box to show them two gold rings: a diamond solitaire and an eternity ring.

'I got the eternity ring for her. I thought it was...' His voice broke, and Emma put her arm around his shoulders.

'She will love it, Jack.'

Miles turned back to the window, his shoulders shuddering.

'We have to be strong, especially now,' Emma said to him. 'Let Judith have the excitement of a wedding to the man she has adored all these years.'

Miles kicked the wall. 'It is so bloody unfair that she is dying.'

'Look forward, Miles, we have to.'

'I wish she had let me bring her to the States; we could have bought time for us all with her.'

'No more talk like that,' Jack said. 'Judy and I were lucky. We loved each other all these years, and for a long time there wasn't a day we didn't have a kind word to say to each other, or a day when we didn't pass a sweet smile. These last few months have been especially precious, and something we never expected. We are lucky; please don't pity us.'

Miles nodded and wished Jack luck with the proposal. As Jack headed out into the hallway, Emma reached and gently rubbed his hand.

'A wedding is just what we need around here,' she said.

They knew Judith must have said yes, because a short while later they heard her shout out and laugh upstairs.

. . .

'How is that poor woman going to have a wedding? She can hardly even walk about these days,' Marsha said the following day.

'We will just have to make sure she has the best day ever.'

Marsha rubbed the tears from her eyes. 'I so want to make her wedding dress. I hope she agrees. Our Judith will look simply stunning in what I have planned,' she said, her voice cracking.

Emma gripped Marsha by the shoulders. 'We have to be brave, we just have to,' she said.

'I know,' Marsha snuffled. 'It's just so hard to think of this place without J.'

'It is,' Emma said.

Jack kicked open the kitchen door, and carried Judith to the bed by the AGA. She was wearing a long blue sequin dress with cap sleeves covered in ostrich feathers. Emma thought she looked like a beautiful, delicate china doll.

'What do you think? With all the weight I have lost, I can finally fit in to a size six, and this long straight dress sets off my figure,' Judith said, holding her hand out to Emma. 'Notice anything different?'

Emma made a big deal of the rings, and they called Miles in from the garden.

'Darling, do you mind?' Judith asked him.

'I am delighted, but when is the big day?'

'We want a simple service by the lake with a champagne reception and a small supper club gathering here,' Judith said.

Marsha, who had been in the drawing room dusting and hoovering, rushed in.

'What is all the noise about?' she asked.

When she saw Judith's rings, she took her hand and kissed it. 'This is a good day. When is the wedding?'

'We thought on Friday,' Jack said.

Marsha gasped. 'Friday? You mean three days from now. How are we going to do that?'

'All that matters is that we are together in front of you, our family and friends, and professing our love for each other.'

Emma looked at Marsha. 'I think Marsha might have some ideas for a wedding dress.'

Marsha was grinning from ear to ear. 'It will be a surprise. I will create the best gown for you, J.'

'I will leave it all to you, my friend. I have every confidence in you,' Judith said.

Marsha clapped her hands and shook herself. 'I can do it – produce a wonderful wedding gown in three days. This is where everything else has been leading me. This is why I am the best seamstress this side of Dublin.'

Judith laughed before turning to Jack and instructing him to carry her to the lake.

'It's time for the last TikTok,' she said, and Emma followed them down to the jetty.

The swans and ducks floated about, too busy pecking at the water and squabbling among themselves to take much note of Judith as she sat on a chair Jack had set out for her. He had also put out a little table for her oxygen carrier.

'How would you like to do this?' Emma asked.

'I will say a little something, that's all. But maybe not so many close ups this time, darling.'

Jack stood to the side, his arms folded, watching Judith's every move.

Emma called 'action', because she knew Judith would want her to use that word.

Judith slipped a small piece of paper from under her neckline and unfurled it slowly.

'Hello friends. Thank you for dropping by. I can say with certainty this will be my last appearance on TikTok. What do you think of the dress? Blue sequins, soft ostrich feathers; it just makes me feel a million dollars.

'Let's concentrate on the good news. I am so happy to tell you all that I am to be married in the next few days, to a man I have loved all my life. It will be a small, intimate affair, and one I will cherish to my last breath.

'I don't have many days left. I suppose I should be telling you all the important things to remember in life. I can only ask you to love each other, grab every opportunity that comes your way, and please, dress well and with pride. *Au revoir*.'

Emma did a close up as Judith blew a kiss. She wanted to scream that it wasn't fair, but instead she called 'cut', and Judith laughed out loud.

'Maybe, just maybe, this one will go viral,' Judith said.

Jack said they had better get her back to the house as it was a little chilly down by the water.

'What are you afraid of, man, that I may die of the cold? You silly, silly, kind and lovely man,' she said.

Jack carried her up the hill to the house, Emma videoing from behind, because she wanted the memory of the two of them ribbing each other and chortling.

THIRTY-NINE

There was a flurry of activity at Killcawley Estate over the next two days. Judith said she would rest up in readiness for the big day, but everybody knew she was not able to leave her bed.

Jack stayed upstairs with her, alternating with Miles and Emma throughout each day.

Emma rang a local restaurant, and ordered all of Judith's favourite food for the wedding supper club meal.

Marsha moved her sewing machine up to the big house because she said she didn't want to miss out on the wedding preparations, even if she had to work day and night to get the wedding dress finished.

Emma saw her pull her car into the courtyard on the first morning of the preparations, and ran out to help her carry in her sewing paraphernalia. Marsha insisted on lifting the machine because she didn't want it to drop on the cobbles.

She told Emma to get the bolt of fabric on the back seat. Emma tugged at the bolt, which was wrapped in plastic, and managed to stagger with its weight across the courtyard to the kitchen table, where she plonked it down.

'Careful, careful, that is the finest silk,' Marsha said, bustling over to tear away the plastic.

Ivory silk embroidered with silver and gold flowers tumbled onto the table.

'I thought Judith said something simple. She hardly expects silk,' Emma said.

'Do you, or do you not know Judith McCarthy? When did she ever dress down in her life? J would be disappointed if I took that nonsense literally.'

'You two know each other inside out,' Emma said, laughing.

Marsha unfurled the silk, letting it slither down the table.

'It's my honour to create a beautiful wedding gown for Judith.'

Emma fingered the silk. 'It's so beautiful. Where did you get it at such short notice?'

'I have had it decades, darling, but there was never an opportunity until now to use it,' Marsha said.

'And you never sewed any of it for yourself?'

'A story for another time; maybe over a coffee, when I have made a start on this dress,' Marsha said, reaching for her basket, and pulling out her notebook.

Emma gasped when she saw the sketch Marsha had done of a simple dress, the silk cut on the bias so it hugged the body, a soft cowl neck and long sleeves tucked into a deep cuff. The skirt flared out into a wide train at the back.

'Simple, and yet so exquisite,' Emma said.

'There's nothing simple about sewing silk, darling. Way too slippery for the needle.'

Marsha dug further into her basket, and pulled out a big envelope. 'I was up all night making the paper pattern. You can help me pin it to the silk. I have to get it cut out this morning, and start the tacking and sewing the long seams by this afternoon.'

Emma watched as Marsha measured, and placed the pattern pieces before carefully pinning them in place.

'Take a few straight pins and start down the other end, like a good girl,' Marsha said.

'Are you sure? I've never done anything like this.'

'You young people these days, no skills. Time you learned, my dear.'

'But not on this important dress. I'll make coffee and you can get organised. I would be afraid of damaging the fabric.'

'Well I'm sure there are a lot of other things to do. I don't have time to chat, so hold the coffee until I have the dress pieces cut out.'

Emma felt she was in Marsha's way, so she retreated to the lake, to map out where the ceremony could take place. Jack had placed a small arch at the end of the jetty and chairs around it. A red carpet was ordered, and Jack had asked a florist to deliver enough roses to cover the arch early on the morning of the ceremony.

She sat for a while on the jetty, and listened to the water lap against the shore. There wasn't much peace anywhere at Killcawley Estate; it was like they were all treading water waiting for the main event, and it wasn't the wedding. She couldn't imagine Killcawley Estate without Judith. Even these days, when she spent most of the time in bed, Judith's presence was felt in every room, and especially here at the lake.

Suddenly, Emma jumped up, and ran up the hill to the house. She didn't want to be alone.

Marsha had cut out her pattern, and was sitting with a mug of coffee.

'You abandoned me, so I took my break anyway. There's coffee in the pot.'

'You cut out all the pieces?"

'Yes, and I have enough to make a cape, which I think I will edge with ostrich feathers. J always liked a bit of bling.'

'You're so good to her.'

'I'm not good enough; I never will be, for what she did for me all those years ago.'

'It must have been something big.'

Marsha took a chocolate biscuit, and bit into it.'

'I'm surprised Judith hasn't told you already; this is probably the last secret of Killcawley Estate.'

Marsha topped up her coffee, and leaned against the work-top, because she was afraid of spilling anything on the silk if she sat at the table.

'Go on, tell me,' she said to Marsha, who put her cup down before starting her story.

'Judith took me into her life, and looked after me when I was at my lowest point. There's nothing better one person can do for another.'

'I had no idea.'

'How could you? Judith, for once, had a bit of discretion.'

'If you don't want to talk about it...'

'Girl, that was years ago. For me, and I hope for J, something good, and a deep friendship, came out of it.'

Marsha stood looking out the window as she continued her story.

'I never married, and now Judith gets to marry a second time. I don't resent it; it's just the way life worked out. I told you I lived in India; I didn't tell you why I went there. I was going out with John Reidy, whose family lived on Killcawley main street. We met at school, and we went out for a few years. He wanted us to marry, but I wanted to see the world first. I was set on going somewhere far away. After I got that out of my system, I knew I would be happy to come back to Killcawley, and settle down.'

'There's nothing wrong with that,' Emma said.

'No, but like everything in life, I regret now that I went

away. I should have stayed at home, and married John. It would have changed everything.'

Marsha stopped to gulp her coffee, before continuing.

'John didn't want me to go, but he supported me, and I went off to work with a charity, a group of nuns in Bangalore. I was only supposed to be gone for eight weeks, but I extended for another four. I had got very attached to the children I was helping and teaching.

'John and I wrote letters to each other, but the post service at that time was so slow and so bad. By the time either of us got a letter, everything was out of date. It was a lonely time, but an exciting time too, if you know what I mean.

'I brought that silk back from India. I knew we would marry. When I was away, I never faltered in my love for John, and I know he felt the same. I bought the full bolt of silk to make sure I had enough for whatever pattern I picked.

'I only found my John had died when I got back home. You see I had already left Bangalore for Delhi, to fly back to London and then Dublin, when the telegram arrived in India.

'John had died in a farm accident. The tractor he was driving tumbled over as he cleared a ditch; the ground went from under the machine. By the time I reached Ireland, John was already buried, the funeral done and dusted, and everybody was wearing black, and in mourning. I couldn't cope. His family blamed me for going away in the first place, and even though my family did not put it in so many words, they blamed me too.'

Emma stood up and made to reach out to Marsha, but she pulled away.

'It was my fault, I was the stupid idiot who thought I needed to see the world, when my whole world was right here in Killcawley.'

'You weren't to know,' Emma said.

'All these decades later, I know that, but at the time, I held myself responsible and it was easier for everyone else to do the same. I thought of returning to India, but somehow the allure of faraway hills had dimmed. I was a mess when I first met Judith McCarthy. We never really knew each other at school – I am younger, not that she would ever admit that.

'I used to go for a lot of walks to kill the time, and I met J. She was doing the same, trying to fill in time, and we got talking. We shared our stories. We always met at the bridge near the park, and one morning when I didn't turn up, Judith went to my house looking for me. She insisted my mother check my bedroom. I had taken so many painkillers, I was passed out on the bed. The doctors later said if I had not been discovered when I was, I probably would have died.

'After that, my mother said I had brought shame on the family, and she farmed me out to an aunt in Bray. It wasn't the worst thing for me; my aunt found me a secretarial job, and J preferred coming into the town, where we could shop and have coffee together. That's how our friendship deepened, and though we bicker, it hasn't faltered.

'Years later, I moved back to the family home in Killcawley to take care of Daddy when he was ill, and after he died, I lived there with my mother. Every now and again, I took out the bolt of silk, thinking I would run up a summer dress, but I wasn't able to even look at it.

'When I moved into the gate lodge, I brought it with me, and now, it seems that I bought it all those years ago to make a wedding dress for my best friend.' Marsha's voice faltered. Emma took her by the arm and led her to the table, where she pulled out a chair for Marsha to sit down.

'You're the best kind of friend,' she said.

'I'm not; if I could give my life for J, I would, and I hope she knows it.'

Marsha sniffed and blew her nose, then said she had to get on with her work.

'I'm going to put my head down, and start sewing; if I'm

going to have this dress ready by Thursday night, I'm going to have to push myself to the limit.'

Emma said she had to check with the restaurant that everything was all right for Friday.

'I hope you ordered the chicken curry; it's J's favourite. She says it isn't as good as mine, but I've never believed her,' Marsha said.

'Jack said you two were quite something; two women going out to eat together, when women didn't do that sort of thing. He said you were the first ladies who lunched in Ireland,' Emma said.

'Slight exaggeration, but we'll take it.' Marsha laughed, her face bright once again.

FORTY

Emma and Marsha were examining the dress and cape on the morning of the wedding when the local florist delivered boxes, and boxes of white and blush pink roses to the back door.

'Go and grab a few hours' sleep or you will collapse at the wedding,' Emma told Marsha.

'I napped during the night. I think, with these lovely roses, I can fashion some class of headgear. It's not an occasion for J if there isn't something silly to put on her head,' she said fondly.

'I love all her hats,' Emma said,

'They're great, and I have always envied her strength of character, that she could walk down the street of an Irish village wearing a concoction more suited to a Paris runway. Believe you me, when I was younger, I begged her to dress down.'

'How did that go?'

'Typical J, she became even more outrageous for a while, so I learned to bite my tongue.'

Marsha pulled out a headband wrapped tightly in the ivory silk.

'I thought if I attached some roses and ostrich feathers, she's silly enough to adore it.'

Emma agreed, and helped put wires through the half-open white roses to twist around the headband. They glued on the feathers.

Marsha placed the headband on Emma's head.

'Beautiful, and ridiculous at the same time, just like our Judith,' she said.

They heard Jack shuffle around upstairs, and they hurriedly covered everything up so he didn't see any of the wedding dress.

When he came into the kitchen, Jack looked tired.

'She had a restless night, and Miles stayed with us right through. There will be a lot of tired people at this wedding.' He sighed.

Marsha poured a coffee, and put it in front of him.

'It is what it is. Your suit was delivered this morning, and tell Miles his is here too.'

'He needs to rest; can you take over, Emma?' Jack asked.

Emma nodded and went upstairs, where Miles was slumped in a chair beside his mother's bed. Judith, her head to one side, was sleeping.

'I can take over for a while, you get some rest,' she said.

'Are you sure?'

'Yes, I will call you an hour before the ceremony.'

He squeezed her hand, and mouthed *thank you*, before leaving the room.

Once Miles had left, Judith slowly opened her eyes, and looked around. 'I kept them shut so he would think I was asleep; poor boy needs to rest, and Jack too.'

'How are you?' Emma asked.

'Dying,' Judith said hoarsely, and gestured for Emma to come closer.

'Sorry about the stupid question,' Emma stuttered as she leaned into Judith.

'What are you wearing for the ceremony?' Judith whispered in between taking breaths from her oxygen mask.

'The dress I bought earlier in the year, light pink.'

Judith shook her head. 'I have the perfect creation for you. Go to the wardrobe on the right, and take out the first hanger. Please, for me, wear the dress today,' Judith said, her voice developing into a rasping cough.

Emma helped Judith to sit up, and plumped up the pillows behind her.

When she had placed a wool shawl over Judith's shoulders, she went to the wardrobe, and opened it.

Taking out a hanger covered in a white sheet, she let the sheet fall to the ground to reveal a sleeveless V-neck silk dress in a blue, she thought looked like the sky.

Judith called her over to her bedside, and lowered her mask.

'Cerulean blue for my good friend, who introduced me to sky-walking.'

'I never heard of such a colour, but it's so like the sky,' Emma said, stroking the silk. 'This dress is so gorgeous.'

'One of Marsha's finest. I ordered the silk and had it delivered to the lodge. She made a copy of an Alexander McQueen; I think it will suit you perfectly. I wanted to give it to you when some occasion arose, and today we have an occasion to celebrate,' Judith said.

Emma began to cry, a tear dropping on the dress, seeping in and staining it a darker blue.

'Don't touch it; it will dry, and with the folds, even if there is a little stain, nobody will see, especially Marsha. Now, try it on,' Judith said.

Emma slipped off her jeans and T-shirt. The dress was cinched at the waist with a full, flared, pleated skirt, which grazed Emma's ankles.

Judith made a circular gesture with her hands, telling Emma to do a twirl, and she did, spinning across the carpet.

'Beautiful. Marsha was a little cross I picked silk from Thailand, rather than India, but it was the colour that did it for me.

It's stunning on you. You need a shawl, which is in the top drawer of the chest over there.'

Emma opened the drawer and took out a cream cashmere shawl and draped it over her shoulders.

'Perfect to ward off any chill breeze from the lake,' Judith said.

Emma sat on the bed. 'I don't know what to say.'

'You don't have to say anything.'

Feeling agitated, Emma wandered to the window to look out at the lake. She could see Jack weaving the roses through the arch, and Miles was helping arrange the chairs for the ceremony later.

'I can't even think about you leaving us, Judith.'

Judith took a long puff of her oxygen before she spoke. 'There, there. Please remember I have had a good life, and I am marrying the man I love. I have done a few things to my will to make sure you and Jack and Marsha are looked after. I particularly want you to have my vintage gown collection, and there is a piece of jewellery I have earmarked for you.'

'I don't expect anything; you don't need to do this,' Emma said.

'Nonsense. Marsha is not doing too bad – she gets the gate lodge for life. And Jack, well, he will forever be part of Killcawley Estate because he will want to be near me in death.'

'How does Miles feel about all this?'

'He drew up the papers for me, and we had it witnessed.'

Emma walked back and sat in the armchair beside the bed. 'It won't be the same, without you.'

'But it will be a blessed relief not to have to do the TikTok videos?'

'Not really,' Emma said, trying not to sob.

'We had such a good time, Emma; these last months would have been so boring without you. I thank you for helping me stay here at Killcawley Estate. God knows what silly New York Miles would have done otherwise.'

Emma made to say something in protest.

'Stay here, get to know Killcawley Miles. Maybe, give love a chance,' Judith said.

Emma didn't know how to respond, but Judith said she needed to rest before taking centre stage one last time.

Emma kissed her on her forehead, and went downstairs. Miles, who was standing in the hall, stopped what he was doing when he saw Emma.

'Wow, you look stunning,' he said.

'Judith had Marsha copy a designer dress for me.'

'They picked the right design for you.'

Emma blushed when Miles offered his hand to lead her down the last few stairs. She thought he was going to say something else to her, but Marsha bustled down the hall to announce she was going home to get ready.

'Judith said she wants to see you in a sari,' Emma said.

'I have a brand-new burnt orange silk one from India, not too flashy – I can't take from the bride.'

Emma said she would tidy up the kitchen, and get the table laid for their wedding supper club.

'Change out of that dress before you tidy up. Also, the restaurant dropped off the food, and I put everything in the fridge, and one or two things on the hob. I will be back in a while to help,' Marsha said, waving goodbye.

Emma moved to go back upstairs to change back into her jeans, but Miles gently pulled her to him and kissed her.

She kissed him back, and they stayed close together for a few moments, until Emma pulled away first. Reluctantly, he let her go, and she lingered for a moment before going upstairs.

. . .

Two hours before the ceremony, Marsha returned wearing her new sari. Emma had decorated the wedding table with roses, and was making a small bouquet for Judith.

'How is she?' Marsha asked.

'Miles went up to wake her; he said he will call when she's ready for us.'

'Hetty arranged a harpist – I just hope she doesn't frighten off the swans; Judith loves those swans.'

Emma thought Marsha sounded a little put out that Hetty had come up with such a good idea.

When Miles came downstairs, he was wearing his top hat and tails.

'Don't you look handsome,' Marsha said, and Emma, blushing because he looked so striking, busied herself with the bouquet.

'We had better show Ms Fancy Pants this dress. Let's hope she likes it,' Marsha said, her voice cracking.

Judith was sitting up in bed, her feet dangling over the edge, when Emma and Marsha arrived at her room.

'Darlings, you're going to have your job cut out for you. I am rather afraid I can't stand on my own.'

'Don't worry, Jack has it all worked out for downstairs, and we will manage here,' Emma said, holding up a special wedding gown bag. Marsha stepped forward, and dramatically unzipped the bag to reveal the long dress, the embroidered ivory silk tumbling on to the carpet.

'Marsha, is that your wedding dress silk?' Judith whispered.

'I can't think of a better way to use it,' Marsha said.

Judith reached out, and squeezed her hand.

'Thank you, my dear friend, but will I fit into it?'

'You're a stick insect, of course you will,' Marsha said, but insisted on doing Judith's make-up and hair first.

'We don't want any smudge on this silk,' Marsha said.

They touched Judith's face lightly with a tinted moisturiser and powder, and a little pink lipstick. They swept her hair into a chignon at the back, held by a mother-of-pearl pin.

When the time came to put on the dress, Emma got Judith to her feet, and held her, while Marsha slipped the gown over her head.

Judith asked to see herself in the mirror, and Marsha pulled it across the room, while Emma helped Judith to stand.

Emma continued to hold her as Judith swayed, the silk falling into place around her body. Judith held up the cuffs, and examined the tiny, silk-covered buttons.

'You know me so well, Marsha; such perfect details. This is an exquisite dress. How can I ever thank you?'

'You were there again and again, when nobody else cared,' Marsha said firmly.

Emma reached for another hanger on the back of the door, and took down the silk cape edged in ostrich feathers. Gently, she draped it over Judith's shoulders.

'I have seen you in a lot of wonderful outfits, but I don't think I have ever seen you look so beautiful. I almost wish I could sneak a TikTok video, but I'm not sure Jack would like that,' Emma said.

Judith chuckled, but was stopped in her tracks when she saw Marsha produce the rose and feather fascinator from a paper bag.

'I made this for you; just shows you should have paid me all these years, instead of going off buying stupidly priced fascinators,' Marsha said as she tenderly placed it on Judith's head, before tilting it to one side.

'Wonderful,' Judith whispered, eyeing herself up in the mirror.

She turned to Marsha, and Emma.

'I'm ready to get married, girls. Thank you both. But first, Emma, go and get your dress on. Miles will be here soon to carry me downstairs.'

Emma left Judith sitting on the armchair, and rushed upstairs to get changed. She quickly brushed her hair, and put on make-up, before stepping into the blue dress.

She knew she should be happy, but today she was overwhelmed with sadness. Hoping to calm down, she wandered to the window to take in the lake. Jack was launching a boat out onto the water. Emma smiled to see the musicians on board. Hetty insisted there had to be music wafting over the lake as Jack and Judith made their vows. Marsha said it would have to be tin whistles, because nothing heavy would be allowed or it would sink the boat.

A harpist and flautist were persuaded to take part, and Jack helped them onto the boat. Peter rowed out with slow rhythmic movements to the middle of the lake.

The swans glided off to the side, watching the small group of people gather at the edge of the lake. Hetty had arranged pots of flowers either side of the arch, around which roses and lilies were intertwined.

Pulling up the sash window, Emma listened to the music float across the water. Tears pricked at her eyelids when she remembered her first time here as she escaped her past. She could never have got through it all but for Judith McCarthy, and Killcawley Estate. It shouldn't be like this, a wedding, and a funeral almost together. Life was bloody unfair, she thought.

Her phone rang, interrupting her thoughts. It was Miles, asking her to come to Judith's room.

Judith clapped when she saw her.

'I have the perfect necklace for you, my darling,' she said, pressing a long velvet box into Emma's hands.

'Open it, and Miles will put it on you.'

Emma gasped when she saw the antique diamond and amethyst pendant. 'I can't take this, Judith,' she said.

'Remember when I showed it to you, and the story I told you?'

'I do.'

'Darling, there is only one person I would like to wear this piece of jewellery, and that is you; our Emma, who taught us all so much about life, and overcoming adversity, as well as a bunch on how to make TikTok videos,' Judith said.

Emma looked at Miles.

'Let me help,' he said, carefully lifting the necklace from the box.

Emma felt his fingers on her neck as he struggled with the clasp.

Tears bubbled up in her, but Judith tutted loudly.

'No crying allowed, Emma; today is a happy day,' she commanded as Miles picked her up to carry her downstairs. Emma followed behind.

Hetty was waiting in the hall by the wheelchair, which she had decorated with roses. Miles placed Judith in the wheelchair. Hetty arranged her dress, and handed her the bouquet of roses, before Miles pushed her slowly down the hill towards the jetty, where Jack and the guests were waiting.

Marsha tugged Emma's shawl, and told her to go ahead, and make sure she had a seat. Jack welcomed the wheelchair, and kissed Judith tenderly, before wheeling her up the aisle under the arch, where they were to exchange their vows.

Marsha bawled, and Emma leaned close to Miles as both Jack and Judith declared their undying love, and kissed passionately. The guests smiled, and applauded, and the music drifted over the water.

The swans were the only birds brave enough to come near shore, the two of them gliding past as Judith collapsed into Jack's arms.

He swept her up, and carried her to the big house, where he lay her down on the velvet couch in the drawing room. Marsha set up the oxygen stand, and Miles placed pillows gently behind his mother's head.

Everyone else lingered outside the front door until Jack gave the all-clear for them to come in. Judith gathered herself, and graciously accepted the congratulations of friends, and well-wishers. Miles popped champagne; Hetty and Emma handed out glasses of bubbly to everyone, before Emma stood on a footstool and called for silence.

'Please can I have your attention. As you know, this is just a short champagne reception to celebrate the wedding of our good friends, Judith and Jack, who we all love so dearly. Miles would like to say a few words, and propose the toast.'

Miles stepped forward.

'Mother, if I thought you could, I would twirl you around this room, and we would dance together. I want you to know how much I love you, and how happy I am that Jack has been a constant in your life, and also in mine.

'Maybe not everyone here knows, but Jack is my biological father, and I am immensely proud of that. I can also say that Stephen would be very pleased today, to see Judith so happy with his dear friend, and to see the light of blissful togetherness in your eyes. This is a good and joyful day at Killcawley Estate. Please lift your glasses to Judith and Jack.'

The group held their glasses aloft, and were calling out the names of the newlyweds, when Judith pulled Jack towards her, and tried to say something in his ear. He managed to catch her in his arms as she slumped against him. The crowd around them parted and, led by Miles, Jack carried Judith upstairs to the bedroom as Marsha rushed off to call the palliative care nurse, and the doctor.

Nobody sat at the table for the wedding supper. Nobody went home. Everybody stayed at the front of Killcawley Estate eager to hear the news of Judith McCarthy. Emma and Marsha divided up the supper club food, and handed out small plates of chicken curry, rice and salad.

Hours passed, and darkness rolled in over the lake.

Miles told people to go home; when there was news to tell, he would make sure everybody was informed. Reluctantly, they drifted away as Jack, Miles and Emma stayed with Judith, and Hetty and Marsha sat in the kitchen, unable to talk, unable to do anything, but wait.

Another day was beginning at Killcawley Estate; the birds were singing, and the sun was stealing across the lake, and peeping in the windows of the big house when Judith took her last breath. Jack kissed her gently on the lips, before waking Miles and Emma to tell them the news.

Emma softly stroked Judith's head, before going downstairs to tell Marsha and Hetty, who were slumped over the kitchen table, asleep.

After Marsha was told, she walked around the big house, and drew all the curtains. Hetty, who days earlier had prepared a black bow, walked down the avenue to tie it on the gate.

Miles called the undertaker, and asked for an announcement of his mother's death to be made. Benny, his head down, wandered off through the walled garden to the wildflower meadows, and the oak tree.

Emma walked down to the lake, and sat on the jetty. Eventually, Miles came, and sat beside her. They held hands, and she rested her head on his shoulder. They didn't need to talk.

EPILOGUE

Every day, the dog wandered about looking for Judith. Benny refused to come into the house, and spent most of his time either on the jetty, or curled up under the oak tree. Every morning when Emma came downstairs, he was at the back door waiting to be fed. He always peered into the kitchen as if he expected Judith to be there, before drifting away when she wasn't.

It was the one-month anniversary of Judith's death. Emma was up extra early to prepare food for the supper club. She left the door open, hoping Benny might mooch in. She was surprised to hear the clip-clop of a horse, and Miles walking Millie across the courtyard. When he saw her, Miles led the horse over to the back door.

Turning from the table where she was chopping an aubergine, Emma noticed he was upset.

'Has something happened?' she asked nervously.

'It's Benny. I found him dead under the oak tree. I guess the old dog couldn't keep going without Mother.'

'Poor thing; we should bury him.'

'I already have; it felt right to bury him where he wanted to die. Benny was always with Mother, when she met Jack under the oak tree.'

Tears rose up in Emma, and she turned back to her chopping.

'I have to get ready for later, and the supper club afterwards,' she said, her voice anxious, and high pitched.

'Let me turn out Millie in the paddock first, then I'll come back to help you,' Miles said.

Emma tipped the aubergine pieces into a roasting pan, and put it into the oven. She was making the red sauce for the topping on the casserole when Miles came back into the kitchen.

'I met Marsha when I started out on the hack – she said she will be up in a while with a beef curry, and a nice dhal and rice.'

'It's not going to be the same, but Jack says we have to continue the tradition.'

'He's right; it's important to continue something Judith considered so special.'

'I suppose.'

He caught Emma around the waist.

'I know how much you miss her,' he whispered,

She nodded, and dipped her head into his chest.

He softly kissed her hair, before pulling away.

'Jack has asked me to set up chairs by the lake, so we can have a little ceremony there when we scatter Mother's ashes.'

Emma watched him go as she made her way to the drawing room to sit, and look at the painting. For some reason, she found solace in the portrait of Judith as a young woman. Maybe, she thought, it was because this is where Jack had placed the urn with Judith's ashes. It had become her place to talk to Judith, to find peace as she adjusted to Killcawley Estate without her.

Closing her eyes, she heard Judith guffawing, and telling her to pull herself together; to start living again. When she opened her eyes, Marsha and Hetty were passing the window, carrying a big box of food. She moved to the kitchen to continue to prepare the supper club dishes.

They had all dressed up in their Sunday best, and Hetty and Marsha wore wide-brimmed hats when they gathered to scatter Judith's ashes just before sunset.

Jack laughed when he saw the others, and asked them to sit down.

'Judy said you would all come dolled up to the nines. Thank you. In the weeks before she died, we spoke on how she wanted this ceremony to play out. For someone who was into the dramatics, she wanted a surprisingly low-key affair with no fancy speeches. When I asked her why, she said in true Judy style, "What would be the fun in having all the accolades, when I am not there to hear them?" After all, she wouldn't be around to steal the show.'

Marsha stood up. 'What do you want us to do, just chuck her in the water?'

Jack put out his hands as if appealing for calm.

'She wants us all to take turns scattering her ashes across the lake, and for us to sit down afterwards together to have a special supper club. She wants us to continue the tradition.'

'It won't be the same without her,' Hetty said, close to tears, and the others murmured in agreement.

'Of course it won't, but we must go on,' Jack said as he opened the urn, and offered a scoop first to Miles. One by one, they walked out along the jetty, and took their turn to sprinkle Judith's ashes onto the lake. The swans glided past, and the ducks bobbed in the water nearby, as the dust that was Judith whooshed across the air. Rays from the sinking sun streaked across the surface as Judith's dust was carried by a light breeze to the centre of the lake, before landing on the water, where it floated, and was brought back to shore.

Emma led the group up the hill to the big house. Jack ushered everybody into the drawing room.

'Judy asked me to say a few words here in the drawing room after she passed.'

He took an envelope from his pocket, and pulled out a slip of paper.'

'Judy dictated this to me a few days before she died. She planned to read it, or have me read it at the supper club reception. She made me promise that if anything happened, I would read it to you as soon as possible, but this seemed a more appropriate time.'

He signalled to the others to sit, and he began to read.

My Dearest Ones,

I want you to know I have lived a full life. Not a perfect life, but a full one. I have had many joys, the greatest being the birth of our son, Miles. Jack's steadfast presence in my life has brought me untold happiness. Being able to marry Jack, and the way you all supported us, has truly brought a great joy to me, and made it the best day of my life.

Nobody is anybody without friends, and I say to all of you, you have been my best friends. Jack, you never wavered in your love for me, and I can tell you, I never wavered in my love for you. My one regret is that soon we will have to part.

Miles, you are the light of my life; there is nothing you have said or done, or could say or do, that would change any of that. I love you completely.

Marsha (note to self, check if she is blubbering, and if she is, tell her to stop sniffling), you are my very best friend. I would never have survived all those years without your sharp wit, your innate kindness and your goodness. We bickered – boy did we argue – but we never stopped loving each other. I always knew, Marsha, you had my back.

Hetty, we fought the good fight together and for that, I will be forever grateful.

That brings me to Emma. Emma, when you walked into my life, I wasn't to know you would become my dearest friend. Stay open now to the many possibilities ahead, and to finding true love. You are part of the Killcawley Estate family now, and this should give you confidence to reach out.

When I am gone, you no doubt will be sad for a while, but it is my hope that every time you look out on the lake, you will remember me fondly, and when you sit down to the supper club, please raise a glass to Judith McCarthy.

There was quiet in the room, except for Marsha snivelling. Emma got up, and asked the others to join her in the kitchen. She handed a bottle of champagne to Miles.

'It's time to toast Judith McCarthy,' she said.

A LETTER FROM ANN

Dear reader,

I want to say a huge thank you for choosing to read this novel. If you did enjoy it, and want to keep up to date with all my latest releases, just sign up at the following link. Your email address will never be shared and you can unsubscribe at any time.

www.bookouture.com/ann-oloughlin

I am in my happy place when I am writing. I love to write about ordinary people often dealing with extraordinary circumstances, and women, who are at their best when supporting each other.

The enduring power of friendship and how family, friends and community can make all the difference are some of my favourite themes.

In this latest novel, you will also find that age should not be a barrier to anything in this life. Meet wonderful Judith McCarthy of Killcawley House who in her seventies refuses to feel old, and she even has a TikTok account. She is joined by equally interesting women of all ages, and there is no stopping them!

I so enjoyed writing this novel and my wish is that you loved reading it. If you did, I would be very grateful if you could write a review. I'd love to hear what you think, and it makes such a difference helping new readers to discover one of my books for the first time.

I love hearing from my readers – you can get in touch on my Facebook page, through X, Instagram or TikTok.

Thanks,

Ann

ACKNOWLEDGMENTS

Words, words and more words. They are all mere words on a page until the reader reads them, and takes them to heart. Thank you dear readers for taking my novels to your hearts. It makes the writing easier to know that these words, shaped into sentences, paragraphs and pages and which make up a novel will be read and enjoyed for a long time to come.

Writing those words can be a lonely business, and I would never do it without the support of my husband, John, and my children, Roshan and Zia. When the words don't come easy, it is to them I turn. Equally, when the words come quickly, and I can't stop to eat, cook or even chat, they don't complain. Thank you guys.

The great team at Bookouture have had my back throughout the whole process, and I thank each and every one of them. Special mention must go to my editor, Ruth Jones for her keen eye and wonderful advice.

My agent, Jenny Brown of Jenny Brown Associates, has always championed my writing and for that, I am very grateful.

If you are new to my work or an O'Loughlin reader, I hope you enjoy your time at Killcawley House.

Ann

PUBLISHING TEAM

Turning a manuscript into a book requires the efforts of many people. The publishing team at Bookouture would like to acknowledge everyone who contributed to this publication.

Audio
Alba Proko
Sinead O'Connor
Melissa Tran

Commercial
Lauren Morrissette
Hannah Richmond
Imogen Allport

Cover design
Debbie Clement

Data and analysis
Mark Alder
Mohamed Bussuri

Editorial
Ruth Jones
Melissa Tran

Copyeditor
Angela Snowden

Proofreader
Liz Hurst

Marketing
Alex Crow
Melanie Price
Occy Carr
Cíara Rosney

Operations and distribution
Marina Valles
Stephanie Straub

Production
Hannah Snetsinger
Mandy Kullar
Jen Shannon

Publicity
Kim Nash
Noelle Holten
Jess Readett
Sarah Hardy

Rights and contracts
Peta Nightingale
Richard King
Saidah Graham

Printed in Great Britain
by Amazon